★ ★ ★ LIBERATOR! ★ ★ ★

The last of the cowering townspeople had been forced inside the building. An *Insurrecto* slammed the door shut while his comrades piled corpses in front of it. Others surrounded the building, aiming their rifles at the windows, while still others seized buckets and ran back and forth from the kerosene barrels, sloshing the flammable liquid on the sides of the building.

Duggan stiffened in horror. "They're going to burn them alive!" Lifting his automatic, he jumped to his feet and started for the building.

He ran twenty-five yards and opened fire at the crowd of men in white. He fired rapidly, six times, feeling the powerful pistol kick in his hand. One or two men fell, and he heard someone shouting wildly in Spanish, "Stop him! Kill him!"

Duggan dropped to the ground.

A prolonged, ragged volley boomed out and Duggan heard the bullets singing overhead. He ejected the clip in his pistol butt and inserted his spare. Then he jumped to his feet and ran forward again, firing as he ran. From behind him he heard his own men open fire—and he dropped to the ground once more. . . .

THE GENERAL

ROBERT LECKIE

BANTAM BOOKS
NEW YORK · TORONTO · LONDON · SYDNEY · AUCKLAND

THE GENERAL

A BANTAM FALCON BOOK / JANUARY 1992

ISBN 0-553-29558-6

Published simultaneously in the United States and Canada

PRINTED IN THE UNITED STATES OF AMERICA

RAD   0 9 8 7 6 5 4 3 2 1

To my dear Kiawah Island friends:

Robert and Constance Degenhart

Doctor Lynn and Jean Freeman

"War never leaves a nation where it found it."

—EDMUND BURKE

SAMAR 1901

CHAPTER 1

"Goddammit, George, she's gone!" Second Lieutenant Mark Duggan swore in anguish. Standing on the wharf on San Francisco Bay, Duggan cupped his hands to his eyes. He saw dozens of ships, many of them sailboats, but could not make out their names. With an exclamation of disgust, he opened the duffel bag lying beside him and pulled out a pair of binoculars. He pressed them to his eyes, focusing on ship after ship. "There she is, George," he said to his bigger companion, standing silently beside him. "The *General Philip Sheridan*. Gone!" There was misery in Duggan's dark brown eyes. "Some pair of shavetails we are! Missed the boat for our first assignment to duty. To *combat* duty! We'll be the laughingstock of the Class of '01!"

"Take it easy, Mark," Lieutenant Meadows said quietly.

"Take it easy! Goddammit, George, I told you we should have left the train at the Nevada washout and come overland by horses. We could've picked up a handcar at the next station and made it on time easy."

Meadows shook his head. His wide gray eyes were calm. "No, Mark. There was no guarantee we'd find a handcar. And we could have gotten lost."

"Lost!" Duggan repeated scornfully. "*Me* lost?" I grew up in those hills! I've tracked trails with Apaches in—"

"Yes, I know, Mark," Meadows said wearily. "You were an Army brat. You grew up on the frontier with the Ninth Infantry. You could ride and shoot before you could read and write. But Mark," he said, his voice gently reproachful, "you know very well we could not afford to take that chance."

"Oh, you and your caution," Duggan snorted. "You're so damn regulation! Sweet suffering Jesus, George, will you please take a chance for once? Just once?" Duggan pointed angrily at the *Philip Sheridan* making slowly for the Golden Gate. "What are we going to do now?"

"Wait for another ship."

"And maybe be reassigned somewhere else and miss the Philippines fighting? Oh, no! Not for me. Now it's me who can't take that chance." He studied the receding ship through his glasses again. "I've got it!" he cried. "I'll send a wire to the *Sheridan* and ask them to stop the ship until we can get out to it by launch."

Meadows stared at his friend. "Mark, you can't really think they'll stop the ship for a couple of shavetails fresh out of West Point?"

"They will when they see the wire is signed 'Duggan.'"

"But what good will—" George Quincy Meadows paused, aghast. "You mean you won't sign your full name and rank, and they may think the wire is an order from your father?"

"Exactly," Duggan replied, his voice proud, his chin lifted defensively.

Meadows placed a reproving hand on his friend's shoulder. "You can't do that, Mark. You'll get into trouble. Real trouble. I mean, this is the Regular Army, now, and it wouldn't be like a cadet's prank at the Academy."

"I'm going to, George!" Duggan burst out, stooping to seize his duffel bag. "I will never let it be said that Mark Duggan missed his first shot at a war." He threw his bag over his shoulder. "Are you game, George?"

Meadows shook his head sadly. "It isn't a matter of being game. It's just not my style, Mark. I can't risk it." He paused, looking pleadingly into Duggan's flashing eyes. "Can't you see, Mark? I'm a nobody. I'm an orphan kid from Buffalo, New York, or wherever it was that I was really born, and I don't have any connections."

"George!"

"Don't be so damn touchy, Mark. I'm the last one to resent the fact that your father's a general. I'm only trying to explain."

Duggan lifted his chin again. His voice was cold and stiff. "What will you do, then?"

"What I said I'll do. I'll go through channels. I'll report to the Presidio and explain what happened and let them take charge."

Mark Duggan stepped in front of his friend and stood silently staring out across the harbor where splashing seals made white question marks on its calm blue surface. He put a finger to his eye to brush away a tear. When he turned to face Meadows again, his eyes were moist and his short full underlip quivered slightly. "Good-bye, George," he said, shyly extending his hand, his husky voice throbbing with emotion. "I . . . I'm sorry I hollered like that."

George Quincy Meadows put out his own hand, conscious, as always, of how Duggan's small fine fingers felt like a child's in his. "Forget it, Mark. But I just wish you wouldn't go through with this crazy scheme."

"I have to, George. Here we are, the two of us, the first ones from our whole class lucky enough to be assigned to the Philippines. I can't stand to think of someone else getting there ahead of us. You know me, George. I just have to be first."

"I know," Meadows said wryly. "I've known that since the day we became roommates and you took the big bureau and the first bath." He grinned, looking down fondly into Duggan's eyes. "For a fellow your size, Mark, you've got more brass—"

Duggan chuckled, withdrawing his hand. "You still haven't gotten over that? Well, at least we're still friends." He glanced quickly out toward the *Philip Sheridan* again. "I can't waste any more time. Good luck, George."

"Same to you, Mark. If the ship doesn't stop, I'll see you at the Presidio."

Duggan nodded. He hitched his bag higher on his slim shoulder and turned to walk briskly down the wharf toward the telegraph office.

Meadows watched him go. In his gray eyes there was a

mixture of sadness and determination. Then he, too, shouldered his bag and turned to walk with long purposeful strides in the opposite direction, toward "channels," the safe and proper way, as he had invariably explained to Duggan, to gain advancement in the Army.

It was a matter of a moment for Lieutenant Duggan to scribble his message on a pad in the telegraph office, after which he hurried out the door to the dock to begin his search for a launch. To his dismay, he found nothing but fishing smacks or whaleboats. Without a wind, Duggan realized, he could never overtake the *Philip Sheridan*. Suddenly, he heard the hiss of steam, and whirled to see smoke beginning to pour from the stack of an ancient little open-decked paddle wheeler. The name *Bay Queen* was painted in bright green on her white stern, and she was gaily decorated with flags and bunting. Mark Duggan took tighter hold of his bag and ran toward a black man in a short-sleeved underwear shirt just then climbing down from the wheelhouse.

"When do you shove off?" Duggan called through cupped hands, raising his voice above the hiss of steam.

"Twelve o'clock, sah."

Duggan frowned. He pulled a gold watch from his pocket. It was an expensive timepiece, shiny new, given to the young officer by his father in recognition of his graduating from West Point with the highest academic record since Robert E. Lee. Duggan was intensely proud of it, but he frowned when he saw that the time was only eight o'clock in the morning. Four hours! He could never wait that long.

"I'll give you five dollars if you shove off now," he shouted.

The black man's mouth flew open in astonishment. "Five dollars! Jes' to ride 'round the bay?"

"No, no," Duggan yelled, shaking an importunate finger in the direction of the *Philip Sheridan*. "Out to that ship out there. I want to catch her."

The pilot shook his head in disappointment. "Cain't do it, sah. *Bay Queen*, she cain't make no mo' than four knots."

"But the ship will *stop*! I know she'll stop!"

The pilot's eyes gleamed and he threw a gangplank up to the dock. "Yassah, yassah—come aboard, sah."

Duggan tossed his bag onto the *Bay Queen*'s deck and jumped down after it. Stooping to retrieve his bag, he paused, an expression of disbelief on his face.

Out on the dock, an American soldier had stopped to peer down at him. From the chevrons on the man's blue wool shirt, Duggan saw that he was a corporal; but the chevrons were in shreds, dangling from his sleeves, his felt campaign hat was missing, as was one of his canvas leggings, and his khaki trousers were torn at both knees. It was the man's face, however, that astounded the young officer. There were bruises on both cheeks, one of his eyes was swollen shut above a gorgeous patch of black and purple skin, and his thick tawny hair was caked with blood and dirt.

"My God, soldier, what happened to you?"

"I dunno, suh. I think I was run over by a brewery wagon, suh, but I jes' cain't recollect how."

"What's your name, soldier?"

"Ames, suh," the corporal replied, suddenly remembering to snap to attention and salute. "Corporal Beauregard Ames." He swallowed, lowering his hand. "Beggin' the lieutenant's pardon, suh, but do y'all have any idea how I can get to that ship out there?" He pointed respectfully toward the *Philip Sheridan*. "That's my ship, suh," he explained. "I was comin' back from town when I got run down by them horses, and she shoved off before I could get back aboard her."

Lieutenant Duggan smiled. "You're in luck, soldier," he said, motioning for Ames to jump down beside him. "That's my ship, too, and I was just getting ready to go after her."

Corporal Ames shook his head in disbelief, grimacing at the pain the movement caused him. "Well, I'll be go to hell," he mumbled, hobbling stiffly toward the gangplank. "If y'all don't mind, suh, rathern'n jump, I'll just mosey down this here plank."

Lieutenant Duggan nodded, then began to laugh. The corporal's rueful expression and his droll insistence on sticking to the transparent story of the brewery wagon struck him as being comical. Fondly, he remembered the noncoms he had known during his boyhood on the western prairies—in particular the grizzled old Irish sergeant who always described his binges as "a fall from grace." As Ames came gingerly toward him, he put out a friendly, steadying hand, just as the deck beneath his feet began to tremble and the *Bay Queen*'s whistle blew. "Tell me, Corporal," he shouted into Ames's blood-encrusted ear, "do you think those horses had been drinking?"

When a humiliated Spain ceded the Philippine Islands to the United States in 1898, President William McKinley announced that it was the mission of America to "Christianize and civilize" the Filipinos. But the Filipinos, who had already been through that process at the hands of Spain 250 years before there was any United States of America, were reluctant to be saved a second time. Moreover, they had been expecting liberation. So they revolted under Emilio Aguinaldo, and there began the bloody, savage three-year war known as the Philippine Insurrection.

It was guerrilla warfare at its cruelest, not at all the kind of fighting to be endured by citizen-soldiers, those short-enlistment Volunteers who had been so helpful in the quick victory over Spain, but who had no stomach for a three-year diet of rain, mud, and blood. Gradually, the Volunteers were replaced by soldiers from the Regular Army.

The Army of that day was half American and half foreign-born. Most of the Americans were farm boys, with here and there a big-city youth who had, more often than not, raised his right hand rather than go to jail. Perhaps sixty percent of the foreigners were Irish. Like their fathers before them during the Civil War, they had come to America expecting employment, only to be told there were no jobs available, only "openings" in the Army.

This was the character of the replacement battalion of about four hundred soldiers that the transport *General Philip Sheridan* was carrying to the Philippines. In command of the troops was a single officer, Captain Alfred Courland, a tall, serious, thoughtful, dutiful man whose insistence upon strict though not cruel discipline was combined with a passion for cleanliness. It was Captain Courland who set the men to work scouring the *General Philip Sheridan*. An old artillery-horse transport, she had been converted to infantry use by order of a War Department genius who either was unfamiliar with the anatomy of a horse or cared nothing for foot soldiers. Topside to bottomside, the *Sheridan* stank of horse dung and urine.

Although the men scrubbed her with lye soap for a week, they could not get the stink out of her, and on the morning that the vessel got under way for the Philippines, an exasperated Captain Courland had the troops' galley moved topside to the main weather deck.

The food was the customary tasteless, though nourishing, blend of pork and beans, and the men, sweating in their heavy blue wool shirts, began to grumble the moment the bugler blew chow call. Holding their mess tins, and their noses, they got into line, chanting in tune to the bugle call:

> "Soupie, Soupie, Soupie
>   Without a single bean;
> Porkie, Porkie, Porkie
>   Without a streak of lean.

One by one the men filed past the big steel pots, extending their mess tins to be filled by the messmen, while mouthing obscene judgments on the quality of the food or the ancestry of the cooks. Private Patrick Durkin was the last in line. He was a huge, red-haired youth, perhaps a trifle bigger than Sergeant Ben O'Rourke, the swarthy, black-haired noncom who was in charge of the morning mess.

"Jaysus!" Durkin exploded, peering into his mess tin in disgust. "There's worms in the soup."

"Worms, is it, Durkin? Ah, but isn't it the grand thing to have two kinds of meat in the single meal. Eat it, lad."

"I can't!" Durkin wailed, rushing to the garbage barrel to spit out the mouthful he had taken. "It's not the worms so much, Sarge, it's the food tasting like the ship smells." He made as though to empty the contents of his mess tin into the barrel.

O'Rourke raised a restraining hand. "Nah, nah, Durkin. None of that. You've got to eat something, lad. Pretend you're a horse and that's a feed bag you're holding."

Making a neighing sound, the redhead gulped a mouthful, made a wry face, and walked over to a capstan to sit down and begin to eat. "Curse of God on that little snake of a corporal," he grumbled, chewing with mechanical distaste, "and him telling me about all the promotions and good pay and the fine food. And not a word, Sergeant O'Rourke, not a single solitary word about there being a war on.''

O'Rourke laughed aloud and strode over to sit down on another capstan opposite Durkin. ''Go on with you, lad. The way you're talking, you'd think you was enlisted by a press gang.''

''Might as well have been. It was in Ellis Island. The immigration officer told me I couldn't get into the country because I didn't have a sponsor.''

''Didn't you?''

''I did. Me own brother, it was. Father Jerry, he's the brains of the family, Sergeant, he got himself shipped to the States not a year after he'd been ordained. Well, I'd been in a bit of trouble at home, see, the bomb in the post office going off ahead of time, and the Peelers had been around to the farm asking questions. So I went up into the Wicklow Hills, until I got word that Father Jerry had written to say there was a job for me as sexton in his church. Well, Sarge, I went near daft with relief. So I wrote to Jerry telling him I was coming over, and took ship for the States.'' Shaking his head sourly, Durkin placed his unfinished meal at his feet. ''I can't eat it,'' he muttered. ''If you could make me believe I was Alexander's warhorse, I couldn't eat it.''

Taking a Bull Durham sack from his breast pocket, he rolled a brown paper cigarette, lighted it, and continued his story. ''When I got to Ellis Island, Father Jerry wasn't there because my ship had arrived ahead of my letter, and by the time he found out about it, it was too late. You see, the immigration officer, this little gnome in a First Communion suit, he tells me I have to go back to Ireland. 'Go back?' I says, not believing my ears, 'Jaysus, man, the Peelers will be waiting for me on the dock with handcuffs and a noose.' 'Now, isn't that too bad,' he clucks, and then he looks over to this corporal at a desk in the corner and winks and says, 'Here's another customer for you, Corporal,' and when I go over and sit down by the corporal, he hands me a cigar and goes out and buys me a big feed, and before you know it he has my left hand on the bible and my right hand in the air.'' Taking a final drag on his cigarette, Durkin flicked the glowing butt over the rail behind him. ''So now I'm a sojer-boy,'' he said glumly.

"Ah, sure, but you'll make a fine one, Durkin," Sergeant O'Rourke said, reaching over to squeeze the redhead's shoulder. "And what would you be doing if you was back in Arklow town? Spreadin' cow flop on the 'taters, that's what you'd be . . ." O'Rourke paused. Beneath their feet the rumble of the engines had ceased, and they could feel the *General Philip Sheridan* slowing. Silently, without wake or bow foam, she slid through the swells until she went dead in the water, a mile or so short of the twin headlands of the Golden Gate and the open sea beyond.

The two soldiers jumped erect and ran to the rail. So did hundreds of others, shouting questions at each other. But there was no explanation, and soon the blue-shirted men went below to resume Captain Courland's tenacious assault on the horse stench. Only O'Rourke and Durkin were left on deck.

"All right, lad," O'Rourke said, pointing to the garbage barrels, "I don't know what she stopped for, but you'd best get busy emptying them barrels over the side."

An hour after the *Sheridan* halted, the *Bay Queen* came under her starboard beam and began to ring her ship's bell furiously. Hurriedly emptying a poised barrel into the water, Durkin set it down and ran to the rail, followed by O'Rourke.

"It's the excursion boat we took around the bay," Durkin shouted. "What's she doing out here, Sergeant?"

O'Rourke shook his head just as a Jacob's ladder went tumbling down from the *Philip Sheridan* onto the *Bay Queen* and a young second lieutenant seized it and climbed nimbly up on deck. Glancing coolly around him, the youth snapped to attention and saluted the moment he saw Captain Courland step out of a hatch and walk toward him.

"Lieutenant Duggan reporting for duty, sir."

To the watching soldiers' surprise, Courland did not return the salute. Instead he stood there, trembling, fists clenched at his sides, the color slowly draining from his face. He spoke to Duggan in a low cold fury. "I have just this moment been informed why this ship was stopped. Lieutenant, by what authority do you stop a ship of the United States Navy carrying troops of the United States Army?"

"None, sir," Duggan said, his face coloring. "I didn't really stop it, sir. I just requested it to wait for me." Captain

Courland's lips tightened, and Duggan rushed on. "I couldn't miss my ship, sir. It's . . . it's my first assignment. You see, our train was delayed by a washout in Nevada, and we—"

"You could have waited for another ship," Courland snapped. Flushing again, recalling George Meadows's similar advice, Duggan said nothing. "But rather than wait and go through channels, Lieutenant, you wired the ship requesting it to stop, and you signed the wire 'Duggan.' "

"Y-Yes, sir."

"So that, everyone aboard this ship being aware that Duggan is the name of the commanding general of American forces in the Philippines, it might just possibly be misconstrued as an order from your father."

Both O'Rourke and Durkin sucked in their breath, and Durkin whispered, "Oh, grand, Sergeant. The cheek of him, the darlin' cheek of him."

Flushing again, but with his large dark eyes still bold and unwavering, Duggan replied, "I can't be sure that that was my intention, sir. . . . I mean—perhaps . . ."

"Perhaps, Lieutenant? Perhaps you need time to reflect. Lieutenant Duggan," Captain Courland snapped, stiffening, "I am confining you to your quarters for the remainder of this voyage. Upon our arrival in Manila, you will appear before a board of inquiry. Please go below."

"Yes, sir," Duggan said, saluting, and he disappeared through the open hatch.

Courland turned to follow him, but his right foot suddenly froze in midair, like the paw of an alarmed cat. He put it down slowly, watching with an expression of amazement on his face while Corporal Beauregard Ames climbed painfully over the rail, clutching Lieutenant Duggan's duffel bag. Courland was so engrossed in studying the corporal's battered face that he did not hear Patrick Durkin's cry of astonishment.

"It's the little snake! It's the corporal who hung me sojer's suit on me."

"Shhh!" O'Rourke hissed.

"We have missed you, Corporal Ames," Captain Courland said in a tone of gentle sarcasm.

"I can explain, suh," Ames mumbled, dropping the bag and snapping to attention. "I can explain everythin'."

"Everything, Corporal. We have received a complete report from the military police. Your, ah, odyssey seems to have started in a San Francisco brothel.''

"I thought it was a school for dancin', suh. Swear to Gawd, I did.''

"And you did resist the civilian police?''

"I was jus' tryin' to get my uniform back.''

Captain Courland seemed to choke. He swung his head up toward the bridge, where the quartermaster stood at the wheel, awaiting the order to resume his course. Courland turned back to Ames with his features in order. "Corporal Ames, you do happen to have a good combat record, and the Ninth Infantry does happen to stand in need of veteran regulars. So I am going to give you a chance to do both yourself and the Ninth some good. You can accept company punishment from me, Corporal, or you can return to San Francisco in that paddle wheeler to face a general court-martial that may land you in Leavenworth.''

Corporal Ames did not hesitate. "I . . . I guess I'll take mah chances with the captain, suh.''

Courland nodded approval. He stepped forward, seized both of Ames's dangling chevrons and tore them from his sleeve. "I hereby reduce you to private," he said, and then, pointing toward O'Rourke: "Please report to Sergeant O'Rourke.''

"Yes, suh. Thank you, suh," Ames said, saluting, before about-facing to approach O'Rourke.

"Stand easy, Ames," the big sergeant said, his black eyes twinkling. "Here," he said, grinning impishly, pointing toward Durkin, "I'd like you to meet an old friend of yours.''

Peering up at Durkin, Ames took an unsteady step backward and swore. "Gawd a'lmighty damn, if it ain't the big greenhorn from Ellis Island.''

"It is, indeed," Durkin said, putting his hands on his hips and glaring down at Ames. "And it's near daft I've been to thank you for all the fine food and good pay and going up the promotion ladder so fast.''

"Lemme tell you, boy, it's faster goin' down," Ames mumbled, glancing dolefully at the discolored patches on his sleeves where his chevrons had been.

Durkin chuckled and was about to reply, but his voice was drowned out by the clanging of the departing *Bay Queen*'s bell. Moments later the three soldiers were showered with hot cinders and began to choke in a cloud of evil-smelling coal smoke floating down from the *Philip Sheridan*'s smokestack. Beneath their feet the decks were trembling again.

Retreating out of the smoke, Sergeant O'Rourke pointed to Lieutenant Duggan's duffel bag lying on the deck. "Get that below, Ames," he said, but before Ames could move, Durkin had hoisted the heavy canvas sack onto his shoulder and made for the hatch.

"He's in no shape to carry it," he said to O'Rourke.

The sergeant clapped an astounded hand to his head and shouted, "Durkin! It's the snake you're helping. Remember?"

Private Patrick Durkin shot a shy, friendly glance at Private Beauregard Ames, who stood as though dazed, swaying unsteadily with the movement of the ship. "Ah, sure, his mother loves him. And now that he's down on the bottom of the heap with the rest of us, I might get to like him myself."

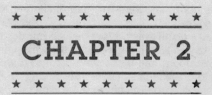

CHAPTER 2

Mark Duggan spent the first few days of his confinement lying on his bunk in his narrow cabin staring dully at the ceiling. Again and again he reviewed the scene on deck with Captain Courland, and each time he went hot with shame and mortification. To be rebuked and punished in the presence of enlisted men!

It seemed to Mark that the career he had dreamed of since childhood was to be cut off before it began. He wondered what his father would think of a son who began his first assignment as an officer under arrest. And his mother? Tears came to his eyes. Mark Duggan still could not think of his mother without weeping.

She had been the mainstay of his life. With the sounds of bugles and marching feet, his earliest recollections were of his mother bending over him at bedtime, the starchy feel of her white muslin dresses, the sweet clean scent of verbena. Until he entered the Academy, each night at bedtime Mark Duggan's mother would lean over him with the remark, "You will be a great man, Mark. Greater than your father, even." Then she would smooth his brow and kiss his forehead. "The world will judge me by you, son. Make the world honor your mother." Kathleen Duggan was with her son at West Point, taking up residence in Highland Park just outside the Acade my gates. From there she supervised his education, reminding him, each night he came to visit her, of his destiny. During the harsh winter of '99, however, she became ill with a severe cold that worsened into pneumonia. Never really able to shake the affliction, she died five months before Mark was to be graduated.

His mother's death was a blow that all but destroyed Mark Duggan. With his father far away in the Philippines, he had no one to lean upon, and he became paralyzed with grief and despair. Unable to attend classes, abstaining from food because he was too proud to endure the sorrowful glances of his classmates, he considered resigning from the Academy—until a letter from his father arrived, sternly commanding him not to betray his mother's aspirations.

Thinking of her now as he lay on his bunk, Mark Duggan felt the hot tears roll down his cheeks. Suddenly he felt dizzy and then nauseous. Leaving his cabin, he staggered down the corridor to the officers' head, where he began to vomit. Still nauseous, he stumbled back to his cabin, flopping facedown on his bunk, arms dangling over the side. My God, he thought, am I going to be seasick?

Another wave of nausea engulfed him, and he felt as though he would vomit again. He tried to sit up, and it was then that he realized that he was not seasick. It was his old affliction, the malaise that sometimes came upon him at critical or dangerous moments. The first time it had seized him was when he was a boy of eight or nine and his father was away campaigning against Geronimo under General Crook. Young Mark had boldly ridden alone out of tiny Fort Selden on the Rio Grande. A few miles outside the fort he had seen one of Geronimo's Apaches riding furiously at him, brandishing a tomahawk. Transfixed with fear, instantly sick, he might have fallen from his horse had he not heard the thunder of hooves behind him and turned to see the approach of a troop of U.S. cavalry riding north from El Paso. The nausea had come again when he received that wretched report card at North Texas Military Academy and his father had snapped angrily: "Mark, you will never make a student!" Again, when he took the examination for West Point, he had been nauseous, though only faintly; but the worst had been during the hazing scandal at the Academy.

As a plebe, probably because of his arrogant self-assurance, Mark Duggan had been subjected to hazing so vicious that he became convulsive. Terrified, the hazers fled, leaving Duggan writhing and twitching on the wooden floor of his tent, his feet beating so loudly against the boards he had to beg his tentmate to hold them in the air so that the officer on duty would not hear. Word of the incident leaked out, and a year later, when another cadet died of similar cruelty, President McKinley ordered a board of inquiry to investigate the scandal. Duggan was called upon to testify.

When the presiding officer ordered him to name his tormentors, Duggan became nauseous. He refused—chiefly because, as his mother had taught him, a Duggan did not lie or tattle. That time, too, his career seemed to be at an end. The officer had sternly insisted that he obey the order—and he had fainted. Fainted fortuitously, as it turned out, for the court had ordered Mark taken to the infirmary, meanwhile summoning another cadet who had no Duggan code to inhibit him from providing the desired names.

Duggan remembered how proud he had been to find the entire corps of cadets admiring him, a lowly plebe, for having striven to preserve its honor, even at the risk of dismissal. Yes, he had stuck to his guns, and he'd do it this time too! He felt his stomach muscles relaxing. Some of his dejection left him. He began to see his present predicament in a more cheerful light. After all, he thought, who could ever *prove* that he had *intended* to make unauthorized use of his father's name. As the defendant, he would not have to take the stand, so he would not need to lie. It would be up to Courland to prove it; that is, if he actually did go through with the board of inquiry. Would he really risk trying the son of the commanding general who reviewed all such proceedings? Duggan began to doubt it. Becoming confident again, he felt his nausea leave him. He hungrily ate the food brought him by an orderly and fell asleep.

In the morning, he visited the ship's library and was delighted to find it abundantly stocked with military history. Clausewitz, Jomini, de Saxe, they were all there, and even the *Memoirs* of Napoleon. So far from seeming ignominious, confinement to quarters now became an unrivaled opportunity to devour the wisdom of the great students of war. So he kept to his cabin, so absorbed with his reading that the only times he noticed the *Philip Sheridan*'s stench was when he was eating, or when, remembering his rebuke in front of the soldiers, he felt himself going hot with shame and remorse.

The closer the *General Philip Sheridan* came to Corregidor, the more Captain Alfred Courland doubted the wisdom of bringing young Duggan before a board of inquiry. Although Captain Courland was convinced, with the rest of self-deluded mankind, that he could not be intimidated, he was also aware that Lieutenant General Duggan was intensely proud of his son. It was common knowledge among Army officers that when Kenneth Duggan was a little-known colonel serving on the frontier, he had spent half his pay cabling congressmen and influential War Department officials in an effort to get his only child into West Point. It had taken two years to do it, chiefly because the young man had grown up on the frontier, where there was little schooling, and he had needed to take a series of post-graduate courses before he could even be accepted as an alternate. Moreover, he might never have seen the plains above the Hudson if the youth accepted ahead of him had not drowned in a sailing accident. Thus, his outstanding scholastic achievements had more than vindicated his father's faith in him. As correct and warranted as Courland's decision might have been—and so he did assure himself—he did not fail to realize that Kenneth Duggan, arrogant and egotistical man that he was, would not take kindly to the officer who brought his son up on charges. Having pondered this reality for two weeks, the captain decided that perhaps the spirited young man had been punished enough, and he sent for Lieutenant Duggan to come to his cabin.

"Lieutenant," he said, after Mark Duggan had closed the cabin door, "it has occurred to me that confining you to quarters has kept you from your men."

"Yes, sir?"

"So I am restoring your freedom. It will be at least two more weeks before we reach Manila. That should be time enough for you to take charge of your platoon. At the moment, Sergeant O'Rourke is in command. You'll probably find him on the fantail."

"Yes, sir. Thank you, sir," Mark Duggan said soberly. He saluted and about-faced, his eyes sparkling, a triumphant grin on his face, and left the cabin. He paused for a moment in the corridor, raising his fists into the air in jubilation. Then he walked slowly up the ladders to the main weather deck.

The sun burst against his eyeballs like an exploding bomb, and he turned quickly away. He shielded his eyes with his hand until he felt that he could stand the light. He saw to his surprise that all of the men had grown luxuriant handlebar mustaches. Barebacked and suntanned, they stood lounging against the rails or sitting atop the hatch covers chatting or playing cards. Duggan's sharp eyes also saw that some of them were becoming flabby around the midriff. Shipboard life, he thought, why doesn't the captain make them exercise?

Duggan found Sergeant O'Rourke sitting with Pat Durkin and Beau Ames on the ship's stern. They had tied their clothes in bundles and thrown them over the fantail fastened to a line, to be washed by the ship's turbulent white wake. Seeing the lieutenant approach, they all sprang to their feet.

"Sergeant O'Rourke, I am Lieutenant Duggan, your new platoon leader," Duggan said with a friendly smile, extending his hand.

O'Rourke took the proffered hand, momentarily startled at the young man's friendliness and easy air of authority. Most shavetails he had seen assuming their first command were either severe and aloof or red-faced and stammering.

"Pleased to meet you, sir," O'Rourke said, and then, pointing to the men beside him, "this here's Privates Durkin and Ames."

"Private?" Duggan asked, puzzled. "The last time I saw you, Ames, you were a corporal."

Ames nodded mournfully, twisting the ends of a gorgeous tawny handlebar. "Cap'n done busted me down to private, suh."

"What did you do to deserve that?"

"I was afraid to ask, suh."

Duggan chuckled and the men laughed. Turning to O'Rourke, Duggan said, "We're going to join the Ninth Infantry, Sergeant. I hear you've served with them before."

"Yes, sir!" O'Rourke's black eyes flashed proudly. "I was with the Ninth in Cuba in 'ninety-eight, in the Philippines in 'ninety-nine, and in China last year during the Boxer Rebellion.'' His swarthy chin lifted. '' 'Tis the finest outfit in the world, sir!''

''I'm delighted to hear you say that, Sergeant. My father commanded the Ninth after the Civil War. I grew up with them in Wyoming.''

''Did you, now?''

The lieutenant chuckled. ''Oh, yes. I'm an Army brat, Sergeant. Bugles and marching feet, those are the earliest sounds I can remember.'' His husky voice rose boastfully. ''I grew up with the Indians too—Apaches and Sioux, Blackfeet and Cheyenne. I tracked trails with them. Sergeant, I can tell you I could ride and shoot before I could read and . . .'' His voice trailed off in embarrassment.

O'Rourke pretended not to notice. Instead he clapped his hands and said, ''Ah, grand, sir—and 'tis lucky we are to have you as our platoon leader.''

''Thank you,'' Duggan murmured, turning as though to gaze out to sea. ''When do you have reveille, Sergeant?''

''We don't, sir.'' Duggan frowned and raised his eyebrows inquiringly. ''Nobody does, sir. The men just get up at seven, in time for morning chow.''

''No roll call either?''

''None, sir. Beggin' the lieutenant's pardon, sir, but none of us figure any of the men are goin' anywhere, so we just—''

''That won't do, Sergeant—that won't do at all. Starting tomorrow, I want you to break out the platoon on deck here at six for reveille. Calisthenics and ten times around the ship—the decks should be clear then—and then you'll break for chow. After chow, Sergeant, back topside to the fantail for school.''

''School, sir?''

''Yes, Sergeant, I've noticed that the men are getting soft around the middle from shipboard life. They could be getting soft in the head, too. So we're going to toughen them up in both places. You, Sergeant O'Rourke, I would like you to hold the first school. You've fought the Filipinos and know what they're like, and I'd like you to tell the men about them.''

''As you wish, sir,'' O'Rourke said respectfully, and then,

to Duggan's astonished delight, the three men, bareheaded and barebacked though they were, came to attention and saluted.

With unruffled calm, Mark Duggan returned the gesture.

Lieutenant Duggan was not unhappy to find that the men in his platoon were out of shape. Because it vindicated his judgement, he was actually secretly pleased to see that most of them were puffing before he had finished leading them through reveille calisthenics, and that no more than half of them could run ten times around the ship. Duggan had himself sprinted the last time around, lapping the field, and he was smiling broadly when he picked up his campaign hat, slapped it against his thigh, and called a red-faced Sergeant O'Rourke to his side.

"Just as I thought, Sergeant. You can't let men lie around like that. The train ride across the country, the layoff on the docks, two weeks at sea doing nothing—it's enough to turn a professional boxer into a marshmallow."

"I'm sorry, sir."

"Not your fault, O'Rourke. It wasn't up to—" Duggan caught himself. "Incidentally, Sergeant, when you break them out tomorrow, make sure they have their Krags with them."

"Rifles, sir?"

"Yes. I'd like them to do calisthenics holding their rifles, and run with them too."

"As you wish, sir."

"And, Sergeant . . ."

"Yes, sir?"

"When was the last time the company had rifle inspection?" O'Rourke blushed. "Not since we left Alabama, sir."

"My God! That was five weeks ago. Do you realize what this sea air can do to the bores of those Krags?"

"I do, sir," O'Rourke said. "But . . . but I—"

"No, no, Sergeant—it's not your fault. All right, 1300 hours. That'll be time enough for them to clean them. At 1300 hours, O'Rourke, we'll hold rifle inspection back here."

"Yes, sir. And the school, sir—I mean, me and the Filipinos." His voice was skeptical.

"Right after morning chow, O'Rourke. Back here."

• • •

Some of Duggan's men were still grumbling when they walked aft after morning chow. Since Captain Courland had abandoned his battle against the horse stench, it had been their custom, along with the men of all the other platoons, to take a siesta in the sun.

"West Pointers!" Beau Ames snorted to Pat Durkin. "They're all alike. Cain't leave the troops alone, without they gotta play soldier all day long."

"Shhh, Beau," Durkin said, pointing aft where Lieutenant Duggan sat on the rail, his campaign hat raked over his right eye, a long gold cigarette holder clamped in his teeth.

Ames grinned. "For a second, I tho't it was Jeb Stuart."

The two men sat down among the soldiers seated cross-legged on the deck.

Sergeant O'Rourke stood above them, rolling a cigarette. Turning to Duggan, he spoke to him in a dubious low voice. "Beggin' the lieutenant's pardon, sir, but are you sure you want me to tell them the truth?"

"I am. I think I know what you mean, O'Rourke, but I can tell you this. I'm no friend of the Anti-Imperialist League. Andrew Carnegie, William Jennings Bryant—that dreadful traitor, Atkinson—they're no friends of mine. I know what our men have to go through in the Philippines, Sergeant. But I think it will be better if you tell them."

"Thank you, sir," O'Rourke said, smiling grimly. "You see, sir—Captain Courland . . . he believes in that 'benevolent assimilation stuff. Not a word against the Goo-Goos. He wouldn't let us say spit against them."

Duggan nodded, puffing on his cigarette. "Go ahead, Sergeant. No holds barred."

"All right, lads," O'Rourke said, turning back to the seated soldiers. "The lieutenant has asked me to tell you about the Filipinos. Only we called 'em Goo-Goos—Goo-Goos and naygurs," he said, cupping his hands to light his cigarette. "Big Bill Taft, he didn't like that. He's the civil governor out there, and he thought we should be more polite toward the Filipinos. Little brown brothers, that's what he called them, and he'd sit on that big sweating elephant ass of his—excuse me Lieutenant—he'd sit there writing out orders we was to stop callin' em Goo-Goos. But we never did." O'Rourke scowled, his black eyes angry. "'Civilize 'em,' he'd say, but we said, 'Civilize 'em with a Krag.' 'Love 'em as thy neighbor,' he'd preach, but we hated 'em.''

"But Sarge," said Beauregard Ames, "I tho't everybody loved each other. Leastways, that was what all the newspapers said.''

"At first, Ames. Right after we kicked the spics out. '*Amigo*,' they called us, turnin' on those phony white smiles. '*Vivo los Americanos*,' they'd holler. That's what they'd say in the daytime, the treacherous scum, but at night they'd be sneaking into your tent tryin' to chop yer dollywhacker off with a bolo knife.''

Some of the troops snickered, and O'Rourke scowled. "What's so bloody funny?" he snarled, his black eyes roving over them angrily. Taking his brown paper cigarette from his lips, he blew on the coal at its tip until it was glowing red. Then, jabbing it angrily at the crestfallen soldiers, he snapped: "See that—that's what they use to put their prisoners' eyes out. And if they didn't burn them out, they'd gouge 'em out and fill 'em with stones.'' One of the men drew breath sharply, and O'Rourke whirled on him. "Face it, lad—this is what you're getting into.'' He flicked his cigarette stub over the side, and put his hands on his hips. "Amigo, eh? Well, pretty soon there were no more amigos. We killed them all. Insurrectos or civilians, we killed them all.''

There were more gasps, and the eyes of all the men swiveled toward Lieutenant Duggan, sitting quietly on the rail. Encouraged by his silence, O'Rourke glared down at the men. "Look, lads, somewhere along the line somebody said you become what you fight. That's what happened to us. If we got shot at from a so-called friendly village, or we found one where our buddies had been tortured and murdered, we burned the village to the ground and killed everyone in sight.''

Pat Durkin was aghast. "Women and children too?''

"I said everyone, didn't I? Well, maybe not always. Maybe just dependin' on what we found. But any male over ten, anybody big enough to swing a bolo, we put 'em away. And maybe if we found a woman or a girl with a bolo in her hand, we killed her too.'' He paused, sensing their dismay. "Ah, sure,'' he sneered, "you wouldn't do anything like that, would you? You read these things in the newspapers or you hear me telling you that they're true, and you say to yourself:

'Not me. I'd never do that.' '' O'Rourke laughed softly. "Of course not, lads—but did you ever read in the newspapers *why* we did it? Did any of them lyin' scribblers of the papers ever tell you about the pits on the trails planted with poisoned spearheads or Goo-Goo head-burnin' or choppin' off a man's pecker and stuffin' it in his mouth or any of the other lovely little tricks? When did you ever read of them takin' a Yank prisoner into a public plaza and settin' him on a sharpened stake—that's right, right up the bunghole—and lettin' him sink on it a few minutes while they soak an American flag in kerosene? Then they wrap the flag around his head and light it. Faith of God, but I've heard from Goo-Goo informers that even some of their own men held their ears to shut out the man screamin' while his head burns off.''

An angry growl arose from the seated circle of soldiers. "The scum!'' Pat Durkin snarled, and Beau Ames exclaimed: "Hell's fiah, Sarge, we ain't never seen none of this in the Stateside papers.''

Lieutenant Duggan slipped off the railing, holding his cigarette holder like a baton. "Of course not, Ames. The American press prides itself on telling the truth. But usually it's only about our own sins, not the enemy's.'' Placing an approving hand on O'Rourke's shoulder, he said, "You mentioned informers a moment ago, O'Rourke. Would you mind explaining to the men what you meant?''

O'Rourke nodded. "It's guerrilla war you'll be fightin', not a regular kind of war at all, with pitched battles and things. It's all patrols and ambushes, like Indian warfare. You can't fight that kind of war without information. Them Insurrectos, now, one minute they're runnin' around in their blue or white uniforms with a Mauser or a bolo in their hands, and the next they hide their weapons and put on pajamas and melt back into the population. Us, with our big noses and white skin, they can see us—but them, all lookin' alike, we can't see them. Christ! Findin' a Goo-Goo in a crowd of Goo-Goos is like findin' a teardrop in a bucket of water. So you bribe one of 'em or you catch one of 'em and give 'em the water cure and he tells—''

"Water cure?'' Durkin interrupted.

O'Rourke nodded again. "That's right. You take a Goo-Goo and you stretch him out on the ground and you fit the end of a hose into his mouth and pump water into him until he swells up like a giant frog, and just when his belly is about two feet above his head and you don't believe he'll take another drop without bustin', you kneel on his belly and force the water out again." He smiled with bitter sweetness. "It don't hurt him permanently, but it does make him tell you who's a civilian and who's an Insurrecto, and maybe even where the Insurrectos are hid—"

"That will be enough, Sergeant O'Rourke."

O'Rourke and Lieutenant Duggan raised their eyes, while as one man the men swiveled their heads to look behind them.

Captain Alfred Courland stood at the rail of the bridge deck. His fingers gripping the railing were white, and his face had the pallor of death.

Mark Duggan found Captain Courland seated at a table in the ship's tiny wardroom. A Filipino messman in a white jacket was pouring coffee from a silver pot. Duggan was relieved to see that the color had returned to the captain's face and that his voice was cordial when he invited him to join him in a cup of coffee.

"Lieutenant," Courland said, "I must tell you that I have been impressed with the way you have taken charge of your men. Calisthenics, running, rifle inspection, school, all these are excellent ways to keep them on their toes." Courland flushed slightly. "Actually, all the men should have been kept on some kind of schedule. I've been too busy myself with administrative work to . . . to . . . And there were no other officers." Courland looked away unhappily, suddenly recalling Duggan's two-week confinement. "However, Lieutenant," he continued, his tone sharpening, "I must also tell you that I cannot permit lectures of the sort Sergeant O'Rourke was conducting."

"Why not, sir?" Duggan asked in polite surprise.

Courland compressed his lips in a prim thin line. "Because I do not subscribe to the 'kill-and-burn' policy which is presently so popular among our officers in the Philippines. I am in complete agreement with Governor Taft. Our purpose is 'benevolent assimilation.' We must lead these people to democracy by our own good example. We cannot get them to follow us by killing them and burning their villages."

"But Captain, how else can you persuade them to lay down their arms?"

"Force and fear will not persuade anyone," Courland replied stiffly, slowly stirring sugar into his coffee.

"All right, sir, I'm sorry I used the wrong word. Compel them, then."

"Compulsion breeds hatred and a thirst for revenge."

"That is true, sir," Duggan said slowly. "At least among the generation that experiences it. But later, sir, after they have laid down their arms and their children and their children's children realize that we really are benevolent and well-meaning, I think then they'll accept democracy."

Captain Courland studied Duggan over his coffee cup. He seemed surprised by the sophistication of the young man's reasoning. Nevertheless, he shook his head. "I cannot agree, Lieutenant. Look at our own Civil War. So far from the scars disappearing, the wounds are still open."

"You would hardly call Reconstruction benevolent, sir."

Courland's eyelids flickered, but he left the sally pass unchallenged. "I began this conversation," he said carefully, "by telling you that I did not want Sergeant O'Rourke infecting my soldiers with his hatred. Our mission in the Philippines now is to bring the people to renounce the revolution and make an oath of allegiance to our country. I do not expect to civilize or pacify a people with troops who hate them."

"But sir, they hate *us*! Aguinaldo keeps telling them that the United States is the mortal enemy of the world's colored races. And they believe him!"

"Judging from O'Rourke's description of them," Courland said dryly, "I can hardly blame them." He shook his head again. "No. Killing and burning will never work. We have to make these people, if not love us, at least agree with us. And American soldiers have to be taught to bear this in mind."

"But this is *war*!" Duggan burst out again. "We are soldiers, not missionaries. These people have weapons in their hands. As long as they do, they are our enemies. Please forgive me if I sound disrespectful, but I'm sure you know what Sherman said about war, what he told the people of Atlanta: 'War is cruelty, and you cannot refine it.' I *want* my men to know this, to know that the Filipinos are very brave and also very cruel, that they can expect no quarter from the Insurrectos and nothing but treachery from the civilians. If I didn't, sir, I would be derelict in my duty.''

Once again the color drained from Alfred Courland's narrow face. ''Lieutenant,'' he said, setting his coffee cup down firmly, as though to signal the end of argument, ''I see that it is not possible to reason with you. Therefore, I am now giving you a direct order: I do not want any Philippine veteran in this command to infect these young soldiers with his hatred of the Filipinos.''

''As you wish, sir,'' Duggan said, getting to his feet, his large dark eyes bold and unwavering. ''But I must also request that you give me that order in writing.''

CHAPTER 3

Thirty-seven days after clearing San Francisco, the *General Philip Sheridan* steamed slowly into Manila Bay, the men aboard her cheering the moment they saw the rock of Corregidor heaving above the blue surface of the water.

The three weeks following the confrontation between Lieutenant Duggan and Captain Courland had been uneventful. There had been, of course, no written order from Captain Courland; neither had there been any more fire-and-brimstone lectures from Sergeant O'Rourke. Silently detesting each other—Duggan convinced that the captain should have been a priest not a soldier; Courland brooding over the proposition that if, as he had heard, Kenneth Duggan was the most arrogant, egotistical man in the U.S. Army, the apple had not fallen far from the tree—they kept out of each other's way and spoke only in the line of duty.

To both of them, the sight of the masts and spars of Cavite Navy Yard rising into view off the ship's port bow, or of the church spires and bell towers of the old Spanish city to starboard, were like the glad portents of liberation. To each, Manila meant separation. Like the men eagerly and noisily crowding the rails, they expected to go ashore to join the various companies of the Ninth Infantry Regiment then operating in northern Luzon, and it did not seem likely that they both would be assigned to the same unit. Manila meant even more to Mark Duggan: he had not seen his father in three years, since before the outbreak of the Philippine Insurrection. Now he would have the chance to visit him at his headquarters.

A few minutes after the *Philip Sheridan* was made fast to a wharf at Cavite, a lieutenant came up the gangplank and handed Captain Courland a sealed envelope. Ripping it open, Courland began to read. He scowled. Raising his eyes over the sheet of paper toward where Duggan stood talking to Sergeant O'Rourke, he called out, "Please come here, Lieutenant." Duggan joined him. "I'm afraid our orders have been changed, Lieutenant. All the replacements are going ashore except you and your platoon. We are to receive another platoon of veterans from the Ninth to form Company C under my command." A shadow passed over Duggan's face, but he said nothing. "We are then to proceed immediately to the island of Samar."

"Samar!" Duggan cried in dismay. "You mean I won't be able to go to Manila? I . . . I had hoped to be able to visit my father." The young man flushed, conscious of the pleading note in his voice. He had been about to add that he had not seen his father in three years, but then, recalling that a Duggan did not beg for favors or play on anyone's sympathy, he lifted his head proudly and said, "Excuse me, sir."

"Quite all right, Lieutenant," Courland said, his voice sympathetic. "I understand. But there is nothing to be done about it. As soon as the ship is cleared and the other platoon comes aboard, we're making for a little port town called Balangiga on the southern tip of Samar." Shaking the paper in his hand, he turned to the officer who gave it to him. "It says here that Samar is in full revolt again. What happened, Lieutenant?"

"There's a man there named Vincente Lucban," the lieutenant replied. "He's half Chinese and half Tagalog. Comes from a wealthy Luzon family and has been a revolutionary for years. About a year ago, he landed at Catbalogan, the Samar capital, with about a hundred riflemen. He took over, said he was governor under Aguinaldo, and called himself a general. Then he began building an army. He made all his men join the Katipunan Society."

"What's that, Lieutenant?"

"It's a kind of bastardized masonry, sir. Secret rites and all that sort of thing. It was founded under the Spanish by a Manila laborer named Bonifacio. When Aguinaldo proclaimed his revolution, he took over the society, and when Bonifacio objected, he was murdered. Aguinaldo said all Filipinos were members of the Katipunan. They take a blood oath to drive us from the islands. Anyone who tries to quit or come over to us is tortured to death."

Courland grimaced. "So the people get it in the neck both ways. If they don't come over to us, *we* kill them; if they do, *they* kill them." He shook his head sadly. "Continue, Lieutenant."

"That's about all, sir. Oh, yes—when Lucban took over, he executed all the Spanish priests and replaced them with native priests. That way, he controls both the church and the state."

"I see. Thank you, Lieutenant."

The officer saluted and went down the gangplank. Captain Courland watched him go, frowning.

Duggan broke the silence to ask, "What was the name of that town again?"

"Balangiga. It's one of a number of coastal towns the Ninth is occupying. Each town forms a military district, with regimental headquarters in Basey up the coast. Our mission will be to subjugate the Insurrectos and pacify the civilians." He pointed toward Sergeant O'Rourke. "You'd better tell O'Rourke to prepare quarters for that incoming platoon of veterans. Tell him to have their platoon leader report to me the moment he comes aboard. Also, I'm giving you half the veterans, and you give the other lieutenant half of your replacements. Work it out between you. In the meantime, I'll be busy getting the other platoons ashore."

"Yes, sir," Duggan replied in a dull voice, unable to conceal his dejection. He walked toward O'Rourke.

"Curse o' God on the bloody luck!" the big sergeant snorted when he heard the news. "There goes me little Carmen. And me thinkin' about no one else half the way over." He smacked his hand with his fist and swore again.

"It can't be helped, O'Rourke," Duggan said glumly, shrugging and moving to the rail to study the buildings that comprised Cavite Navy Yard. There was little to see, except for an occasional victoria dashing through the streets drawn by spirited little Filipino ponies. Duggan noticed that there was not a Filipino in sight. He sighed, and went below to write a letter to his father.

A half hour later, feeling the ship shudder with the renewed murmur of the engines, he realized the *Philip Sheridan* was about to get under way. Quickly ending the letter, he sealed it in an envelope and hurried topside.

It was raining now. The departing men wore black slickers and had pulled their gray campaign hats low over their faces. They went silently down the ramp, and Duggan handed his letter to the sergeant who brought up the rear. Then he heard the tramp of approaching feet, and saw the platoon of veterans come into view. His spirits rose. These were regulars! He could tell by their easy, confident strides; the careless slouch of their campaign hats. Unlike the replacements just departed, their Krag rifles were slung upside down to keep out the rain. They came aboard and fell in, automatically forming ranks until their sergeant brought them snapping to attention.

A familiar voice said, "Fall them out, Sergeant—I've got to go below to report."

Duggan's mouth flew open in astonishment and incredulity. It *was*! It couldn't be, but that was George Quincy Meadows standing there.

"George!" he cried out in amazement. "George! How in blazes . . . ?"

Grinning, Lieutenant Meadows walked toward his astounded friend. "Lieutenant Duggan, I presume?" he said, putting out his hand. Duggan took it mechanically. "No, I didn't fly here, Mark." Meadows went on, obviously enjoying himself. "I did just what I said I'd do. I got another ship. Only this was a cruiser. The *Brooklyn*. They told me at the Presidio she was due to sail that night. She was just getting up steam when I came aboard her." He looked around him disdainfully. "Hell, Mark—she's got to be at least twice as fast as this old tub." He sniffed and wrinkled his nostrils. "What's that awful smell?"

"Horses," Duggan answered dully, a note of resentment in his voice. "She used to be a horse boat."

"Well, she sure moves like a mudder. I got here more than

a week ago.'' He put a friendly hand on Duggan's shoulder. ''And do you know, I've really been enjoying it. After four years of coming in second, Mark, I finally got somewhere ahead of you.''

It was still raining when the *General Philip Sheridan* crept cautiously into the tiny shallow harbor at Balangiga. Wary of running aground, the skipper halted his ship about a half mile offshore. The men cheered when they heard the anchor chains go clanking down the hawse pipe and the loud splash of the anchor hitting the water.

All of the eighty men and three officers of Company C were on deck. In slickers and campaign hats they stood silently at the port rail, staring glumly at the shoreline, dimly visible through the sheeted gray rain. Mark Duggan and George Meadows stood together. Although Duggan had recovered from his pique at having been beaten to the war, he had to struggle very hard to conceal his resentment at the fact that Captain Courland had made Meadows his executive officer. He realized, of course, that Courland probably would have preferred anyone—the devil himself—to Mark Duggan, but still he was inwardly bitter that he, the First Captain of the Cadet Corps, now had to take orders from a classmate to whom he had always given them. He had noticed also that George seemed to sympathize with the captain in his tirades against ''the kill-and-burn mentality,'' or in his reiterated promises that ''we are going to prove that you can pacify a people without bayonets.'' Peering through the rain, Duggan wondered if his friend was trying just a little too hard to ingratiate himself with the captain.

The *Philip Sheridan*'s whistle shrieked. As though by signal, the rain stopped and a light wind began to shred the mists. Five minutes later the American soldiers could see boats putting out from shore. There were perhaps two dozen of them, outrigger dugout canoes called *barotos*. The men in the *barotos* were short and stocky and dark-skinned. They wore white pajama tops and unbleached cotton pants. Some of them had on wide-brimmed straw hats with broad red bands. The Americans called to them cheerfully, but the Filipinos did not answer: they merely stared back in sullen silence.

"Ain't they the darlin' little fellows," Sergeant O'Rourke exclaimed, to the loud laughter of the men around him. "You're in Goo-Goo land for sure, lads."

Captain Alfred Courland frowned, but he said nothing, watching as the *barotos* parted to allow the passage of a barge rowed by a half-dozen men. Two men dressed in white cotton suits and shiny black top hats sat in the barge. Between them was a priest, obviously a native Filipino, in a black soutane. He held a gold-headed cane, his badge of office. The barge stopped under the transport's port beam, and the three men began to climb the Jacob's ladder.

Turning to the two lieutenants beside him, Captain Courland snapped, "Don't let any of the men make any smart remarks about those top hats. In fact, you'd both better fall your men in and bring them to attention. I want to impress these people."

Both officers moved to speak to their sergeants. In a moment the commands rang out. "First platoon, fall in! Ten-shun! Second platoon, fall in! Ten-shun!" The soldiers formed a lane down which the three Filipino officials walked toward the waiting Captain Courland.

"I bring you greetings from my government," Courland said, speaking in Spanish. He had learned it in Cuba, and it was roughly, though often incorrectly, understood by his officers, both of whom had studied it at West Point.

The heavier of the two men in top hats bowed. "We welcome you, *Capitan,* and we thank you." Bowing again, he said, "I am Pedro Machado, *presidente* of Balangiga. This," he said pointing to his companion, "is Miguel Gomez, the chief of police, and this," pointing to the priest, "is Father Luis." Both men bowed, and Courland returned the gesture.

"We have come, *Presidente,*" Courland said, "to protect you from the Moro pirates and Insurrectos."

"Moros, yes, *Capitan,*" Machado said, nervously glancing shoreward. "Insurrectos, no. There are no Insurrectos in Balangiga."

"I am glad to hear that. Then there should be no trouble in getting the people to take the oath of allegiance to the United States?"

"None, *Capitan.*"

"Excellent. Are there quarters available for my command?"

"It is my pleasure to offer you the use of the *tribunal*, the city hall, for your headquarters. And Father Luis," he said, motioning to the priest whose hand had unconsciously strayed to one of the sores on his thin, pockmarked face, "has graciously donated the convent for your use as a barracks."

"You are very kind, gentlemen. You may be sure you will not regret our coming. We are here to help you, *Presidente*, not to hurt you."

Machado bowed silently, and Courland smiled, coming toward the three men with outstretched hand, cordially shaking hands with each of them. The Filipinos, however, did not smile. They bowed again, and turned to climb over the rail, going slowly down the Jacob's ladder into the gently bobbing barge below. The rowers pulled their oars and the barge made for the shore, followed by the *barotos*, sliding away as silently as they had come.

A few minutes later the *Philip Sheridan*'s winches began to whine, swinging boats out on their davits and lowering them into the water, while the black-slickered men of Company C hurried below for their rifles, bedrolls, and ditty bags. Cargo nets were thrown over the side, and the soldiers began clambering over the rail to go down into the waiting boats, cursing when their clumsy Krags bumped against the backs of their heads or caught them under the ear.

"Duggan," Captain Courland said, "I want you to go ashore in the first boat and find the *presidente*. Ask him if we may borrow his barge. It'll be a great help getting the ammunition ashore. Especially the Gatling."

"Gatling!" Duggan exclaimed, his large eyes gleaming. "Do we have a machine gun, sir?"

"We do, indeed—and frankly, I don't know what the devil to do with it, or with the one-pounder they gave us. They're both defensive weapons, Duggan, of no use at all on patrols. You couldn't pull them a hundred yards through the jungle. And the Gatling's so tricky to operate, I doubt if we have a soldier in this command who can do it."

"Yes we do, sir—Private Ames in my platoon. He was in a Gatling battery in Cuba." Duggan called to Beau Ames, just swinging his leg over the rail. "Ames, can you handle a Gatling?"

"I sure can, sir," Ames said, coming back over the rail and advancing toward the two officers. "I served under ol' 'Gatling' Parker at San Juan Hill." He looked up to see a cargo boom swing overhead carrying a stubby round steel tube mounted on a caisson with oversize wheels and thin wooden spokes. "There she is!" he cried, "an' she looks like she's one of the latest models too."

"Excellent, Ames," Courland said. "You will take charge of the Gatling after it comes ashore. It'll be your personal responsibility, and it may get you started toward getting your stripes back."

"Yes, suh. Thank you, suh."

Turning to Meadows, Courland said, "You stay aboard, Lieutenant, and take charge of unloading the supplies and ammunition. Remember, bullets, first, and then the beans." He rolled his eyes. "Thirty thousand rounds of rifle ammunition! My God, that's four hundred rounds a man. What are they looking for—a bloodbath?" Shaking his head, he walked to the rail and began climbing down the cargo net.

Like most Filipino towns, Balangiga was hardly more than a cluster of about two hundred nipa huts, built on stilts six feet high for coolness and safety from the sudden floods that so frequently flashed down from the hills. The huts surrounded a central plaza of beaten earth, on which were located the town's only two masonry structures: the *tribunal* and a combination church-convent with a bell tower. The buildings were side by side, a hundred feet apart, facing toward the bay perhaps a hundred yards away, with the *tribunal* to the right of the church-convent. To the right of the *tribunal*, perhaps another hundred yards away, was a small river, cold and swift, running between steep banks covered with thick, tangled vegetation.

Many of Balangiga's population of about a thousand had crowded down to the bay shore to watch the *Americanos,* led by Lieutenant Duggan, wading ashore from boats that could not pass over the last fifty yards of shallow water. Holding their rifles and ditty bags aloft, stooped under the weight of the bedrolls on their backs, the blue-shirted soldiers called to each other cheerfully, happy to feel solid ground beneath their feet for the first time in two months, and to be finally free of the *Philip Sheridan*'s horse stench.

"Have the men stack arms," Duggan said to O'Rourke, "and pile their bags and bedrolls on the beach." Then the lieutenant strode up to the *tribunal*. He found President Machado in the police station, arguing loudly with the police chief, Gomez. He knocked on the door, and when it was opened by the *presidente,* he bowed and said in imperfect Spanish, "The *capitan* wishes to know if he may borrow your barge."

"You speak Spanish, *Teniente*?" Machado asked in surprise, glancing uneasily back at Gomez, who sat at a table holding a bottle of *tuba,* a beer made from fermented coconut palm.

"*Un poco,*" Duggan said, smiling cheerfully when the *presidente* peered suspiciously into his eyes.

Deciding that the young American officer had not overheard his argument with the police chief, Machado smiled himself and bowed. "You are most welcome to the barge, *Teniente*. I will send word for the rowers."

"*Gracias, Presidente,*" Duggan said, and turned to walk back to the beach.

Machado watched him go, scratching his jowls. He closed the door and sat down opposite Gomez. "Miguel," he said, his eyes thoughtful, "from now on, when we speak to each other in front of the *Americanos,* we speak in Tagalog."

"*Muy bien,* Pedro," the chief replied, throwing back his head to tilt the bottle of *tuba* to his lips.

A few minutes after Duggan had returned to the beach, the *presidente*'s barge arrived. Calling for one of Company C's two Maccabebe scouts—Tagalog-speaking mercenaries who had served the Spanish and now worked for the Americans—he sent the man out to the boat to oversee the unloading of the ammunition.

"There'll be no trouble getting the stuff ashore," he said to O'Rourke. "But how in blazes will we carry it up to the *tribunal*? Each box holds a thousand rounds, and that's close to fifteen hundred pounds." He scratched his head and glanced around him. "Do you think you could scare up some pack animals?"

O'Rourke shook his head, grinning. "If it's pack animals

you want, sir, it'd be easier to teach your men to crap when they walk." Duggan chuckled and O'Rourke slapped his thigh. "Shank's mare, Lieutenant, that's how we'll do it."

The huge boxes, however, were too heavy, and too many men were needed to lift one, so that they got in each other's way. In the end, the resourceful O'Rourke seized one of the mess tents that had come ashore, rolled the box over onto it, and had the soldiers, ten men abreast, drag it up to the *tribunal*.

By noon chow all the ammunition was safely stored in the *tribunal*, together with thirty spare Krag rifles boxed in cosmoline. After chow, the one-pound cannon and the Gatling were rowed ashore. There was some enthusiasm when the little cannon was pulled onto the beach, but when the shiny, sinister-looking machine gun came rolling through the surf, the watching soldiers burst into cheers. Even the Filipinos dropped their reserve, chattering excitedly and pointing to the weapon in childlike awe with cries of *"Ametralladora!"* "Machine gun! Machine gun!" President Machado stood there, too, his black eyes gleaming with interest.

Beau Ames seized the trailer with the warning, "Don't nobody get no sand or saltwater on mah sweetheart." Machado sidled closer and the soldiers crowded around Ames while he explained how the gun was operated. "Y'see, it's got six barrels, an' they turn as they fire." He showed them the drum feed, like a wheel of cheese, that fed the gun, and the crank that fired it, and as he talked, the *presidente* came still closer to the circle. Aware of Duggan watching him thoughtfully, he lifted his shoulders and walked up the beach to the plaza.

"How many rounds a minute does it fire, Beau?" Private Durkin asked.

"A thousand."

Durkin rolled his eyes. "Jaysus, you could fire off all the ammo we unloaded in half an hour!"

"You could. But you'd get mighty tired reloading the drums. Tell you what, Pat, I'll teach you how to run it. Maybe you'll get that promotion I done promised you."

Durkin grinned and slapped him on the shoulder. "Ah, sure, you little snake, your blood's worth bottlin'!"

Between them, the two men pulled the Gatlin up to the convent, turning it around so that its muzzle pointed toward the bay. Opposite it, in front of the *tribunal,* stood the little cannon, also sighted bayward.

By noon all the supplies were safely ashore and stored in the *tribunal,* followed by Lieutenant Meadows and the rest of the soldiers riding in a *baroto.* Now the *General Philip Sheridan* turned toward the sea, her whistle shrilling and shrieking, and the yelling, sweating soldiers ran down to the beach to say their farewell, waving their campaign hats derisively and shouting.

"Safe home, *Phil Sheridan!*" Pat Durkin shouted. "God's speed to ya, P.S.—old Piss and Shit—may you drown in the Horse Latitudes!"

"Oh, no, don't *sink!*" Beau Ames cried in mock horror. "She'll stink up the seven seas."

The soldiers returned to the plaza, where Captain Courland set them to work building raised wooden platforms over which the mess tents were erected. Wood-burning stoves were placed inside and the tent flaps were kept rolled up so that the dining soldiers could see around them. Next day, they began partitioning off the interior of the *tribunal* into a storeroom, an orderly room, a headquarters room, and a commissary where they might buy tobacco and toilet goods. Upstairs became a barracks, with two rows of twenty cots along opposite walls. Moving to the convent, the soldiers built quarters for the officers as well as a small infirmary—Company C had no medical officer as yet, although a surgeon had been promised, and the infirmary was in charge of a medical sergeant. Finally, to complete four days of hammering and sawing, Courland had the men section off part of the plaza for a parade ground, raising a flagpole above it.

The garrison at Balangiga was "in."

Next day, eager for combat, to test himself and his men against the Insurrectos, Mark Duggan led his first patrol into the wild, mountainous jungle beyond the town. He found no one. Nor did he see anyone the following day. Again and again the soldiers of Company C shouldered their packs and slung their rifles and went slogging and sliding along slippery trails behind and to either side of the town, searching, searching, searching for an invisible enemy, but finding only frustration and misery. Often, on prolonged patrols of two or three days' duration, the men would enter the sunless, dripping jungle sunburned and dusty, only to return bleached and washed, white-faced and soaking, their flesh slimy where it was covered by clothing, puckered where it had been exposed to the rain. And if it did not rain in the rain forest—if they did not seem to be immersed in water and the sound of it falling, spouting, streaming, gurgling—then it dripped. The forest steamed, and they went stumbling along the trails swathed in the misty pale light that seemed to float between the floor of the jungle and its roof.

So great was their misery on patrols that they did not notice the magnificence of the country, the sweep of the mountains, the splendor of the chains of lakes that would burst upon them around a turn in the trail, or the blue of the narrow rivers that went twisting and turning through the valleys, tumbling into the canyons in frothing white waterfalls. They saw only that the mountains were a tangle of fern, creeper, and vine that tripped them and flung them on the cruel cutting rock beneath, or that sometimes they had to cross the same river a dozen times in chest-deep water, their rifles held high with the leeches sucking on their flesh and the clouds of insects buzzing and biting around their heads—and they cursed and cursed and cursed the country.

Exhausted and frustrated, they dared not relax, for there was always the fear of ambush. The amigos were out there, they knew, for often, winding through the fields of tall grass with only their heads and shoulders in view, they would find their progress impeded by grasses tied together or slashed brush interlaced and knotted. Sometimes, at the heads of passes or the mouths of canyons, they would be halted by barricades of mud and logs—and then there would be shots, and they would flop down in the mud and prepare for battle. But it never came—only the crack of Mausers, never the flash of the bolo or the screams of the Insurrectos that they had been trained to expect.

At night, crouching wearily on the mountaintops, bathed in moonlight with the high glittering southern sky swinging slowly overhead, they gazed in fascination down at the dark jungle roof below them, watching the moving lights beneath it and knowing that the amigos were down there.

The knew also that the civilians were against them. The paths leading into and out of the tiny villages or barrios were sown with sharpened bamboo stakes hidden beneath the leaves. One day, when Duggan's patrol passed out of a barrio with the lieutenant, Ames and Durkin forming its "point," Durkin stepped on one of these "dragon's teeth." He yelled and fell when he felt the point penetrate his shoe and pierce his foot. He went down with his big arms flailing, also knocking down Ames and Duggan—just as a volley of shots crashed out from the jungle on the right. The bullets tore Duggan's campaign hat from his head and sent it sailing into a bush.

But the lieutenant did not notice. "Down!" he shouted. "Down and fan out!" Squirming on their bellies, the soldiers formed a skirmish line. Duggan took Ames and O'Rourke with him in an attempt to get around the unseen enemy's right flank and trap him. Once again they found no one, nothing but matted grass where the Insurrectos had lain, and empty cartridge shells lying gleaming in the bush.

Disappointed, Duggan returned to Durkin's side. He was surprised to see the big soldier grinning.

"What's the joke, soldier?"

"That, sir," Durkin said, pointing to the lieutenant's bullet-riddled hat hanging on a branch. "From here on in, sir, you've got a charmed life."

"How's that?"

"Because they already used up all the bullets with your name on them."

Duggan smiled, striding to the bush to seize his perforated hat and clap it proudly on his head. "Durkin, when you can laugh with a hole like that in your foot, you're a true soldier."

Ames cut a sapling and made a stirrup crutch for Durkin. He helped his friend to his feet and put his shoulder under his arm while he hobbled along on the crutch. "Gawd almighty damn, Durkin," Ames grumbled, panting under the big man's weight, "when in hell's the Lawd goin' to start makin' little micks?"

Although the men chuckled, they were still enraged when they returned to the barrio.

O'Rourke argued angrily. "Jesus, Lieutenant, they must have known about the ambush. They probably helped set it up. Let us burn the rathole down."

Duggan shook his head. "It's against the captain's orders. No villager is to be harmed in his person or his property. The captain was explicit. There will be no killing and burning in his district."

O'Rourke said nothing. Neither did the men. But their sullen hot eyes were eloquent of their growing resentment. Their attitude secretly pleased Lieutenant Duggan as he led them back to Balangiga. He strode ahead of them with his heart bursting with the fierce proud joy of the warrior. He had been shot at! He had been attacked! He had lost no one and driven the enemy off! He had proven himself to himself and knew that he would never show fear. And what had Durkin said?

"From here on in, sir, you've got a charmed life."

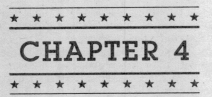

CHAPTER 4

Mark Duggan was convinced that someone inside Balangiga was warning General Lucban of the approach of the American patrols. It was incredible that they had not seen a single Insurrecto, only the barred or barricaded trails and those random phantom shots. It was as though Lucban were the mongoose and the Americans were the cobra. He was dodging and ducking, wearying the cobra, waiting for the moment when he might strike and seize the cobra's neck in his jaws.

Duggan's suspicions had been confirmed the day he took a patrol to the east of Balangiga, only to be recalled by a courier from Captain Courland. He returned to the village just as two Filipinos jumped into a *baroto* and began paddling swiftly up the coast, eastward.

Of course, Duggan realized, the ambush near the *barrio* seemed to challenge his mongoose-and-the-cobra theory. But that incident also puzzled him and made him uneasy. Judging from the sound of the volley, the width of the matted and trodden area, and the number of empty cartridges, there must have been at least twenty Insurrectos—enough to have wiped out his entire patrol. Yet they shot only at himself, Ames, and Durkin. His hat and the limited number of bullet-holed trees proved that. What, then, marked the three of them? He could not say. At night, lying in the hot and stuffy little room he shared with George Meadows, the croaking murmur of the jungle in his ears, he went sleepless attempting to isolate what the three of them had in common, or in trying to deduce who Lucban's ally in Balangiga might be. Finally he took his misgivings to George Meadows.

"I think it's the *presidente*," Mark said one night as they sat outside the convent smoking, staring at the faraway winking of the huge jungle fireflies.

"Machado?" Meadows asked in mild surprise. "I doubt it, Mark. He's been very cooperative. Machado and the captain have become very close. They confer every day."

"That's just it! They're too close. Machado must know more about the captain's plans than we do. I wouldn't be surprised if he isn't keeping Lucban fully informed." George said nothing, dubiously silent. Mark rushed on. "Machado was very interested in the Gatling gun the day we brought it ashore, and when I went to borrow the barge, he acted very suspiciously, as though he and the police chief had been saying things they didn't want me to hear."

"But Mark," Meadows said, puffing thoughtfully on a big-bowled pipe, "if they know where you're going to be, why don't they set a trap for you?"

"That's what bothers me. Of course, even when they have the element of surprise, they never do well. They don't have our firepower. Bolos are just no match for rifles. But then," he said, flicking his cigarette stub from his holder, "they had plenty of rifles the day they tried to wipe out my point." He ground out the stub beneath his boot. "Damn, George, I think they're after something bigger than a patrol or two."

"Such as?"

"A massacre."

"A *massacre*? Mark, please! I know you don't think much of Captain Courland, or at least you don't share his convictions. But even you will admit he's alert. He's taken all the precautions. Security patrols every day, besides your combat patrols, sentries all over the place twenty-four hours a day, the cannon and the Gatling loaded and locked. He's even cleared a field of fire around the town at least two hundred yards wide. Hell, Mark—a man trying to get into Balangiga would have as much concealment as a fly on a windowpane. If

Lucban is as well-informed as you say he is, he must know this. He'd never try it.''

"Not directly, no," Mark Duggan said musingly. "Besides, a frontal attack is not their style. They like trick plays." He grinned in the dark. "Like the Navy football team."

George Meadows chuckled. "They almost got away with it. Lucky for us their end got to his feet too soon. Otherwise the sleeper play would have worked."

"Lucky for you, you mean. From heel to hero in one interception—and it landed you on Walter Camp's All-America."

"A lot of good that does me out here," Meadows said ruefully. "Anyway, Mark—you might be right. Why don't you talk to the captain about it?"

"Maybe I will," Duggan said, pausing as the sweet sad notes of taps floated through the still night air. "Maybe I will."

Captain Courland was in conference with the *presidente* when Lieutenant Duggan entered the orderly room. Mark could hear them conversing in Spanish behind the closed door of the captain's office.

"Would you tell the captain I'll be back?" Duggan said to the sergeant on duty, and strolled to the open door of the *tribunal*. To his left he could see Ames and Durkin working on the Gatling gun outside the convent. Walking toward them, he saw they had broken the machine gun down and were cleaning the barrels.

"How's it going, Ames?" he asked.

"Right good, suh. Pat can take her apart blindfolded now, jes' about as good as I can. But I'd still like a chance to test-fire her."

"Good idea, Ames. I'll speak to the captain about it." Duggan turned toward the *tribunal*, watching as Pedro Machado stepped out of the building into the sunlit plaza. He removed the coat of his white cotton suit, slung it over his arm, and came toward the lieutenant.

"*Buenas dias, Teniente*," Machado said, bowing graciously.

"*Buenas dias, Presidente*," Duggan replied, with a nod that was barely civil.

"Your *capitan*," the *presidente* said, shaking his head in mock ruefulness. "He has a passion for cleanliness, no?"

Machado pointed to the rows of nipa huts ringing the plaza. "He tells me I must clean them up. Get rid of what he calls 'the mess.' "

"They are kind of dirty, sir," Duggan said.

"It is their custom, *Teniente*. They throw everything underneath the hut. They do not mind the smell."

"But there is the danger of cholera."

"So the *capitan* has said." The *presidente* extended both hands palm upwards, lifting his shoulders in a gesture of futility. "But they will not understand that. I told the *capitan* they will not like it if the soldiers make them do it." Duggan made no reply, and Machado pointed to the Gatling and said: "*La Ametralladora,* how fast does she shoot?"

Duggan hesitated, suddenly aware of the *presidente's* true purpose in striking up a conversation. But he was trapped. "A thousand rounds a minute."

"*Madre de Dios!*" Machado exclaimed. "Mother of God! Are you serious, *Teniente*?"

"I am," Duggan said, glancing anxiously away toward the *tribunal*. "If you will excuse me, *Presidente*. The captain...he is expecting me."

Machado bowed, and Duggan turned to stride swiftly toward the *tribunal*. Inside, he found the captain's door open and went in.

"I was just talking to Private Ames, sir," Duggan said, sitting down opposite Courland. "He says Private Durkin is familiar with the Gatling now, and he'd like to test-fire the gun."

Courland examined the young officer suspiciously. "Do you mean a public demonstration?" he asked sharply, and when Duggan nodded, he snapped, "This is an attempt to cow the townspeople!"

"Not at all, sir. It's merely a precaution. The gun is new and should be tested."

"Where would you do it?"

"It would be safest on the bay, sir. There's a couple of old *barotos* on the shore. We could mount a sheet on one of them for a target, tow it out onto the bay and let it float free for Ames to shoot at. It would be safer that way, and it would be over before the people knew what was going on."

"Let me think about it," the captain said, preparing to rise from his chair. "Is that all, Duggan?"

"Ah, no, sir . . . I really came to see you about something else, Captain." Duggan quickly detailed his misgivings about the *presidente* of Balangiga.

When he had finished, Courland ran a long thin hand through his blond hair. "Lieutenant," he said gently, "I'm afraid these daily patrols are unsettling your judgment. No, please don't be offended," he said soothingly. "I am fully aware of your courage and leadership ability. But that sort of thing, day after day, it's got to be nerve-wracking, and it may tend to make a man exaggerate what he sees—even what he doesn't see." He leaned back in his chair. "I have to tell you, Lieutenant, that the *presidente* has been the very soul of cooperation. Why, just a minute ago, when I spoke to him about the filth under the huts, he didn't like it. It's a sore point between him and his people. Even so, he promised to bring in laborers from the *barrios*, people who have taxes to work off. They'll do it, he promised. So you see, I just can't believe he's a traitor."

"He wouldn't think it treachery, sir. He'd consider it loyalty to Lucban."

Courland was momentarily silent. "Are you suggesting that he has deliberately been deceiving me?"

Duggan flushed. "I wouldn't want to put it that way, sir."

"It can't be," the captain said, speaking as though he were thinking aloud. "Why, the *presidente* has done as much to create an atmosphere of mutual trust in my district as I have. Maybe more. It was Machado who took me around the town's perimeter to show me all the likely avenues of attack, where to place barricades and the sentries. Why, he was the one who suggested collecting all the rice in the district and bringing it here. And it was the ration of rice that got the village people to come in and take the oath of allegiance."

"Has the *presidente* taken the oath of allegiance?"

Courland frowned. "Not from me. When I asked him— him and Gomez and Father Luis—they said they'd already taken it."

"Sir," Mark Duggan said slowly, choosing his words carefully, "with all due respect, may I suggest that you ask them to take it again? Surely they couldn't object. You could hold a big public ceremony in the plaza. With the troops drawn up and the colors flying, all the people in the district watching, you could administer the oath to the three of them.''

Courland's voice was cold. ''And what earthly good would that do, Lieutenant?''

''It might show everyone who was boss, sir.''

Alfred Courland swore. ''Goddammit Duggan!'' he cried in exasperation. ''Will you never understand what I am trying to do? I am trying to create an atmosphere of mutual trust and confidence. And I can't do that by setting up some kind of American raj. We've got to treat these people as equals. That's what democracy's all about—equality—and if we want these people to accept it, then we've got to treat them that way.''

''I wasn't suggesting lording it over them, Captain,'' Duggan said stiffly. ''I merely—''

''That will do. Matter of fact, I'm placing a different interpretation on your patrol reports. I think the Insurrectos are gone. We're succeeding with the people, and without the people to supply and shelter them, they can't operate. So, for the time being, there will be no more punitive patrols. From now on, you will take charge of security patrols, Duggan,'' the captain said, ignoring the look of incredulity on the lieutenant's face. ''And one more thing, I do not want the men taking their weapons to chow with them anymore.''

Duggan sprang to his feet with a swiftness that sent his chair spinning backward. ''No *arms*?'' he cried in a tone of disbelief. ''My God, Captain Courland, are you out of your mind?''

''Lieutenant Duggan, I am going to pretend that I did not hear that remark.''

''All right, Captain, I apologize. I shouldn't have said it. It's only that . . .'' Duggan's voice trailed off in exasperation. ''Captain Courland,'' he said pleadingly, ''you must be aware that we are on the frontier. Those soldiers can't sit in those open tents unarmed, surrounded by people that might turn on them at any moment. Why . . . when I was a boy on the Wyoming frontier, my father never let his men go anywhere unarmed. They always—'' Duggan fell silent. The set, stubborn look in the captain's eyes told him that he had said the wrong thing—again.

"I am telling you for the last time, Lieutenant," Courland said coldly, "that I am trying to create an atmosphere of mutual trust and confidence here. An armed soldiery suggests neither. Therefore, except for sentries and men on patrols, I do not want my men to carry weapons in public. Is that clear?"

"It is, sir," Mark Duggan said stiffly, and turned to stride quickly from the room.

The soldiers of Company C soon discovered that the one relief from the wearying tedium and monotony of garrison life was the combat patrols they had detested. With punitive patrolling suspended, there were no distractions whatsoever. Life in Balangiga was a boring round of sentry duty and work details, conducted listlessly in alternating hells of heat and rain. At one time or another everyone came down with malaria, and the medical sergeant had to send weekly *barotos* up to Basey for quinine. For dysentery he could do nothing, nor for dhobie-itch, nor the jungle's myriad flukes and fevers. Worse than disease was the deadly homesickness that sometimes drove men insane; they would go up to Basey in a *baroto,* bound and gagged.

The food was merely nourishing, a bland, tasteless unvarying diet of canned bacon, canned "willie," hardtack and black coffee. Any attempt to spice it with native fruit or pork inevitably filled the infirmary with sick soldiers.

There was no recreation, at least not after Captain Courland's program of cleansing Balangiga, both physically and morally, became an obsession with him. At first the soldiers had enjoyed the Sunday cockfights held in the public plaza. But Courland was sickened and shocked by what he considered the cruelty of the cockpit and the immorality of the betting. He went to Father Luis to ask him to stop them.

The little *mestizo* priest had shrugged. "It is true, *Capitan.* Cockfighting is the sport of the devil. But you might as well ask a dog to stop barking as to ask a man of Samar to give up his bird." He smiled mirthlessly. "There is a saying, *Capitan.* If a man's hut catches fire, he will save his gamecock first—before everyone, *Capitan,* even his wife and his children."

Unable to stop the Sunday cockfighting, Courland prohibited his soldiers from attending "these immoral and cruel spectacles."

He also put an end to their custom of bathing naked in the bay. Overhearing some of the Spanish-speaking girls making giggling comparisons between the size of the Americans' genitals and those of their own men, he immediately put out an order that all soldiers must henceforth wear trousers while swimming. That same order also prohibited the men from drinking *tuba*.

The girls, however, continued to worry Captain Courland. They matured early—at thirteen or fourteen—and were most seductive in the bright thin cotton dresses drawn tight around their bodies to display the curve of their small firm breasts and hips. The dresses were also slit at each side, revealing a flash of bare brown flesh from ankles to buttocks. The bored, homesick American soldiers could not take their eyes off them, and Captain Courland, fearing an ugly incident, went to speak to Father Luis to persuade him to make the girls wear more clothes.

"This is how they dress," the priest said with a shrug. He stood in the shade of the church's bell tower, his hands invisible beneath his long black soutane.

"But, Padre—this is a matter of impurity. Doesn't the Catholic Church insist on observance of the Sixth Commandment?"

"The Sixth?" the priest repeated absently, raising a hand over his eyes to shield them from the sun. "Oh, yes—adultery." He dropped his hand to finger one of the pustules on his face. "We try, *Capitan*, but it is a hot climate." He shrugged again. "Most of the girls are pregnant when I marry them. Often, they do not know the identity of the father of their first child. But it is all right, *Capitan*. They all attend Mass and receive the sacraments." Father Luis pinched the sore and winced, fumbling beneath his soutane for a handkerchief to remove the pus and blood oozing out of it.

Courland averted his eyes, sighing. "If you would just say something to them."

"I will, *Capitan*," the priest replied unconvincingly, putting the handkerchief out of sight again, and Captain Courland strode back to his office, so worried about the possibility of rape, that he addressed the entire company on the subject at reveille the following morning.

"Any attempt to cultivate a so-called friendship with any of the young women in this district," he said, "or any actual bodily contact such as touching or kissing or caressing, will be construed by me as rape. And I warn you, I will order the guilty soldier executed on the spot."

The men broke ranks silently, their faces white with suppressed rage. They waited until they were seated at the mess tables inside the tents and saw Captain Courland enter the convent before their anger became vocal.

"Nigger-lovin' son of a bitch!" Beau Ames snarled beneath his breath. "There ain't enough Goo-Goo girls in the world to be worth the life of one American soldier."

Pat Durkin nodded, chewing distastefully on a mouthful of hardtack and greasy bacon. "It is Captain Clean he is, whiter than the snow and purer than the Virgin Mary."

"You mean Captain Turncoat," Ames snapped. "Who's side is the bastard on, anyway?"

Durkin saw Sergeant O'Rourke approaching, and he glanced at Ames warningly and kicked him under the table.

O'Rourke glanced at them in suspicion. "All right, let's go, you two. They've got the sail mounted on the *baroto* and they're waiting for the test-firing to start."

Captain Courland had hoped that the Gatling might be test-fired out of the sight of the people of Balangiga, but the moment Ames and Durkin unlocked the chain securing the weapon to a block of concrete and began rolling it down to the bay shore, hundreds of curious Filipinos gathered in excited, chattering groups on the beach. President Machado, Chief Gomez, and Father Luis were among them. Machado came to stand beside Captain Courland, a few feet behind the gun. Out on the water, the *baroto* rigged with a square white sheet was set adrift from its tow.

Crouching behind the Gatling with Pat Durkin beside him, Beau took careful aim.

An ear-splitting chatter burst from the gun, while a golden stream of empty cartridges fell tinkling from its side. On the bay, the sheet quivered as though struck by wind, and scores then hundreds of holes appeared in it. On the shore, many of the astounded Filipinos put their fingers to their ears or their hands to their mouths in fright.

"I'm gonna stitch her, suh," Ames cried above the chatter. Raising and traversing the weapon, he cut a three-foot square out of the sheet. A cry of delighted astonishment broke from the onlookers, and then the gun was silent.

"That's all, suh," Ames said to Duggan. "We shot off one drum, and lemme tell you, suh—she's a beauty."

"Excellent, Ames, that was beautiful shooting." Duggan turned toward Courland expectantly.

"Very good, Lieutenant," Courland said. "Have them take it back to the convent and clean it." Duggan nodded and moved toward the two soldiers.

"*Madre de Dios!*" Machado exclaimed, shaking his head in wonder. "Who could attack such a gun? It is not possible."

"No, it isn't," Courland said absently. "Matter of fact, the man who invented it thought the weapon so frightful it would put an end to war."

Machado's voice was musing. "It must be difficult to train so many men to shoot it."

"It would be if we trained them all. There's just the two of them, right—" Courland caught himself, glancing in momentary suspicion at the Filipino standing beside him. But he was reassured by Machado's innocent smile. Nevertheless, he spoke in English when he turned to Duggan and said, "Lieutenant, it might be a good idea if we taught a few more men how to fire the Gatling. Will you attend to that, please?"

"I will, sir. Starting tomorrow."

CHAPTER 5

"We can wait no longer, Miguel," Pedro Machado said softly.

The two men sat inside Balangiga's little church. Father Luis was in the pew in front of them, twisted around to face both the two officials and the front entrance. It was cool and murky inside the church. The smell of melting wax was in the air, mixed with the faint fragrance of frankincense and the lingering, heavier body odor of the people. Talking softly, the three men watched the guttering candles in ruby-red glass cups throw flickering shadows on the white plaster walls.

"If we do not move at once, it will be too late," Machado repeated. "The *capitan* is going to train more machine-gunners." He stared at Chief Gomez reproachfully. "You should not have missed them, Miguel. General Lucban was not happy. He gave you half the rifles in the district, and you did not kill them."

"I tell you it was an accident. An instant before we fired, they fell down. The big man stepped on a stake and fell into the others." Gomez swore, ignoring the priest's frown of displeasure. "How can we get at them again when they no longer go on patrol? If we kill them here, it will alarm the *capitan*."

"Can you not blow up the machine gun or roll it into the bay?" Father Luis asked.

Gomez shot him a pitying glance of contempt. "There is a sentry, Father—and the gun is chained to concrete."

"But why can you not capture it?" the priest persisted.

"*Capture* it?" Machado repeated scornfully. "*Madre de Dios!* It shoots one thousand bullets a minute! They would make chopped meat of us, even without their rifles. We would be like lead soldiers storming a stove." The *presidente* shook his head grimly. "Come, Miguel," he said to the chief pleadingly, "you must think of something. The gunners must go."

The police chief shook his head in despair. "I can think of nothing."

For a few moments the two officials sat in their pew in gloomy silence, until the priest opposite them gave a little gasp and cried. "The girls! The *capitan* worries about the girls!"

Machado and Gomez exchanged glances. "Are you all right, Father Luis?" Machado asked in concern.

"Of course!" the little priest snapped petulantly. "You do not understand. Some time ago the *capitan* came to me to ask me to make the girls wear more clothing. He said the way they dressed excited his men. He was afraid of an ugly incident—rape, perhaps—something that would turn the townspeople against him." Father Luis shrugged. "What could I do? He was unhappy, the *capitan*. So he threatened his men that if they so much as touched one of the girls, he would execute them."

"Go on, Father," Machado urged, and the priest shook his head. He turned to look at the crucifix over the altar. The flickering candlelight threw his bony, hawkish profile, enlarged and grotesque, against the plaster wall. "It is not for a priest of God to make such recommendations," he murmured.

The *presidente* nodded. "I understand, Father," he said softly, getting to his feet and looking down at his companion. "Well, Miguel—do you know of two willing young ones?"

"Do I?" the police chief replied with a lecherous grin.

"Good. Now, Father Luis, you will please write to General Lucban for us. Tell him the attack will take place the day after the Gatling-gunners are shot.'' Machado smiled wickedly. "We will inform His Excellency of that regrettable event. We will need fifty bolomen. Let them drift into town just before dawn the morning of the attack. They must dress in women's clothes so that the *Americanos* will not come too close to them. They will go to the church. We will also need two hundred bolos, Father. They can bring them to the church in a coffin.'' He smiled grimly, his own bulky figure now silhouetted against the wall. "There will be a funeral that morning, Father. Many people will be there. You will issue them bolos. Tell General Lucban that we will also need sixty strong men dressed as laborers. They will bring their picks and shovels with them. They will appear just after dawn.

"Tell the general also that there are thirty thousand rounds of ammunition, perhaps a hundred rifles, a cannon, and a machine gun that will soon be his. And you may tell His Excellency, Father Luis, that Father Luis Menendez has been of great assistance in this project.'' The priest inclined his head graciously, and Machado paused, pondering. "That is all, Father. And you will tell His Excellency I pray daily that God may preserve him for many years.''

Outside the church, Machado spoke to Gomez. "The day before the attack, Miguel, you will tell the *capitan* that there are American prisoners in the village of Tacbalahap. He will send out a patrol to rescue them, I am sure. It is a day's march, and will take at least twelve men out of the garrison.'' He smiled his nasty smile. "It will also remove the troublesome *teniente*. You will be in charge of the laborers. Bring them into the plaza as the *Americanos* are marching to the morning meal. After the soldiers are seated, the laborers will disarm the sentries. And then,'' he said, his black eyes glittering, "the bolos will sing.''

Beau Ames and Pat Durkin had found a sanctuary. It was a deep pool beneath a waterfall about a mile upriver along the steep little stream that ran beside the *tribunal*. Because it was unknown to anyone else in Company C and seldom visited by the townspeople, the two soldiers swam naked in the pool without fear of being seen. They would climb out on a smooth stone recessed in the cliff about six feet under the cataract and dive into the plunging water, letting it seize them and drive them down deep beneath the surface of the pool.

On the Sunday following the conference in the church, Ames and Durkin decided to have a picnic at the pool. They wheedled some hardtack and a rare jar of jam out of the mess sergeant and traded a sack of tobacco for six quart bottles of *tuba*.

"We'll let the *tuba* cool in the pool while were swimmin', Pat," Ames said as they slipped into the scrub surrounding the town and began walking along the riverbank. A half hour later, red-faced and sweating, they arrived at their private paradise. Immediately stripping off their clothes, they dove into the water to cool off.

"What the bloody hell, Beau," Durkin said, "why wait for the beer to cool? Let's drink it now."

"Right good thinkin'," Ames drawled, grinning, and the two crawled back up the bank and opened the *tuba*. They drank quickly, and soon they were relaxed and happy.

But then Beau scowled. "Gawd almighty damn! What I wouldn't give to get laid. I sure would like to spread the legs of one of them little Filipino gals."

"Nah, nah, Beau," Durkin said in mock reproach. " 'Tis a mortal sin you're thinkin' of."

" 'Course it is. Anything that feels that good jes' has to be that bad." Beau's eyes twinkled. "You ever been laid, Pat?"

Durkin blushed. "Almost. One time I had little Bridget Flynn up against a tree. But she wouldn't lift her skirts. She said her body was a temple of the Holy Ghost."

Ames choked on his *tuba*. "Oh, my God!" he spluttered, wiping his chin.

" 'Tis difficult gettin' yer pecker wet in Ireland, Beau," Durkin said ruefully. "All them girls being under the priests' spell. In Lent there's no fuckin' at all, in or *out* of wedlock."

Ames groaned. "What do you do for kicks?"

"Drink and fight. Drink and sing."

"Well, that ain't all bad. But it sure don't beat screwin'. Where I come from in Alabama, screwin's a way of life. Hell's fire, Pat, I was laid when I was fourteen."

"Fourteen! Jaysus! When I was fourteen I still thought it was only for makin' water."

"It was the church organist," Beau said dreamily. "I used to pump the organ for her. Pretty soon I was pumpin' her. She took me to her house and gave me gingersnaps and cider. We was in the kitchen, and don't you know she leaned over and grabbed me by the pecker. Wow! I thought my head was comin' off. She give me a quarter. After that, I used to go to her house every Sunday after church." Beau sighed. "But then she died."

Durkin bowed his head. "God rest her soul," he murmured, solemnly crossing himself.

"It was an accident. She'd just finished playing the Death March at a funeral. She went to cross the street and the hearse horse kicked her in the head." Beau sighed again. "I sure missed them quarters. An' she made the best gingersnaps!"

Now it was Durkin who choked on his *tuba*. "How about a song, Beau?"

"In a minute. I was just thinkin' about my real gal. Betsy King. She was the daughter of the sergeant major back in Camp Robinson in Wyoming. She was only fifteen, but hell's fire, how she loved to screw. Swear t'God, Pat, she had a tight little snappin' pussy like it was lined with honey. A pair of tits like scoops of vanilla ice cream with pretty little pink cherries in the middle. We used to meet in a cave out at Comanche Bluff, until her old man followed us out there one day. Thank God we both still had our clothes on when he came bustin' in roarin' and swingin' his saber over his head."

"Y'mean he was going to cut your head off?"

"Naw. Ol' Kit King was meaner'n that. I believe he'd've cut my pecker off, if I hadn't had my clothes on."

"What'd he do?"

"He slapped poor Betsy across the face and sent her home bawlin' and then he kicked my ass all the way back to camp and put me on a wagon that took me down to the train station and out to the replacement depot in San Francisco." Beau paused in disgust. "That's why I'm out here in the asshole of the universe, and I can tell you, Pat, I sure do wish I could get laid."

"Forget it, lad. Not with Captain Clean in command. C'mon, let's sing a song."

"The one about him?"

Durkin nodded, and the two soldiers opened two more bottles of *tuba* and began to sing.

> *Women, if we went swimmin'*
> *You'd know the reason*
> *He makes us wear pants*
> *be*—cause
> *Majors, have only got one ball*
> *Colonels, have two but very small*
> *Privates, has got the* Privates—
> *And Captain Courland has no balls at all.*

Laughing in delight, they opened two more bottles and began to sing another song:

> *Hi-diddle-de-deen, my name is Captain Clean*
> *I cleaned the Goo-Goos with a hose*
> *I picked the niggers' dirty nose*
> *Hi-diddle-de-deen, I'm clean as my latrine.*
>
> *Hi-diddle-de-dure, my name is Captain Pure*
> *I've got the girls in iron tights*
> *My pecker's just for water rights*
> *Hi-diddle-de-dure, a virgin I'm for sure.*
>
> *Hi-diddle-de-doe, my name is Captain No*
> *No booze, no girls, no dirty words*
> *No chow that isn't fit for birds*
> *Hi-diddle-de-doe, I love the Goo-Goos so.*

The *tuba* was gone now, and the two men got unsteadily to their feet.

"C'mon, Pat," Ames said, walking tipsily toward the waterfall. "I've gotta cool off." He climbed carefully onto the stone ledge. "Swear to God that pool must be fifteen foot deep," he shouted, cupping his hands to his lips to make himself heard above the roar of the waterfall overhead. "This time I'm gonna hit bottom!"

Bending his knees, Ames sprang off the ledge, followed by Durkin a few seconds later. They surfaced together shaking the water from their hair. Ames was spitting water. "What happened, Beau?" Durkin yelled.

Ames shook his head woefully. "I just got scared, that's what. It was so cold and dark down there, I—"

They heard feminine voices above them. Then giggling . . . Two Filipino girls stepped out of the brush and came to the riverbank to peer down at them. They giggled again, standing sideways to the men and moving their hips suggestively. Ames and Durkin could feel a rising warmth in their genitals.

"Go away!" Durkin shouted, waving his hand at them. "Leave us alone, for Jaysus sake!"

The girls turned to face them, smiling. They stooped to seize the hems of their bright skirts, lifting them waist high.

A bellow of lust broke from both soldiers at the sight of the black curly hair nestling in the triangle of their tan crotches, and they came splashing out of the water like stallions, water streaming from their sleek bodies, penises erect and throbbing, running up the riverbank to where the now-silent girls awaited them in the tall grass.

"The priest is here, Captain," the orderly sergeant said.

Alfred Courland looked up from his desk in surprise. "Send him in, Sergeant."

Father Luis glided into the office, his hands, as usual, concealed beneath his rustling black soutane. His thin, pocked face was grave. "*Capitan,*" he said in a low voice, looking down at Courland, "two of my girls say they have been raped by your soldiers."

Alfred Courland stiffened in his chair. "You are sure, Father?" he asked in an anguished voice. "The priest nodded, and Courland said, "Where are the girls?"

"I will get them, *Capitan.*"

Turning with a faint swish of his skirts, the little priest went to the *tribunal* door and called, "Maria, Yeyi, come in, please."

The girls entered the office, walking slowly, arms stiff at their sides. They stood silently beside Father Luis, their downcast eyes red and swollen, as though they had been weeping. A faint aroma of onions suggested nothing to Alfred Courland. He sat staring dully at them, his cheeks seeming to sag in despair.

"Show the *capitan* where they hurt you," Father Luis said softly.

Slowly, with maidenly demureness, they lifted their skirts. Courland sucked in his breath at the sight of bluish bruises and reddish-brown blobs like thumbprints on the insides of their thighs.

"The girls say they were very strong," the priest said.

"Can they identify them?"

"Oh, yes." Father Luis paused, a thin finger straying nervously to the sores on his face. "They said one was a big man with red hair and the other smaller with brown hair. They had mustaches."

"They all have mustaches," Courland snapped irritably, arising and coming around his desk. "Sergeant," he called into the room, "have Lieutenant Meadows break out the company." Grim-faced, he turned back to the priest. "Where did it happen?"

"By the waterfall. The men were in swimming. They had no clothes on."

"Naked?"

"Yes, *Capitan*."

A familiar set, stubborn look came into Alfred Courland's eyes. "We'll see," he murmured. "Come with me, all of you."

He strode outside, going directly to the sentry on duty at the cannon, motioning to the girls to step up and examine him. When they shook their heads, he went next to the sentinel at the Gatling gun, and thereafter to the five other soldiers standing guard at their posts around the village. Satisfied that the sentries were innocent, Courland strode to the parade ground where Company C was drawn up in front of Lieutenants Duggan and Meadows, and Sergeant O'Rourke.

"Follow me," he said to the priest and the two girls, and walked slowly down the front rank.

In the middle the girls stopped and pointed to Beau Ames. "*Este hombre*," they said in unison. "This man."

"Private Ames," O'Rourke bellowed, swallowing, "three paces forward—march!"

Astonished, beginning to sense his predicament, Ames stepped forward and came to attention.

At the end of the third rank the girls found Pat Durkin. "*Ese hombre*," they said, pointing accusingly. "That man."

"Private Durkin," O'Rourke shouted, his eyes moist, "front and center!"

With soldierly swift strides, Durkin stepped out of ranks and took his place beside Ames. Studying the two of them, observing their white faces and trembling limbs, Mark Duggan guessed what was happening. Then he heard the captain ask the girls in Spanish: "Are you sure?"

"*Si, Capitan. Estas son los hombres.* Those are the men."

Captain Courland bowed formally to the girls. "Myself, my command, and my country offer our apologies for what has happened. You may be sure we will do all that we can to make recompense." Turning to Father Luis, he bowed again and said, "You may be sure, Father, and you may tell the *presidente*, that these men will be punished to the extreme."

"The extreme, *Capitan*?" Father Luis murmured.

"Yes—the extreme," Courland replied grimly.

"Thank you, *Capitan*," the priest said, and glided back toward the church, holding the hand of each girl on either side of him.

"Dismiss the company, O'Rourke," the captain said.

"Commm-pany, disss—missed!"

The soldiers broke ranks, murmuring in nervous excitement. They drifted back to their details and duties, sometimes turning to shoot curious or pitying glances at the two men standing alone on the parade ground.

Captain Courland stepped toward the accused pair. "Privates Ames and Durkin, you have been identified as the men who raped those two girls at the waterfall yesterday afternoon. Do you have anything to say in your defense?"

"Yes, suh," Ames said, speaking through clenched teeth. "It ain't true."

"It's a bloody lie!" Durkin burst out. "Those goddamned Goo-Goos asked for it! They came down to the waterfall where we were swimming and—"

"With your trousers on, Durkin?"

The big redhead flushed. "No, sir," he mumbled. "It's lonely there, and we didn't think anybody'd—"

"You are aware of my prohibition against swimming naked? You are? Then continue."

Durkin began to plead. "Captain, you've got to believe us. We were alone and they came onto the bank and began waggling their hips. I hollered at them to go away. And then, God's truth on it, sir, they pulled their dresses over their bloody heads and there they were standing there mother naked. What could we do, sir?''

"What *did* you do?''

Durkin blushed, and Ames spit out the words with a snarl. "We gave 'em what they wanted.''

"Penetration?''

"All thee way!''

"That will be enough, Ames,'' Courland snapped, his face whitening. "Sergeant O'Rourke, take these men to the guard room. Lieutenant Meadows, you'd better send for Father Luis, and break out the company again. Duggan, form the firing squad. Twelve rifles, a live round in every other one.''

"My God, sir!'' Duggan cried. "You can't be serious!''

"Never more. And this time, young man, I will advise you to keep your own counsel.''

"I will do no such thing!'' Duggan flung out hotly, advancing toward Courland to confront him with flashing eyes. "You heard those men say that those girls asked for it. How much provocation can a man stand? Or is it that you're so obsessed with placating these people that you prefer the word of a pair of tarts?''

"That's enough, Lieutenant,'' the captain said, his voice ugly and his jaw set. "I am not going to allow two irresponsible soldiers to ruin all the good work that's been done in this district. And *that*, is *final*!''

"No, it isn't, Captain,'' Mark Duggan said, leaning forward, his voice low and controlled. "I am not going to let you sacrifice these men on the altar of 'mutual trust and confidence.' If you do not send them to Basey to stand trial as you should do, if you execute them, then I will go to Basey to prefer charges against you.''

Alfred Courland was shaken. He glanced across the plaza to watch Father Luis hurrying toward him, his cassock held high in one hand. Opposite him, returning from the *tribunal*, came Sergeant O'Rourke. "All right, Lieutenant,'' he said, his voice thick with rage and hatred. "They will go to Basey. And so will you, to account for the insubordination you have shown me since the moment you came under my command.

Sergeant,'' he said, swinging on the astonished O'Rourke, ''please take Lieutenant Duggan to the guard room.''

The priest came up, and Courland said, ''Father Luis, I have changed my mind. I am sending the accused men to Basey to stand trial.''

''To Basey?'' the priest repeated in dismay. ''They will not be executed?''

''Not until after they have been convicted. We will need the girls to testify.''

''They will be leaving soon?''

''At dawn tomorrow.''

''I see,'' the priest said slowly, his anxiety giving way to relief. ''When will you need the girls?''

''Not for a week or two, until after the court-martial is formed and the charges are written up.''

Smiling reassuringly now, Father Luis nodded. ''Perhaps it is better this way, *Capitan*. The people will be pleased to know that justice will be served. I will tell the *presidente*.''

''Thank you, Father.'' Captain Courland said.

''Captain,'' the orderly sergeant said, ''the police chief was here. He asked me to tell you that he has been informed there are American prisoners in a village called Tacbalahap.''

''In our district?'' Courland asked in surprise.

''Yes, sir. He said the Insurrectos captured them in ambush outside of Basey last week. They were taking them to Lucban's headquarters at Rosario, but they had to leave them in Tacbalahap, to go on another operation.''

''Good,'' Courland said, striding to the wall to study a map of his district. ''Are they under guard?''

''No, sir—but three are wounded.''

''I see,'' Courland said, frowning as he put a finger on the map. ''A full day's march, at least. Did Señor Gomez say how long the Insurrectos would be away?''

''Two or three days, sir.''

''Excellent—then we have time. Sergeant, please find Lieutenant Meadows and tell him to take a squad and three stretchers out to Tacbalahap. Immediately.''

''Yes, sir.''

Captain Courland went into his office and sat down at his desk. He flushed, remembering Duggan's remark about ''the altar of trust and confidence.'' Insolent shavetail! But then he put Duggan out of his mind. After all, everything was going well: There had been no demand for summary execution, and any insinuation of his being a ''nigger lover'' would certainly be discredited by his prompt rescue of the wounded Americans. Moreover, in the morning Gomez was bringing in the laborers to clean up the filth beneath the huts.

CHAPTER 6

Next day, O'Rourke loaded his prisoners into a *baroto*. However, swarms of sharks had entered the warming waters of the bay, and the frightened Filipino paddlers refused to push off. So Captain Courland told O'Rourke to take his charges up the coastal track to Basey.

An hour outside Balangiga, O'Rourke halted his prisoners and told them to take a rest. They all sat on a fallen coconut palm tree, tugging their canteens from the pouches at their belts and tilting back their heads to take long swigs of water. O'Rourke slipped his pack from his sweat-stained shoulders and dropped it on the ground. It fell heavily, with a metallic clanking, and the sergeant's prisoners glanced up in surprise. O'Rourke grinned and opened the pack. He pulled out three .45 automatic pistols and handed one to each of them.

"Didja think Ben O'Rourke'd let you go walkin' through Goo-Goo land unarmed?" He shook his head and grinned again. "Not bloody likely."

"Very thoughtful of you, Sergeant," Mark Duggan said, standing up to stuff the pistol inside his belt. He looked down at the two soldiers sitting in despairing silence beneath him. "Don't worry, men," he said, putting a hand on Ames's shoulders. "I'm going to defend you personally."

Ames tried to smile. "Thank you, suh. An' thanks a million for savin' our lives."

Durkin nodded in agreement. "You do believe us, don't you, sir?" he asked eagerly.

"I do." Duggan took off his campaign hat to wipe the sweat from his forehead with the back of his forearm. He replaced it and said, "Sergeant, we'd better be moving if we want to make Basey before dark."

O'Rourke arose. His eye fell on the bullet holes in the lieutenant's hat. "You still wear that hat, sir—the one they shot off your head that day?"

"I do, indeed. I'm as proud . . ."

Mark Duggan paused, aghast. *That* was it! He stared down at Ames and Durkin. "Ames, are you two the only ones in Company C who can fire the Gatling?"

"Guess so, suh. We ain't had the time to train nobody else."

"My God, O'Rourke," Duggan cried, whirling on the astounded sergeant. "The company's in danger! Real danger!"

"Sir?"

"On the patrol that day, when they shot at the point, they were trying to kill Ames and Durkin. I used to think they were trying for the three of us, and I couldn't put my finger on what we had in common. But now I realize that I just happened to be in the target area. It was Ames and Durkin they wanted. The gunners! They're terrified of the Gatling, sergeant, and I can see now they were afraid to try anything so long as it was operative."

Sergeant Ben O'Rourke turned to look back in the direction of Balangiga. "This morning in the plaza, sir." he said, his voice rising in excitement. "Before we left, I noticed there were a lot of women going to church. Some of them carried little coffins, baby coffins. The sentries let 'em go. After what happened to Ames and Durkin, none of us wanted to go near a Goo-Goo woman." O'Rourke turned again to face the young lieutenant. "Still, sir, I had to check. So I made one of 'em open the box, and sure enough, there was a dead baby inside. The women began hollering something about fever and cholera, so I took my revolver butt and nailed it shut as fast as I could."

"Cholera? There wasn't any epidemic in the district."

"I know, sir," O'Rourke said, nodding grimly. "And the woman was big and she carried that heavy coffin almost as easy as I did. All of the women were big, sir."

"Bolomen!"

"Right, sir—bolomen dressed as women so we wouldn't go near 'em, and them coffins must have been full of bolo knives!"

Lieutenant Duggan saw it all clearly now. It was indeed the "trick play" he had feared. Himself and the gunners out of the way, George Meadows and a full squad off on a wild-goose chase, the company weakened, the church crammed with bolomen and bolos, the "laborers" coming in—and the men of Company C sitting down to eat unarmed . . .

Mark Duggan seized his pistol and pointed it toward Balangiga. "We're going back!"

Although the sun had been up for an hour, the plaza was deserted, except for the soldiers of Company C filing slowly into the mess tents. They held mess tins in their hands, and they were grumbling, cursing the fierce heat that was already making them sweat. Captain Courland could hear them as he stood in the doorway of the convent, eagerly searching the perimeter of the plaza for signs of the laborers Police Chief Gomez had promised. Seeing a flash of white along the beach to the right of the *tribunal,* Courland's face brightened. They were there—perhaps sixty of them, clad in white pajama suits and wearing wide-brimmed hats with broad red bands. Courland saw with approval that they carried their own picks and shovels. Gomez keeps his word, he thought gratefully, watching the police chief advancing toward him at the head of the column.

All of the soldiers were inside the mess tents now, and Gomez halted his workers in the middle of the plaza. He spoke a few words which Courland could not hear, and the men broke up into gangs, moving off toward the huts surrounding the plaza and the sentries on guard there. Courland sensed no danger; rather, he was smiling as Gomez came toward him with a smile and an outstretched hand. But the hand held a pistol, and Alfred Courland had time only to gasp before the men following Gomez hurled themselves forward, overpowered him, and bound him to the high wheel of the Gatling.

"Prop him up, amigos," Gomez said, bending his head to light a cigar from the match held in his cupped hands. "I want him to see the show."

A scream rose from the plaza. A "laborer" passing the Gatling gun had knocked the sentry's rifle free with a spade, and then, seizing the weapon, had driven the bayonet deep into his stomach. Turning the blade upward, he ripped the stricken man up to the breastbone. The soldier toppled over, clutching his stomach. Blood and intestines oozed through his fingers.

All around the plaza, now, there were screams while Gomez's "laborers" fell upon the other sentries, braining or decapitating them with picks and shovels.

Courland shut his eyes and struggled against his bonds, actually pulling the gun caisson after him. Exhausted, he sank back against it in despair, his eyes forced open by the screams that he could not shut out of his ears.

Fleeing American soldiers were being cut down by wildly yelling bolomen. Courland could hear the whistling of the heavy steel blades and the chunking sound they made when they cut through flesh or bone.

More than eighty of the bolomen burst into the mess tents. They came through every open side. Unarmed, surprised, the Americans fought back with knives and forks, with fists and chairs. They threw their cups of hot coffee or plates of steaming hash into the faces of their assailants. They seized the thick bolos in their bare hands, sometimes succeeding in wrenching the bloody blades free, more often losing their fingers and then limbs and heads. Very quickly, the floors of the mess tents became a slippery, sodden, scarlet mess.

Some of the soldiers were able to escape through the open sides, and these were the ones Courland saw being cut down. Others ran to the *tribunal* where the rifles were stacked, but in their wild rush to gain the second floor, they brought the stairs crashing down. They fell in a tangled mass of blue and khaki, and most of them were hacked to pieces by the pursuing bolomen. A few ran to the beach and swam out into the bay. But the bolomen put out after them in *barotos* and overtook them. Standing erect in their swaying boats, they swung their bolos down with such force that they cut off the arms raised to ward off the blow, tumbling off balance into the bay. But when the bolomen saw the black shark fins gliding through the water toward them, they scrambled in terror back into the *barotos*, paddling furiously for shore. Behind them the boiling, splashing white water gradually turned red.

It was over in fifteen minutes. Perhaps ten soldiers had escaped the massacre by hiding in the jungle. None of the townspeople suspected of cooperating with the Americans were so fortunate. Execution squads organized by Pedro Machado went from hut to hut, seizing the screaming suspects by their hair and dragging them to the square, where, their trembling lips moving in prayer and supplication, they were forced to their knees and made to bend their heads for the decapitating stroke. At each flash of the blade, as each head fell to the ground from its carmine-spouting stump, the onlooking Insurrectos cheered wildly.

Father Luis, standing alone outside the church, gravely moved his hand in the sign of the cross, intoning, meanwhile, the formula for conditional absolution.

'Absolvo peccata te . . . I absolve thee of thy sins . . .''

Eventually the Insurrectos grew hoarse and bored with the executions, but a great shout arose from their midst when they saw the *presidente* walk into the plaza carrying the American flag pulled down from the *tribunal*. He handed it to one of the men and pointed to one of the barrels of kerosene Captain Courland had procured for burning the town's garbage. Grinning cruelly, the man nodded and ran to the barrel to soak the flag inside it. Another Insurrecto began sharpening a stake.

With Gomez at his side, Pedro Machado walked toward Alfred Courland, who was slumped against the caisson wheel. The captain had lost his mind. His face had collapsed. It was no longer the face of a rational creature, but rather the smooth, blank, uncaring face of an idiot child. Machado stooped to seize and shake him.

"Come, *Capitan*," he said, pointing toward the sharpened stake now buried in the center of the plaza, "we have saved the best for the last."

No one saw Lieutenant Duggan and his men enter Balangiga from the woods along the little river. The huts around the town were deserted, and the four Americans slipped silently between them, moving toward the plaza unobserved. Coming to the last row of huts, they crawled up on the garbage heap beneath one of them and studied the square. For perhaps a minute they lay gaping in horrified incredulity.

The plaza was covered with sprawling bodies, with heads and legs and arms and headless torsos. Thick pools of blood glinted scarlet in the sun. It was a scene of horror so complete, so obscene, that it was at first difficult for them to believe it. So somber and so still, it seemed unreal, it might have been that they had stumbled upon some ghastly world where maniacal giants tore human beings apart with their hands. Only the sticky-sweet smell of blood and the black cones of angrily buzzing flies rising from the mouths and ears and eyes of the dead compelled them to accept the reality of what they saw.

"Mother of God!" Sergeant O'Rourke exclaimed in a low, shocked voice. "They're all dead."

Lieutenant Duggan nodded in anguish, the tears forming hot and salty in his eyes. Soon they were all weeping softly, until they saw the crouching charred figure in the center of the square that once had been Captain Alfred Courland. Then, a fierce and burning anger seized them and their hands tightened on their pistol butts. O'Rourke started forward, but Duggan put a hand on his wrist and pointed toward the bay where perhaps fifty *barotos* were pulled up on the beach. Beside them was the *presidente*'s barge. Then Duggan pointed to the *tribunal*.

Pedro Machado stood there, shouting orders and waving his arms. He turned to a column of about a hundred Insurrectos, all of whom were now armed with captured Krag rifles, and pointed to a throng of townspeople herded together in the plaza. The men lowered their bayoneted rifles and encircled the Filipinos, prodding and pricking them with bayonets and driving them inside the *tribunal*. Meanwhile, other groups of white-clad Insurrectos were harnessing ropes to the backs of teams of thin, bony caribou yoked together in pairs. Shouting at the poor beasts, beating them with the flats of their bolos, they forced them to drag the huge heavy boxes of ammunition toward the bay. Another team of caribou was harnessed to the cannon, while a second was led slowly toward Chief Gomez, who stood bending over the Gatling gun, pushing it, going over it with his hands, apparently trying to discover how it operated.

"That's it!" Mark Duggan cried in dismay. "The guns and the ammo. That's what they wanted, probably even more than the massacre. See, O'Rourke," he whispered, his fingers tightening around the sergeant's wrist, "they're going to take it all away by boat." He shook his head grimly. "Sergeant, if Vincente Lucban ever gets his hands on a hundred rifles, thirty thousand rounds of ammunition, a cannon, and a machine gun, he'll make a bloody hell out of Samar. We've got to stop them!"

"Jaysus, yes, sir—but how'n the bloody hell can just the four of us do it?"

"I've got a plan," Duggan said, his dark eyes gleaming in excitement. Turning to Ames and Durkin, he asked: "Is the Gatling ready to fire?"

"Yes, suh," Ames replied. "An' there's another full drum inside the convent door."

"Excellent. I want the two of you to get under the hut opposite the Gatling. Wait there until you hear firing. Then run as fast as you can for the Gatling." He paused, searching their faces. "Who's the best pistol shot?"

"Me, suh," Ames answered.

"As soon as you get close enough, or as soon as you see that Gomez has spotted you, you stop, Ames, and bring down Gomez. Durkin, you just keep on running. The moment you get to that gun, open fire. Ames, after you've shot Gomez, you make for the convent and that spare drum." Both men nodded soberly, and Duggan turned back to O'Rourke. "I'm going to create a diversion, Sergeant. I'm going to start crawling toward the cannon. You cover me. After I've gone about fifty yards I'm going to jump to my feet and start shooting at them. Then I'm going to run toward the cannon as though I intend to capture it. After five seconds, which will give them time enough to react, I'm going to fall down again—which is when you start shooting at them. Just bang away, O'Rourke, that's all—the idea is to distract them while Ames and Durkin are making for the Gatling." He looked steadily into the eyes of each of the two gunners. "All clear?" They nodded silently. "All right, you two, move out. I'll give you five minutes."

Ames and Durkin slid down the heap of filth on their bellies. They began running with bent heads toward the last hut. Duggan and O'Rourke lay quietly together. Suddenly Mark Duggan felt dizzy. He stomach turned over, and he shuddered as the first wave of nausea convulsed his body. Oh, my God, he prayed, not now . . .

But then a strong hand squeezed his shoulder and O'Rourke's rough voice was in his ear. "Look, Lieutenant—look!"

His blurred vision clearing, Duggan saw that the last of the screaming, cowering townspeople had been forced inside the *tribunal*. An Insurrecto slammed the door shut while his comrades began dragging corpses toward it and piling them in front of it. Others surrounded the building with raised rifles pointed at its windows, while still more seized buckets from a pile and ran back and forth from the kerosene barrels to slosh the flammable liquid on the sides of the building.

Mark Duggan stiffened in horror, his nausea forgotten. "They're going to burn them alive! I can't wait any longer!" Lifting his automatic, he slid down the garbage heap.

As he crawled toward the *tribunal,* he could hear the yelling of the Insurrectos growing louder in his ears. Someone— Machado, perhaps?—was shouting: *"Fosforos! Fosforos!"* Who has the matches? Duggan began to crawl faster.

Behind him, Sergeant Ben O'Rourke lay on his belly, his pistol in his hand, his eyes moving from the lieutenant's back to the crowd in white clothing milling around the *tribunal*. An incongruous patch of black came into the corner of his eye, and he turned quickly to see Father Luis step out of the church. Holding his soutane skirts above the bloody earth, the little priest stepped gingerly across the plaza, as though headed for the charred figure of Alfred Courland. O'Rourke sucked in his breath. Father Luis was on higher ground between the two buildings. At any moment he would be able to see Lieutenant Duggan!

"Holy God!" O'Rourke breathed aloud, "What would me sainted mother think, her own darlin' son killin' a priest of God?" Crossing himself solemnly, he picked up his pistol in his right hand and snicked back the slide with his left. Then, resting the barrel on a coconut, he led the priest a trifle and squeezed the trigger. Instantly, the small black figure flew up into the air and fell backward out of sight.

Mark Duggan heard the pistol shot behind him and guessed that some new, unexpected factor had caused O'Rourke to shoot. Although he was only a quarter of the way to the *tribunal*, he nevertheless jumped to his feet and ran toward the cannon. The Insurrectos did not see him immediately. They were gazing in astonishment at the fallen priest. Duggan ran another twenty-five yards and opened fire at the crowd of men in white. He fired rapidly, six times, feeling the powerful pistol kick up in his hand each time. One or two men fell, but then he saw Pedro Machado turn toward him and heard him yell, *"El teniente! Parale! Matale!"* Stop him! Kill him!

Duggan dropped to the ground.

A prolonged, ragged volley of perhaps thirty seconds' duration boomed out. Duggan heard the bullets singing overhead. He ejected the clip in his pistol butt and inserted his spare. He crawled forward and to his right, closer to the cannon. He jumped to his feet and ran forward again, firing as he ran. From behind him, he heard O'Rourke open up—and he dropped to the ground once more.

Ames and Durkin were sprinting toward the Gatling gun. O'Rourke's first shot had set them prematurely in motion. Chief Gomez had been distracted by the death of Father Luis, and then, again, by the appearance of the American lieutenant.

Only when Duggan dropped out of sight did he sense his danger. Whirling, he saw the two American soldiers closing on him. His cigar fell from his lips as he tugged his pistol from his belt and opened his mouth to yell in warning. He never closed it again. The bullet from Ames's .45 entered it and came out his neck, leaving a hole as big as a baseball.

Now Durkin was on the gun. In an instant, it was firing . . . shaking . . . chattering . . . Insurrectos were toppling . . . piercing screams rose above the rattle of the madly spinning Gatling. Then Ames was inside the convent, running out bowlegged beneath the weight of the second drum. He knelt beside Durkin, waiting for him to eject the first drum, then he put his own steel wheel into place. In the process, neither man noticed that the Insurrectos had begun to throw down their rifles in terror, holding their hands high.

"Me rindo!" they cried. "I surrender!"

But the Gatling began chattering again, until the two soldiers heard Sergeant O'Rourke bellowing: "Ceasefire."

An eerie quiet descended upon the plaza, broken only by the groans of the wounded or the hoarse, rattling cry of the dying. O'Rourke had joined Lieutenant Duggan, who had walked toward the cowed Insurrectos.

Duggan shouted at them in Spanish. "Lay down your arms! Lay down your arms in the center of the plaza, or we'll open fire again!"

The men in white suits ran forward and threw their weapons crashing on the ground. There were perhaps fifty of them. The rest had fallen under the deadly scything of the Gatling gun. O'Rourke formed the survivors in a square between the two buildings. Then he ordered Ames and Durkin to unchain the machine gun and emplace it opposite him. Next, he took a half-dozen prisoners and set them to work freeing the *tribunal* door of its barricade of corpses. When it was done, Duggan walked to the door and pulled it open.

"You are all free!" he shouted. "Come outside!"

The townspeople of Balangiga came surging out into the sunlight. Some of them stumbled and fell to the ground, the pressure of the bodies behind them was so great. A few weeping women sank to their knees in front of Duggan and sought to kiss his hand. He pulled them gently to their feet. Some of the men began a wild cursing of the captive Insurrectos and ran for the heap of rifles and bolos. But Sergeant O'Rourke restrained them.

"Where is Machado?" Duggan asked O'Rourke.

"Search me, sir. He ain't among the prisoners."

Duggan frowned. He turned and spoke in Spanish to the civilian men, and three of them jumped forward to look for the *presidente* among the heaps of bloodstained bodies in white. They found Pedro Machado lying beside the cannon, feigning death. O'Rourke pulled him roughly to his feet and slapped him hard across the mouth. Staggering backward, Machado spat out teeth and blood. O'Rourke seized him by the throat and clenched one huge fist.

"O'Rourke!" Duggan cried angrily. "Do you want to be like they are?"

Dropping his hands, the big sergeant muttered, "Sorry, sir," and released the *presidente*.

Machado tried to adjust his white suit, which, like his face, was smeared with mud and blood. He put a finger to his lips, already beginning to swell, and winced. Then he shrugged. "A few teeth. What do they mean, when you are about to die?"

"Not yet, *Presidente*," Duggan said coldly.

"You are not going to kill me? That is not wise. I would kill you. I wanted to kill you this morning, *Teniente*. But the stupid little priest, he would not allow it. He said it was enough to have you out of the way." He stared at his men under guard. "Stupidity," he mused bitterly, "it is the thing you cannot guard against. Stupidity and pity. Together, they will destroy you."

Lieutenant Duggan removed his campaign hat and pointed to the bullet holes in it. "You tried to kill me, then?"

"*Si, Teniente*. But the police chief, he was not a good shot. None of them are good shots," he muttered in disgust. "They understand so little, they knock the rear sights off the rifle barrels." He lifted his shoulders wearily. "Well, *Teniente* . . . ?"

Duggan pointed to the *tribunal*. "You and your fellow criminals are going in there. No, we are not going to do to you what you tried to do to your countrymen. We are going to hold you for trial. You will see why I do not kill you, *Presidente*. In my country it is the law, not men, that passes judgment. You will be given a fair trial, and it will only be after you have been convicted by the testimony of free men, it will only be then, *Presidente*, that you will be executed." Turning to O'Rourke, he said, "Get them going, Sergeant."

Once the captive Insurrectos had been imprisoned in the *tribunal*, with Pedro Machado carefully locked up alone in the guard room, Duggan placed selected civilians armed with bolos on guard outside the windows and ordered Ames and Durkin to cover the front door with the Gatling gun. Then he and Sergeant O'Rourke made a tour of the massacred garrison.

Much as they had thought themselves inured to slaughter and to cruelty, they were nevertheless appalled and sickened. The floorboards of the mess tents were slippery with blood. Limbs and chunks of flesh lay everywhere. Some soldiers were still seated, slumped forward, their severed heads lying on the tables, still attached to their bodies by the skin of their throats. Others had been boiled bodily—alive or dead, they could not tell—in the scalding hot water of the cleaning barrels. Outside the tents they found mutilation upon mutilation: penises cut off and stuffed into mouths, bodies disemboweled and stuffed with human excrement or strawberry jam or the gouged-out eyes of other victims . . .

"Let's kill them, Lieutenant," O'Rourke pleaded, "all of them. In the name of God and for Jaysus's sake, let me burn the *tribunal* down. They'll burn in hell, anyway, the scum!"

"No, O'Rourke—they're going to live to hang."

The two men walked slowly toward the charred figure in the center of the plaza. There was movement to their left, down near the *barotos* drawn up on the beach.

"Ames!" Duggan called, dropping to his knee with O'Rourke, "Turn the gun toward the bay." Then he saw soldiers in worn blue shirts and khaki trousers and the familiar figure of George Meadows. "At ease, Ames!" he cried joyfully, "It's Lieutenant Meadows's patrol returning."

The two men waited while Meadows and his men trudged up to them. "Patrol, halt!" Meadows shouted. "Fall—" he began, and stopped in stunned silence. Cries of horror and outraged curses broke from the lips of the returned men. George Meadows's homely face turned white. Tears came to his eyes.

"My God, Mark, what happened?" he cried, rushing up to his friend.

"What I predicted, George," Duggan replied, unable to resist the temptation to gloat. "A massacre."

"What . . . what's that?" Meadows asked, aghast, pointing to the black figure between them. In horrid fascination, he put out his pistol to touch the volutes of the dead man's charred nostrils, recoiling in horror when the entire nose collapsed in a puff of ashes.

"That was Captain Alfred Courland, George," Duggan said bitterly, "the late author of the policy of mutual trust and confidence."

Meadows shuddered and shook his head sorrowfully. "I don't think you're being very kind, Mark. No man deserves to die like that."

"Perhaps not. But he fought as softly as he thought." Mark Duggan's voice hardened in contempt and he swept his finger from the plaza to the mess tents in an accusing arc. "If you'd like to see what happens to men who follow soft-hearted leaders, George, just take a walk around the garrison."

George Meadows stepped back a pace, startled by the ferocity in his friend's voice.

"And one other thing, George," Duggan added, his large dark eyes flashing again with the old pride and arrogance.

"Yes, Mark?"

"I'm in command now."

★ ★ ★ ★ ★ ★ ★ ★ ★ ★ ★ ★ ★ ★ ★

MEXICO

★ ★ ★ ★ ★ ★ ★ ★ ★ ★ ★ ★ ★ ★ ★

CHAPTER 7

It took a week for a transport to carry the survivors of the Balangiga massacre and their Insurrecto prisoners to Cavite Navy Yard in Manila Bay. During that period, Lieutenant Mark Duggan spent hours working on recommendations for four Medals of Honor: for Sergeant O'Rourke, Privates Ames and Durkin—and himself. When he had finished writing and rewriting them, like a professional author, he handed them to George Meadows as the two youths sat drinking coffee in the ward room.

"See what you think of these, George."

Meadows read the recommendations, puffing thoughtfully on his big-bowled pipe. Occasionally he frowned. Glancing up at last, he tried to smile.

"A little purplish, I'd call it."

"How do you mean, purplish?" Duggan shot back petulantly.

"Don't get excited, Mark," Meadows said soothingly, putting down his pipe and picking up his coffee cup. "I only meant that there's an awful lot of words like 'heroic' or 'valorous' or 'intrepid' in it."

Duggan flushed. Trying to conceal his wounded vanity, he drew his gold cigarette holder from his pocket, fitting a cigarette to it and lighting it with affected casualness. "What words would you use, George?"

"I don't know. Probably, I couldn't write one of these. You know me, I was never very much for eloquence."

Duggan smiled with gentle scorn. "Ah, but Tacitus said that eloquence is mistress of all the arts."

"Tacitus!" Meadows snorted. "The trouble with you, Mark, is that you read too much."

"And you don't read enough. Anyway, George," Duggan continued, picking up the papers, "are you going to forward these with your endorsement?"

A stubborn scowl darkened George Quincy Meadows's homely face. "No, Mark, I am not."

"Whaaat?"

"I am not, because I personally saw none of this happen."

"But you saw the result!"

"I did, and I have told you again and again how much I admire what you did."

"Then why don't you forward these recommendations?"

"Because I didn't *see* this happen. Supposing I were to be questioned about it? What could I say?"

"Same old George," Duggan muttered bitterly. "Never take your finger off your number."

"Mark!"

"Oh, all right, George—I'm sorry. But sometimes..." Duggan picked up the papers and stood up, removing the cigarette from his holder and crushing it out in an ashtray. "I'll find some other officer to present these."

"Who could that possibly be?" Meadows said, puzzled.

Duggan grinned and said, "Mark Duggan."

"Mark!" George cried in consternation. "You're going too far! To recommend yourself for the Medal of Honor is presumptuous enough, but then to endorse it yourself... That's...that's much too much...even for a...for a..."

"Even for a Duggan?" Mark asked tauntingly. He was about to add that it would be a Duggan—his father—who would or would not forward the recommendations to the President with his approval, but decided not to rub it in.

Nevertheless, the four recommendations were in a manila folder Mark held as he walked down the gangplank after the transport docked at Cavite. Mark immediately made for his father's headquarters in "the Palace" in nearby Malacanan Park. Reaching it, he nodded to the sentries presenting arms at his approach and bounded quickly up the stairs. Inside, a sergeant took him to the general's appointments captain. Saluting, Duggan lifted his chin proudly. "Lieutenant Duggan requests permission to see General Duggan, sir."

His heart actually pounding, it was moments before he realized what the captain was saying.

"I am sorry, Lieutenant, your father is no longer in the Philippines."

"He's . . . he's not here?"

"No, Lieutenant." The captain's tone was gentle. "General Duggan has been assigned to command of the Department of the Pacific, with headquarters in San Francisco. He took ship two weeks ago."

Mark Duggan felt terribly lonely. It was as though fate were conspiring to prevent his seeing the only person on earth he loved. Unaware of the captain eyeing him anxiously, he walked dejectedly to a straight-back chair and sat down. He glanced dully at the folder in his hand. He looked around him for a wastebasket. What did it matter now? he thought resentfully.

Mark glanced up. The captain had come back. "General Carley would like to see you, Lieutenant."

"General Carley!"

"Yes, he replaced your father. Do you know him?"

Duggan nodded. Amos Lorenzo Carley! For an instant Duggan felt dizzy. He was a boy again, riding alone out of Fort Selden . . . The Apache was galloping after him, brandishing his tomahawk . . . He was getting nauseous . . . A bugle call pealed behind him, followed by the thunder of many hooves . . . and then Major Carley had his horse by the bridle and was cursing him in a red-faced rage . . . What a dressing down he had given him! Mark had been so embarrassed that he'd almost wished the troopers would leave him alone again. Later on, however, after dinner with Mark and his mother, Major Carley had relented and had spent the evening entertaining them with stories of his service with the Sixth Cavalry during the Civil War. And now he was in command in the Philippines, Mark mused, smiling as he entered the general's office and came to attention before him.

"Sit down, boy," the general grunted, pointing to a chair.

He spat a tinkling stream of tobacco juice into a brass
spittoon beside his desk. "Heard all about you down at
Samar," he said, wiping his graying mustache with the back
of his hand. "Made your daddy proud, I'll tell you—he heard
about it, too, just before he left." General Carley scowled,
ignoring the young man's murmur of gratitude. "Goddam
volcano we're sitting on, boy. Some day, it's going to blow
sky—" General Carley broke off, looking up irritably as the
captain rushed into the room.

"Dreadful news, General!" the captain cried. "President McKinley has been shot! They say he's dying! Teddy
Roosevelt is hurrying to Buffalo to take the oath of office!"

"Thank God!" Carley shouted, springing erect and tug-
ging at his general's sash. "I—I mean, thank God the
President was not killed." He spat into the spittoon again.
"But let me tell you, Captain—T.R. is a *fighter!*" Unable to
conceal the delight in his voice, he turned on young Duggan.
"Didja hear that, Lieutenant? We're going to have a Rough
Rider in the White House." He struck his hands together
gloatingly. "That'll put a finish to all this mollycoddling."
General Carley straightened his sash again and sat down.
"That'll be enough, Captain," he growled. "Just keep me
posted on the latest reports." He turned his bright blue eyes
on Mark Duggan, who was recovering the scattered papers
that had spilled from his folder when he, too, jumped to his
feet at the captain's announcement. The empty folder lay on
General Carley's desk. The general could read the address:
Commanding General, Philippine Islands . . .

"Those are for me, boy?" he asked, pointing to the
papers.

"Ah, no, sir . . . I mean, yes, sir . . . I was going to give
them to my fa—to General Duggan."

Young Duggan was blushing violently, and the general
eyed him suspiciously. "What are they?"

"R-R-Recommendations for the Medal of Honor."

"Who for?"

"Sergeant O'Rourke and Privates Ames and Durkin—the
men who were with me at Balangiga."

"That's only three," the general growled, extending a
hand for the papers in the obviously mortified young man's
grasp. "Who's the fourth?"

There was an embarrassed silence, during which Mark

Duggan felt the hot color rising from his neck to his cheeks. He wondered if his face was now as red as the general's campaign-beaten flesh.

"Me, sir," he said in a small voice.

Amos Carley shook his head in wonderment. "You do have a habit of sticking your neck out, don't you, boy? I've often wondered what that hellion of Geronimo's would have done to you if we hadn't happened by." With slow deliberation he put three of the sheafs of papers back into the folder and returned it to Duggan. "Give these to Captain Macy on your way out, and tell him to forward them to the President with my approval. This one," he said, carefully tearing it in two, "I'm filing," and he dropped it into his wastebasket.

Mark Duggan was aghast. Momentarily, his dark eyes flashed, and he opened his mouth to expostulate, only to be silenced by a single hard look from the general.

"Listen, boy," Carley said, leaning back to aim another brownish stream at the spittoon, "you cain't go putting yourself in for the only medal this country gives out. Hell's damnation, in the Navy and Marine Corps they just ain't any medals for officers. They say officers is *supposed* to be brave. Anyway, cain't you get somebody else to put you in? How about the other shavetail was down there with you?"

"He refused, sir. He said he didn't see what happened and couldn't swear to it."

General Carley shrugged. "That's that, then. But let me tell you, boy, you'd be the laughingstock of this here army if I let you go through with this." His tone now was persuasive and avuncular. "Besides, when it gets out you put in three enlisted men for the medal and left yourself out, you'll get yourself a reputation for modesty as well as bravery." He paused, a sly look on his foxlike face. "Somethin' new in the Duggan family, boy, eh? Modesty." He snickered, and even the crestfallen Mark Duggan had to smile weakly at this rare sally from the humorless Amos Carley.

"As you wish, sir," Duggan said with a heavy sigh. "I really wouldn't have done it, General Carley, if it weren't for the fact that I thought I'd never get another chance. I mean, Aguinaldo has been captured, and it looks like the war's over."

"There'll be other wars, boy—you mark my words."

"America? I mean, ours is a peace-loving country, sir."

"So we keep telling ourselves. Only we ain't done nothing else but fight since the Pilgrims landed at Plymouth Rock. First it was the Indians, then the Spanish in the south and the French in the north. Then the French and the Indians and the British twice and then the Mexicans, after which we fit each other, then the Indians again and a second shot at the Spanish, and now the Filipinos." General Carley drew breath. "That's a peck of fightin' for a peace-lovin' nation. And let me tell you somethin' else, boy, there's goin' to be plenty more." He swung in his chair and gazed out the window moodily toward the graceful palm trees in the park. "I never had the schoolin' you've had, boy, but I've read history. We're in for a peck of trouble."

"How is that, sir?" Mark asked, puzzled.

"Simple. All this talk of Imperialism, Manifest Destiny, the Open Door policy in China, it boils down to one thing. Internationalism. No more isolation, boy—much as they preach about it. We're in the pit with the rest of 'em—France, England, Russia, Germany—all the fighting cocks of Europe. Up to now, we done all of our fighting at home, leastways on our own continent. But we're involved overseas, now, Lieutenant Duggan, and I think a soldier your age can look forward to a lot of sailing. We humiliated Spain, and the proud old powers of Europe didn't like it. No, sirreee, bob, they didn't like it! We annexed Hawaii and then we took the Philippines, and now we've got a Pacific commitment ten thousand miles from home."

General Carley leaned back as though to spit, changed his mind and leaned forward again. "Worse'n that, the powers of Europe have gone loco. They've got huge conscript armies that keep gettin' bigger and bigger, and they're spendin' like crazy in an arms race that has to end in a big blow-off somewheres. No, sir, boy, don't you worry none about gettin' a chance in another war. I can tell you it's guaranteed." General Carley sat erect, straightening his sash. "It's guaranteed because Europe is suffering from its worst disease since the bubonic plague." Deliberately pausing for effect, he waited for the startled young man's questioning glance, and then pronounced a single word:

"Militarism."

CHAPTER 8

"He said militarism," Captain Mark Duggan said, looking up from his newspaper to stare at his father across the breakfast table, "and he was right."

"Who was right?" Kenneth Duggan asked irritably, brushing the perspiration from his white walrus mustache. It was an extremely hot day in Washington, and the general had already removed his dressing robe, sitting at table in a very unmilitary set of white spongee pajamas.

"General Carley," Captain Duggan replied, and then, pointing to the newspaper: "Twelve years ago he predicted all this."

"All what?" his father snapped. "Really, Mark, you are developing an annoying habit of speaking in riddles."

"All this mobilization. He said Europe had gone mad with militarism, and he predicted exactly what is happening today. You know, Father, I've often wondered how a rough old Indian-fighting soldier like Amos Carley could have had such foresight."

"Strange you should say that," the general mused. "So many people underestimated Amos. Jeb Stuart for one. Geronimo for another. I never did. When I was on the frontier, I noticed that most cavalry commanders had whiskey bottles in their saddlebags. Amos had books."

"He told me he had read history," Mark Duggan said, returning to his newspaper. "Anyway, Father, just listen to these figures: The Russians are estimated to have 115 divisions; the French, sixty-two; the Germans, eighty-seven; Austria-Hungary, forty-nine; the British aren't mentioned, but it must be representative, even if they do spend more on their navy; and then the smaller countries. All told, Father, Europe musters 335 infantry divisions alone. That's between five and six million men! Add the cavalry and field artillery and the headquarters and service troops, and you've got another million. That's seven million men under arms! Good Lord, if they ever get at each other's throats, there will be the greatest slaughter."

"Probably," General Duggan said. He picked up a piece of toast and began to butter it. "All it needs is a spark. But I don't think we're in any danger. The Atlantic is a pretty wide moat." He bit into the toast and began to chew. "Mexico, Mark, that's our trouble spot. Now that Huerta's gotten away with murdering Madero, he might try attacking us just to get the Mexicans behind him."

"Is that why the Second Division is concentrating on the Texas border?"

"It is. A warning, Mark—and from the War Department, I might add. Not our fat friend in the White House." Mark Duggan was inwardly amused. His father never lost an opportunity to ridicule William Taft, the man who had removed him from power in the Philippines. "Much as I dislike Woodrow Wilson," the general continued, "I'm glad to hear that he is against Huerta."

"Do you think Wilson will be a good President, Father?"

"No," Kenneth Duggan snapped, beginning to stir his coffee. "How could he be? He's a Democrat." The general sipped his coffee. "By the way, Mark," he said, looking up, "I spoke to General Field yesterday. You will soon be assigned to the General Staff."

"Wonderful!" his son exclaimed, his dark eyes gleaming. "How did you manage it?"

"I may be retired, Mark, but I still have some influence. Leonard Field and I are old friends. We were with the Rough Riders together in Cuba."

The hall door opened and Sergeant Patrick Durkin came

into the kitchen. "There's someone to see you, Gen'ral, sir," he said. "A Doctor Marsden."

Kenneth Duggan glanced up in surprise. "Marsden? What's he doing here?"

"Wasn't he your old Civil War surgeon, Father?" Mark asked.

"Yes, with the Eighteenth U.S. But I already told him I wouldn't be able to speak at the reunion. Besides, President Taft is coming." He looked at his pajamas in dismay. "Well, I certainly can't see him like this. Show him into the drawing room, Durkin, and tell him I'll be with him in ten minutes."

"Yes, sir," Durkin said, and disappeared into the hall. A few minutes later the general followed him and went upstairs to dress, after which Durkin returned to the kitchen and began clearing the breakfast table.

"Jaysus, it's hot!" Durkin exclaimed, running a hand through his thick red hair. "'Tis only March, but it must be ninety degrees already."

"Is it really, Pat?" Duggan asked politely. Heat did not bother Mark Duggan. Even then, he sat in the kitchen of his father's home, fully dressed in a civilian suit, without so much as a bead of perspiration on his lips.

"How do you do it, sir?" Durkin asked, shaking his head wonderingly. "You could be sitting there in hell, and you'd never sweat."

"Low pulse rate, Pat."

Durkin snorted. "Is that the name of it, sir? Jaysus, I've heard other officers swear they'd give their eyes out to be able to parade in the heat as cool and creased as yerself."

Duggan smiled. "Tell me, Pat—have you ever heard from Ames?"

Sergeant Durkin shook his head. "He's not much of a letter writer, sir. All I hear is that he's living in Alabama somewhere. On his father's farm."

"And O'Rourke?"

"That one?" Durkin exclaimed, grinning. "Sure, O'Rourke thinks a pen is a place to keep pigs in. He went back to Ireland, Captain. They tell me you'll find him in the village pub every night, wearin' his Medal of Honor and fillin' the place with dead Goo-Goos."

Captain Duggan chuckled. Then his dark eyes became

anxious. "Tell me, Pat—how is my father's health? He seems unusually irritable lately."

" 'Tis the asthma, sir. On days like this, he can scarcely breathe, it's that fierce."

Duggan frowned, and then, seeing his father enter the kitchen wearing his full-dress uniform, he sprang to his feet in alarm. "Father," he cried, "where are you going?"

"To the reunion," the general said.

"But I thought the President was going to address the men."

"He sent his regrets. Too hot for him, I guess, the fat tub of lard. Marsden asked me to come in his place."

"But, Father—you're not well. Sergeant Durkin just told me that days like this are the worst for you."

"Sergeant Durkin is your orderly, not my physician," the general said dryly. "Besides, the men want me. It's their fiftieth reunion, the last they'll ever have, and they want to be together with their old regimental commander." He turned to Durkin. "Sergeant, please bring the carriage 'round."

"Yes, sir," Durkin said, and went out the back door to the stable.

Mark Duggan sighed unhappily. "You won't reconsider, Father?"

General Duggan shook his head, turning to go into the front hall, where he stood before a full-length mirror, carefully adjusting the sword at his side. He took his braid-thick hat from a console table and placed it under his arm. Mark went before him to open the front door, recoiling from the wave of hot air that flowed into the room.

They heard the clip-clop of horse's hooves and saw Durkin come rolling slowly down the drive in a victoria.

"I was thinking, Father," Mark said slowly, "why don't you invest in a motor car?"

"Absolutely superfluous," his father replied. "Besides, even if I wanted one, I couldn't afford it." He grimaced. "In America," he said archly, "a general's pension is scarcely more remunerative than a postman's."

"I read in the newspaper this morning that President Taft is replacing the White House carriages with a fleet of automobiles."

General Duggan grunted. "I can think of no man in the world more in need of motive power." The thin lips beneath the drooping white mustache moved mockingly. "At least the automobiles will get him out of the White House quicker."

"I know you despise him, Father—but he did make General Field chief of staff."

"He didn't know what he was doing," Kenneth Duggan snapped, and strode down the walk to his carriage. He got in, still holding his hat under his arm, and Durkin shook the reins gently. With apprehensive eyes, Mark Duggan watched the little bay horse begin to move daintily down the long slope of Connecticut Avenue.

Captain Duggan reentered the house. In the hall, he stopped to check the gold watch his father had given him for his graduation. He frowned. Not nearly time enough to write the letter to George Meadows and still make it to the War Office before noon. Betsy King always left her desk promptly at noon, and Mark had made up his mind that today, the last day of his furlough from Fort Leavenworth, he would conquer his puerile shyness and ask her to lunch with him.

But what about George? Mark had not written to him since Meadows, still a first lieutenant, had returned to the Philippines. Mark did not like to admit that his friendship with his West Point classmate had cooled. True, both were enthusiastic about the "new Army" being created by General Field, and the "Preparedness" campaign training civilians at their own expense to be the officers of America's own conscript army. Otherwise, they had little in common. Wherever Mark Duggan had served, exclusive of his studies at the Leavenworth schools, he had commanded troops. George Quincy Meadows had never led men in the field. He was always a general's aide, a staff officer, or an instructor. He excelled as a planner, a compiler of reports, an inspector of other men's commands. He had become the type of officer that Kenneth Duggan had taught his son to loathe: a desk soldier.

Standing before the hall mirror, Mark Duggan decided that he would not write to George. No, he would not fill a letter with false commiseration for George's failure to rise in rank. Instead, he would wait and let George break the ice, he thought, returning the watch to his pocket. Glancing into the mirror, Mark frowned again. Five or six years ago his fine silken brown hair had begun to thin, and now, standing before the mirror with the noonday sun flooding into the hall, he could see his scalp. Grimacing, he carefully placed a straw hat on his head, then went outside for his walk to the War Office.

Three blocks from the baroque old War Department building on Pennsylvania Avenue, Mark passed the New Willard Hotel. He paused. The Willard was Washington's most fashionable hotel, and also its most expensive. Maybe he'd take Betsy King there for lunch? He went inside to make a reservation.

To his surprise, he saw the regimental colors of the Eighteenth U.S. Infantry hanging from the balcony above him. They're having their reunion here? he wondered. Someone in Father's old outfit must have money. Nevertheless, he was delighted, and when he saw from the lobby clock that he still had ten minutes, he decided to drop in on the fiftieth and last reunion of the Eighteenth U.S.

The room in which the affair was being held was small and extremely hot. Many of the forty or fifty silver-haired veterans had taken off their blue uniform coats and had draped them over the backs of their camp chairs. They sat there, in white singlets and blue suspenders, mopping their foreheads with huge red bandanas. Standing quietly in the back of the room, Mark could see that perhaps half of them had canes. Their chins were propped on hands folded over the heads of the canes and they leaned forward, listening intently to General Duggan.

He stood erect. The armpits of his uniform were stained black with perspiration, but he made no move to wipe his glistening brow. He spoke earnestly, in a low voice that sometimes throbbed with emotion. He was leading them again in the long charge at Chickamauga . . . They were changing front at Atlanta . . . marching through Georgia with Sherman . . . Some of the old soldiers began to weep. Suddenly, Kenneth Duggan's eyes flashed and he turned to a tall, stoop-shouldered officer seated to his right.

"Let us, above all, remember our dead!" he cried. "Let us salute the first to fall, our regiment's first gallant martyrs to the cause of freedom. Let us call the roll, Chaplain Maynard, and let us pray for them: Corporal Daly, Private Ingrams, Priv—''

Kenneth Duggan clutched his throat and toppled forward. The chaplain caught him as he fell, lowering him gently to the ground. A gasp rose from the old soldiers, struggling to their feet. Horrified, Mark ran forward to his father's side. But Dr. Marsden was there before him, kneeling over his crumpled body. The regimental surgeon arose.

"Comrades," he said quietly, "your old commander is dying."

"Oh, my God!" Mark cried, falling to his knees beside his father. He clutched his hand, feeling it already turning cold in his. He heard his father gasping, and he put his ear to his mouth.

Faintly, the hoarse, gasping voice whispered, "Mark . . . I . . . am going . . . to . . . join . . . your mother . . ."

"Yes, Father, yes," Mark sobbed. "Tell her I love her."

Mark felt a slight pressure on his hand, and then the failing voice again: "Mark . . . carry on . . . the name . . . our . . . family name . . . Carry it . . . higher . . . Mark . . ."

That was all. Mark knew that it was all, and he stood erect and came to attention, watching as a man in a captain's uniform took the regiment's battle flag from the wall and gently wrapped it around his father's body. Now all the soldiers were standing at attention, silver heads erect and proud, canes lying at their feet.

Behind him, Mark heard Chaplain Maynard begin to sing. His father had told him of Chaplain Maynard's voice, which had inspired Colonel Duggan's men around a thousand camp-fires. The chaplain was singing "The Battle Hymn of the Republic," that magnificent song that Kenneth Duggan once said was "well worth the war."

> Mine eyes have seen the glory
> Of the coming of the Lord . . .

Every voice took up the chorus, old men hymning their general to his reward, tired voices growing stronger as the shouts of "Glory, glory, hallelujah!" went reverberating around that hot and stuffy room. Mark stood there listening, rigid at attention and the hand salute, tears streaming down his face.

When they came to that great crashing conclusion: "His truth is marching on!" he did not hear them. Nor did he notice the bowed white heads watching him as he went striding from the room. In his heart he seemed to hear other voices, his mother whispering, *"You will be a great man, Mark,"* and Private Durkin chuckling, "From here on in, sir, you've got a charmed life," and then his father's dying command:

"Carry the name higher."

CHAPTER 9

Like everyone else in the offices of the General Staff in the War Department, Betsy King was shocked and saddened by the news of the death of General Duggan. Betsy had not known the general, but she had heard Mark speak of him frequently. In fact, she had rarely heard Captain Duggan speak affectionately of anyone else but his father. Of course, he did talk about his dead mother constantly; but that was more like reverence—adoration, even—than affection. But of his father, Mark often spoke fondly; proudly quoting his judgments of men or events, chuckling at his acid gibes at President Taft.

Betsy had confidently been expecting Mark to ask her to lunch with him that day, and was even prepared, if his courage should fail him on this last day of his furlough, to put the words into his mouth. She had been angry and frustrated when he failed to appear.

Betsy King you're a fool! she had thought bitterly, setting your cap for a man who touches your hand like a boy delivering Valentines. How could someone his age, looks, intelligence, and prospects in life be so shy? It wasn't as though he was one of those other kinds of men. No, she knew he was masculine. Betsy King liked men. She preferred their company—even in the plural—to the company of women.

But what made Mark Duggan so reverent? Why did he seem to want to kneel beside her rather than sit beside her? Probably his mother, she thought jealously: Lady Virtue wrapped in a thousand yards of white muslin sprinkled with five pounds of verbena. Betsy slammed her desk drawer shut with a bang that sent heads swiveling in her direction. She ignored them, absorbed as she was in self-recrimination. *What did I do to scare him off?*

Next morning, she read in the newspaper of the general's death. It was on the front page, just under the stories about President Wilson's inauguration that day. At first she was shocked. It was only after the news made Mark's absence explicable, that she felt relief; he hadn't asked her to lunch because of what had happened to his father.

In mid-morning Captain Duggan came into the office. He was pale, and yet his dark eyes and bearing seemed prouder than ever. Seeing the black band of mourning on the left sleeve of his uniform, Betsy King burst into tears.

Mark hurried past her into the chief of staff's office. General Field, just rising from behind his desk, was in full dress. Mark realized that he was probably on his way to the Capitol for the inauguration, and glanced anxiously at the wall clock.

"That's all right," General Field said, interpreting his glance. He came toward the captain and extended his hand. "Mark, I'm sorry," he said gently.

"Thank you, sir. But he could not have hoped for a better death."

"Speaking to his old soldiers? No better way."

"He was a great admirer of yours, General."

"And I of him." Now it was General Field who glanced at the clock, and Captain Duggan spoke up quickly. "I've come to ask a favor, sir. Would it be possible to forego burial in Arlington Cemetery?" The chief of staff seemed surprised, and Mark rushed on: "My father always wanted to be buried beside my mother, sir."

"I see. And yet...a simple ceremony for Kenneth Duggan...?"

"I know he was fond of honor and glory, sir—but he loved my mother."

"Well said, Mark. But why don't we give him full military

honors—after all, he was retired as a lieutenant general, the highest rank since U.S. Grant—and then you can arrange for a private burial.''

''Excellent!'' Mark cried in delight. ''Just what my father would have wanted.''

The general nodded, and Mark left his office.

Outside, his eyes fell on Betsy King. She was standing by a window, watching the inaugural bands and marching units forming below on Pennsylvania Avenue. She wore a full-length dress of a sober and sensible gray, which, though severe, nevertheless set off her full breasts and slender waist. Betsy had been surprised to discover that the modest dresses she'd worn after Mark began to visit the War Office actually did more for her figure than the tight, bright clothes she had formerly worn. She was even more startled to realize that no one, least of all Captain Duggan, seemed to notice when she put aside the lemon rinse and the peroxide and became a natural ash-blond again. Sensing someone behind her, she turned and saw Mark advancing toward her.

''I . . . I'm so sorry, Captain Duggan,'' she murmured, holding out her hand.

''Thank you, Miss King,'' he said, taking her hand with customary deference and quickly releasing it.

''It must have been a terrible experience.''

''It . . . it was. But it was inspiring too. It . . . it was grand . . .'' Betsy King was astonished. *''Grand?''*

''I'll explain, some day,'' Mark said, his voice trembling with emotion. ''I . . . I don't trust myself to tell you, now.''

Betsy nodded sympathetically.

''Miss King, I really don't know how to ask you this, but would you do me the honor of attending my father's funeral with me?''

Her eyes widened and she struggled to suppress her amazement. ''Why . . . why, of course, Captain. I'm flattered.''

''Not at all. I will be back tomorrow morning with the time and date.'' He put out his hand shyly and Betsy took it. Then he was gone.

Incredulous, Betsy stared at the door closing behind him. A funeral for their first date! The first time he asked her anywhere, it was to his father's funeral! She felt an impulse to shake her head, but checked herself when she became aware that half of the eyes in the office were fixed on her. Pretending not to notice, she walked gracefully back to her desk, sat down, and began to type. Only then did she remember the mourning band on Mark Duggan's left sleeve. Three months, she thought with sudden dismay, they usually mourn for three months! And I'll bet he doesn't ask me out again until he takes it off.

Betsy King was right. With the circumspection that was of the essence of his Episcopalian heritage, Mark Duggan remained in mourning for three months. Some of the older ladies in the War Office thought it was admirable of the young captain to carry his grief openly on his sleeve, especially in an age when tradition was everywhere being mocked and young people had no respect for their elders. Betsy King found it exasperating. Outwardly, however, she was gentle and understanding with him.

They saw each other almost every day, since Mark had been assigned to the General Staff as the junior officer of the thirty-eight member, policy-making board for the U.S. Army. Because Captain Duggan did not rate a secretary, and because he threw himself into his work with an energy that raised a mountain of paper on his desk, Betsy volunteered to do much of his secretarial work, frequently staying with him after hours. They ate coffee and doughnuts, they chatted, their hands touched, their eyes met; sometimes, even, their bodies brushed, but there was not the slightest breach of rectitude. Betsy King was beside herself. She could not believe that any man as masculine and seemingly as virile as Mark Duggan, could spend night after night alone with her and put not so much as a finger on her wrist. Where did he get such self-control? Though furious, she at least took comfort in the realization that no other woman was getting close to him.

Meanwhile, her desire grew daily—especially when she could observe him in action. It was not so much the swift incisiveness of his mind that impressed her, or his enormous knowledge of military history. Rather, it was his invincible poise and incredible self-confidence. He never became angry or flustered, even though, as the junior member of the board, he repeatedly challenged officers twice his age and three times his rank. Sometimes she had to keep herself from applauding, as on the day the board discussed reopening and increasing the number of "Preparedness" summer camps for students in the Officers Reserve Corps.

The discussion began after the chief of staff congratulated Brigadier General Homer Bean, chief of training and operations, on the conduct of the first camps the preceding summer. It was quickly agreed that four more camps should be opened, again for students or other young men who could pay their own way during the six-week training program.

"Very good, gentlemen," General Field said, placing his pencil on the next item on the agenda. But then, glancing down the end of the long table, where Mark Duggan sat, he noticed a frown on the young captain's forehead. "Something displeases you, Captain Duggan?"

"Well, yes, General Field," Duggan said, rising to his feet and fixing his dark eyes on General Bean. "With all due respect, I think it may be a mistake limiting the training to people who can afford it."

"And how is that, Captain?" General Bean asked coldly.

"Well, you see, sir, I was assigned to the western camp last summer, the one at Monterey. It was at the Del Monte Hotel, overlooking the Pacific Ocean." Mark's lips tightened. "A beautiful place, General Bean, but no place to train troop commanders." General Bean's neck reddened visibly, but Captain Duggan continued in a calm voice. "There were over a thousand trainees. All fine fellows—idealistic, full of enthusiasm, patriotic. But they were also a bunch of bluebloods. I never saw so many Rolls-Royces and Pierce-Arrows in my life. They looked on it as a lark, sir—a holiday. Playing at war by day in the salt sea air, dancing and drinking and dining in the Del Monte Hotel at night. They were as naive as the Union Army marching down Pennsylvania Avenue to take Richmond—bands, flags and flowers, pretty girls kissing zouaves in baggy red pants. Then the dreadful reality, the mud and blood of Bull R—"

"Please, Captain," General Bean interrupted. "Much as I admire your eloquence, not to say histrionics, I still find nothing like this in my reports."

"My report was written for General Eberts, sir."

"I still find nothing of the kind from the Western Department in my files." The general's voice had risen sharply, but

Duggan merely bowed politely and continued: "I am sure you did not, sir—but if you will allow me to describe one incid—"

Now it was the chief of staff who interrupted. "Go ahead, Captain," he said. "Briefly."

Bowing slightly, Duggan said: "One beautiful day, I lectured my platoon in the morning. The afternoon was to be devoted to close-order drill. But at noon all the wives and sweethearts drove out from San Francisco. They had picnic hampers full of delicacies and champagne. They had a great time eating and drinking under the oak trees, but then, after the women left, I tried to fall them in for close-order drill. They laughed at me. They said I had to be out of my mind if I thought they'd drill in the hot sun after a lunch like that." Fixing General Bean with his dark eyes, he spread his hands wide and said, "There was nothing I could do, sir. I had no authority over them, let alone control. They were civilians, and they were paying their way. They considered themselves my equal, a gentleman like themselves." Captain Duggan drew breath, shifting his gaze to General Field. "Based on this incident, and similar ones, I would recommend, sir, first, that candidates for the Officers Reserve Corps either be paid, or at least not charged; second, that the new camps should be located in hard climates and rough terrain; and third, that all drilling and physical training be conducted by noncommissioned officers."

Betsy King watched intently as General Bean leaned back in his chair, letting out his breath slowly while the color rose again above his collar.

"Really, Captain Duggan," Bean said in a tired voice, "I wonder where you think we will get the money to pay these people."

"I don't know, sir. Perhaps Congress would—"

"I see," General Bean said, lifting a hand, his voice eloquent with the disdain of a general toward a presumptuous captain. "And as for putting the new camps at the back of beyond, I get the impression, Captain, that if you had your way, you would burn down all the barracks in the country."

Momentarily, there was an awkward silence in the room, as though the members of the General Staff were embarrassed by the unequal contest developing before them. Mark Duggan, however, seemed unaware of the pause. "General Bean," he said easily, "if I may quote Napoleon. Maxim Fifty-eight: 'The first quality of a soldier is the ability to support fatigue and privations; valor is only secondary. Poverty, privation, and misery are the school of the good soldier.'"

An uglier silence ensued. Homer Bean turned scarlet, and General Field glanced quickly at the wall clock.

"Gentlemen," Field said softly, "let us adjourn for lunch."

A scraping of chairs followed, and the room emptied out. Betsy King remained, cleaning ashtrays and straightening out the papers and pencils scattered across the conference table. Seeing Captain Duggan standing in the doorway watching her, she went up to him. "You were wonderful! Honestly, simply wonderful!" Then she started, noticing that the familiar mourning band was missing from his sleeve.

He followed her eyes and laughed. "Thank you," he said. "And for those kind words, Miss Ki—I mean, Betsy, I am going to ask you to lunch."

They went to the New Willard. Mark quickly led Betsy across the lobby to the room in which he had last seen his father alive. They entered, and Mark pointed silently to the wall, on which a brass plate had been mounted.

> IN THIS ROOM
>
> ON MARCH 3, 1913
>
> LT. GEN. KENNETH DUGGAN
>
> COLLAPSED AND DIED
>
> WHILE ADDRESSING THE 50TH AND LAST REUNION
>
> OF THE MEN OF HIS CIVIL WAR REGIMENT
>
> THE 18TH U.S. INFANTRY

Betsy King's eyes were moist when she read the inscription. Turning to Mark, she said: "That was very sweet of you. You must have been very fond of your father."

"Yes, I was—but more proud than fond. Remember the day after he died, when I came to the office to see General Field? I said then that his death had been grand, and you were surprised. I said that some day I'd explain what I meant." He took her arm and escorted her back to the lobby. "Well, that was it—all those white-haired old soldiers singing, and my father lying there dead. It . . . it was terrible . . . but it was also magnificent and inspiring."

They entered the dining room and sat down beneath one of the huge glittering crystal chandeliers that only recently had been wired for electric lights. The waiter brought their menus, took their drink orders, then left.

"Do you know, Betsy, I was going to ask you to lunch here the day it happened."

"Really?" Her eyes were wide with feigned surprise.

"Yes. But when I went inside to make the reservation, I saw that the . . ." His voice trailed off. "Not even my mother's death affected me as much," he continued, motioning for the waiter. "I was with her when she died too."

Betsy reached for her menu, momentarily at a loss for what to say.

"She gave me a motto to remember too," Mark added, fixing Betsy King with the intense gaze of his dark eyes. "She told me I would be a great man."

This time Betsy was not embarrassed. Impulsively, she put out her hand to touch his. "I . . . I think you will, Mark," she said shyly, and then, as the waiter set down their drinks, she lifted the menu and exclaimed, "Hot dog! Oysters Rockefeller!"

Mark Duggan burst out laughing. "I take it you like seafood?"

"Do I? And the girls in the office told me they have the best seafood in the District. Ummmm . . . lobster, clams, and soft-shell crabs. I'll take the seafood plate, Mark."

"You're not as shy as I thought you were, Betsy."

"Not really. I'm from the west, you know, and they don't have much time for lollygagging out there."

Mark laughed again. Glancing up at the waiter, he said, "I'll just have ham and scrambled eggs."

Betsy looked at him in amazement. "Don't you like seafood?"

"Not very much. It doesn't agree with me."

"But they have so many other delicious dishes on the menu! If you like eggs, why don't you try the eggs Benedict?"

Captain Duggan shook his head, still smiling, pleased at her interest in him. "I'm afraid not. I don't have the toughest stomach in the world. I guess a lifetime in the mess hall ruined my taste for good. I'm an Army brat, you know, Betsy. I grew up on the frontier. When I was a boy, I tracked trails with—"

"You *are*?" Betsy exclaimed in delight. "So am *I*!"

"You're joking."

"No, I'm not. My father was General Field's orderly. How do you think I got my job in the War Department? I wrote to General Field and mentioned my father's name, and he asked me to come east."

"Where were you living then?" Mark asked, sipping from his drink.

"Outside Camp Robinson in Wyoming."

Mark put his glass down, incredulous. "Now I know you're joking. I grew *up* in Camp Robinson. That's where the Indian scouts taught me to ride and shoot. I could ride and shoot before I could read and write."

"So could I!" Betsy burst out proudly. "And I rode bareback, too."

"I bet you did," Mark said in admiration. "Say, did you ever go out to the cave under Comanche Bluff?"

"Sure, I did. All the time. I used to play dolls there when I was a little girl."

"I don't believe it!" Mark said in mock scorn. "Betsy King play dolls?"

"Well, I guess I was a bit of a tomboy," Betsy said, blushing. Mark smiled with pleasure, unaware that Betsy was coloring at the recollection of the grown-up game she had played there with Corporal Beauregard Ames. How sweet it had been, how broken-hearted she had been when her father had shanghaied Beau to the Philippines. She could still remember his thick honey-colored hair, and his Alabama accent, as slow and sweet as molasses. She'd cried for a week when he was transferred out to the Philippines.

"Is something wrong, Betsy?"

"Not really. I was just thinking of how General Bean looked at you this morning. Do you think he'll have it in for you?"

"Why should he?"

"Well, you certainly made him look sick this morning."

The waiter brought their food. After he left, Mark said, "I did? I hadn't intended to."

"He was real mad. I was watching him. And when you quoted Napoleon, he looked like he wanted to kill you. Didn't you know that General Bean can't take criticism?"

"No, I didn't," he said slowly. "But I never consider things like that. I just speak my mind. That's the great thing about General Field. He always listens."

They fell silent, Mark picking at his food mechanically, Betsy eagerly addressing her lobster. Mark studied her fondly, unaware that for perhaps the first time in his life he was relaxing with a woman and enjoying it. "Say, you really do like seafood, don't you?" he exclaimed, noticing that Betsy had carefully cracked every red tendril of the lobster on her plate.

She laughed. "Sure do. I always dreamed of coming east and eating seafood. I knew I'd love it, just reading about it. The first time I bit into Maryland crab, I thought I was in heaven." She surveyed the wreckage on her plate in mock dismay. "After this, I ought to be able to swim back to the office."

Mark chuckled, getting to his feet. "You've got a great sense of humor, Betsy," he said, helping her from her chair. "That's what I like about you."

That's *all*? She snorted to herself as she stepped demurely in front of him and preceded him out of the dining room.

A year to the day after the death of General Duggan, Betsy and Mark announced their engagement and began to compile a guest list for their wedding. They worked at the table in the living room of the dead general's home. It had been bequeathed to Mark, and they planned to live there following their honeymoon. Mark was surprised to see that Betsy was inviting only a few of the girls from her office.

"Don't you know anyone else?" he asked.

"Not in the east. The few living relatives that I do have are all west of the Mississippi." Betsy did not add that she was not so foolish as to invite any of the young men she had known before she met Mark. "But you'll more than make up for it," she continued, running her eyes over her fiancé's list. "My, my, Mark—don't you know anyone under the rank of colonel?"

"Well, yes," he replied, his face serious. "There's George Quincy Meadows. He's still a first lieutenant."

"Who's he?"

"He's my old West Point classmate. We were in the Philippines together."

"Funny, I never heard you mention him before."

"No? That is strange. He's back in the Philippines now. At Fort William McKinley."

"Well, he'll never make it to the wedding, then. It would certainly take him all of six weeks to get here, and it's only a month away."

"True. But I still want to send him an invitation."

"All these generals, Mark. Do you really know that many?"

"Of course. Most of them are friends of my father's. They were all captains and majors when I was a boy."

"Wow! Look at this list of sword attendants. Six generals, no less—and fourteen stars!"

"Betsy, when you walk under that arch of swords, all the stars in the heavens wouldn't be enough for you."

"Well, I don't know, Mark. To tell you the truth, I'm getting a little nervous. I never dreamed I'd be married by a bishop. The Right Reverend Wilfrid William Williams, Episcopal Bishop of Washington. Wow! That's a little too rich for a little old southern Baptist like me. You know, Mark, I'm glad you're not a Catholic. If you were, you'd have me up in front of a cardinal."

"If I were, Betsy King, I'd have you up in front of the pope."

She laughed. "I believe you would," she said, picking up a pen and beginning to address the heavy white envelopes stacked on the table in front of her.

The ceremony was performed in the West Point chapel. Betsy King, who was given away in marriage by General Field, was calm and beautiful in a long white wedding dress of heirloom lace. Captain Mark Duggan, though pale and slightly nervous, was strikingly handsome in his dress uniform. He had planned to wear a top piece, but had been dissuaded by Sergeant Durkin.

"Nah, nah, sir," Durkin had said, "if yez put one of them on yer head, you'll have to keep it there for life—and change it with the seasons of life, too, sir."

Instead, Mark had carefully combed his hair a little forward so that the thinning area would not be so noticeable.

The wedding went off smoothly, both bride and bridegroom going through the responses in clear, controlled voices. Outside the chapel, Betsy cried a little when she saw the six generals standing on the steps, resplendent in brass and braid, their glittering drawn swords presented overhead to form a wedding arch. She recovered quickly, however, when she saw the bank of photographers, all from the big New York newspapers, aiming their cameras at her.

The reception at the Officers' Club was in the best of taste. There was a buffet lunch similar to the one served after the Army-Navy football game: a profusion of salads and hors d'oeuvres heaped in silver serving dishes. Black stewards in starched white aprons and tall white chef's hats, carved turkeys, hams, and huge steamboat roasts of beef. Champagne flowed freely, and the first toasts were given to Betsy and Mark, standing alone together on the dance floor, by General Field.

"To the bride, ladies and gentlemen," he said bowing to Betsy with a fond smile, and lifting his glass. "The rose of old Wyoming has come to full blossom in the East." And then, to Captain Duggan: "He has stars in his eyes today, but believe me, they will soon be on his shoulders too."

A murmur of approval, mixed with the tinkling of glasses and the smacking of lips, moved through the gathering; and then the West Point band began to play. The first number was "The Wyoming State Song" in honor of Betsy, and then "Old Soldiers Never Die" for Mark, after which the newlyweds danced the first dance to the tune of "My Old Kentucky Home." After they had finished, Betsy and Mark moved among their guests, hand in hand.

They soon discovered that almost all the talk among the officers present—there were no civilians, and Mark was keenly disappointed that the Secretary of War had sent his regrets—was about President Wilson's intervention in Mexico a few days before. Wilson had refused to recognize the regime of General Victoriana Huerta, on the ground that

Huerta not only had murdered President Madero, but was now also trying to kill constitutional government. When one of Huerta's officers had arrested a paymaster and several sailors from an American warship, Wilson promptly asked Congress for authority to enforce his demand for "unequivocal amends." But before Congress could act, it was learned that a German ship was steaming toward Vera Cruz with a load of ammunition for the Huerta government. With that, Marines landed in Vera Cruz to seize the city and hold it for the arrival of General Homer Bean at the head of an expeditionary force of 7500 men.

"About time, too, I'd say," Major General Amos Lorenzo Carley was saying to a circle of attentive listeners as Captain Duggan came up to introduce his bride. "I always wondered why Wilson didn't let the Second Division loose over the border." He paused to acknowledge Mark's introduction. "You're a good picker, boy," he said, measuring Betsy with a twinkle in his normally frosty eye.

"And you are a good predicter, sir," Mark replied.

General Carley grinned. "You remember that, eh? Well, it's taken longer than I thought. But the volcano's ready to blow now, boy. That crazy kaiser, rattling his saber, calling himself Admiral of the Atlantic Ocean—the British don't like it one bit, I'll tell you."

"Do you think there'll be war with Mexico?" Mark asked, and Carley shook his silver head. "Not unless Huerta finds some sucker to buy him the beans and bullets he's going to need." He paused. "C'mon, boy—what kind of talk is this on your wedding day?"

Mark smiled. So did Betsy. They moved on to other guests. Soon it was dark. The band began to play "Here Comes the Bride," and Betsy advanced toward the dance floor to throw her wedding bouquet to the small group of unmarried girls gathered in the center. Then she turned to follow Mark out the door and outside to Sergeant Durkin, waiting in the victoria. He drove them to the Thayer Hotel, where they were to spend the night.

They stepped inside their suite and embraced.

"My dearest," Mark said. "My wife."

"My husband," Betsy murmured, hugging him. She stepped back. "Shall I . . . shall I undress . . . ?"

"If you like," Mark said, blushing. "I'll go in the bathroom and wait."

"When I turn down the light, you can come in."

Mark nodded and closed the bathroom door behind him. Betsy undressed quickly, carefully hanging her wedding gown in the closet. She examined herself nude in the mirror, drawing in her belly and running a hand over it. Putting on her nightgown of Chantilly lace, she went quickly to her bag, opened it, and took out a small vial. She pulled down the bedcovers and opened the vial. It contained duck's blood which she had bought in the market a few days ago. She sprinkled a few thick drops on the immaculate white sheet and waited for the stain to sink in. God forgive me, she prayed, as she lay down in her nightgown and pulled the covers up to her chin. But why take chances? Then she reached up a hand to turn the kerosene lamp down low.

"Mark, I'm ready."

He came into the bedroom. He was wearing his old gray bathrobe from cadet days, with the big gold and black A sewn on it. "Do you . . . do you want to talk a little, or do you want me to join you?" he asked.

"Join me, Mark. I love you."

She closed her eyes, hearing the rustle of his clothing as he removed his robe. She lay quivering, hungry for the feel of his hand between her thighs, the pressure of his lips on her breast. But it did not come. She opened her eyes and looked at him. He lay beside her, unmoving, gazing at her ardently.

"My dearest," he murmured.

"Mark, don't you want to take off your pajamas?"

He arose. She closed her eyes again, listening to the whisper of silk. He lay down once more, still unmoving. She reopened her eyes, looking into his dark eyes, full of ardor.

"Come, Mark," she gasped, reaching down to guide him into her. Oh, Lord! she thought, feeling the inert body above her beginning to quiver faintly, do *I* have to do it?

CHAPTER 10

Betsy King—it would be several days before she began to think of herself as Betsy Duggan—awoke before Mark. It was early. She could hear a cardinal singing and see the dawn mists of the Hudson shredding outside her window.

Betsy gazed fondly at her sleeping husband. I love you, Mark, she thought. And now I am really and truly the wife of the dashing Captain Duggan, the officer that everyone at the War Department said was destined for high command. Since her early childhood, she had dreamed of becoming an officer's lady. On every post, on almost every Saturday night, she would leave the wretched family shack on this or that "Soapsuds Row" and run to the Officers' Club. She would climb a tree or find some hiding place from which to watch the officers arriving with their ladies, who wore long evening gowns. Now she would be leading the dance. Gazing once again at Mark, she imagined all the exciting posts he would hold, all the wonderful places she would see. Everyone at the War Department seemed to think there would be a big war in Europe. Perhaps Mark would be sent there as an observer, and they would live in Paris or London or Vienna. Maybe, Betsy thought, after our honeymoon is over, I'll start studying French. A French-speaking wife would be no small asset in Paris.

Suddenly, Betsy thought of their first moments together. She tried to put it out of her mind. After all, he had awakened later on and she had succeeded in arousing his passion. He was just shy, that was all, too much the product of genteel tradition, of wife-and-mother worship. She smiled gently, lightly touching his noble forehead with her fingertips. I will teach you, Mark. It's all very well to act like a general on the parade ground. But in bed, my dearest, it's more fun to behave like a private. She traced the line of his eyebrow with her finger and his eyes fluttered and flew open.

"Good morning, husband," she said, and he put her hand to his lips.

"My dearest."

"All right, Captain," she said, grinning impishly. "You're senior, here. Who gets to use the bathroom first?"

"You go, Betsy. I'll wait."

"As you wish, sir," she said, throwing him a mock salute. She swiveled around to put her feet on the floor and arise. Behind her, she heard him gasp.

"Betsy!" he cried. "What's that stain on your night-gown?" She craned her neck around and pulled the material forward. "My goodness, it's . . . it's blood!"

He looked beside him in horror, seeing the bloodstains on the bedsheet. "My dearest! Oh, God—what a brute I am! Did I . . . did I hurt you, Betsy?"

"I didn't even notice. I knew something was supposed to happen, but I forgot about it. I guess it did." She blushed. "You know, I rode bareback so much when I was a girl, I always wondered . . ." Betsy giggled. "Now you *have* to marry me, Mark."

Mark Duggan smiled. He came around the bed to embrace her. There was a discreet knock on the door.

"Call for Captain Duggan," a voice said.

Betsy darted into the bathroom while Mark quickly put on his gray robe and opened the door. A bellhop stood outside.

"Sorry to bother you, sir, but the War Department in Washington is on the telephone downstairs."

"Tell them I'll call right back."

"Sorry, sir. They want to hold the line. They said they had too much trouble getting through on a Sunday morning."

"All right. I'll be right down." Frowning, Mark closed the

door and began to dress. Betsy came out of the bathroom in alarm.

"What is it, Mark?"

"The War Department is on the line downstairs. I'll be right back."

Betsy sat down on the bed, her hand at her throat in apprehension. She was still there when he returned five minutes later. He was scowling now, and her heart sank.

"General Field wants to see me."

"When?"

"Tomorrow morning. We'll have to take a sleeper from New York tonight."

Betsy's lips quivered and she began to cry. He rushed to her side.

"Mark, it's our honeymoon!" she wailed. "What about Martha's Vineyard and Cape Cod?"

"We'll have to cancel," he said grimly. "Betsy, dearest, please believe me, there's nothing to be done. General Field was emphatic. He told me to convey his apologies to you, and I told him I was sure you would understand."

"I guess I have no choice," she said poutingly.

"Betsy, I'm a soldier!"

"Oh, I know, but how many honeymoons does a girl get?"

He looked at her in exasperation. "Betsy, you're a soldier's daughter and should know better." He tried to smile. "You should know that before I married you I had another mistress."

"Whaaat?"

"Yes, my country. The United States of America. She is still my mistress, Betsy." He came to her and put his hands on her shoulders. "You know the poem, 'To Lucasta on Going to the War'?" He smiled fondly. " 'I could not love thee so much, dear, loved I not honor more.' " Pointing to his gray cadet bathrobe lying over the back of a chair, he continued: "Even at the Academy, dearest, you see it: 'Duty. Honor. Country.' "

Betsy nodded dully. She removed his hands from her shoulders and walked stiffly into the bathroom. She looked into the mirror, into the misery in her eyes, at her tear-streaked cheeks, and wondered: Is that the way it's going to be? Duty? Honor? Country?

And then me?

• • •

"Captain," General Field said, "when I arrived in Washington Saturday night, there was an urgent message for me to call the Secretary of War immediately. I did, and Mr. Garrison requested an immediate conference. He was worried about the situation in Vera Cruz. He said there was every possibility of war with Mexico, that a field army under my command might have to be sent there to back up General Bean. In that case, we would need to know the lay of the land, the availability of transport, food for the men, fodder for the horses, and so on. Which means that I will need a personal observer down there. And I can think of no one better than yourself."

"Thank you, sir!" Captain Duggan exclaimed in delight, springing to his feet. "When do I leave?"

"Immediately. There's a supply ship leaving Norfolk tonight. You'll have time to pack and say good-bye to your wife . . . And by the way, please tell her that my wife and I will stop by tonight to take her to dinner." He shook his head ruefully. "I didn't much enjoy wrecking her honeymoon, I can tell you that."

"She's a soldier's daughter, sir. She understands."

"Perhaps. But she's also a bride. Well, it couldn't be helped." He arose and extended his hand. "Good luck, Mark."

"Thank you, sir."

"And remember, as my personal emissary, you are answerable only to me and the War Department."

"Yes, sir. I understand, sir."

The voyage down the Atlantic coast and around the tip of Florida into the Gulf of Mexico was uneventful. A week after leaving Norfolk, Captain Duggan and Sergeant Durkin stood at the rail of the freighter *Adams* and watched the sun setting behind Mount Orizaba, the snowcapped mountain peak above the city of Vera Cruz.

"We've been here before, Pat," he said, drawing his gold cigarette holder from a breast pocket and fitting a cigarette into it.

"How's that, sir?" Durkin asked, shielding his eyes against the sun's glare.

"Over sixty years ago, in the war with Mexico, Winfield Scott landed here with ten thousand men. From Vera Cruz he marched on Mexico City." Captain Duggan blew smoke thoughtfully. "Scott was an organizing genius and he won an empire for his country—yet they gave the presidency to Taylor."

"Who was that, sir?"

"Zachary Taylor, another Mexican War general. He couldn't compare to Scott, Pat, but he was popular. Old Rough 'n' Ready, they called him, while Scott was known as Ol' Fuss 'n' Feathers. That should tell you something."

"I don't folly you, Captain," Durkin said, watching in enchantment as the red ball of the setting sun came closer to the glistening white peak of the mountain.

"It's simply that in America, Pat, a man with presidential aspirations must be careful not to seem too polished or professional. Here was Scott, our first scientific soldier, and there was Taylor, an ordinary plugger—but Ol' Rough 'n' Ready never made the mistake of seeming superior. So they put him in the White House."

Sergeant Durkin let out his breath in delight. The sun had touched the snowcap. "God's truth on it, sir, if yez'll look close enough, you'll see her steam."

Captain Duggan chuckled. "All right, Pat, you'd better get our gear. We'll be going ashore in a lighter."

Sergeant Durkin nodded and went below, reappearing above deck a few minutes later laden with duffel bags. He dumped them into a boat slung beneath a pair of davits. Captain Duggan quickly opened his own bag and drew out a battered campaign hat, clapping it on his head. "Remember this, Pat?" he asked with a grin.

"Jaysus! It's the one they shot off your head a dozen years ago."

"It is indeed," Duggan said, removing it and proudly fingering the bullet holes. "It's my war bonnet, Pat, and I intend to wear it every time my country goes on the warpath."

Durkin grinned, his sooty blue eyes gleaming. He helped the captain into the boat and clambered in himself. The coxswain signaled the bos'n's mate, the winches began to hum, and the boat was swung out on its davits and lowered over the side. Once in the water, the coxswain opened the throttle and pointed his prow shoreward. Captain Duggan and his orderly sat silently at the gunwales, watching the city come closer. They could see women in parasols and men in white suits and sombreros strolling along the beach.

"Not much of a war, sir," Durkin shouted above the roar of the motor.

Duggan nodded and pointed to the crumbling ramparts of a huge stone fortress on a reef across the bay. "Fort San Juan de Ulua," he yelled, cupping his hands. "It was supposed to have been impregnable, but Scott sailed right by it."

Now the coxswain cut his motor and the gently pitching boat slipped up beneath a wharf. Durkin vaulted onto the boards and helped the captain up beside him. An American army captain came toward them with outstretched hand.

"Captain Duggan?"

"Correct," Duggan said, taking the proffered hand.

"I'm Captain Delchamp, the provost marshal here. Headquarters asked me to pick you up."

"Very kind of you, Captain Delchamp."

"Not at all. If you'll just bring the gear, Sergeant. I have a staff car waiting." Captain Delchamp was about to say more, until he noticed Captain Duggan's campaign hat. "That's not exactly regulation headgear, Captain."

Duggan chuckled. "It's my good-luck hat, Captain. It was shot off my head on Samar thirteen years ago."

"You served on Samar?"

"Yes." He pointed to Durkin, shouldering their bags. "Sergeant Durkin won the Medal of Honor there."

To the astonishment of both men, Captain Delchamp snapped to attention and saluted. "I was formerly a Marine officer," he explained. "Whenever a veteran of Samar came into a Marine officers' mess, the C.O. always arose and said, 'Stand, gentlemen, he served on Samar.' "

Captain Duggan smiled. "Leave it to the Marines," he murmured, getting into the rear of the staff car. Durkin put their bags beside the driver and got in next to him, then they pulled away. For a few minutes Duggan studied his surroundings: the tree-lined cobblestone streets crowded with horses and horse-drawn vehicles, the whitewashed storefronts, the crowded sidewalks.

"Seems pretty quiet," he said.

"It is. Huerta's people are nowhere in sight. Of course, the civilians hate us. Not openly, of course, just cold and distant. Can't say that I blame them. No one likes an occupation, especially not by gringos. But they don't trouble us. Actually, the sawbones are the only people who are busy down here, what with the brothels and the *vomito*."

"*Vomito?*"

"Yellow fever. Of course, it's not nearly as bad as it was in Scott's day, thanks to Walter Reed. But it's still around, and now is the worst time of year for it."

"I see."

"Otherwise, we just sit here and wait for someone to make the next move."

Duggan nodded, his dark eyes studying the clip-clopping, neighing, sweating animal traffic that engulfed them and slowed their staff car to a crawl.

"They don't seem to have heard of the horseless carriage down here," he said.

"No. Matter of fact, Captain, transport is probably our biggest problem. We have plenty of our own horses, and there's more in the city, but Huerta seems to have rounded up all the mounts in the province. All the locomotives are gone too. There's plenty of rolling stock, but no loc—"

"No rail transport?" Duggan looked at Delchamp, aghast. "My God, supposing we did have a war. How could we supply a field army marching on Mexico City?"

Delchamp shrugged. "Search me. That isn't my can of worms, anyway, Captain. I'm just in charge of sobering up the drunken doughboys my MPs pull out of the whorehouses. Here we are, Captain—this is headquarters." He pointed to an imposing three-story baroque building facing on an open courtyard with a fountain playing in the center of a round formal garden. "Used to be the post office, but now it's General Bean's HQ. The duty officer inside will take care of you and the sergeant."

"Thank you, Captain," Duggan said. He got out of the car and preceded Durkin through the plaza. Inside, a second lieutenant assigned Captain Duggan an office and issued him a map of the occupation zone.

"Will you be needing a Spanish-speaking guide, sir?" he asked.

Duggan shook his head. "That won't be necessary. I can get along fairly well in Spanish myself. But we will need some mounts."

"As you wish, sir. The stables are at the rear of the building."

Duggan nodded, and the two men followed an orderly outside. In five more minutes they were mounted and riding slowly about Vera Cruz, visiting all the outposts, wound like a cordon around the city. At each of them, Captain Duggan questioned the commander on his mobility. Very quickly he discovered that the American expeditionary force could move no faster than its soldiers' feet.

"My God, they're immobile," he muttered to Sergeant Durkin as they trotted back to the heart of the city. "They're infantry up against a mounted army. They're relying strictly on their own animal transport and a few city horses." He shook his head grimly. "They can't move."

"Do you think Huerta can kick us out of Vera Cruz, sir?" Durkin asked, reining in his horse as an American army artillery wagon rumbled by, raising a cloud of dust.

"Not on your life," the captain answered, pulling the brim of his campaign hat low over his face as a shield against the white dust settling on them. "But we can't mount an attack against him, either, not without rail or motor transport to move our artillery and supplies."

The following day, the two men stayed within the city, visiting the railroad terminal. They found the car barns full of rolling stock—freight and passenger cars—but the roundhouse was silent and empty. Disturbed, Captain Duggan returned to his hotel to write his first report to General Field.

I consider the absence of adequate transportation to be the most critical problem in Vera Cruz and the most serious obstacle facing an American field army in the event of full-scale war. The cavalry units have adequate remounts, but there are no replacements for the wagon horses. Motor transport exists only at the regimental level, and, worst of all, there are no railroad locomotives. Huerta has not only cleaned the countryside of animal transport, but has also taken all the locomotives. Obviously, if he gives battle, he will fight a war of movement against our hopelessly immobilized forces. We may hold Vera Cruz, sir, but we are actually only holding an island in a hostile sea. Without transport, we cannot leave the island without sinking . . .

Captain Duggan paused, pencil at his teeth. He started erect and swung around in his chair when the door flew open and Sergeant Durkin burst into the room. His red hair was rumpled and there were greasy black streaks on his face. But his blue eyes shone.

Captain Duggan suspected him of drinking. "Pat—" he began sharply.

"A glass or two is all, sir." The big sergeant grinned and put a huge hand in the air as though he were taking an oath. "'Twas me personal reconnaissance I was on, sir, and the situation required a glass or two." He drew his hand across his mouth and grinned again. "I've got him in the stables, sir, sobering up in the horse trough."

Duggan shot to his feet. "*Who* do you have in the horse trough?" he cried in alarm.

"The fireman, sir. The Mexican fireman. You see, sir, it occurred to me that whoever drove them locomotives out of town probably lived near the railroad terminal. I was going to speak to you about it, but seeing you busy on your report, I decided to reconnoiter on me own. So I rode back to the terminal and began scoutin' the local *posadas*." Durkin's eyes gleamed. "Glory be to God, sir, but there he was in the second stop, a little greaser sitting at the bar, daft drunk and babblin' away in ten different directions. Who else but a railroad fireman would stink of coal like he was born in a mine, I says to myself, so I sidled closer and bought the little darlin' a couple shots of tequila. Just to be sociable, sir, I bought meself a few. Jaysus, sir, in another minute I'm beginning to hear words like *ferrocaril* and *locomovil,* and then he's on his feet pounding his chest and tellin' the whole bar how him and Huerta made fools—*tonto,* sir, that's the word for it—out of the *idiota* gringo devils. Jaysus save me wit, Captain, but doesn't the whole damn *posada* fall on their bellies laughin', and that was when I put the little laddy under me arm and brought him here."

"Didn't anyone try to stop you?" Duggan asked, his voice full of incredulity.

"Well, sir, the barman had something like that in mind, so I give him a little love tap under the chin."

"And the others?"

"I had my forty-five out, sir."

Captain Duggan was about to shake his head disapprovingly, but then he sighed. "I guess you did the right thing, Pat. Anyway, good work—*excellent* work." He reached for his campaign hat. "Let's get over to the stable."

Sopping wet and shivering, a huge Army horse blanket wrapped around his thin shoulders, his long black hair plastered against his skull and his huge mustache drooping beneath either side of his chin like limp shoelaces, the little Mexican sat on a stool in the stables while Captain Duggan interrogated him in Spanish.

He told the captain that his name was Eduardo Lobo, that he was a fireman on the Alvarado and Vera Cruz Railroad, and that he had indeed helped to drive one of the locomotives out of Vera Cruz to a roundhouse at the other end of the line in Alvarado.

"*Cuantos locomoviles?*" How many locomotives?

"*Seis.*"

Duggan's eyes gleamed. "Are they still in Alvarado?"

"*Si.*"

Duggan smiled, but then he frowned. "Why not farther away? I mean, why did you not take them all the way to Mexico City?"

"There was not enough coal, *Capitan.*"

"I see." He stared thoughtfully at the Mexican. "How would you like to make two hundred dollars American?"

Now it was the Mexican whose eyes gleamed. "In gold, *Capitan*?" he asked slyly.

"In gold. All you have to do is lead us to the roundhouse in Alvarado. Agreed?"

"*Si.*" The Mexican's fingers strayed to his damp mustache. "There is a handcar. It is how I came back to Vera Cruz. We can take this handcar to Alvarado and back."

"Excellent!" Duggan exclaimed, striking his hands together jubilantly and turning to Sergeant Durkin. "Put him in a clean Army uniform, Pat, and take him up to your room. Don't let him out of your sight.''

"As you wish, sir."

"I'm going to speak to Captain Delchamp."

The provost marshal was impressed with Captain Duggan's discovery. "Those locomotives would come in mighty handy if it ever came to full-scale war."

"I know. But we have to be sure they're there. So I'm going out to take a look."

"When?"

"Tomorrow night. Can you take care of security for me?"

"Of course. I'll put you through Captain Walker's outpost line. That's where the railroad tracks are." Delchamp frowned. "Are you going to speak to General Bean about this?"

"I don't think I need to. My instructions from General Field seem to cover this contingency."

Delchamp frowned again. "I don't know, Captain. They're awfully touchy about so-called incidents down here. Anything that might start a war . . . The hills out there are swarming with guerrillas and bandidos, Captain. Maybe you should talk to the inspector general."

"Who's he?"

"I don't rightly know. He's new here, just came aboard a few days ago. Only a first lieutenant, too, which isn't a helluva lot of rank for an inspector general. But General Bean seems awfully high on him."

"Where can I find him?" Duggan asked, getting to his feet. Captain Delchamp pointed to the corridor and said, "Two doors down on the left. And good luck, Captain. I'll let Walker know that your party will be coming through tomorrow at dusk."

"Thanks a million," Captain Duggan said, shaking hands. He turned and went out into the corridor.

Two doors down on the left, the door was closed. Captain Duggan knocked.

"Come in," a familiar voice called, and Mark Duggan paused in astonishment. It can't be! he thought. Not again! Inside, George Quincy Meadows was just putting a match to his big-bowled pipe when Mark Duggan threw the door open and entered.

"Welcome to Mexico, Mark," Meadows said, putting down the pipe with a grin.

"George! I thought you were in the Philippines."

"I was, up until two months ago. I thought I was headed for duty on the border with the Second Division, but when we came through the Canal and stopped at Galveston, they pulled me off the boat and shipped me down here." Meadows grinned again. "Looks like I beat you to another war, Mark."

Mark Duggan smiled a weak, unconvincing smile. "Guess so," he murmured. "General Bean must think a lot of you, George, making you inspector general with just one silver bar on your shoulder."

"I knew him in Leavenworth," Lieutenant Meadows said, picking up his pipe again, and lighting it this time. "He was one of my students." His teeth ground hard on the stem. "From what I've seen of the Spanish War deadwood around here, even a plebe could outswim them." His eyes strayed to his shoulder insignia. "Nine years a first lieutenant," he said bitterly. "I've taught colonels and generals, but I'm still a first looey. I tell you, Mark, if it hadn't been for this Mexican affair, I would have left the Army and gone into business."

"I can't say that I blame you, George," Duggan said gently. "Promotions come harder and harder. And Congress gets stingier and stingier. Meanwhile, up on top, the arteries get harder and harder." He shook his head ruefully. "General Field tried to break that logjam up there, but even he couldn't do it."

Lieutenant Meadows nodded, sighing. He leaned back in his chair. "We'll see," he murmured. "Anyway, what's on your mind, Mark?"

Speaking quickly, gesturing with his cigarette holder, his voice low and husky with emotion, as it always was when he proposed a daring scheme, Duggan explained his plan. After he had finished, Lieutenant Meadows laid down his pipe and stared at Duggan meditatively for perhaps ten seconds.

"As you say," he began slowly, weighing his words, "that kind of information could turn out to be invaluable." He paused, pursing his lips, his homely face a study in concentration. "But I do not think it would be worth the risk."

"Risk? Risk of what, George?"

"An incident. Washington does not want war, Mark. The

President and the State Department are hoping that some other Mexican leader may force Huerta out. Someone like Carranza. I have heard that they are actually helping Carranza. So, you see, any incident..." He shook his head apprehensively.

"I understand," Duggan said evenly. "But the Secretary of War seems to think that there will be war. And in that case, this intelligence . . ." He lifted his shoulders eloquently. "Besides, George, my orders from General Field are very clear on the point of obtaining vital information."

"Then you plan to go ahead with it?"

"Yes."

"Then I must tell you, Mark, that I am strongly advising against it, and that I am going to inform General Bean of our conversation."

Duggan rose slowly to his feet. "If you see it that way, George," he said stiffly, "then it is your duty to speak to the general. If he wants to see me," he continued, taking his campaign hat from the chair beside him, "I will be in my quarters." Nodding, he strode from the room, pausing momentarily outside the door before walking quickly down the corridor and reentering the office of the provost marshal.

"Captain Delchamp," he said to the startled officer behind the desk, "I've decided to move sooner."

"Yes?"

"You'd better tell Captain Walker I'll be coming through at dusk tonight."

When Mark Duggan entered Sergeant Durkin's room, he found him playing cards with his captive. Eduardo wore an Army uniform so big that he had been compelled to roll up the cuffs of both his blouse and trousers. He seemed dwarfed and waiflike beside the huge sergeant.

His lips parted in a flashing white smile when Durkin pointed at him and said, "Eduardo and me is gettin' to be real good butties, sir. Especially after I relieved him of them toys he was carryin'." He jerked a finger toward the bureau on which a small pistol and a slender sheathed knife lay. "And here I'd been thinkin' 'twas only us, sir, the Scots and the Irish, that carried a *skin dhu*."

Duggan smiled. "A stocking dirk, eh?" He stared at Eduardo, who looked away. "He's clean now, Pat?"

"Oh, yes, sir."

"Good. Now, Eduardo," Duggan said speaking in Spanish, "you search us." Eduardo glanced up in surprise. "That's right, Eduardo—go ahead."

Eduardo rose and came shyly to the captain. He ran his hands over his clothes and withdrew a wad of currency, a handful of gold coins, and Duggan's cherished gold watch and his cigarette holder. From Durkin's pockets he took more currency, a rosary of ivory beads and silver cross—which seemed a pleasant surprise—a combination knife, and a sack of Bull Durham tobacco. He gave the knife back to Durkin and put the other objects on the bureau as directed.

"You see, Eduardo," Captain Duggan said. "We now carry nothing of value on our persons. If you try to lead us into a trap, you will get nothing for your treachery. All we have is our weapons," he said, pointing to the .45 automatics in holsters at his and Durkin's hip, "and this flashlight." He lifted the shiny long instrument in his hand. "So it is now essential for you to ensure our safe return. Otherwise, you do not get your money. *Comprendes*?"

"*Si*," Eduardo said, his face clearing. "But, *Capitan*, can you not give me a little of the *dinero* now?"

"If you like," Duggan said, going to the pile of gold pieces on the bureau. "I can give you fifty now and the rest on our return." Eduardo nodded, swallowing, extending a hand greedily. "But if you take it now, Eduardo," Duggan said, "and something happens to us . . . and the Huertistas find you in our company with this gold on you . . ." He paused significantly, drawing a finger across his throat. Swallowing again, Eduardo nodded and handed the money back to Duggan.

The captain took it, placing it in a bureau drawer with the other objects, locking it and putting the key in his pocket.

"Let's go," he said, putting on his campaign hat.

He led them outside and down to the lobby, where he left the drawer key with the orderly on duty. Then they walked across the street to the stables, obtaining mounts and riding silently through the deepening dusk to the position held by Captain Walker. They left their horses in his care and climbed carefully through the barbed wire across the railroad tracks and began walking rapidly, tie by tie, south toward Alvarado.

A half hour later they came to a bridge across the Jalapa River. Eduardo held up a hand.

"It is here, *Capitan*," he whispered, pointing to a ditch below the tracks. "There, do you see it—the handcar?"

In a few seconds Duggan made out the outlines of a wooden platform lying on its face with its iron wheels reaching for the night sky like an upended monster centipede. The captain whistled under his breath. "My God, Eduardo, it must weigh seven or eight hundred pounds!" Trying to keep the suspicion out of his voice, he asked casually, "How did you get it down there?"

Eduardo grinned in the dark. "You do not trust Eduardo, eh, *Capitan*? You think he is too little to do that?" He chuckled and walked to the other side of the tracks, stooping to seize a railroad tie and pull it toward him. "You see? I park the handcar up there." He pointed up the grade toward the bridge. "Then I put this here. I start the handcar. She rolls down the grade. I jump off, and—*caramba*—she jumps off."

Now it was Duggan who chuckled. "All right, Eduardo, I believe you. C'mon, Pat," he said, scrambling down the embankment. "Let's see if you can move it."

"It won't be easy," Durkin muttered, following him down with short, braking steps. He grasped one end of the handcar and lifted. It rose a few inches. "Maybe I can fishtail her, sir," he grunted. "If you and Eduardo will just hold on to me gorgeous behind." They put their hands at his back, bracing him, and Durkin lifted one end, pulling it up the incline, and then the other. Five minutes later he had the vehicle on the tracks, where he turned it rightside up.

All three climbed aboard. "This is the mount, *Capitan*," Eduardo began, pointing to a pair of facing handlebars in the center of the platform.

"I know, Eduardo—I pumped many a handcar when I was a boy in the American west."

Surprised, Eduardo nodded and sat down facing the rear. Durkin took the seat opposite him, and both began to work the handlebars, pumping them up and down alternately, see-saw fashion, turning the crank-and-cog mechanism that powered the wheels. With a screech of steel on steel, the handcar began to move. Slowly, it climbed the grade to the bridge.

Beneath them, the dark coil of the Jalapa River was barely visible. Captain Duggan glanced upward in alarm. Black clouds were scudding low across the sky. The night was turning squally. Thick raindrops pelted them. They could see flashes of lightning ahead.

"Hurry, men," Duggan urged.

Durkin nodded, grunting. "What can she make, Captain?"

"Downhill, maybe thirty miles an hour, twenty on the level. This one seems to be in pretty good shape, so we should do close to that."

They clattered along rapidly, shooting across bridge after bridge, culvert after culvert. *Clank-clank,* went the handle-bars; *clack-clack,* went the wheels. Soon they had left the snakelike Jalapa behind them, emerging on a plain. Road crossings replaced the bridges and culverts, and at each of them, it seemed, they could hear the drumbeat of horse's hooves. Sometimes, in the thickening storm, a flash of lightning would illuminate bands of horsemen galloping across the tracks in front of them, or reining in skittish horses frightened by the sound of the approaching handcar. Then the reenveloping darkness would obscure them both from each other's sight.

"The country must be alive with Huertistas," Captain Duggan muttered, standing beside the panting Eduardo.

"Not Huertistas, *Capitan*," Eduardo gasped, releasing his handlebar to run his wrist across his perspiring brow. "*Bandidos. Bandidos y desterrados.* It is bad. These carrion live off the country people. They rape and rob and kill, and there is no one to stop them. My country is in agony, *Capitan*," he said with gentle sadness. "Mexico is like a woman in labor."

"Maybe someday she will bring forth a man," Duggan said, placing a consoling hand on Eduardo's shoulder. Suddenly both men realized that they were gaining momentum. Durkin was pumping his handlebar madly. Duggan could feel the force of the wind pressing the brim of his hat against the crown. They were swaying dangerously . . . and then there was a piercing scream of tortured steel and the car slowed down. Eduardo had hit the foot brake.

"*Madre de Dios, Capitan!*" he yelled. "Tell the big one the handcar does not fly."

Duggan cupped his hands to his lips to shout at Durkin to

ease up, only to see, in another lightning flash, perhaps a dozen riderless horses standing near a crossing below them. Men in high sombreros, with bandoliers slung across their chests, were rolling a huge stone toward the tracks.

"*Bandidos!*" Duggan cried warningly. "Pour it on, Pat! Eduardo, get pumping!"

The car lurched forward, gathering speed, swaying once again, the wheels screeching. Duggan drew his pistol and cocked it, putting his face into the wind, peering into the darkness. Probably the same bunch we saw at the last crossing, he thought: They rode around to head us off. Ten more seconds. He counted slowly to himself: *one thousand* . . . *two thousand* . . . *three* . . . He raised his pistol and fired . . . *eight thousand* . . . he fired again . . . *nine thousand* . . . This time a scream, and then a loud crash and the handcar shuddered, leaping as though it would jump the track. But the wheels held to the tracks. Neighs and high-pitched horses' screams, shouts and curses and shots rose around them. Soon they were rattling down the grade, rolling onto a straight stretch at a speed of perhaps thirty-five miles an hour.

A half hour later the rain stopped. The skies began to clear. In five more minutes they rolled alongside Alvarado's deserted streets and saw the dark bulk of the roundhouse looming ahead of them. They stopped and dismounted. Eduardo swung open the huge roundhouse door and they went inside.

Duggan switched on his flashlight, whistling in delight when he saw the locomotives standing there. Three of them, he saw immediately, were little switch engines, of no use to an army. But the other three were big road-pullers, apparently in good condition.

"Excellent, Eduardo!" Duggan exclaimed, clapping the Mexican on the shoulder.

"*Gracias,*" Eduardo murmured, swinging up into the cabin of one of the locomotives. "Will you give me your flashlight, *Capitan*?"

Duggan handed it over, the beam swinging eerily across the roundhouse roof. Eduardo pointed the light into the coal tender and peered inside. "That is strange," he muttered. "There is not very much coal." He climbed down and inspected the other two engines. They also were low on coal. "Perhaps *los ciudadanos*"—the townspeople—"took the coal for their stoves." He jumped down from the last locomotive and returned the flashlight.

"That's no problem, Eduardo," Duggan said, switching off the beam. "We're not taking them anywhere. I just wanted to verify their existence. Come, we'd better get going before it gets light again."

Hoofbeats pounded outside the roundhouse. Shrill, yipping yells rose in the night. Shots rang out and bullets spanged off the iron hides of the engines.

"Bandidos!" Eduardo yelled, throwing himself down.

Duggan drew quickly and fired from the hip at a rider galloping into the roundhouse with leveled pistol. He fell, a hoarse, echoing death cry issuing from his lips, and Sergeant Pat Durkin ran quickly forward to push the heavy steel door shut and slam the bolt. More bullets spanged off steel, against the door this time, and some shattered a few of the door's high glass windows.

Duggan stooped to seize Eduardo and pull him erect. He pushed the muzzle of his pistol into the pit of flesh beneath his ear and cocked it with a menacing click. "Eduardo?" he asked softly.

"No, no! *Madre de Dios, Capitan,* I do not betray you. I am with you, I swear it!"

"How did they get here so fast? How did they know?"

"You forget, *Capitan,* the line ends at Alvarado. We could only be going here. They must have forded the river. It is a shortcut, *Capitan.* And the railroad makes a big swing around Alvarado. It would not be difficult if they rode hard."

Duggan paused, still not convinced. "What do they want?"

The answer came from outside the roundhouse. Evidently, a bandit had crept up to the steel door. Now, his voice came through the broken windows.

"Throw out your guns and come out with your 'ands up," he called in perfect English, except for a slight accent. "You will not be harmed. We do not want to kill you, Excellency. We want to 'old you for ransom."

"Not a chance!" Duggan cried.

"Do not be foolish, Excellency. You cannot get away. We have your 'andcar, and the only way out of the round'ouse is through this door."

Duggan paused. "Let me think it over," he shouted, to Durkin's immense surprise.

"As you wish, Excellency. We 'ave the time, we 'ave food, and we 'ave water. You 'ave none of these."

With slow deliberation, Duggan swung his flashlight beam around the perimeter of the roundhouse, looking for a door or opening of some sort.

"It is true, *Capitan*," Eduardo whispered. "There is only the front door." The beam settled on the body of the fallen bandit.

"How about him, sir?" Durkin asked eagerly. "Maybe we can hold him hostage."

Duggan shook his head. "He's dead, Pat. You know they don't live when they holler like that." Duggan turned to Eduardo. "Can you run a locomotive?"

"*Si*. But there is so little coal, *Capitan*. We would not get very far."

"Yes, but there is some coal in all of the tenders. Enough for one engine?"

"*Si*," Eduardo said, his eyes gleaming.

"Good. Eduardo, you climb up on top of the first engine, the one we're taking, and keep watch through the windows. I'll cover the door. And you, Pat," he aimed the finger of light at a coal basket lying against the wall, "you start transferring the coal."

Durkin strode quickly to the wall, seizing a shovel as well as the basket, and began to shuttle back and forth between the engines with a full load of coal balanced on his shoulder. Soon he began to hum in rhythm to his movement, and then to sing verses from "Finnegan's Wake."

> *Tim Finnegan lived on Watkin's Street*
> *A gentleman, Irish, mighty odd*
> *He had a thirst both rich and sweet*
> *And to rise in the world he carried a hod!*

Each time he pronounced the last word, he threw down his shovel and swung the loaded basket onto his shoulder, dancing a jig across the floor to the tender of the locomotive where Eduardo stood watch, meanwhile singing the chorus of the song:

Whack fol the dah, now dance witcher partner
Welt the floor, yer trotters shake,
Wasn't it the truth I told you?
Lots of fun at Finnegan's wake!

With the final word of the chorus, he emptied the basket into the tender with a crash, dancing back to another tender to refill it. Perhaps ten minutes after he had begun, the voice of the bandit leader outside came floating through the windows.

"Are you ready to come out, Excellency?"

Duggan paused, climbing up into the engine and pointing his flashlight into the coal tender. "How about it Eduardo, do we have enough?"

The Mexican shook his head unhappily. "We need fifteen minutes more, *Capitan*. Unless you want me to help the big one."

Duggan shook his head. "No, you have to keep watch." He climbed up beside Eduardo and called, "You forget something. We have one of your men as hostage. We will trade him for our liberty."

"Let me talk to 'im. José, are you all right?"

"He can't talk," Duggan yelled. "He is badly wounded. He needs immediate help."

"That is too bad. But I think he is dead, *señor*. And if he is not, then you had better kill him. He is no good to us anymore. Come, Excellency, you 'ave five more minutes."

Duggan turned to Eduardo. "If you start a fire in the boiler now, will the steam give us away?"

Eduardo shook his head. "I will not let off steam until we are ready to go."

Hoofbeats sounded outside again, and Duggan said, "They're up to something. You'd better get started. I'll stay up here."

Eduardo jumped down into the cabin, swung open the firebox door, threw in paper and kindling, and ignited a fire. A few minutes later he began shoveling coal inside. It caught, a fine blue flame rippling across its shiny black surface, and Eduardo slammed the door shut.

Atop the cabin, Duggan stiffened. It was growing light and he could see horsemen returning, dragging a long heavy object. At first Duggan thought it was a tree, but then he saw it was a power pole. They probably pulled it down with horses and lariats, he thought; and then, seeing them using lariats to fashion a kind of sling between two teams of four horses each standing in tandem, he realized that the pole would become a battering ram.

Duggan drew his pistol and took careful aim at the first horse on the right. He fired. It fell with a short gurgling scream, pulling the second horse down with it. Shouting in anger, the bandits drew their own pistols and fired. Bullets broke through the windows, shattering all the center ones. Duggan dropped quickly into the cabin. The firing ceased, and he crawled back on top of it again. He could see nothing, but he could hear voices and movements, closer to the door this time. He realized that they had moved in close under the windows so that he no longer had a field of fire. He looked at Durkin, staggering, now, from tender to tender, sweat coursing in rivulets down his coal-caked cheeks. He thought of having Durkin stand next to the door, so that he could climb onto his shoulders and shoot down through the windows. But then he saw that the bandit captain had thought of the same tactic, but sooner. A window to his right now framed a sallow, swarthy face, and a pistol muzzle was coming through it. Duggan flopped quickly back into the cabin, and the bullet whined harmlessly overhead.

There was a smashing, shuddering crash. The roundhouse door buckled inward slightly, showering the floor with shattered tinkling glass. Duggan stared apprehensively at the door's iron hinges, already sprung.

"Are you ready, Eduardo?" he asked.

"Not really, *Capitan*, but I guess we can try it."

"Well, we can't stay here," Duggan muttered, as another crash sent the door sagging inward. Cheers and yips of approval rose from the bandits.

"All aboard, Pat," Duggan called to Durkin, and the big redhead dropped his basket and swung, sweating, into the cabin.

Eduardo opened the throttle slowly. Steam came hissing angrily from the stack, then showers of hot cinders that drove him back from the side window.

"It is not very good coal, *Capitan*," he said ruefully.

He pulled back harder on the throttle lever. A thick hot jet rose to the ceiling. It bounced off and spread out in thick white coils. Soon the roundhouse was filled with steam and smoke.

"Let's go, Eduardo," Duggan said.

The Mexican nodded and began backing slowly into the shed. When he had given himself a hundred feet freeway, he stopped and reversed gear. He moved forward, gathering momentum. Halfway down the track a third blow from the battering ram buckled the door. Eduardo pulled back on the lever. The engine picked up speed. Duggan seized the bell cord and began ringing the bell.

"It'll panic the horses," he yelled.

Panting steam, driver bars pumping, huge black wheels turning, bell clanging, the great iron vehicle struck the sagging door with a reverberating crash that shook the entire building, forcing the three occupants of the cabin to cover their ears.

The locomotive burst out into the open, rolling down the track, pushing the snagged steel door ahead of it until the door finally stood on its end and snapped in two, one part falling atop the cabin with a monster clanging sound before sliding off. Duggan had heard screams, human and equine, when the locomotive burst free. Now, turning to look back, he saw horses and men writhing on the ground. Perhaps five or six surviving bandits were running for their mounts.

"Hurry, Eduardo!" he urged.

"No, *Capitan*," Eduardo panted, slowing the engine. He pointed wildly ahead. "The switch! I must close the switch!" The engine was merely coasting now, and Eduardo jumped down. He lost balance momentarily, but caught himself and sprinted bowlegged for the switch ahead. Duggan looked back. A mounted bandit had drawn his pistol and was aiming at Eduardo. He fired.

Eduardo tumbled forward, but staggered quickly erect, holding his elbow. The engine's great wheels were only a few yards from the open switch. Duggan watched them close the gap in dread. Eduardo reached the lever, grabbed it, and pulled backward. The tracks moved with a click, and the engine clattered through, just as Durkin leaned down from the cab to seize Eduardo under the armpit and swing him aboard.

''We've made it!'' Durkin cried jubilantly, his white teeth flashing in his soot-smeared face.

''Not yet, Pat,'' Duggan said, gazing grimly out the window at the band of horsemen galloping parallel to the locomotive. The bandits were staying prudently out of pistol range, and Duggan made no attempt to fire.

''If they take that shortcut back, they can still head us off,'' Duggan said. ''And if they get a big enough rock on the track—''

''Against a handcar, si, a locomotive, no,'' Eduardo said, sitting in the engineer's seat, holding his elbow. Blood was seeping through his fingers, and his eyes were clouded with pain. Duggan came at once to his side. He took Durkin's knife and cut holes in the sleeve of Eduardo's blouse. He closed the knife, slipped it through the holes and twisted it to draw the cloth tight in an effective tourniquet.

''That'll stop the bleeding,'' he said, ''but I'm afraid your elbow's shattered.'' He patted Eduardo's shoulder. ''We'll get you to an Army hospital as soon as we get back.''

Duggan returned to the cab window, starting when he saw that one of the bandits leading a riderless horse had galloped ahead of the others. He was well in front of the locomotive and was now veering to his left toward the railroad tracks.

''Speed it up, Eduardo!'' he cried. ''Don't let that fellow reach the tracks ahead of us.''

''Why not, sir?'' Durkin asked, rushing to his side.

''The spare horse—he's going to kill it on the tracks to block us!''

Eduardo pulled back on the lever and the engine surged ahead. Duggan rested his pistol barrel on the window ledge and took aim. Then he changed his mind.

''Don't shoot, Pat. You might accidentally drop the spare horse on the tracks. Anyway, we're gaining. See, he's turning away!''

The bandit had indeed abandoned his plan. He had let the riderless mount run free and was galloping back the way he had come. Soon, all five bandits turned and rode back toward Alvarado.

''They're quitting!'' Duggan cried in delight.

Eduardo nodded, easing up on the throttle lever. ''Once

they were twelve, *Capitan,* now they are five. *Bandidos* do not like to have casualties."

Duggan said nothing, watching the mounted figures grow smaller until he could no longer see them or their dust. An hour later the engine was in the outskirts of Vera Cruz. Eduardo brought it to a puffing halt a hundred feet outside Captain Walker's outpost line. Duggan climbed down from the cabin. "I'll tell them to roll back the barbed wire so's Eduardo can take the locomotive to the terminal," he told Durkin. "Then you get him to a hospital."

A smile of triumph on his face, Captain Mark Duggan strode proudly down the tracks, returning the salutes of the sentries who greeted him, and hurried to Captain Walker's post of command. Inside, he was surprised, even chagrined, to see that the captain barely listened to what he was saying.

"I said I found the locomotives, Captain," he repeated irritably, "and brought one of them back."

"Yes, yes," Walker replied absently. "Wonderful work, Duggan. But I guess you haven't heard about Sarajevo."

"Sarajevo?"

"I just heard about it an hour ago. Archduke Ferdinand of Austria and his wife were assassinated there yesterday."

CHAPTER 11

Mark and Betsy Duggan sat on the boardwalk at Atlantic City, holding hands, watching the reflection of the dying sun behind them sparkle on the distant rim of the horizon, listening to the roar of the high white surf boiling up on the sand. Again and again the white waves formed, rolling in and breaking with a sharp snapping sound, leaving the mark of the sea on the edge of the land. Betsy and Mark sat there silently, holding hands while the purple dusk glided in to enfold them; they were content.

They were on their honeymoon at last, having chosen the Jersey shore rather than Cape Cod because it was closer to Washington. Mark had returned from Mexico in July. His report so impressed General Field that the general recommended him for the Medal of Honor. The chief of staff also made good on his promise to "make it up" to Betsy. He gave Captain Duggan a month's leave, and the newlyweds entrained for Philadelphia and the Jersey shore two days after Britain declared war on Germany.

"It's going to be a dreadful war," Betsy said, breaking the silence. "Do you think we'll get in it, Mark?"

"No. Not yet, anyway. It's much too early to tell. It isn't even a week old yet."

"I know. But the Germans are moving through Belgium so

fast. And the awful atrocities they're committing! It's so horrible! Most of the war correspondents are saying that the Germans will be in Paris in another week.''

''They always say silly things like that at the start of a war, Betsy. The Union Army planned to be in Richmond in a week. But it took four years.''

Betsy shuddered. ''I certainly hope this war doesn't last that long,'' she said. ''The awful weapons they have to kill each other! It's mass slaughter! Machine guns and . . . and artillery . . .'' She shuddered again, turning to gaze at him. He watched her, graceful in her white cotton dress and broad-brimmed hat of white silk, and thought that in the dusk she looked like a figure in a cameo.

''That's true,'' he said quietly. ''I read in the *Inquirer* this morning that the Germans have a huge 16.5-inch gun that fires an eighteen-hundred-pound shell nine miles. Big Bertha, they call it.''

''Is that very big?''

''Biggest ever, Betsy. That's what knocked down the Liege forts and opened the road into France for the kaiser.''

''The kaiser! I hate him! The pompous little sneak!''

Mark chuckled. ''That's your English blood talking, Betsy.''

''It is not! Anyway, I'm proud that I'm one hundred percent English stock. And I think the war is all the kaiser's fault. All his posing and strutting. If he had only kept his mouth shut.''

''It isn't such a good idea to take sides, Betsy,'' Mark said slowly. ''It's not good for the country. It's divisive. I think that's what Wilson meant when he said we should be impartial in thought as well as action.''

''Oh, *him*! I'm beginning to dislike Woodrow Wilson. Did you ever see him smile? Those horrid horse teeth? It's hideous. Imagine *kissing* Woodrow Wilson? Ugh!'' Betsy glanced back at the seashore to where a couple in bathing suits were approaching the surf hand in hand. ''Anyway, how can anybody be impartial in thought?''

''True. But even Teddy Roosevelt said he wasn't going to take sides. Maybe we have too many hyphenated Americans in our country, Betsy. German-Americans, Italian-Americans, Irish-Americans . . .''

''What does Sergeant Durkin say about the war?''

"When he brought me my shoes this morning, he gave me a big wink and said, 'Albion's woe is Erin's weal.'"

Betsy laughed. "I like him, Mark—he's funny."

"And loyal."

"Yes." Betsy paused, watching the bathers enter the water. "Mark," she called softly, squeezing his hand in hers.

"Yes, dearest?"

"Why won't you go swimming with me?"

"I tell you, Betsy, it's not you or the water. I used to swim all the time when I was a boy. But that was different. Now I'm a grown man, an officer—perhaps soon a general. I would feel ridiculous in a bathing suit."

"Oh, you and your dignity," Betsy said teasingly, squeezing his hand again. "Nobody else seems to mind being seen in a bathing suit."

"I do. Can you imagine Napoleon or Alexander in a bathing suit?"

Betsy giggled. "I can't." She giggled again. "Or the pope?"

"Betsy, you are incorrigible."

She got to her feet, looking down at him fondly. He wore a straw hat and an immaculate white linen suit. His profile silhouetted in the dusk made her realize that she had yet to meet a man to equal his dignity. Still in a teasing mood, though, she continued in a sly voice, "Do you know what we should have done, Mark? We should have rented a lodge on some lonely lake in the Maine woods. Then we could have gone swimming all the time and you wouldn't have had to worry about a bathing suit."

He looked up at her in a mixture of amazement and amusement. "You would have made some Apache chieftain an exemplary squaw," he murmured, rising to kiss her lightly on the cheek.

"Ugh," she said, patting her belly. "Squaw heap big hungry."

He laughed, taking her arm. "Let's see, it's Wednesday night, isn't it? Isn't that the night they have the lobster buffet?"

"Don't I know it!" she exclaimed, lifting her skirt slightly as they walked across the wide street between the boardwalk and their hotel. "All those goodies in aspic!" She smacked her lips. "Mmmm."

"Be careful, dearest. I am not certain of this, of course, but it is entirely possible that you might have put on a pound or two while I was in Mexico."

"I know," she said ruefully, passing a hand across her waist. "But there really wasn't much else to do." She squeezed his hand again. "Now that you're back, I think I'm going to start studying French."

"What on earth do you want to do that for?"

"You never know, you might be sent to Paris as an observer. Having a wife who spoke French would be a big help. Anywhere, in fact. It's the language of diplomacy. Besides, there isn't anything else to do. And you won't let me go back to the War Office."

"Absolutely not," Mark said, nodding politely to the uniformed doorman holding open the door for them. "But French . . ." He shook his head wonderingly and followed her inside.

Upon their return to Washington, Betsy, true to her word, enrolled in French courses at Georgetown University, while Mark resumed his work on the General Staff. To his keen disappointment, he found that the War Department had rejected General Field's recommendation for the Medal of Honor. A complaint had been received from General Bean to the effect that Captain Duggan's escapade "might have started a war," and this had influenced the board against approving the recommendation. Enraged, Duggan protested in writing to the chief of staff, and was promptly summoned to his office.

"I don't think this is a good idea, Mark," General Field said, pointing to the protest on the desk before him.

"May I respectfully ask why not, sir?"

"General Bean uses some very strong language in his complaint. Even indiscreet language, I would say, to say nothing of his personal letter to me."

Duggan blushed, recalling the stormy interview with General Homer Bean two days after his return from Alvarado. He could still hear the general's cold voice: "I had always thought that Kenneth Duggan was the most arrogant and egotistical man I ever knew—until I met his son."

Now, Captain Duggan said, "Yes, sir, I understand, sir. I had an interview with him in Vera Cruz. It was not exactly friendly."

"It would not be wise to pursue the matter further, especially not over the objections of an officer of General Bean's standing. They seem to think you deliberately hoodwinked them down there. There's a report from Bean's inspector general claiming that you led them to believe you were going out the night of June tenth, and then went out on the ninth, just to prevent them from stopping you."

George again! Duggan thought bitterly, and then aloud: "That's not true, General."

"I'm sure it isn't. I'm sure there was a misunderstanding somewhere. I still think that what you learned was and is of great value. However, under these circumstances . . ."

"I withdraw my protest, sir."

"Good. Now, there is something I would like you to do, Mark. I would like you to act as the General Staff's intelligence officer for the European War. I'm having large maps of both fronts fixed to the wall outside my office. Each day, with whatever information you can gather, I would like you to post the progress of the war, and the positions of the opposing armies."

Duggan beamed, his resentment against General Bean and George Meadows forgotten in this new opportunity to excel. "Thank you, sir," he said, getting to his feet.

Each morning, relying upon newspaper reports or information from the State Department, Duggan charted the war. Using black-headed pins for the Germans, red for the Russians, and white for the Anglo-French and their allies, he maintained an amazingly accurate and informative "situationer" for the benefit of his august colleagues. One morning in late August he mounted his small stepladder armed with black pins to portray the latest gains of the German armies plunging down from Belgium into France. Affixing them, he stepped back to examine the situation, and fell from the ladder. He scrambled onto all fours, and paused in amazement. He whistled. From the floor, he saw what was not so easily apparent from eye level: the German strategic plan in France!

To his left, western France, he saw that the Germans were

driving at a southwest tangent that would carry them west of Paris. To his right, the Franco-German border, he saw that the French were on the attack. My God, it's another Leuthen, he thought: but Leuthen on a gigantic scale!

Beside him, he heard a voice say: "Look at this, Leonard, it looks like the Germans have got a Cannae up their sleeve."

"Oh, no!" Duggan exclaimed. "Not Cannae at all. It's more like Frederick the Great at Leuthen." Turning to explain, he stared straight into the cold blue eyes of Brigadier General Homer Bean. "I...I'm sorry, General," he stammered. "But if you'll let me explain."

"Explanations seem to be a specialty of yours, Captain Duggan," General Bean snapped, and Duggan glanced appealingly from him to General Field, standing beside him.

"I don't quite see the resemblance between this and Leuthen, Mark," General Field said slowly. "That was Frederick against the Austrians, wasn't it?"

"Yes, sir. Marshal Daun, Seventeen fifty-seven. But you see, sir," he said excitedly, pointing to the German spearhead, "they're just beginning to get below Paris. And if you'll examine it closely, sir, their right wing is just starting to turn east. If they get east of Paris, sir, they will have scooped the French capital into their net."

"True. But I still don't see the resemblance."

"Here, sir," Duggan continued, pointing eagerly to the east. "See? The French are on the attack. If the Germans there fall back before them—lure them, that is, into Germany—then the other, stronger German wing charging east from Paris will smash right into the French rear. They'll catch the French between two fires, front and rear, and destroy them!"

"My God!" General Field breathed. "You may be right!" He gazed thoughtfully at General Bean. "I wonder if I should pass this along to the State Department..."

"To be relayed to London and Paris?" General Bean countered. "The Germans might consider that a violation of neutrality, Leonard. Besides," he said, staring coldly at Captain Duggan, "you'd think Sir John French and Marshal Joffre might have an idea of what's going on." Snapping a final hard glare at Duggan, he preceded General Field into the chief of staff's office.

Duggan said nothing. He was engrossed once again in the

map. Morning after morning he stood there, placing black pins lower and lower in France, trembling with suppressed excitement at a maneuver that seemed to him one of the most daring in all history, and on the greatest scale. But then, in the last days of August, he was puzzled to see the Germans just above Paris beginning to turn to their left. On the eastern front the Germans had hurled the French back. As September began, the Germans turned sharper left, *above* Paris.

"They've muffed it!" Duggan groaned that night to Betsy.

"Who muffed what, Mark?" Betsy said, putting down the French textbook she had been studying.

"The Germans. They were bringing off the most brilliant offensive stroke I've ever seen, and today they lost their nerve."

"Are you for the kaiser, Mark?"

"Of course not. But I'm a professional soldier. I admire excellence. I couldn't help but admire what I was seeing. And then . . ." He grimaced in disgust. Seeing the perplexed look on her face, he seized her notebook and pencil and quickly sketched the western front for her. "See, if they'd've gone below Paris and charged east—they'd've won the war in another week. But now they're *above* Paris with their right flank exposed."

"What does that mean, Mark?" Betsy asked, still puzzled.

"The Allies now have the opportunity to roll up the German flank. Even Joffre will see that."

"But perhaps you were wrong, Mark. Maybe General Bean was right."

"Nonsense!" he cried, looking at her in astonishment and reproach, as though she had just committed an act of treason. "General Bean didn't know what he was talking about. I couldn't believe it when I heard him say Cannae. That was Hannibal against the Romans two centuries before Christ. Cannae was a *double* envelopment, not a single encirclement like Leuthen. But every fool of faint knowledge I have ever met insists on comparing every battle ever fought to Cannae."

"I always knew I married a brain," Betsy said proudly. "But now I know I married a genius."

Mark smiled. "You're right. I am a genius," he said simply, and then, drawing a small leather box from his pocket, he handed it to her and said, "General Field seems to think so too. He gave me this today and told me it was really for you.''

Betsy opened the box. ''Oak leaves!'' she exclaimed in delight. ''Mark, you're a major!'' She came to him, standing on tiptoe to remove the double silver bars from his shoulders and replace them with the gold oak leaves. Then she kissed him full and hard on the mouth.

''Mark, you're a major, now,'' she said softly, tears filling her eyes. ''And soon I will be a mother.''

In the months that followed, Betsy Duggan sometimes wished that she were not pregnant, or at least that she had not told her husband about it. He would not let her alone. He smothered her with attention, with kindness, with affection. He hired a housekeeper to do the cleaning and cooking. Each night, he brought home special foods prescribed by medical officers attached to the War Office. Liver was good for the blood . . . a pregnant woman needed iron . . . Major Wurzer recommended that she drink porter . . . One night he brought her a white cashmere scarf which he said he wanted her to wear every time she went outdoors.

''This is ridiculous!'' Betsy stormed. ''It isn't even fall yet. You're treating me like I was some kind of Eastern hothouse plant. I'm a mountain flower! I don't curl up or wilt at the first cold wind. I'm strong! I'm healthy! You said yourself I was fit to be an Apache squaw.''

''I was only joking,'' he said with an indulgent smile. ''And besides, I'm only trying to make sure that the baby will be as healthy and strong as you are.''

Mark was also obsessed with the idea of having a son. With characteristic single-mindedness, he ruled out the possibility of a daughter. He immediately had what had once been his own bedroom done over in blue and white for the baby, while buying a crib, layette, bureau, blankets, and curtains in those colors.

''Build me a son, Betsy,'' he would say to her at bedtime, his voice low and throbbing with emotion. ''Build me a son who will be strong and gentle, brave and pure, truthful and just—a son who will carry the family name even higher than I will.''

Sometimes, the ardor of his large dark eyes and the passion

of his entreaty would bring tears to her eyes, and she would kiss the hand that caressed her cheek. At other times she resented the nightly litany. Much as she honored him for his nobility of mind and for actually trying to practice the virtues and ideals which he cherished, she felt that she should not be held responsible if the baby turned out to be neither masculine nor messianic.

Betsy also resented the fact that Mark would no longer come to bed with her. He said that he was afraid that he would harm the baby. She could not convince him otherwise, and so she went unrequited in her desire for sexual satisfaction. Betsy was not lewd or nymphomaniacal. She was an unusually well-balanced woman who saw nothing wrong with the marital act. Unlike many of her contemporaries, she did not believe that the man should have all the pleasure and the woman all the pain.

"Are you going to come in with me?" she asked one night as he took off his gray cadet bathrobe before going to bed.

"No, Betsy, I'm sorry. I don't think we should take any chances."

"But Mark, Captain McCarthy said there wasn't any danger until the last month or so."

"You *asked* him?" he countered, aghast.

"Of course. He must know how I got this way."

"Yes, of course," he mumbled, turning away in embarrassment. "As a matter of fact, I, ah . . . I asked Major Wurzer about it. He said that normally there was no danger. But there was always a chance that something might happen."

"Damn Major Wurzer!" Betsy snapped in irritation. "I'm sick of his prescribing for my pregnancy. Captain McCarthy is my doctor. And besides, if you ask me, Herr Doktor Macher Wurzer wants everyone to live in an incubator."

Mark said nothing, quietly turning off the light and getting into his bed. In the morning, as usual, he awoke before Betsy, breakfasted lightly on orange juice, toast, and coffee, and walked a brisk two miles to the War Department. By eight o'clock he was once again in front of his war maps, studying newspaper reports, reading State and War Department estimates prepared for his benefit.

Unknown to Major Duggan, his diagnosis of German intentions had been correct; and, as he had suspected, someone—

fat and fumbling Helmuth von Moltke, the German chief of staff—had indeed lost his nerve. By weakening the wing that was to have wheeled around Paris, in order to strengthen the Eastern Front, Moltke aborted the German plan. There were not enough reserves to relieve the fought-out troops moving down on Paris, As a result, the Germans turned above the city, and when the Allies saw the enemy flank exposed, they struck at it to launch the famous and decisive First Battle of the Marne.

Watching the march of his colored pins across his maps, Major Mark Duggan sensed that this battle, though occurring so early in the war, was decisive. His was a sure, swift military mind. He understood war and he knew combat. He divined immediately that Germany must win at the Marne, must overwhelm France in order to drive Britain into the sea, whereupon she could defeat Russia at her leisure. When the fugitive French government came creeping back to Paris, and "Papa" Joffre proclaimed an Allied victory at the "Miracle of the Marne," Major Duggan walked home from the War Department sunk in thought. Germany has had it, he thought; if I were the kaiser, I'd sue for peace.

At that very moment in Berlin, the German General Staff was indeed recommending that course to Kaiser Wilhelm. But the German emperor flatly rejected this wise and expert advice, fired von Moltke, replacing him with Erich von Falkenhayn, and demanded that the Western Front duplicate the string of stupendous victories being won in Russia.

Now, charting the war day after day, Major Duggan watched the Germans try to turn the Allied left flank, while the Allies sought to get around the German right. Thus, both armies were making sideways lunges in the same direction: toward the North Sea. This mutual maneuver became known as the Race to the Sea, and not even the kaiser or the Allied war chiefs were more disgusted than Major Duggan when it ended in a tie. The German right and the Allied left were anchored on water, while the opposing flanks at the other end rested firmly on the Swiss mountains. To escape each other's artillery, both sides dug in. They constructed elaborate facing networks of trenches which zigzagged four hundred miles from a corner of Belgium on the North Sea all the way across France to Switzerland.

"They've set warfare back a thousand years," Duggan moaned one October morning, sitting in the kitchen while Sergeant Durkin brought him breakfast. "They've created a front without flanks. How can you maneuver when millions of men face each other in fortifications miles deep?"

"Couldn't they try a breakthrough, sir?"

Duggan shook his head. "Too many men, too much barbed wire, too much artillery, too many machine guns." He downed his orange juice in three equal gulps—the way he always drank it—and reached for his first piece of toast. "I'm afraid the machine gun has frozen the front, Pat," he said, moodily sipping his coffee. "You see, the problem in combat is how to move *exposed* firepower against *entrenched* firepower. It was difficult enough in the Civil War, when the new, accurate, long-range rifle gave the defense a decided advantage, but now, to attempt to move exposed soldiery against entrenched guns is murderous madness." He shook his head again, reaching for his second—and last—piece of toast: his unalterable quota. "I'm afraid someone will try it, though," he said.

Once again Major Duggan was right. On October 20, 1914, the Germans made the first attempt to break through the enemy's line. It was called the First Battle of Ypres, and it raged for weeks, until it was finally smothered by a series of freak November blizzards. The casualties: 250,000 men.

Duggan was aghast. He read the figures with unbelieving eyes and looked at his map of the Western Front in disbelief. The black pins representing the Germans had moved forward perhaps 1/32 of an inch, indicating a gain of roughly two miles, and then had moved back again. So had the white Allied pins, in an abortive Anglo-French counterattack. They're back where they started! Duggan thought in dismay; and a quarter-million human beings are dead or maimed!

"It's awful, I know!" Betsy said in agreement that night. "Why don't they stop it?"

"I don't know. Perhaps they're too close to it and can't see what's coming. But if they keep this up, it's going to be a dreadful, dreadful war, Betsy. Worse than that, it's going to be a senseless one. Just mutual mass slaughter, that's all. Here," he said, looking searchingly around the living room, "where's your notebook?"

"I don't know," Betsy said, her knitting needles clicking on the blue wool baby boots she was making. "Since I dropped French for knitting classes, I don't know where I put it."

"Oh, well, I'll try to explain without a map. The point is, the only way either side can make this a war of movement again is to break through the opposing line. But there is just no way either side can do it. The troops simply cannot move fast enough through the enemy trenches. The spearheads pierce the outer lines, of course. But each time they do, their progress is slower. Finally, the spearheads are exhausted. And that is when the fresh enemy turns on them to pin them down while his artillery breaks up the oncoming reserves behind them. Now, there is a dent or a bulge in the enemy's lines. That is called a salient. The fresh enemy hammers at the sides of the bulge, the shoulders of the salient, trying to cut off the pinned-down spearheads. When the spearheads realize this, they withdraw. And they get chewed up worse going out than they did going in." He shook his head in gloom again. "It's . . . it's just not war. And I'm afraid we're going to see a lot more of it."

Betsy shuddered, putting down the completed bootie and picking up another ball of wool. "From what you say, I'm glad we're staying out of it."

"I guess so." He glanced at the wool in her hand sharply. "Betsy, is that *pink*?"

Betsy blushed. "Well, yes, it is," she stammered. "You can't be sure. I know how much you want a son, Mark, but you know as well as I do that it could be a g—"

"Never!" Mark exclaimed, standing erect and coming to her side. He gently took the pink ball from her hand and replaced it with a blue one. "All my life, Betsy, I've believed in my destiny. And I haven't been disappointed. You've *got* to believe! And I just *know* our first child will be a boy. Even to think otherwise would be to doubt my destiny." He bent to kiss her forehead. "Of course, I want a daughter too. A girl just as beautiful as you are. But the first child just *has* to be a boy."

Betsy shrugged in resignation. But then an impish light flashed in her eye and she picked up the pink ball again and put down the blue one. "All right, Mark, then you certainly won't mind if I knit a pair of booties for the daughter later on, the one who's going to be as beautiful as I am.''

"I'm not going to say you win, Betsy," he murmured in grudging admiration, "but I will admit that you are unbeatable." He looked at her with troubled eyes. "Are you sure you're well enough to attend General Bean's reception?"

"Of course!" She got to her feet and went into the hall, standing in front of the full-length mirror to run a hand across her stomach. "I don't show hardly at all," she called. "Don't forget, I'm only in my fifth month. If I wear that green dress with the shirred skirt I wore the first night in Atlantic City, nobody will notice." She came back into the living room. "Besides, if you think I'm going to miss a chance to go to the White House—"

"I thought you despised Wilson."

"Well, he is the President. And I haven't seen General Field in so long." Her eyes gleamed. "I'll bet *everybody* will be there."

"Probably. The President's making this big fuss over General Bean just to show the world—especially Germany— that we won't stand for any more interference in Mexico. Now that Huerta's out and Carranza's in, and our people are leaving Vera Cruz, he can claim a pretty creditable diplomatic victory."

"Is that so?" Betsy murmured absently, putting her hand on her stomach again. "You know, I think I'm going to try on that green dress."

The following night, Sergeant Durkin drove them to the White House. They joined a cavalcade of horse-drawn conveyances moving slowly down Pennsylvania Avenue. Betsy was astonished by the opulence of some of the carriages, gleaming with gold leaf and lacquer. Because many of the members of the diplomatic corps were the scions of the noble houses of Europe, their escutcheons were embossed on the sides of their coaches and their drivers and footmen wore their livery. Before and behind them, Betsy and Mark could hear the snorting of high-spirited horses and the ring of horseshoes on the pavement, while the avenue appeared to be a garden of waving red, green, and blue plumes rising from the burnished helmets of mounted military attachés.

"I'm glad you came, after all," Mark said, as they rolled slowly toward the tall white portico where black stewards in white tie and tails and white gloves helped the arriving guests from their carriages. "This is a sight you should never forget, and I doubt if you'll ever see it again." He gestured around him. "This, this style of life . . . it's disappearing, Betsy. The motor vehicle is sure to change it, for one thing. But it's not so much internal-combustion engines as war. War never leaves society where it found it. And this one in Europe is the most shattering ever. All these people . . ." He gestured again. "These dukes and duchesses and counts and princes . . . the dynasties . . . they're dying, Betsy. Their world is being shot to pieces by machine guns and Big Berthas."

Betsy nodded, watching the portico where a short dumpy woman in a sable coat and blue velvet dress was being helped from her coach. The light fell on her exquisitely coiffed red-dyed hair and sent a shower of sparkles arching from a huge diamond tiara.

Betsy gasped. "I don't know, maybe it isn't such a bad thing. I mean, they're so useless . . . and spoiled . . . I'm glad they're going."

"They weren't so bad," Mark said musingly. "And they did give us beauty, and, for a while, order. Of course, like everyone else, they eventually confused the means for the end. Order became order for order's sake, even if it meant injustice. But who will replace them? You know the biblical story about the man from whom the unclean spirit went forth, only to be replaced by seven more wicked spirits? 'And the last state of that man becomes worse than the first!' "

"Well, I'll be switched," Betsy snorted. "An Episcopalian easterner quoting the bible. I thought it was only us Baptists read the Good Book."

Mark chuckled. "You read it, all right—with blinders on. I hope thine eye never offends thee, Betsy. It's much too pretty for plucking out."

"Go on with you. Anyway, I say freedom will replace them."

"Freedom, eh? Well, I'm for freedom too. Only sometimes it gets out of hand. You can have too much freedom, Betsy. And when freedom becomes perfect among imperfect men, you've gone full cycle back to anarchy. That's what those fellows in Russia are talking about. Freedom for all. Freedom for all and bread for all. But it won't work, you surrender some freedom. You want freedom, you give up a little bread.''

''My, but you're philosophical tonight.''

''Perhaps,'' he said. ''But I'll tell you this, it won't be freedom, Betsy. And it won't be bread either. Do you remember that in the last presidential election a million Americans voted Socialist? That's out of fourteen million who voted. And the Wobblies say they're going to destroy capitalism and the wage system. That's all right with me, if they have something better. But they don't say what they'll put in its place. Neither do the Russian Communists. They just prefer what is not to what is, that's all—whatever it may be.''

''What do you say it will be, Mark?''

He shrugged. ''God knows. But it won't be freedom and it won't be bread. That I know. Probably, it'll be a little bit less of both.'' He took his gloves from beneath his uniform belt and started drawing them on his hands. ''Here we are, dearest,'' he said.

When General Field saw Betsy approaching on Major Duggan's arm, he stretched his arms wide and left his place beside the President to come and kiss her on the cheek. Then he took her to the head of the reception line to introduce her to the President. To her surprise, Betsy found Woodrow Wilson extremely attractive and charming.

''If the chief of staff can kiss the beautiful young ladies, why cannot his commander-in-chief,'' the President murmured, bending to kiss her. For a second surprise, so did General Bean.

''We miss you at the War Office, Mrs. Duggan,'' he said, and then, to Mark: ''Congratulations on your promotion, Major.''

Walking self-consciously beside Mark, Betsy became so aware of the eyes of everyone upon her—the recipient of such marks of affection from the President, the chief of staff, and the guest of honor—that she barely noticed the white-and-gold elegance of the East Room in which the reception was being held. She recovered her composure, however, after

Mark introduced her to the Spanish ambassador and brought her a drink from a tray proffered by a White House steward.

Betsy was delighted to see how animated her husband had become. The discussion in the carriage seemed to have stimulated him. Wherever he moved, with Betsy at his side, radiant and beautiful, he became the center of a circle of attentive listeners, European as well as American. His theories about what was happening on the battlefields of Europe, what was likely to happen once the worst of wars was over, came spouting from his lips, spiced with illustrations or analogies drawn from his exhaustive knowledge of military history, sparkling with an occasional sally of wit. Even the President stood listening for a few minutes, pushing out his underlip thoughtfully; and once, the German military attaché. Betsy was also startled to see Mark drink so much. Normally, he was a most temperate man, content with one cocktail made of gin and orange juice before dinner. At public affairs he would take a drink from a tray and carry it with him all evening, putting it down barely half finished. Tonight, he drank at least three highballs. He even mixed himself another when they arrived home, exhilarated and happy, already rehashing the high points of their wonderful evening.

When they went upstairs to their bedroom, he came to her and shared her bed. It was the only time during her pregnancy that he came to her, and he reproached himself bitterly for that single lapse. Four months later, when the baby arrived stillborn, he wept openly at Betsy's bedside, telling her it was his fault that their son had come into the world dead.

CHAPTER 12

The boy was named Kenneth Duggan and buried beside his grandmother and grandfather in the family plot. Betsy cried softly, like a keening small animal, when she saw the tiny white casket lowered into the ground, and Mark quickly put his arm around her and led her away from the grave.

Nevertheless, it was Betsy who was first to recover from the shock and grief of the stillbirth. Mark grieved on. It was not so much the loss of the baby, whom, after all, they had never known, and who, without personality or shared experience, was hardly more than a name to remember. No, it was not something possessed and lost that troubled Mark, but a far more poignant sense of deprivation: something that might have been—and was not.

For this he constantly reproached himself. He could not rid himself of the morbid conviction that if he had not been guilty of that single deviation from the rule of continence, the baby would have lived. He accused himself of having betrayed his destiny, and he came to dread the marriage act, approaching it with concealed repugnance. But Betsy soon became aware of his reticence and guessed the reason. Wisely, she said nothing, afraid that to bring it into the open might give substance to her fears. Mark also realized that his was an unhealthy habit of mind, and he spoke of it to

Major Wurzer one morning as they sat in the War Department coffee shop.

The major, a short, stocky, bald-headed man in his forties, had studied in Vienna under Kraft-Ebbing and later Sigmund Freud. "You must stop persecuting yourself, Macher," he said, with that slight hissing accent derived from his Milwaukee boyhood. "If you do not stop, soon you make yourself impotent. It seems to me you are unconsciously acting out a kind of wish-fulfillment. And it is bad. It could ruin your marriage, Macher. The best thing that could happen to you is that your wife becomes pregnant again and you have a strong, healthy baby."

Mark nodded. "I'm sure you're right. And yet . . ." He grimaced and shook his head.

"You still blame yourself, Macher?" Wurzer said, sipping loudly at his coffee. "Perhaps you would like to come to me for psychoanalysis?"

"No, thank you. I mean no offense, Major, but I really don't put much faith in that sort of thing."

Now it was Wurzer who grimaced, putting down his cup and clapping a pudgy hand to his bald forehead. "America," he sighed, "sometimes she is so forward, and sometimes so backward. You do not trust the metronome, eh, Macher? And does your barber pull your teeth?" Mark tried to smile, and Major Wurzer got to his feet, petulantly brushing coffee cake crumbs from the lapels of his uniform. "Maybe some day you change your mind," he murmured. "In the meantime, you must try to have another baby."

Although Mark realized that the major had given him excellent advice, he still could not master his inhibition, and between this, his preoccupation with the war, and the long, tiring days that he put in at the War Department, he did, as Major Wurzer had predicted, become impotent. Years later, looking back on this period in his life, Mark was astonished to find that he could remember nothing from it. It was a complete blank. Half a year seemed to have disappeared from his memory. Between the stillborn birth of his son and the sinking of the *Lusitania* in May 1915, he seemed to have lived in hibernation.

It was the shock of the *Lusitania* sinking that ended Mark Duggan's obsessive brooding on the death of his child. Like almost all Americans, he was outraged by the torpedoing of the British passenger liner, especially after he learned that General Amos Lorenzo Carley was one of the 128 Americans who went down with the ship. General Carley had booked passage to London as an agent of an American munitions firm negotiating contracts with the Allies.

Even Major Otto Wurzer was dismayed by the German U-boat's sneak attack. "Ach, he is a madman, the kaiser," he said to Mark in the coffee shop. "He has ruined all chances of keeping American neutral."

"You weren't exactly neutral yourself, Major," Mark teased.

"Yes, I admit I was pro-German," the rotund physician said. "But before I was pro-German, I was always a loyal American. Now, when I see my country turning against the kaiser, I guess I turn too." He looked at Mark inquiringly. "Do you think we'll get in it, Macher?"

"I'm afraid not. I honestly think that now is the time for America to intervene. I think General Field was right in saying we should join the Allies. If we go in now, perhaps our immense productive capacity and our manpower might bring the war to an end in another year. But if we continue to wait . . ." He shook his head ruefully. "They'll just continue to slaughter each other."

"Yes. Perhaps you are right. But I do not think the American people want to go to war."

"You're right. They don't. They're pro-British now, or at least anti-German, and even if British propaganda keeps them that way, they still don't want to fight."

"That was what the President said: 'There is such a thing as a man being too proud to fight.' "

"Wasn't that disgusting?" Mark asked angrily. "Sometimes I wonder about that man. But it's true, the people really aren't ready for war."

"No," Major Wurzer said moodily, "not until that *dummkopf* of a kaiser makes himself more madness."

Mark nodded, watching the waitress, who came to remove their luncheon dishes. She was blond and shapely and she reminded him of Betsy. Suddenly, he felt an overwhelming desire to be with his wife. Yearning for her, he realized with horror and remorse how completely he had neglected her.

"You're right, Doctor," he said, getting to his feet and putting away his cigarette holder.

"Yes? You agree the kaiser is a *dummkopf*?"

"No. I'm talking about trying for another baby."

Mark came to Betsy that night. She held him in her arms with tears of joy in her eyes. She knew he had fully recovered from the trauma of the stillbirth, and hoped he would now be his old cheerful and attentive self. Three months later she told him she was pregnant again, and Mark was pleased. Although he did not speak of it openly, he confidently awaited the arrival of another son.

But the baby was a girl. Mark wanted to name her Elizabeth, after Betsy; but Betsy insisted that she be called Virginia, after his mother. On March 9, 1915, she was christened Virginia Elizabeth Duggan. Betsy was happy. She laughed with delight when the Episcopalian priest put the salt on the baby's tongue and she squalled aloud and screwed up her mouth in a wry little rosebud.

That night, with Virginia safely asleep in the room that Mark had had redecorated in pink and white, they drank champagne and ate the lobster that Sergeant Durkin cooked for them. For once, Mark overcame his dislike of fish, and found that he actually liked lobster. They went to bed, more content than they had been since their honeymoon in Atlantic City. They were awakened, however, by the voice of a newsboy crying outside:

"Extra! Extra! Read all about it! Mass murder in New Mexico!"

Mark arose, hurriedly pulled on his gray West Point bathrobe and ran downstairs to buy a paper. In the flickering gas light of the streetlamp, he read that a Mexican bandit captain named Pancho Villa had led a raiding party into Columbus, New Mexico, and killed nineteen Americans.

Once again, Woodrow Wilson intervened in Mexico. Under the terms of a protocol negotiated with the Carranza government, he ordered Brigadier General John J. "Black Jack" Pershing to lead the Punitive Expedition—seven regiments of cavalry—across the border in pursuit of Pancho Villa. And once again General Leonard Field sent Major Mark Duggan south as his personal observer.

"Does it *always* have to be you?" Betsy wailed when she heard the news. "I thought General Field was supposed to be our friend."

"It's a wonderful opportunity," Mark said. "Remember, the last time I came back from Mexico, I made major. Who knows, there may be silver leaves in this one. Besides, this time you'll have Virginia. And I'm getting another housekeeper."

"I don't *want* a housekeeper!" Betsy burst out in exasperation. "I can take care of the house myself. The last time you got a housekeeper, I wound up taking care of her too."

"All right, my dearest. You are the original Apache squaw. Just the same, there's going to be someone from the War Office dropping by every day to be sure everything's all right. Now, let me say good-bye to Virginia."

For the second time in three years, Mark Duggan and Patrick Durkin took ship from Norfolk. They sailed around the Gulf to Houston, and then overland by train and horseback to the bare, sunburned hills of Chihuahua Province. They cantered into General Pershing's headquarters at about dusk on May third. A tall, well-built first lieutenant with the thick, coiled gold braid of a general's aide-de-camp on his shoulder helped Major Duggan from the saddle.

"Lieutenant George Peyton at your service, sir," he said, his white teeth flashing in his sunburned face.

Duggan nodded absently, his eyes traveling over the encampment of tents, neatly pitched in precise, mathematical rows. "Major Duggan, here," he murmured, and then, seeing the pearl-handled pistol swinging low at the lieutenant's hip, he grinned. "Is that the new cavalry issue?"

Lieutenant Peyton grinned in return. "Not exactly regulation, sir. But if you'll pardon a first looey's impertinence, Major, neither is your hat."

Duggan laughed aloud, lifting his dust-covered campaign hat from his head. "It's my war bonnet, Lieutenant. It was shot off my head on Samar fifteen years ago. And Sergeant Durkin here told me then that I'd have a charmed life."

" 'Tis God's truth, sir," Durkin said, addressing Peyton.

"With the one volley, they used up all the bullets with the major's name on 'em."

Peyton chuckled, but then an expression of dawning recognition crossed his face and he said: "Samar! Then you must be *that* Duggan. Goddammit, Major, I read about you when I was a freshman in high school."

Duggan smiled, opening his mouth to say something, but pausing when the roar of airplanes overhead made it impossible to speak. Peyton glanced up, too, his hand on the white butt of his pistol.

"Aero Squadron," he shouted.

"Are they effective?" Duggan yelled back.

"Very. Too goddammed effective, if you ask me, sir. All my life I've wanted to be in a cavalry charge, but it looks like those bimbos up there have made that sort of thing a thing of the past."

"I don't know, Lieutenant," Duggan said musingly, watching the aircraft drone away. "There will always be a need for shock effect."

"True. I heard General Pershing say the British were experimenting with some kind of land battleship. Something they call a tank."

"Yes. They're already coming off the production line. Maybe that's what's needed to break the stalemate over there. *Protected* shock, armored shock—not horses, and certainly not foot soldiers."

"I agree, sir," Peyton said, pointing toward a big, double pyramidal tent pitched in the center of the encampment. "If you don't mind, sir, General Pershing is expecting you."

When Mark Duggan saw Black Jack Pershing seated behind his desk, he remembered how his father used to describe him as "a man made for monuments." Ramrod straight, with features that seemed to have been chiseled from marble, he was impeccable in gleaming leather and breeches. His face was as expressionless as when Mark had first met him in his father's office in the Presidio. Mark was still a cadet then, and Pershing was a cavalry captain, just returned from Cuba, where command of a troop of black cavalry had earned him his nickname. Mark remembered how Pershing had congratulated him on his academic record and for being First Captain at the Point. "We First Captains have to stick together," he had said, and then, to his father: "I have a feeling Mark and I will meet again." Well, here it was.

"Mark, we do meet again," Pershing said, rising with extended hand and a rare thin smile.

"I knew we would, sir," Mark said, taking the general's hand, and then the chair indicated to him.

"I am going to attach you to my staff," Pershing said, his face impassive again. "If you discover something you think may be of value to the War Department, please inform me of it before passing it along."

Startled, Duggan was about to protest that he was responsible to no one but General Field, until he felt Pershing's flinty blue eyes watching him expectantly. "That way, Mark," the general continued, "there will be no chance of any misunderstanding such as might have existed at Vera Cr—"

"Excuse me, General," Lieutenant Peyton cried, rushing into the tent. "There's a couple of Carranzistas outside who want to see you. They say Villa's attacking a town not far from here."

"Are they armed?"

"They were, sir. But they gave me their weapons."

"Send them in."

Peyton nodded and left. Major Duggan arose to follow him, but General Pershing held up a hand. "Stay here. I may need your Spanish."

Nodding, Duggan sat down, watching intently as Lieutenant Peyton ushered two Mexicans in mud-stained white shawls into the room. The two men stepped forward awkwardly, holding their sombreros in their hands, bowing stiffly. Then they burst into excited Spanish, and Pershing nodded toward Duggan.

"They say the town is Cusihuiriachic. Cusi, they call it. It's thirty-six miles from here. It's a Carranzista stronghold, sir, but he says the Villistas outnumber them."

"How many?"

Duggan turned to the Mexicans to translate, and they rolled their eyes wildly, speaking in agitation again.

"They say they drove them off but there must be at least five hundred of them, all mounted."

"Is Villa there?"

"They say no, sir, but three of his top lieutenants are. Cruz Dominguez, Julio Acosta, and Antonio Angeles."

Black Jack Pershing put his ham swordsman's hand to his

bristling brush of a mustache and gazed thoughtfully at the Mexicans.

"Those three, eh?" he mused aloud. "All right," he said with sudden force, "tell them I'll send help. Tonight."

Duggan translated, and the two Carranzistas broke into flashing white smiles of gratitude, pouring out their thanks in elegant compliments to the general. Pershing inclined his head slightly in polite acknowledgment and dismissed them.

"Peyton," he snapped, "get Major Walton in here."

A few minutes later a short, bowlegged man with extremely broad shoulders and an enormous nose strode into the tent.

"Walton," Cushing said, "I want you to take six troops of the Eleventh Cavalry, a machine-gun platoon, and the Apache Scouts, and ride with these Carranza men to whatever town it is they say is under attack. Drive them off. Also, bring back whatever information you can on the location of Villa and his main body. There are three of his lieutenants there. Try to capture them."

"Good, sir," Walton said. "When do we ride?"

"Before dark," Pershing said, glancing up when Lieutenant Peyton stepped toward him.

"Excuse me, General," Peyton said, "but I heard this morning that Lieutenant Sherry of the Apache Scouts was hurt this morning in a fall."

"Well?" Pershing snapped, as though irritated by such trivial reports.

"Would it be all right if I took his place, sir? I've ridden with the Apaches be—"

"All right, fire-eater, go ahead," Pershing grumbled.

"Me, too, sir?" Duggan asked.

"Why you?"

"My Spanish might be useful, for one thing, sir. For another, I might learn something of the enemy's tactics."

Black Jack Pershing grunted. "Doubtless."

Outside the general's tent Major Walton swung aboard his horse and galloped off, waving his campaign hat in a flourish of farewell.

Peyton grinned. "He sure loves to swing that hat."

"He can ride," Duggan said admiringly.

"He sure can, sir, and he can fight too."

"Good. Mind if we ride with you and your Apaches, Lieutenant?"

"Be honored. Here, Major, I'll take you to the Apache camp."

They walked on in silence through the fading twilight, until they came to a cluster of not-so-precise tents, from which the pungent odor of roasting meat issued. Duggan paused momentarily, sniffing the familiar smell. "Horse meat!" he said with a chuckle. "Where do they get the horses to eat?"

"Steal 'em, I guess," Peyton replied. "They're Apaches." He pointed toward a wrinkled old Indian standing by the horse trough. His hair hung in two braids from beneath either side of his campaign hat as he examined the shiny new .45 automatic pistol he held in his hand.

"That's First Sergeant Chicken, Major," Peyton said. "He'll take care of you."

Mark Duggan gasped in astonishment. He strode toward the old Apache with outstretched hand and a wide grin on his face. "Sergeant Chicken!" he exclaimed. "You remember me?" Chicken shook his head wonderingly, and Mark cried: "I'm Mark Duggan! Captain Duggan's son."

"Huli!" Sergeant Chicken chortled with a toothless grin. "You damfine man now, Markie."

Duggan laughed and seized the Indian's hand in delight. "You old horse thief! Remember the time in El Paso you gave me a pony, and when my mother found out where you got it, she made you take it back?"

The Indian displayed his gums again in merriment. *"Huli!* She mad that day, Markie. She holler hard! She say me make you Apache. Make you miss school. Ride and shoot, 'stead of read and write."

Major Duggan smiled in fond recollection. "They're both dead now, Chicken, both my parents," he said, sobering.

Sergeant Chicken bowed his head momentarily. "We all go, Markie," he muttered. "Me old man now. Me no look good no more. Soon they put dirt on Chicken's eyes." He shrugged, glancing up at the circling planes of the Aero Squadron. "White man find new way to kill," he said, pointing upward. "Too much bad. I glad I die, Markie. No good."

Duggan put an arm around the old man's shoulders. "I think you've got one more fight in you, Chicken," he said,

and the Indian's faded eyes twinkled again, just as the bugle
call to mount pealed through the encampment.

Instantly, there was an uproar compounded of hoofbeats
and whinnying horses, cursing troopers and cries of command,
the slap of steel barrels on leather and the thud of bodies
hitting saddles. In a few minutes it was quiet again, except
for the creak of leather and the snuffling sound of hooves
pawing the soft powdery soil.

The bugles blew "Forward!" and the three hundred troopers of the Provisional Squadron moved out slowly, in columns
of fours. Gradually they increased their pace, until, with the
descent of night, they were riding at the gallop. The dirt road
hummed with the drumming of twelve hundred hooves. Soon,
the machine-gun platoon fell back, slowed by the old-fashioned
Benet-Mercier machine guns they were hauling. Choking,
invisible clouds of alkali dust raised by the main body ahead
of them descended on the gunners and mule drivers. Cursing,
they pulled their yellow cavalry scarves up over their mouths.

Up ahead, Major Duggan thought he heard a strange,
tinkling noise around him. "What's that clinking sound,
Peyton?" he asked, reining his horse alongside the lieutenant.

"Cartridges. The men's bandoliers are worn clear through
and the cartridges keep falling out."

"No new bandoliers?"

"Not with this penny-pinching Congress."

Major Walton rode up and shouted, "Get your scouts
moving out, Peyton. We could be riding into a trap."

In the darkness, Peyton saluted smartly and called to First
Sergeant Chicken. With high Apache cries, the scouts urged
their ponies at a faster pace up the road.

There was no ambush along the way, however. At midnight
the tired mounts of the Provisional Squadron clattered through
Cusi's deserted main street. Lights showed only in the *posadas,*
from which the troopers could hear music, the laughter of
women, and the shouts of intoxicated men. Bullet holes in the
low white adobe buildings along the street attested to a recent
battle, or at least an exchange of shots.

Major Walton was dismayed. He sent for Major Duggan
and the Carranzistas. "Tell them I want to know what's going
on," Walton snapped angrily, and Duggan turned to relay his
request. The two Mexicans dismounted and entered one of

the *posadas*. Ten minutes later they returned with reports of a big battle in which the Villistas were driven off.

"How many casualties?" Walton asked in a tone of disbelief.

"None," Duggan replied with a grin.

"I never heard of so many goddamned bloodless battles in my life," Walton muttered, fingering his big nose. "All right, where'd the Villistas go to?"

"A ranch called Ojos Azules. It means Blue Eyes. It's about twenty miles from here."

"Good," Walton exclaimed, his eyes gleaming. "Maybe we'll catch them in their beds."

"You'll need a guide," Duggan said. "These men say they don't know the way."

"Goddamn!" Walton swore, striking his gauntlets into his open hand. "Let's get one, then. We can't waste any more time."

Unfortunately, all the Carranzistas had gotten drunk celebrating the big "victory," and it was three hours before one of them could be sobered up to act as guide. By the time Walton and his weary troopers arrived at Ojos Azules, it was already daylight. Walton could see the rim of a brazen sun rising slowly above the edge of the eastern sky. It shone on the low buildings and adobe huts of the ranch, about a mile away across an open field. Walton contemplated the field in disgust.

"Christ!" he groaned. "We can't move over that. We'd be like flies on a windowpane."

"What about the road?" Duggan said, pointing to the yellow ribbon stretching away from them.

"You mean a charge?"

"Why not?"

"Hell, yes, why not!" Walton exclaimed, and sent his orderlies flying to summon his troop commanders. "Troop A will charge down the road," he told them. "The others will peel off right and left to ride around the ranch." He looked at Duggan. "What time is it, Major?"

Duggan reached for his gold graduation watch. "Quarter to six," he said.

Walton nodded. "That'll be all, gentlemen."

Orders to mount shattered the desert stillness. The troopers swung aboard their horses, canteens clinking against saber hilts.

"Draw pistols!"

They drew. Steel slipped from leather holsters with the sound of a kiss. They pointed their flat, ugly automatics skyward. The bugles blared and the Provisional Squadron charged.

Lieutenant Peyton led his advance guard pounding down the road. Major Duggan and Sergeant Durkin followed, grinning at the shrill yipping of the Indians. First Sergeant Chicken leaned forward on his mount, feeling the power flowing through the beast between his legs. The thin little pony's breath came noisily. Sergeant Chicken's ears were ringing with the drum of hoofbeats. His hair braids stood straight back from beneath his hat like black sticks. Ahead of him he could see the ranch at Ojos Azules. No one stirred.

Peyton raised his hand and signaled to the left. The Apaches plunged off the road into a cornfield. Duggan and Durkin followed. Now, the drumming of the hooves was muffled in the softer underfooting. Some of the horses reared in fright from the corn stalks that menaced their underbellies like a field sown with spears.

"Dismount!" Peyton cried, and the Apaches leaped from their saddles, seizing their rifles and scuttling low through the field to form a line of skirmishers.

Durkin moved to follow, but Duggan put out a restraining hand. "No, Pat, let's stay up where we can see better," he said, turning to watch as A Troop's horsemen went galloping past.

They came thundering on in columns, reins loose in the extended gallop, dirt clods flying in the air, hooves drumming, red-and-white guidon pennants streaming backward with their swallowtails as rigid as metal. The troopers leaned forward, pistols at the ready; the horses ran with stretched-out heads and tails distended, rumps bunched and rocking in time. Major Duggan watched in admiration, his eye on the ranch's open gate. There was still no movement there. Suddenly, a quarter mile ahead of him, he saw two men rise from the earth and run toward the ranch. They were goatherds. Even as Duggan drew his automatic, he realized they were out of pistol range. To his left he heard a report and one of the Mexicans fell.

Sergeant Chicken had opened fire. He bolted his Springfield

to eject the empty cartridge and slam another one into the breech. He raised the rifle again. The second man was a vanishing speck over his open sights. Chicken squeezed the trigger again, and the second man staggered and fell. But it was too late. Alarmed, now, the Villistas came swarming out of Ojos Azules. They came running out of doorways, somersaulting out of open windows, leaping from flat-topped rooves. Some were naked, others half dressed. They were terrified. They ran bowlegged, as horsemen do, for the hills behind the ranch where hundreds of horses were tethered.

Major Duggan wheeled his horse and rode at full gallop across the cornfield, making for the open gate. Not all the Villistas had fled. About thirty of them on top of the main ranch building laid a heavy fire into the cornfield and down the road toward the approaching A Troop. Another ran across the patio to bar the gate. Duggan spurred his horse. If the gate were closed, the troopers could never overtake the fleeing Villistas. They could jump it, of course, but only one or two at a time. Bullets whispered around Duggan, pealing shrilly when they hit a stone and richocheted. He felt one tug at his blouse. His horse beneath him was sobbing. Duggan could see the fleeing Villistas struggling up the hill slope toward their horses. Behind him he could hear the thunder of the charging troopers.

Bullets were kicking up spurts of dust along the road. But not a trooper had fallen. On the rooftop, Duggan saw the high crown of the Villistas' sombreros as they rose to aim and shoot. Behind him he heard the scream of a horse. Now the Mexican was hauling the gate shut and barring it. To his right Duggan saw that the road was barricaded with high barbed wire on either side. No one had brought wire-cutters, and there was no way the cavalrymen could ride into the Villista rear to cut them off. The entire squadron would have to come through the gate. It had to be opened. . . .

Now Duggan was coming at the gate. He bent low and struck his pony savagely. The beast gathered its muscles and sprang from the ground. Up, up, and up they went, and as they reached the apex of their arc, Duggan could see the Mexican kneeling, wildly bolting his rifle . . . taking aim . . . Lifting his left arm, Duggan rested his right wrist on the other and fired. The Mexican fell. Now, man and beast were on the downward arc, landing, driven forward by the force of their fall, steadying, righting—and galloping on again.

In the cornfield, Sergeant Chicken saw them land. "*Huli!* Damfine jump." Then the bullets sang around him once more and he pressed his old brown face into the earth again.

Duggan reined his horse around to ride back to the gate. A mounted Mexican charged at him brandishing a pistol. The Mexican fired and missed. Holding his fire, Duggan waited until the man's momentum brought him even with him. Then he leaned from the saddle, stuck his pistol under the man's armpit, and fired. Blood stained the man's white blouse. He screamed and fell, one foot caught in the stirrup. His terrified horse ran for the patio fence and leaped it. But the body he was dragging caught on the rail and pulled him down on top of it in a screaming, struggling heap.

Wheeling, Duggan rode back to the gate, dismounted, and seized it to swing it open. Aghast, he saw that it was firmly secured. A half-inch pin had been bent around a ring. Seeing the small sledgehammer that the Mexican had used to batter the ring, he grasped it and swung hard at the pin. But it merely turned inside the ring. Duggan could hear the thunderous approach of A Troop, and he looked around him wildly for something heavier.

"Faith o' God, give it to me, sir," a voice above him shouted, and he saw Sergeant Durkin's huge figure swing out of the saddle and clamber over the gate. The big redhead took the sledgehammer and struck one stupendous blow at the center of the pin. It snapped in two, and Durkin swung the gate open. A half minute later the horses of A Troop came thundering through.

Because of the narrowness of the patio, the troopers were unable to dismount and deploy under the rooftop. Instead, they galloped past, swiveling in their saddles to fire their pistols, then riding on to pursue the Villistas struggling up the hill. As they passed, there were screams on the roof. One Villista staggered to his feet, clutching his throat. He pitched forward to the ground. Now the rooftop defenders joined the general flight. As they did, they were slaughtered: shot or sabered to the earth when they sought to escape on foot, caught in a converging fire when they attempted to hold out behind a stone barricade.

Major Walton would not allow his men to tarry for the slaughter. He wanted to capture the three Villista leaders: Angeles, Dominguez, and Acosta. Waving his hat, he urged his troopers up the hillside. But their horses were blown. They were compelled to dismount, opening rifle fire at long range.

Major Walton rode up, hat in hand. His face was streaming sweat, beads of it running down his big nose. He mopped his brow with his yellow cavalry scarf, watching glumly as the gradually dwindling specks to the south finally vanished beneath the horizon. Reluctantly, Walton turned to his bugler and ordered him to sound the recall.

By ones and twos the troopers rode slowly back to the patio and the open space beneath the hill. Walton dismounted and walked after them, glancing up when he heard a roar of laughter from a cluster of cavalrymen outside the ranch house door.

"What's so funny, Peyton?" the major snapped irritably.

Peyton pointed to four obviously overjoyed Mexicans standing beside the door. "Those are Carranzistas, sir," he explained. "They were due to face the firing squad this morning. They were so grateful to be freed that one of them offered to execute those prisoners over there." He pointed to a group of half a dozen dejected Villistas tied to the patio fence.

Walton laughed. "What did you tell him?"

"I said I was sorry, but I had to decline his charitable offer."

Chuckling again, Walton turned to greet Major Duggan, coming up to join them. "Nice work, Duggan," he said. "That gate could have held us up. They might have all gotten away."

"About eighty enemy dead, Major," Duggan said. "Probably two or three times as many wounded or dying. Dominguez and Angeles are dead."

"How about Acosta?"

"He must have gotten away."

"Goddammit!" Walton swore, striking his palm with his gauntlets again. "I wanted to bring at least one of them back with me."

"Don't worry," Duggan said. "Our Carranzista friends tell me that Acosta will never be able to get more than twenty men to follow him again. Not after this defeat. Villa will get a black eye out of it too.'' He smiled again. ''A black eye at Blue Eyes.''

Walton's response was a mirthless grunt. ''I'd still have liked to have given Black Jack a present.''

Lieutenant Peyton came up and saluted. ''I have our casualty report, sir,'' he said.

Walton's chin came out. ''Let's have it.''

''Four dead ponies,'' Peyton said proudly, ''a few holed hats and blouses, but not a hole in a trooper.''

''None?'' Walton cried in mixed amazement and relief. He swore again. ''They've got one helluva nerve starting a war when they shoot like that. Here, Lieutenant, please inform Captain Chalfant that I want C Company to stand picket duty.''

Walton walked back to his horse to pull a notebook from his saddlebar. Holding it against the animal's rump, he began writing his report.

Peyton turned to leave, but Duggan held out a hand. ''Congratulations, fire-eater—you got your charge, after all.''

''Right,'' Peyton said, his white teeth flashing. ''And it may be the last one of all time too.''

''Probably so,'' Duggan said musingly as Peyton walked away. He looked around him. All over Ojos Azules the weary troopers were fishing battered cooking gear from their saddle rolls and setting up the individual messes characteristic of the campaign. Duggan noticed that their breeches were worn through at the knees and in the seats. Their campaign hats, though jaunty, were tattered and trail-stained. Everything about the cavalry seemed old, he thought, listening to the far-off drone of the planes of the Aero Squadron. His eyes fell on First Sergeant Chicken, squatting before a fire of cottonwood twigs.

The Apache was roasting a chicken.

''They named you well,'' Duggan said, chuckling. ''How long did it take you to find the henhouse?''

Sergeant Chicken looked up and grinned. Beneath his campaign hat, his wrinkled brown face seemed even older.

''Well, old friend of my boyhood,'' Duggan said, laying a fond hand on his shoulder, ''you've lived long enough to see the last cavalry charge in history.''

''Huli!'' First Sergeant Chicken said. ''Damfine fight!''

FRANCE

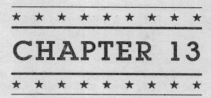

CHAPTER 13

The night was squallish. Rain gusted in sheets down Pennsylvania Avenue, forcing thousands of people crowding the sidewalks to turn their backs to the wind. Occasionally, a fitful flicker of lightning against grumbling low clouds sent a jagged pale gleam of light along the wet black pavement, and when a close crash of thunder followed, children cried out in fright.

The crowd was silent, waiting patiently for the appearance of the President's Packard limousine. They had read in the newspaper that he'd called an extraordinary joint session of Congress for that night, and they were certain he would ask for a declaration of war against Germany.

A clatter of hoofbeats from the direction of the White House was heard. The onlookers began to cheer. Woodrow Wilson could hear the applause faintly as he and his wife drove slowly toward the Capitol, surrounded by two troops of cavalry. Wilson's long white face was paler than usual. Furrows of anguish cut deep into his high forehead as he reflected bitterly on his failure to preserve American neutrality.

As late as January 1917, not long after the recall of Black Jack Pershing and the Punitive Expedition from Mexico, he had said: "This country does not intend to become involved in this war. It would be a crime against civilization for us to go in.''

Again and again, on those dreadful nights when his terrible headaches made sleep impossible, he would pace the bedroom floor and explain to his wife, Edith: ''If we cease to be neutral, the whole civilized world will be on a war footing. The world's last powerful neutral will have taken sides, and there will be no one left strong enough to bring about a reasonable, negotiated peace.'' Shuddering, he would hold his pounding head in his hands and moan: ''My God, why won't the kaiser stop his madness?''

But Kaiser Wilhelm would not. On February 1, 1917, he ordered resumption of unrestricted undersea warfare. Next, he tried to persuade Mexico to attack the United States. His offer of alliance was intercepted by the British, who skillfully exploited it to enrage the American people. Still, Woodrow Wilson fought for neutrality—until American merchant ships began to sink with German torpedoes in their vitals. On March 16 the *City of Memphis* and the *Illinois* were sunk by German submarines, and that was the end of American neutrality.

Now, two weeks later, Thomas Woodrow Wilson, twenty-seventh President of the United States, drove through the night rain to utter what had once seemed to him the unutterable call. Louder, now, he heard the cheering.

''They're *applauding*,'' he muttered in horrified disbelief. ''Think of what they're cheering, Edith. Tonight, I am going to ask for the death of our young men, and they're applauding that. How horrible the war mentality is. Why does the world love a fight so much? Can't they see what I'm leading them into—the brutality, the ruthlessness, the wanton destruction of war? The end of tolerance, of reason?'' Again, he held his aching head in his hands.

His features were composed, however, when he stepped from his limousine and ascended the Capitol steps. More cheers broke from thousands of people gathered on the steps, beneath the floodlit dome. Inside the House, the applause was thunderous, especially from the packed and overflowing galleries.

Major Mark Duggan stood at the gallery rail. He had

been an early arrival, quivering with excitement as he watched the floor below filling up with senators and representatives, justices of the Supreme Court and cabinet officers. All of official Washington was there, their eyes bright with excitement. Everyone seemed to have a small American flag in his lapel. Everyone, of course, except Senator LaFollette of Wisconsin. Major Duggan watched him standing alone, his arms crossed, his bulldog jaw set in grim disapproval. He, too, had fought to keep America out of the war; but for pacifism, not for neutrality. Now, his cause lost, he glanced around him belligerently, making Major Duggan smile to himself. Who is more bellicose than a pacifist? he thought wryly: Be for peace, or I'll kill you!

Major Duggan leaned over the balcony for a glimpse of the President. He noticed how pale his features were, and wondered if he were suffering from another headache, remembering the last time he had seen him.

It was the day of little Virginia's first birthday. Betsy had baked a tiny cake for her daughter. She put a single candle on it and placed it on the tray of Virginia's high chair. For perhaps ten seconds Virginia studied the cake and the lighted candle with roundly solemn blue eyes. Then she made the rosebud mouth that so delighted Mark, sucked in her cheeks, and blew the candle out. Betsy clapped her hands and laughed till she cried, after which she and Mark drank a hasty glass of champagne so that he could hurry back to the War Office, where he had to stand the General Staff's night watch.

Major Duggan had not been back in his office five minutes before he received a telegraph reporting that Major General Homer Bean, the man informally chosen to lead an American Expeditionary Force if America entered the war, had just dropped dead in the St. Anthony Hotel in San Antonio. Duggan was aghast. Secretary of War Newton D. Baker was dining alone with the President that night and had left orders that he was not to be disturbed. But this, Duggan thought grimly, is surely an emergency; and he hurried to the White House.

Secretary Baker glanced up in irritation when Major Duggan entered the family dining room, led by a steward. The

President's inquiring glance, though sharp, was friendlier. Duggan snapped to attention and saluted. Staring straight ahead into the gilded convex mirror crowned with an eagle hanging on the yellow wall above the green-and-white marble mantelpiece, he cried: "Mr. President, I regret to report that General Bean has just died of a heart attack."

Exclamations of dismay broke from both of them, and Major Duggan remembered how the reflection of Secretary Baker in the convex mirror exaggerated his froglike appearance.

"Good Lord, Newton," the President had said, "who will lead the Army now?"

Baker paused. His small eyes sunk in purplish pouches were thoughtful behind his thick spectacles. Suddenly he turned to Duggan. "Who would you pick, Major?"

"General Pershing, sir."

Baker nodded, and the President said quietly, "He would be a good choice, Newton. We'll have to give it some thought." Returning to Duggan, he said, "Thank you, Major Duggan. You were wise in coming here straight away." Duggan saluted and left, just as the President began to dictate a letter of condolences to Mrs. Bean.

Watching Woodrow Wilson now, almost a month later, Duggan was struck by the contrast between the pale drawn man beneath him striding quickly toward the dais and the relaxed, almost jovial President of that evening. In four weeks he seemed to have aged ten years.

A sudden, expectant hush came over the chamber as the President ascended the dais. Speaking clearly, he began to enunciate the insults and injuries inflicted upon the United States by Germany since the sinking of the *Lusitania*. He described the alternatives short of war left to him, and then, raising his voice, he exclaimed:

"There is one choice we cannot make, we are incapable of making: We will not choose the path of submission."

Thunderous shouts reverberated around the House. Chief Justice White lifted his hands above his hoary head to grasp them together in the prizefighter's vaunt of victory.

Wilson waited for the storm of approval to subside. "The world must be made safe for democracy." Again the House erupted, drowning his words in sound. Again he waited. "To such a task we can dedicate our lives and our fortunes, everything that we are and everything that we have, with the pride of those who know that the day has come when America is privileged to spend her blood and her might for the principles that gave her birth . . ." He swallowed and straightened. "God helping her, she can do no other."

A roar of applause rose from the floor of the House. It engulfed the President. Never before had he been so acclaimed, and he stood there in astonishment. At the gallery rail, Major Mark Duggan found himself on his feet with everyone else, pounding his palms together and shouting.

"War!" they roared. "War!"

And Major Mark Duggan also shouted, "War!"

"General Pershing will see you now, Major," the captain said.

Duggan arose from his chair with a smile. It had been only a few days ago that President Wilson had appointed Pershing Commander-in-Chief of the American Expeditionary Force. At once, a delighted Mark Duggan had obtained an interview with the general.

"We meet again, Mark," Black Jack grunted as Duggan came into his office and saluted. "What's on your mind?"

"Combat, sir," Duggan answered, grinning as he sat down. "I'd like to serve with the First Division in France."

Black Jack frowned and shook his head. "Sorry," he grunted.

"But, sir!" Duggan cried in dismay, leaning forward in his chair. "There's no one else of my rank in the Army with my combat experience. Just a battalion, sir," he pleaded. "I'd love to command a battalion. I'd rather lead a battalion in combat than be President of the United States."

"I believe you, Mark. And I'm sure you'd always take your objective. But you're needed where you are." General Pershing shook his head grimly. "If we're going to move and supply the AEF, we're going to need a General Staff that understands logistics. I'm afraid too many of our senior officers there don't know what it's all about. They're still feuding with the old bureau chiefs. So you are needed, Mark, where you are," he concluded in a tone of finality.

Realizing that the interview was over, Duggan concealed his disappointment and got to his feet. "Thank you for seeing me, sir," he said, saluting before about-facing and striding from the room.

He paused in the anteroom, his shoulders slumping momentarily—until he saw George Meadows seated in a chair reading a newspaper. His mood suddenly turning playful, he stole up to him, pretending to read a headline from the front page of Meadows's folded paper: "George Meadows to Command First American Units in France."

Down came the paper, with a sharp, whipping sound, and Meadows's startled look quickly changed to one of good humor. "I might have known it'd be you, Mark," he said evenly.

"I see you finally made captain, George," Mark said. "Congratulations."

"Thanks. It took a war to do it, though. Twelve years with single silver bars," he said, shaking his head in disbelief. "I tell you, Mark, they never felt heavy."

"What brings you to Washington?"

"Black Jack," Meadows said, moving his head toward the general's office. "You might say he inherited me after poor General Bean passed on. I was his deputy operations officer for the Southern Department. Now he wants me to be the same for the First Division."

"Dammit, George, are you going to beat me to another war?"

A grin creased Meadows's homely face. Then he sobered. "Mark, that business in Vera Cruz—there's no hard feelings?"

Duggan shrugged. "Why should there be? You did your duty as you saw it, and so did I."

He paused, about to add that he was getting used to it, anyway, but changed his mind. Meadows observed the pause, but said nothing. There was an awkward silence. Both men looked away, and both were relieved when the captain at the desk announced that General Pershing was ready to see Captain Meadows. They shook hands with a cordiality distinguished by its lack of comradely warmth, and parted.

You may beat me to the war again, George, Mark Duggan thought, watching the general's office door close behind his old friend, but I'll still beat you to the combat zone.

"You shouldn't be so depressed, Mark," Betsy Duggan said the night that Black Jack Pershing and his staff—George

Quincy Meadows among them—sailed secretly for England. "I should think you'd be proud to know that General Pershing thinks you're so indispensable to the General Staff."

Mark Duggan scowled. "Soldiers don't grow great commanding desks," he said grimly. "They only flourish in the field." He pulled the belt of his gray cadet bathrobe tighter around his waist and studied his wife, seated opposite him in their living room. "One good victory, Betsy, is worth a thousand glowing fitness reports." He scowled again. "George Meadows is very skillful at the fitness-report game, but he's yet to see a shot fired in anger."

"Why are you so bitter against your old friend?"

"I don't know," he said moodily. "Maybe it's because he's turning out to be the sort of staff officer my father taught me to loathe."

"Could it be because he beat you to another war?"

Mark chuckled mirthlessly. "Three in a row, Betsy. But he still hasn't beaten me to a battlefield." He shrugged. "Oh, I don't know. George is all right in his way, I guess. But he's just so cautious . . . so careful not to make a mistake. I guess I never noticed it when we were kids at the Academy. But after we were commissioned, it really showed through. It's almost . . . it's almost like toadying. That's just not my way, Betsy."

"I know Mark. I've seen you in action, you know. There is probably no officer in the American army more adept at alienating his superior officers."

Duggan's chin lifted. "Not on purpose, Betsy. For principle. And I think I may have done it again today." She glanced at him in alarm and he tried to smile. "You know that I've been a minority of one in trying to persuade the General Staff to approve use of the National Guard in France. Well, we had the final round today. They all voted to send only 500,000 men overseas, all regulars. I voted against it. I told them that it was a mistake to ignore the citizen-soldier, the traditional American fighting man since the days of the minutemen. I told them how much my father had admired the volunteer regiments of the Civil War. He commanded regulars himself, but he sure thought highly of outfits like the Twenty-fourth Wisconsin, the Fifth New Hampshire, the New York Sixty-ninth—especially the Sixty-ninth. I said the Guard should call for volunteers and train them for combat. I told them it was a mistake to limit our ground forces to half a million men. I said a force that small would never weigh the scales of war in favor of the Allies." He paused, aware that his voice had risen and was throbbing with emotion.

"What did they say?" Betsy asked.

He shrugged. "Nothing. They just looked at me with those silvery stone heads of theirs and brought the question to a vote. It was twenty-nine to one." He compressed his lips grimly. "Then I think I made a mistake. When the recommendation came to me for my endorsement I wrote on it that I disagreed with it completely. I said to send only a half-million men to France was to send a boy on a man's errand. I said that to depend on regulars alone and ignore the huge potential of the National Guard—a force in being—was a hidebound repetition of the blunders of the Spanish War. Then I said that if this recommendation was approved, I wished to be relieved of service on such a purblind board." He shook his head a little wistfully. "My language may have been a little strong, and I guess I'll be hearing about it soon."

Betsy Duggan glanced at her husband in alarm again. "You did it on purpose!" she shot out accusingly.

He shook his head. "Not on purpose, dearest—on principle. I said that because I believe it. What can I lose, anyway? A desk? And I might gain a battalion." His jaw lifted once more. "I tell you, Betsy, the Duggans have been in every American big shoot since colonial times, and I'm not going to be the first to sit one out."

Betsy said nothing, although her eyes were full of anguish and apprehension. She was too much a soldier's daughter, a soldier's wife, to say what was in her heart: What of me? What of me and Virginia? The telephone rang in the hall and she rose to answer it.

"It's for you, Mark—the Secretary of War."

Startled, Mark went into the hall. His face was ashen as he took the receiver from Betsy's hand.

"Duggan here, sir," he said, unconsciously coming to attention. "He did? I'm sorry to hear that, sir." He stood listening for a few more moments, still ramrod straight in his bathrobe. "When, sir? Yes, sir—I'll be right down." He hung up and turned to Betsy, his face still white. "The chief of staff approved the General Staff's recommendation. He forwarded it to Secretary Baker. The Secretary wants to see me. Immediately.''

Betsy's hand went to her lips.

''You'd better have Durkin bring the staff car around,'' Mark said, untying his gray bathrobe. ''And I'd better get back into uniform.''

Newton D. Baker sat hunched in a huge black leather chair. He did not look up when Major Duggan entered his office, continuing to read the General Staff's policy paper while smoking a big, sweet-smelling pipe. Major Duggan's stomach began to turn. He imagined that Baker was studying his endorsement. He felt the nausea rising. At last the Secretary looked up and removed his pipe.

''I agree with you, Major,'' he said quietly. ''I think you're absolutely right. So does the President.''

''Thank you, sir!'' Duggan said, elated, the nausea gone and forgotten.

''I do not, however, approve of your intemperate language.''

''I...I'm sorry, sir,'' Duggan stammered, flushing. ''I...I'd been working hard, and I was just so desperately opposed to this proposal that I guess I—''

Baker held up a hand. ''Very well. I have ordered the chief of staff to destroy your endorsement. I also assured him that I would reprimand you in person. Consider yourself reproved, Major.''

''Yes, sir. Thank you, sir.''

''Now, the President has asked me to put your ideas into effect. I would like to do something to dramatize them, something that would electrify the country. Do you have any suggestions, Major?''

Duggan's eyes gleamed. ''I do, indeed! There are too many divisive forces at work in our country, Mr. Secretary. All kinds of hyphenated Americans, socialists, Wobblies, pacifists. Let us do something truly unifying, sir. Let's create a *national* division!'' His voice beginning to throb, gesturing dramatically as he spoke. ''We could form one division of National Guard units from every one of the forty-eight states. Just think of it, Mr. Secretary: infantry from, say, New York; artillerymen from Virginia; cavalry from Kansas—and so on. All the different states, all the different creeds and colors— but all American! I tell you, sir, it would stretch across the country like a giant rainbow!"

"Excellent!" Secretary Baker exclaimed, clapping his hands together. "The Rainbow Division! That's what we'll call it." Putting his pipe down on his desk, he walked around behind it to stand there, studying his lineage book. "The Forty-second Division is nothing but paper. That should be just the outfit."

Duggan nodded. "Who would command it, sir?"

"It would have to be Brigadier General Parker Phann," he said slowly.

"Isn't he close to retirement, sir?" Duggan asked anxiously.

"He is. But he's next in line for divisional command. And with his political connections, I just don't dare jump anyone over him. If I did, the telephone would never stop ringing."

Duggan nodded. He was aware that General Phann's position as chief of militia required close association with the National Guards of all the states, where he met and befriended many influential politicians.

"I understand, sir," he said. "But with a division commander as old and inactive as General Phann, may I suggest that you give him the youngest, finest colonel in the Army as his chief of staff."

Secretary Baker nodded. He smiled slowly, putting a finger to his heavy glasses. "I am, Major—I'm giving him you."

"Me!" Duggan cried, flabbergasted. "But he rates a colonel, sir!"

"He's getting one," Baker replied, sitting down in a chair and drawing a blank commission from his drawer. "I take it that you want to remain in the infantry, Colonel Duggan," he asked gently, beginning to write.

"Yes, sir. The Duggans have always fought on foot."

Standing there silently, listening to the scratching of the pen on foolscap, he remembered his father's dying words and felt his eyes go moist. He took the commission the Secretary handed up to him and read it.

"*Colonel* Duggan," he said aloud, the hot tears falling quickly from his eyes. "You know, sir, my father was a colonel at nineteen. And I'm already thirty-nine. If I want to catch up with him, I'd better get a move on."

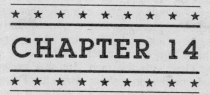

CHAPTER 14

The Rainbow was truly a national division. It did not have units from all the states, but it did have troops from twenty-six of them: infantry from New York, Ohio, Alabama, and Iowa; artillerymen from Indiana, Illinois, and Minnesota; machine-gunners from Pennsylvania, Wisconsin, and Georgia; mortarmen from Maryland; engineers from California, North and South Carolina; signalmen from Missouri; military police from Virginia; supply trainmen from Texas; ammunition men from Kansas; cavalry from Louisiana; and ambulance and field hospital men from Tennessee, Michigan, New Jersey, Oklahoma, Colorado, Oregon, Nebraska, and the District of Columbia.

Colonel Mark Duggan was delighted with the composition of the organization that he would always consider *his* division. He was not, however, as pleased with the conduct of the Rainbow's commander, General Parker Phann. General Phann seldom ventured outside of the comfortable headquarters that was the first structure to rise above Camp Mills, Long Island. He became known as "Parkyer Phanny." The men also called him the "Parker House roll," in tribute to what was probably the roundest paunch in the American Expeditionary Force.

Much as Colonel Duggan despised General Phann for his indolence and self-indulgence, he also realized that the general's inactivity was his own opportunity. Gradually, he took the actual command of the Rainbow into his own hands. Each time newly-arriving units pulled into the railroad terminal at Camp Mills, Colonel Duggan was on the platform to greet them. Wearing his bullet-riddled campaign hat, impeccable in whipcord breeches, gleaming leather puttees, and Sam Brown belt, a swagger stick under his arm, he would introduce himself to each unit commander, shake hands with all the officers, and chat with the men. He was present at every outfit's review or demonstration: when the Doughboys fired for record on the rifle range or when the "cannon-cockers" calibrated their field pieces; he watched the signal men learning to lay communication wire, and was the first to ride over the engineers' first bridge; during the Rainbow's first field maneuver in the mud of a driving September rain, he rode beside a truck driver hauling ammunition to the simulated "front"; and it was he who visited the soldiers sent to the division's new field hospital suffering from pneumonia or dysentery. Eventually, inevitably, the men of the Rainbow came to think of their outfit as Duggan's division; and no one was surprised, one raw overcast day in mid-October, to see that it was "Dug" who stood alone on the reviewing stand to review the Rainbow for the last time before the division took ship for France.

The infantry came first, followed by the artillery. Sergeant Patrick Durkin, standing below Colonel Duggan and a little to his right, watched the approach of the 168th Regiment—the old third Iowa—with the disdainful eyes of the old regular.

"Yez'll never make a silk purse out of a sow's ear," he muttered contemptuously beneath the music of the regimental band playing "Iowa." "Jaysus!" he swore when the men, hearing the order "Eyes right!" gave instead the hand salute. "Look at them mother's mistakes."

Next came the 167th Infantry—the old Second Alabama— with its band playing "Dixie." Even Colonel Duggan could not conceal his dismay when the Alabama forward ranks collided with the Iowans, who had unaccountably halted and begun to mark time. Then the Alabama commander gave the order, "Rear march!" just as the 165th—the old Sixty-ninth New York—came swaggering up, the wind whipping their famous regimental banner of green silk with a gold harp and the gold legend "Erin Go Bragh!" emblazoned upon it.

Neither Colonel Duggan nor Sergeant Durkin could believe what they heard. The New Yorkers' band was playing "Marching through Georgia," and from the vicious jabs that the huge kilt-clad drum major made with his enormous, knob-headed, shillelaghlike baton, it was obvious to both that the "Fighting Sixty-ninth" was spoiling for a fight.

A wild yell of outrage rose from the ranks of the Alabamans. They had heard the detestable, hateful song. From the New York Irish came a roar of delight. Instantly, the men of both regiments threw down their rifles and tore the flat-brimmed steel helmets from their heads. With high, yipping, rebel yells, the Alabamans wheeled and attacked. The New Yorkers closed. Rich brogues rose from their lips impetrating Heaven and the Virgin for a smash to the jaw.

A general melee ensued. Within minutes the struggling, swinging Doughboys were smeared with mud and blood. Bodies came hurtling from the mass, only to be turned around by their officers, encouraged, and sent tottering back into the fray. Now the bands of both regiments stood to the side, the New Yorkers playing "The Irish Washerwoman," and the Alabamans "Pop Goes the Weasel."

Colonel Mark Duggan realized it was useless to attempt to be heard above that cacophony of music, screams, and curses. Instead, he ran down the steps of the reviewing stand to tell Durkin to run to the New York band and tell them to play the National Anthem. He put his hand on Durkin's shoulder just as a blond Alabama sergeant came staggering toward them. He was limping and blood was streaming from his nose. Nevertheless, he turned and started back to the brawl again, screaming in a thick southern accent, "You dirty gawd-damned micks! We licked y'all down in Dixie, and we'll do it again in your own backyahd!" With a growl, Durkin darted forward. He seized the Alabaman's shoulder with his left hand, spun him around, and raised a ham of a right to finish him off.

"Glory be to God!" he cried in delight, dropping his hand and hugging the man. "It's himself! It's me darlin' little snake!"

"Ah'll be go t' hell," Beauregard Ames muttered, drawing

a muddy cuff across his bloody upper lip. "If'n it ain't the big harp." Seeing Colonel Duggan beside him, an expression of disbelief came into his round blue eyes and he came to attention.

"Do we *always* have to meet this way, Ames?" Colonel Duggan murmured. Then, seizing each by the shoulder, he said, "Quick! Tell the bandmasters to play the National Anthem and stop this disgraceful riot."

Durkin bounded off, Ames hobbling after him. The music stopped. A few moments later the strains of "The Star-Spangled Banner" burst out, played with a certain plaintive sheepishness that was not missed by the now-silent soldiers. Slowly, they released each other. Their apprehensive eyes swiveled toward the slender, ramrod-straight figure on the stand above them. They retrieved their rifles and helmets and resumed ranks.

It was quiet on the parade ground at Camp Mills. Colonel Mark Duggan stood there, tight-lipped, straight, and silent, for perhaps five minutes. He really did not know what to say. After all, these were the men he had trained, the soldiers he would one day help to lead against the Germans. Certainly, two months was never time enough to turn raw recruits into trained soldiers, to mold an efficient, modern division 26,000 strong. But he could not ignore what he had seen: a divisional review turned into a bloody brawl in front of the reviewing officer. But what was he to do: put two entire regiments into the guardhouse? Recommend the relief of their commanding officers? On the very eve of their embarkation? Duggan let out his breath.

"You will all return to your quarters," he cried in a trembling voice, "and you will remove your Rainbow Division patches from your shoulders. And you will not put them back on until the day I see you do to the enemy what you have just done to each other."

And then, to symbolize his own disgust and dismay, he put his hand to his shoulder and tore his own patch away.

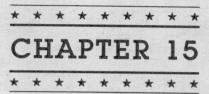

CHAPTER 15

It was a tense and uneventful voyage from Hoboken to St. Nazaire. Uneventful, because no enemy appeared, above or beneath the cold gray sea; tense, because the enemy's appearance was dreaded every waking moment.

All the ships of the convoy were so overcrowded that the men were allowed above decks only forty-five minutes a day. Otherwise they stayed below, in stuffy, foul-smelling holds, playing cards, reading, chatting, writing letters, or catnapping in canvas bunks slung four tiers high. It was tedium spiced with terror: the swift silences seizing them all upon the sudden movement of the ships, the inexplicable changes of course, the shrill piping of "General Quarters" down the ventilating shafts at every submarine scare, the endless booming of the six-inch guns of the convoy warships shooting at towed targets of simulated periscopes.

Thirteen days out of Hoboken, twenty-four hours away from the Loire and safety, Allied wireless informed the convoy that its ships had been spotted by German submarines. The U-boats were moving in for the kill . . .

Not a captain left his bridge. Throughout the long, cold, North Atlantic night, they stayed there, zigzagging their ships. "Rudder left . . . rudder right . . ." In swaying crow's nests high above the weather decks, shivering lookouts searched the obsidian surface of the sea, watching for broken patches of water where periscopes would be. They saw none. In the pale light of a misty drizzling dawn, they saw instead the lights of Belle Isle—and then the wide gray ribbon of the ancient Loire stretching away to St. Nazaire and safety.

Minutes after the ships docked, the troops began marching down the gangplank. They clambered into the tiny French boxcars that were to be immortalized as *le quarante et huit*, "the forty and eight," suitable for holding forty men and eight horses; providing, of course, that neither were too large or too fastidious. They stank, of course, of horse dung and urine. Even the foot soldiers of the Rainbow, gay again, now that the tedium and terror of the sea voyage were behind them, could not behold them with affection.

Once embarked, the infantry rolled off to training camps in Toul, just east of Paris and south of the front. The artillery chugged away west to the Breton peninsula and the French Military School, where they would receive further training as well as their quotas of French field pieces, the famous seventy-fives and the 155 heavyweights. They and the other units completing similar specialized training would rejoin the Rainbow at its headquarters at Vaucouleurs, in the heart of Lorraine, the country of Joan of Arc.

Colonel Duggan stood at the rail of the *Covington*, watching the men file slowly down the gangplank. Sergeant Durkin stood beside him. Sergeant Beauregard Ames, who had left his farm and fourteen-year-old son in the care of his father the day he enlisted in the 167th Alabama, was not there. Upon examination, his leg, injured in the brawl—now legendary in Rainbow traditions as "the Battle of the Hicks and Micks" —was found to be broken, and Ames had to go to the hospital to have it set. He would not be able to rejoin the Rainbow until the cast was removed.

"Let's go, Pat," Colonel Duggan said as the last Dough-boy stepped onto the soil of France.

"Yes, sir," Durkin said, picking up both his and the colonel's duffel bag and following Duggan down the gang-plank. They walked toward the train shed where they could see eddying clouds of thick white smoke and smell the sulfurous odor of burning coal.

A voice called, "Mark," and Duggan turned to see George

Quincy Meadows hurrying down the wharf toward him. The big man stuck out his hand with a grin.

"Welcome to France, Mark," he said.

"Yes, I know, George," Duggan replied with a weak smile. "Three in a row, now, eh? And I see you've already made major. Pretty quick, George."

"Yes, but not as quick as you, Colonel Duggan. Anyway, I was afraid I'd miss you. We had a flat tire on the way out from Chaumont and I—"

"Chaumont? I thought you were with the First Division."

"Not anymore. I'm at GHQ, now. Assistant G-3. Black Jack asked for me and I had to go." His voice was wistful. "I didn't want to. I thought that I was finally going to see some action." He shrugged. "Well anyway, Mark, that's why I'm here. G-3 hears that your ships are loaded with supplies and equipment."

Duggan's eyes gleamed and he lifted his chin proudly. "Right. Before we left I made certain that the Rainbow would be self-sustaining. Except for the artillery the French are giving us, we don't need anything. New machine guns, new uniforms, shoes, gas masks, rolling kitchens, blankets, tin hats, beans, and bullets—everything! We've got enough supplies to last us for six months."

"So we heard," Meadows said musingly, and then, his voice sobering, "I'm sorry, Mark, but you're going to have to give most of it up."

"What? What do you mean, 'give it up'? It's *ours*!"

Meadows shook his head. "No, it isn't. It's the AEF's—and we need it for the other divisions already overseas."

"What do you mean, 'the other divisions'? Let them get their own supplies. That stuff is *mine,* George, goddammit. I scrounged the country for it. I pulled every War Department string I knew. I even made a personal call on Secretary Baker to get those new machine guns and forty thousand extra pairs of shoes. And now you're telling me you're going to give it to someone *else*. No way, George—not on your life."

"I'm sorry, Mark," Meadows said doggedly. "But the other divisions are in short supply and they've got to have it."

Duggan compressed his lips in exasperation. His handsome face was white with rage. Struggling to control himself, he fitted a cigarette into his gold holder and lighted it, jabbing the air with it as he spoke.

"In other words, George, the inefficiency of their own staff is about to be rewarded, and my own efficiency and foresight is to be punished. Is that the way it is?"

"Mark," Meadows said pleadingly, "Why must you always twist things that way? It's very simple. Those three divisions are going to be the first to go into the trenches, and they have to be fully equipped. Besides . . ." He paused, his eyes miserable.

"Besides what?"

Meadows swallowed and looked away. "Your division is not going to be an active one, Mark."

Duggan stared at him in disbelief, his hands white at each end of his swagger stick, bending it as though he would break it. "Go on, George," he whispered.

"General Pershing is forming the first American Corps. G-3 had recommended that it be formed by the First, Second, and Twenty-sixth divisions. The Rainbow is to be a replacement division for that corps."

The stick snapped in Duggan's hands, and he swung around and hurled the parts savagely into the bay. He whirled back to face his old friend. "You mean the men that I have trained are to be the cannon fodder for other outfits?"

"Please don't put it that way, Mark—you are a professional soldier, the same as I am, and should understand these things."

"And you, dear friend, companion of my youth," Duggan snarled, his voice hoarse and cracking, "you concurred in this recommendation?"

Major Meadows lifted his shoulder and said nothing. Colonel Duggan spun on his heel and strode toward the train shed. Durkin followed.

"Mark," Meadows cried in dismay. "Don't take it this way. Where are you going?"

"To Vaucouleurs. To Vaucouleurs and General Phann and the cablegraph office," he cried in a choking voice. "We'll see who really runs this man's army."

At Vaucouleurs another blow awaited Colonel Duggan. To form his staff he had carefully combed the Regular Army for the youngest, ablest, most aggressive officers he could find. Most of them were West Pointers or graduates of Virginia Military Institute. At Vancouleurs he found that thirty of his thirty-four staff officers had been transferred to other divisions. It's all George Meadows's doing, he thought bitterly: I can see now that he was always jealous of me, that he could never forgive me for having a three-star general for a father.

General Phann was as angry as Duggan. "It's a plot to make the National Guard play second fiddle," he snarled as his chief of staff entered his office. Phann's little blue eyes crackled in his florid face. "They want us to train men that they can siphon off into the regular divisions. They'll get all the glory and we'll get all the headaches. Well, Duggan," he snapped, "I tell you I'm not going to sit still for it."

"What will you do, sir?"

"I am not without friends in Washington. And you, Duggan, I'd appreciate it if you'd use your influence with the Secretary."

"I will indeed," Duggan said, returning to his own office.

During the next few days cablegraph after cablegraph sped beneath the ocean from France to the United States. A week later General Phann summoned Duggan to his office again.

"General Pershing wants to see me," he said, his fleshy face ashen, his blue eyes pale and watery. "I understand that he's been getting a lot of noise from Washington. I've been told he's hopping mad." Phann paused to blow his nose, swinging around in his chair to gaze out the window at snow flurries swirling outside. "Ah, Duggan... Would you, ah, mind going to Chaumont in my place?" He coughed. "You see, I have this miserable cold and we're supposed to be in for a blizzard."

"Of course, sir!" Duggan exclaimed, getting to his feet. "I'll leave this afternoon."

Back in his quarters, Duggan called for Sergeant Durkin. "Get a staff car from the motor pool, Pat," he said. "We're driving to Chaumont." He paused, looking around him with a frown. "Have you seen my war bonnet, Pat?"

"Not since you broke the day of the brawl, sir."

Duggan groaned. "You're right. I took it down to Washington with me for Mrs. Duggan to fix. I must've forgotten it." He shook his head in self-reproach. "I've *got* to have it! I've gotten so superstitious about that damn bonnet that I'm actually afraid to go into battle without it." He picked up a writing pad from his desk and seized a pen. "I'll send her a cablegraph right away."

"Excuse me, sir, but I think I've got a better idea. Sergeant Ames will be taking ship soon. Why not have him pick it up and bring it here in person? Sure, it'll be safer that way, sir."

"Good. You take care of it, Pat. Send Ames a cable as soon as we get to Chaumont. It'll get to the States faster from there."

Black Jack Pershing was not friendly. "What are you doing here, Mark?" he snapped. "I sent for Phann."

"He's sick, sir."

Black Jack sneered. "Is that what he calls it?" he said, his voice cold with contempt. "Very well, Mark, since you have chosen to be your general's shield, here it is." He leaned forward, the gray eyes beneath the gray eyebrows stony. "This playing politics has got to stop. Your division is to furnish replacements for the First Army Corps. You and Phann personally will stop trying to put pressure on me from official Washington. Is that clear?"

"It is, sir," Duggan murmured, feeling faintly nauseous. "But may I respectfully ask why it has to be us?"

"Because you have an inactive commander, because you have not yet begun to train here as a division, because you have not yet received your artillery and other material, and because you have a complete backup of personnel for the other units."

Duggan swallowed. "I understand, sir. But may I respectfully suggest why the Rainbow should not be used for replacements?"

Black Jack Pershing sat opposite Duggan, cold and still as a statue. His gray hair and gray brush of a mustache seemed to have been chiseled from granite. "Two minutes, Mark," he said.

"Thank you, sir. First, the problem of the inactive commander . . . I think, sir, with all due respect, that this is a problem you can handle yourself." Pershing's eyelid flickered, and Duggan guessed that General Phann's career was at an end. "Second, ours is the first division to arrive here complete. Our training has been basic soldiering, sir, none of that trench-and-bomb baloney.'' Pershing's eyelid fluttered again, and Duggan, realizing that he had scored a point, grew bolder. "It's also true, sir, that we've been in the papers a lot and made a lot of friends. For us to disappear might raise some eyebrows." Black Jack's mouth became a cold thin slit, and Duggan felt faint again. Deciding that he had already passed the point of no return, he rushed on. "As you know, General, the 165th Regiment is the old Fighting Sixty-ninth. Actually, it's the Friendly Sons of St. Patrick in khaki. President Wilson is already not too popular with the New York Irish. Some of the things he's said . . . If he had said them before the election last year, he never would have won. I doubt very much if the President wants to alienate them furth—''

"Mr. Wilson is a lame-duck President," Pershing snapped irritably.

"I know, sir. But he is still a politician, a Democrat—and the Democrats need those forty-seven electoral votes in New York State."

Pershing grunted and said nothing. Duggan's confidence returned, and he continued: "Finally, sir, I honestly believe that if you used the Rainbow for replacements, the War Department would reverse you. If you asked the War Department for permission to do it, sir, I believe that it would be denied."

For the first time since he had known Black Jack Pershing, Mark Duggan saw his expression change. Just for a moment, a split second, a look of incredulity came into his eyes. But they were cold and unblinking again when he said, "Mark, I always thought that your father was the most arrogant and egotistical man I had ever met, until I met his son.''

"I . . . I'm sorry, sir," Duggan murmured, his voice faltering.

"You are *sorry*? You sit there, a divisional chief of staff, a colonel, and you tell me, the commander of the American Expeditionary Force, a general of the armies, that if you don't get what you want, the politicos will be on my back. And then, when I rebuke you, you tell me that you're *sorry*?''

"I . . . I didn't mean it in quite that way, sir.''

"It comes out that way, Mark," Pershing snapped.

Duggan looked away in misery, certain that he had failed.

"General, I honestly believe what I have just said," he said in an apologetic tone. "If I may, sir, let me tell you of an incident with Secretary Baker. I was in his office when he created the Rainbow Division. When he told me that he was choosing General Phann to command it, I reminded him that General Phann was close to retirement age. He answered that he was aware of the general's age and inactivity, but he dared not risk a fight with his influential friends by passing him over." He paused, fixing General Pershing with the direct gaze of his large dark eyes. "I do really believe now, sir, that if you were to relieve General Phann and replace him with someone . . . someone with the right name . . . and let it be known that the Rainbow would remain an active division . . . I really do believe that this would be understood and accepted in Washington."

Black Jack Pershing placed his heavy black spectacles over his eyes and bent his head over the papers on his desk. "That will be all, Mark," he said in a dry, noncommittal voice.

Colonel Duggan arose, saluted, and left, driving back to Vaucouleurs in silence. Three days later a directive went out from General Headquarters in Chaumont to the effect that the next division to arrive in France, the Forty-first, would serve at supply depots in the rear; and the next, the Thirty-second, would furnish replacements for the other divisions.

"We've sold it!" Colonel Duggan cried jubilantly when General Phann summoned him to his office and reported the good news.

"Yes, Duggan, you Judas!" General Phann snarled, his florid face white with rage. "And you also sold me! Tomorrow I am to be relieved of my command and replaced by Major General Michael J. Corrigan of New York City." His voice choked and he brandished the directive in his hand. "Michael J. Corrigan of New York City!" he snarled. "D'ya think I can't read between the lines, Duggan? You saved the Rainbow, yes. You saved it by selling me down the river for a pack of dirty Irish micks!"

"That may be, General Phann," Duggan said quietly, getting to his feet and staring at his livid commander in contempt. "And the 165th may be, as you say, a bunch of dirty Irish micks." He turned and went to the door. "But, General—they can fight."

• • •

Sergeant Beauregard Ames decided to walk from Union Terminal to the colonel's home on Connecticut Avenue. He couldn't afford to take a taxi, not on his pay. Colonel Duggan's hat wouldn't be much to carry anyway, and it was a beautiful late November day, full of the golden light of autumn. Besides, Washington was Ames's favorite city. He loved its white buildings and monuments, its parks and circles and wide streets.

He was sweating just a little under his tight-fitting Dough-boy's uniform when he strode up the Duggan walk. Taking off his overseas cap, he ran a hand through his thick tawny hair and lifted the knocker.

Betsy Duggan heard the knock with surprise and pleasure. She had so few visitors. Putting down her glass of white wine, she came quickly to the door and opened it.

Ames looked at her in amazement. "Jesus Christ and General Jackson!" he swore. "It cain't be. Is it really you, Betsy?"

"Beau!" Betsy cried. "Beau Ames! What are you doing here?"

"I've come to get the colonel's hat. What're y'all doin' here, Betsy? Y'all work for the colonel's missus?"

"I do not!" she shot back angrily. "I *am* the colonel's missus," she said proudly. "Colonel Duggan is my husband."

Ames was astounded. He ran a hand through his hair again. "I'll be go t' hell," he muttered disbelievingly. "It cain't be. Kit King's little girl married to my commandin' officer."

"We met in the War Office," Betsy said, almost defensively. "We've been married almost four years." She stepped aside. "Would you like to come in, Beau?"

He nodded. "Thank y' kindly," he murmured, and walked past her through the hall and into the living room.

He sat down, and Betsy asked, "Would you like a glass of wine?"

"Don't mind if I do, Betsy," he said, and she poured him a glass from a decanter and handed it to him. He sipped it, studying her. "You sure turned into a beautiful woman, Betsy," he said. She blushed and he went on. "You remember the cave under Comanche Bluff?"

Betsy turned scarlet. "Stop, Beau," she said. "I was hardly more than a little girl then."

He sighed. "I ain't never seen no little girl come up to you since."

"Please, Beau . . ."

"I sure hated to leave Camp Robinson. I think I was goin' to ask you to marry me, Betsy. But then I got orders to report to the Presidio." He sighed again. "I sure missed you. When I was out in the Philippines, out there on those night patrols, I used to think of you. What it was like back there under Comanche Bluff. I swear t'God, Betsy, it was the only thing kept me from goin' loco like some of them other Doughfoots in Balangiga."

"*Balangiga?* Were you in Balangiga?"

"Sure. That's where I met the colonel. 'Course, he was only a second looey, then."

"He never told me."

"Why should he? He was an officer and I was an enlisted man. Besides, how would he know I knew you?"

Betsy nodded. She got up from the sofa to pour herself another glass of wine. Ames watched her thoughtfully.

"You sure startin' early on that stuff," he said.

She glared at him in resentment, sitting down again. "I won't have another one until dinnertime," she said, pouting. "Besides, it's so boring now that Mark . . . the colonel is gone. My little girl is in a nursery and I have a housekeeper to do the chores for me. So . . ." She shrugged and took another sip.

"You'd best be careful. You know what happens to officers' wives when they ain't got nothin' to do."

"I know, Beau—they become drunks or whores. But you won't find me playing games with good-looking enlisted men like some of the ladies I've known."

Ames grinned. "Same ol' Betsy," he drawled. She studied him, running her eyes over his thick tawny hair, remembering how plunging her fingers into it used to excite her so. How she loved to comb the golden hair on his forearm and see it ripple like wheat in the sun.

"Oh, Beau!" she cried suddenly. "Why didn't you even say good-bye?"

"I couldn't. I wanted to, but they wasn't any way without

lettin' your daddy know. An' I hardly had time to pack my bag before they had me up on the wagon and down to the railroad station.''

''I cried every night for weeks. You could at least have written to me.''

''An' have your daddy start askin' questions?''

She fell silent, moving a hand out impulsively toward the wine decanter, then drawing it back. Beauregard Ames rose, went to her and lifted her gently to her feet and put his arms around her and kissed her. She kissed him back, hard, thrusting her taut belly into him, clutching him desperately at the back of his head. He stooped as though to slip his hands under her dress, but changed his mind and swung her off her feet and carried her out into the hall and up the stairs to her bedroom.

When Beauregard Ames brought Colonel Duggan's hat to Vaucouleurs, he also brought him a thick gray cashmere muffler that Betsy had knitted for him. It had a large black-and-gold A sewn on it. Mark was delighted. He had been troubled by sore throats caused by the raw French winter, and he thought the muffler would keep his throat warm. He wore it like a cravat: wound around his neck inside his wool trench coat, but fluffed up in the V of the coat so that the black-and-gold A was visible. He also pinned up the right side of the brim of his campaign hat to the crown, Rough Rider style, and wore it set at a rakish angle. So attired, his cigarette holder jutting from his mouth, a new black-lacquered malacca swagger stick beneath his arm—a gift from Sergeant Durkin on his fortieth birthday—he was indeed a dashing, singular figure as he roamed the lines of the Luneville-Baccarat combat sector, where the Rainbow's four infantry regiments were being introduced to battle under French supervision. Soon his soldiers were calling him ''the Dude'' or ''Dandy Dug.'' They did not do it derisively, but rather with laughter and affection. Swaggerer that he undoubtedly was, he did not cherish his gleaming leather puttees so much that he would not descend into the muck and watery slime of their trenches.

Although the men of the Rainbow had not yet received their baptism of fire, they had indeed been christened in mud and misery. They had become, like their allies and enemies, anonymous steel moles dwelling in trenches dug four to six feet below the surface of the earth. In the rear face of the trenches were the shallow, drafty dugouts in which they lived. Here, blinking in the sputtering light of candles stuck into dirt walls, their nostrils full of a unique reek compounded of unwashed flesh, excrement, urine, cigarette smoke, and dank earth, they scratched at the "cooties," those ubiquitous lice that infested the uniforms of all soldiers one day after they entered the trenches. They slept, munched hardtack, wrote letters home, cleaned their rifles, and frequently, bracing their backs against walls shuddering beneath the impact of enemy artillery crashing harmlessly overhead, they wondered bitterly why "Horseface," as they had contemptuously christened President Wilson, had decided that *he* would make "the world safe for democracy" by sending *them* into the "mad monotony" of this dullest, dirtiest, yet bloodiest of wars. Except for cards and cigarettes, there was no recreation; although occasionally one of the giant rats of no-man's-land, bloated with human flesh, would fall splashing into the trenches, and then, with cries of loathing and of hate, the Doughboys would rush to skewer it on their bayonets.

One day in early February of 1918, Colonel Duggan and Sergeant Patrick Durkin stood in the trenches of the New York Sixty-ninth, watching a party of soldiers chase a monster frog down the zigzagging line of the traverses. Croaking in fright, the terrified creature went leaping over the muck, until a tall corporal spitted it and swung it, grotesque and wriggling, over the parapet and into the snowy anonymity of no-man's-land.

"Ah, sure, 'tis the grand sport, indeed," Durkin muttered in contempt. "But wait'll you try stickin' them can openers into the heinie-koplotzes over there."

"They'll be trying it sooner than you think, Pat," Colonel Duggan murmured, jumping lightly down into the communications trench running perpendicular to the front and leading to the division's farmhouse headquarters a few miles to the rear. Duggan paused, flicking his swagger stick at a gob of gray mud stuck to his puttee. "General Guerard told me today he wanted the Rainbow to see action."

"A full-scale attack, sir?" Durkin's blue eyes were wide.

"No, Pat—not yet. Just a raid. The general wants a few prisoners, and he also wants to test the men."

"When, sir?"

"Tomorrow midnight. Those lads chasing the frog, that's the company General Corrigan selected." Duggan fitted a cigarette into his gold holder and lighted it, idly straightening the A scarf at his throat. "And, Pat," he continued, his dark eyes twinkling, "we'll be going with them."

A slender sickle moon glinted faintly through wispy dark clouds scudding across the face of no-man's-land.

Mark Duggan glanced up at it anxiously. "Let's hope it doesn't clear," he muttered to the tall, one-armed French colonel standing beside him.

Colonel Baudin nodded silently, watching the burly Americans climbing over the parapets to fan out and lie down in the muddy snow of no-man's-land. Both their faces and their bayonets had been blackened to avoid reflecting light. The French colonel, whose armless left sleeve was tucked neatly inside his belt, observed these facts approvingly. He wondered if all Americans were so big and muscular. Perhaps, in the ancient time, the Franks were like that—the Paladins of Charlemagne, the knights of Charles Martel. He lifted his shoulders in a tiny shrug. Size, he thought wryly, unconsciously putting a hand on his empty sleeve and then withdrawing it quickly, what does it matter now—with machine guns.

The last of the Doughboys had left the trenches. Above Duggan and Colonel Baudin the sergeants were stringing out the jump-off tapes. The tapes were studded with aluminum disks every two feet, to keep them from sinking out of sight, as they had at Ypres. Now the sergeants straightened and put their whistles to their lips.

Below them, Colonel Duggan studied his luminous wristwatch. "One more minute," he said to the French colonel, and stepped aside to allow him to precede him up the parapet. Baudin nodded and started forward with a smile. He had heard that the handsome American colonel was an officer of great élan, and he was eager to see him and his men fight.

The two men climbed out of the trench and turned expectantly toward the dark horizon behind them, just as it erupted into a blaze of light. An enormous roar followed. The ground beneath their feet shook. Overhead, the air was alive with a wild wailing of the steel banshees speeding toward the enemy. Ahead of them they could see yellow flashes and hear the faint staccato of exploding shells.

A cheer rose from the inert men around Duggan, and the sergeants shouted at them angrily.

"Shut up, you mother's mistakes!" Durkin hissed. "D'you think yer at a football game?"

The men subsided, snickering. Other, lighter voices joined the iron clangor to the rear, and Duggan realized that three different calibers of artillery were bombarding the enemy sector chosen for the raid.

The French colonel nodded, seeming to read his thoughts. "It is the box barrage," he explained, his liquid Gallic accent seeming to caress the last syllable. He bent with his baton to draw a box in the snow. "To the rear," he said, pointing to the back line, "the one-fifty-fives. There is no escape for the Boche. On the sides, the one-oh-five—and to the front, the seventy-fives." He clapped his hands together. "No one can get to them. They are nailed into a box of steel." Duggan nodded, and Baudin continued. "In five minutes, we advance. In ten, the seventy-fives lift and the front of the box is open to us. Comprehend you?"

Duggan nodded again and turned to Durkin. "Tell Captain Baugh I'd like to speak to him." In a moment Durkin returned with a short, barrel-chested officer. His fiery red mustache bristled on his blackened face. Colonel Duggan noticed that the captain had a bayoneted rifle slung from his shoulder, and he smiled in the dark. "Going to join the fun yourself, eh, Baugh?" The captain grinned and nodded. "Do you have your bangalore torpedoes?" Duggan asked, and the captain nodded again. "Good. Put them in the front of your column. We'll advance in a column of twos until after they've blown the wire. Then we'll fan out and go in. The signal to attack will be a green Very light." He tapped the Very pistol at his hip, and the captain nodded a third time. "Good," Duggan said. "We move out at exactly twelve-ten."

The captain saluted and returned to his men. Two minutes later whistles blew and the reclining Doughboys arose. They formed two columns, each with a hand on the shoulder of the man before him, moving out lockstep so that they would not get separated and lost. The sergeants walked beside them, softly barking orders and warnings.

"Stay away from them shell holes. You kin drown in one of them."

"You there, Ryan—what the hell you doin' chewin' hard-tack in ranks?"

"For the juice, Sarge—I'm very fond of the juice."

"Shaddap, wise guy—an' close up. Get your hand off Berkley's ass and put it on his shoulder. You think yer in the Greek army?"

"Aw, Sarge, I was just pickin' dingleberries, thas' all."

A chuckle rippled along the line, and the sergeant's voice cut across it like a whip. "I said, *shaddap*!"

The men fell silent. Behind them the sound of their own artillery became fainter while the exploding shells ahead grew louder.

A quarter hour later the two columns halted and a runner came hurrying back to Colonel Duggan. "We've reached the enemy wire, sir."

"Good," Duggan said. "Please tell Captain Baugh to start clearing a path."

The runner turned and hurried back the way he had come.

Up ahead, soldiers began slipping bangalore torpedoes—lengths of pipe stuffed with explosive—under the barbed wire barring their path. They lighted the fuses at the end and raced back toward their comrades, shouting, "Fire in the hole!" At once, the men flopped down, some of them covering their ears. There was a roar and flash of flame ahead. Pungent smoke drifted skyward and filled their nostrils. But a path now lay open through the wire.

"Move out," the sergeants called, bellowing through cupped hands to make themselves heard above the crashing of the cannonade, now only a hundred yards away across the trembling earth. Slowly, the men filed down the lane, fanning out to either side of it and going down on one knee to peer up the long dark slope crested with red and yellow flame.

"Unsling rifles!"

They took their weapons from their shoulders, thrusting them out before them, preparatory to the charge.

"Check your gas masks."

Their fingers moved to their necks to feel the straps from

which the ugly boxes containing their respirators dangled at their breasts.

No more orders . . . Only silence now, silence like a caesura standing still between the rumbling flickering to their rear and the flash and crash ahead. Now, a light wind was shredding the clouds overhead and the sickle moon was shining through. . . .

Colonel Duggan glanced anxiously at his watch. He slipped his Very pistol from its holster and turned to look to the rear, waiting for the red rocket signaling that the seventy-fives had ceased firing and the front of the box was open. He studied his men kneeling at the foot of the slope.

"No," he said. "Let's get closer."

"You do not fear the friendly fire?" the French colonel asked.

Duggan shook his head. "We may lose a few men," he said grimly. "But it's worth the risk. I want to be in on them before they can use their Maxims." He turned to Durkin. "Tell Baugh to get the men halfway up the slope and lie down. Tell him I want my Doughfeet to go in yelling."

Baudin nodded approvingly. "You are brave, mon colonel. But better than that, you are audacious."

Both men fell silent, walking slowly in the trace of the Americans trotting forward. They held their rifles hip high in their right hands, their lefts clutching the grenades at their belts. Soon they were clearly silhouetted in the explosion flashes ahead: ugly, even awkward figures in their flat steel helmets and lumpy overcoats. Colonel Duggan caught his breath, feeling his stomach turn, the nausea rising. One short round, he thought. . . .

A soldier tottered backward, clutching his stomach and sinking to the ground. Another seized his thigh and sat down. Duggan whirled. The sky behind him was black . . . opaque . . . until a speck of red appeared, growing larger and hanging over no-man's-land like a giant star. Duggan turned and fired his Very pistol above and slightly ahead of the advancing Americans. The flare burst and caught them in an eerie, greenish light. Racing over the hill crest, the Doughboys heaved their grenades into the silent trenches ahead of them, hurling themselves onto the ground until the detonations ceased; and then, with wild yells, they leaped down among the enemy.

The Germans had been expecting the attack. They were elite *Stosstruppen* of one of von Ludendorff's crack *Sturmbataillones,* and they had known, moments after the four curtains of concussion, that steel and flame isolated them from the rest of the front, that they had been singled out for a raid.

Within moments they had dragged their Maxim machine guns to firing platforms below the parapets, and had then scurried back within the safety of the dugouts. There they sat out the bombardment, waiting for the moment when the front of the box lifted, to return to their battle stations and riddle the enemy raiders before they could reach the trenches. The front did lift, and they did dash from their dugouts, and that was when the American grenades fell among them.

Half of them were killed or maimed by that chain of explosions. In the light of a series of flares sent skyward by Colonel Duggan, Sergeant Durkin could see bodies in field gray and coal-scuttle steel helmets sprawled grotesquely beneath the gun platforms, or draped lifelessly over the Maxim barrels, their arms flung out protectively; faces blackened or blown away, arms gone, limbs gone. Hoarse dying screams or pitiful pleading cries of the wounded filled his ears as he led the yelling Doughboys toward the surviving half of the enemy, stunned, yet rallying bravely around a young lieutenant who flailed at them savagely with the flat and sometimes the edge of his sword.

"Leave him be!" Durkin bellowed above the continuing roar of the three sides of the barrage still isolating the trench from the front. He pointed his rifle at the young officer, whose jaunty little trench cap had fallen from his head, revealing a mop of angelic blond ringlets. The youth gazed unflinchingly at the huge American advancing on him with outthrust bayonet, and he tugged a Luger pistol from his belt.

"He's the prize, lads!" Durkin yelled, ducking a rifle butt swung at him by a figure in field gray and driving his blade deep into the screaming man's belly. "He's the pick of the bloody litter!" he roared, bracing his foot against the collapsing German's middle and yanking his blade free. Bloody entrails dangled from it as Durkin plunged through the melee toward the blond young officer. Lifting his Luger, the German calmly took aim. An American helmet, skimmed at him by the tall corporal who had skewered the frog the day before, struck his hand and knocked the pistol free. A huge balled fist—Durkin's—crashed into his temple, and he fell senseless to the ground, one of his eyes popping from its socket. Durkin bent and swung the unconscious youth onto his shoulder.

"Prisoners, men!" Colonel Duggan shouted. "We want prisoners. If they won't quit, kill them!"

Cries of "*Kamerad!*" arose all along the trench.

Quickly, the Americans herded their prisoners together and drove them, hands clasped over their bare heads, over the parapet, across no-man's-land and back to the lines of the Rainbow.

Jubilant, laughing Doughboys crowded around Duggan after he and Colonel Baudin jumped into the trenches of the Sixty-ninth. Their prisoners had already been despatched down the communication trench, bound for General Guerard's headquarters, and the French, in grateful exchange, had provided the Americans with wine.

The Doughboys had their heads thrown back and bottles tilted to their lips when Duggan dropped among them, and they ran up to him to seize his hand and pound him on the shoulders.

"We did it, Dug, we did it!" they cried, to the astonishment of the French colonel. "Goddammit, Dug, we showed those Jerries how to fight."

"You did indeed," Duggan said, grinning, and then, to the French colonel's further amazement, the Doughboys began to sing.

"Are you daft?" Sergeant Durkin shouted at them, pushing them away from Duggan and toward their dugouts. "For the love o' God, d'you want the heinies to drown you out with a seventy-seven serenade?"

Still chuckling and singing, they disappeared into the dugouts. Captain Baugh stepped up to Colonel Duggan. He came to attention and handed Duggan a small square of cloth he held in his hand.

"The men would be very happy if you would put this back on, sir," he said, his moonlike face turning the color of his mustache.

Momentarily puzzled, Duggan suddenly realized that the object in his hand was the Rainbow Division's shoulder patch; indeed, the very one he had torn from his shoulder that unhappy day at Camp Mills.

"I will indeed, and with pride," Duggan said, tears forming in his large dark eyes. To his surprise, Colonel Baudin also stepped up to him. "Here is something else for you to wear, mon colonel," he said, fastening a medal to the breast of Duggan's tunic.

Looking down, Duggan saw that it was the Croix de Guerre. Then Duggan saw another object on his coat. It was nestled inside the A of his cashmere scarf. With horror and rising nausea, Duggan realized that he was looking into the delft-blue eye of Durkin's brave young prisoner.

CHAPTER 16

The third morning that Betsy Duggan became sick, she realized that she was pregnant. She had been vaguely aware that her menstrual period was late, but had not given it any significance until that dreadful third morning when she swayed, clutched the basin in the bathroom, and began retching.

Whose child was it?

It had been mid-October when Mark sailed for France, and mid-December when Beauregard Ames had . . . had come to Washington to get her husband's hat. But Mark had not been near her since late September, and it was now February. . . .

It was Beau's baby.

Betsy Duggan knew that it was Beau's. Staring dully at her haggard face in the mirror, her soul writhed in repentance and remorse. Her fingers drummed on the sink, counting the months of Mark's absence. *One, two, three, four . . . One, two, three, four . . .*

And she was only two months pregnant.

"No!" she screamed, covering her face with her hands. "Oh, my God, *no!*"

Sobbing, she turned and ran into the bedroom and threw

herself on the bed. Outside the door, she heard Mrs. Watkins, Virginia's governess, calling to her.

"Are you all right, Mrs. Duggan?"

I'm all right, Mrs. Watkins. I . . . I just shinned my ankle, that's all. Is Jinny dressed?"

"Yes, ma'am, she's having breakfast, now. And then I'm going to take her out in the stroller."

"Very good, Mrs. Wa—" she began, quickly putting her hand over her mouth and rolling over when tears welled up within her again. She lay there, facedown, the sheets wet with her tears, her muffled sobs gradually subsiding until at last she fell asleep. An hour later she awoke, perplexed to find herself in bed again—until she remembered, and the black night of despair engulfed her once more.

Why? she wondered bitterly. Why had she done it? She loved Mark. She had always been faithful to him. Why had she gone to bed with Beau? Betsy Duggan knew why; but she could not admit it to herself, especially not now. She did truly love and honor her husband. But she hungered for Beau. Everything about him—the musky smell of his body, his honeyed hair, his soft voice and mocking eyes, the firm, smooth texture of his skin—everything about him aroused her. Despairing, Betsy sensed dully that she could not allow herself to be near him.

What was she to do?

Betsy could not think. She passed her hand over her forehead with a weary gesture. Getting to her feet, she returned to the bathroom and threw cold water on her reddened eyes. She dried them, put on a dressing gown, and went outside to the landing.

Guessing that Mrs. Watkins and Virginia were still outside, she ran downstairs to the dining room, seized a decanter of sherry and a glass, and hurried back upstairs. She sat in the gold velvet chair beside the dresser and began sipping sherry. The liquid seemed to suffuse her body with warmth, soothing her. She felt that she could think now.

An abortion! That was it! But who would do it? Captain McCarthy, her doctor, was a devout Catholic and would certainly refuse. And she could not approach Major Wurzer. She despised him, and, anyway, he would probably tell Mark.

But who? Some strange doctor? Betsy had heard of women bleeding to death at the hands of brutal, clumsy abortionists. No, she thought. Even the word appalled her.

She drank again and her eyes brightened. Of course! She would sail for France, go to Paris, have Mark meet her, sleep with him—and then, a premature baby! It was a deception, of course, Betsy thought with a sham sense of guilt, just like her ruse of the duck's blood on their wedding night—but it would preserve their marriage. And she would never, never, never . . .

Jumping to her feet, she hurried downstairs to the hall telephone to call her friends at the War Office. An hour later, defeated, she crept back upstairs to the velvet chair and the sherry. No one but the military or military supplies could cross the ocean, she had been told. Drinking once more, she thought wildly of stowing away. But that was ridiculous!

Simple.

It was so simple, so absurdly simple, why hadn't she thought of it before? Mark would certainly not be home again until the war was over. And that would not be for at least another year. All the officers said so. They said that with Russia out of the war and in the hands of the Bolsheviks, the Germans were able to transfer huge masses of men and guns to the Western Front. Even with America on the Allied side, it would take some time for American aid to take effect. Her fingers drummed on the marble dresser top. Good. He would certainly not be home before the end of the year, and in the meantime she would find one of those places the church maintains for wayward girls and arrange to have the baby there. They could put it out for adoption. Her fingers drummed once more. That would be in September.

In the meantime, she would keep to the house, watch her weight, and be careful to stay away from neighbors. She would have to let Mrs. Watkins go, of course, poor thing—but Mrs. Watkins knew that Mark had sailed in October. She would get another governess for Jinny, one who wouldn't know.

It *was* simple. Really simple, she thought, reaching for the decanter again, frowning when she saw that it was empty. Oh, yes, everything was going to be all right. Mark would never know. And she would be so good to him, she really would. She would make him so happy. She would bear him the son he desired so ardently. Betsy glanced again at the empty decanter. Momentarily, she began to despair once more, wondering if she actually could carry it off.

Until she remembered that there was another bottle of sherry in the dining room breakfront.

Betsy Duggan had been correct in her belief that the Germans would renew their offensive in France. In the spring of 1918, reinforced by the forces freed from the Eastern Front, the German High Command launched an assault upon the French on the Allied right. It was intended merely as a diversion, to lure Allied strength away from the left, where the true blow was to fall. To the German's surprise, their troops crashed through the weary French in unheard-of gains of seven or eight miles a day. Soon the triumphant Germans were within fifty miles of Paris and the French government was preparing to flee. But then the Americans stopped the German spearheads in Belleau Wood and Chateau-Thierry. At once, General Pershing moved to save Paris by throwing three of his best divisions into the fight. One of these was the Rainbow, ordered to entrain from Lorraine toward Champagne.

Colonel Duggan drove immediately to Charmes and other railheads in the rear of the Baccarat front to prepare for movement of the division. Next day the men of the Rainbow came marching into Charmes. Rather, they slouched in. They had been at the front for four months. Their glazed, unseeing eyes were sunk deep in the sockets of their gaunt, windburned faces. Mud-caked overcoats hung on their emaciated frames in ragged folds, and some of them had dirty toes sticking out of worn and broken boots.

Watching them march slowly up the loading ramps into the waiting trains, Duggan remembered the tons of equipment George Quincy Meadows had taken away from the Rainbow after its arrival in France. Thousands and thousands of spare boots and blankets and overcoats. They could have been issued to the men the moment they came off the line. Then they wouldn't have looked like spooks, he thought bitterly. No, they'd look like what they were: the best damned soldiers in the AEF. Suddenly, Duggan caught sight of a limousine rolling slowly into town. It was a black Rolls-Royce, and four red stars flew from the square white pennant flying from its fender.

My God! Duggan groaned. It was Pershing!

Tall, severe, and as elegant as the machine he was leaving, Black Jack Pershing picked his way carefully through the rain-filled shellholes in the pavement and approached the awed men of the Rainbow. Behind him, the silver leaves of a lieutenant colonel on his shoulders, came George Quincy Meadows. Black Jack looked searchingly at the men entering the trains. He spoke to them gently. But his piercing eyes were flashing when he spun on his heel and bore down on Colonel Mark Duggan.

Ten feet away from him, he began to shout. "Duggan, this division is a goddammed disgrace! The men are filthy scarecrows! They don't have an ounce of discipline or esprit. It's the worst goddam outfit I've seen since I came to France!"

Duggan was aghast. The men had heard every word! They had come to a halt on the ramps and were watching tensely, listening.

"But General—" he began.

Pershing cut him off with an impatient gesture of his riding crop, and snapped, "No buts, Duggan." His eyes roved contemptuously over Duggan's jaunty campaign hat and knotted gray scarf. "What's this ridiculous getup you've got on?" he sneered. "Don't you want to look like an officer?"

"Sir," Duggan went on pleadingly, his eyes falling on George Meadows standing silently behind Pershing. "We've just come out of the line."

"I don't care where you've been. No staff officer worthy of the name would let his men walk around looking like that."

Mark Duggan swallowed. He caught sight of Meadows again, and thinking of all the Rainbow's requisitioned equipment, he blinked back the tears of rage springing up behind his eyes.

"D'ya hear me?" Pershing cried, slowly pounding his palm with the riding crop. "I want this division cleaned up. I'm holding you personally responsible for it. And when I see these men again in Champagne, they'd better not look as sorry as they do today." He fixed Duggan with his steely gray eyes and let his rasping voice come out deliberately slow and cutting. ''Or you'll be sorry.''

Black Jack Pershing turned and walked back to the Rolls-Royce, followed by Meadows. Duggan watched the driver carefully backing his immaculate machine out of the mud and squalor of the square. These were the results of the war, and the contrast struck him forcibly: a ruined French town with its pot-holed streets and blackened chimneys standing gauntly among rotting corpses and the rubble of buildings, and the gleaming Rolls-Royce and its impeccable occupants, disdainfully departing from their handiwork. For a moment, Duggan had an insane impulse to pull out his pistol and shoot that hateful vehicle full of holes.

This division is a disgrace! Filthy scarecrows! Worst outfit! Mark Duggan thought bitterly of the long, dark months of misery in Luneville and Baccarat. He remembered the poison-gas barrages—no less than eleven of them, in the first of which he himself had almost died. There were six or seven hundred gallant men who lay buried in the soil of Lorraine, and another fifteen hundred Rainbow soldiers who had bled there. And this is their reward, he thought—to be publicly insulted by perfumed commanders smelling of desk polish and saddle soap. He shuddered, still unable to believe that John J. Pershing could be guilty of such contemptible callousness; but then, hearing the muttering of the men, hearing them curse the ''Iron Commander'' and ''Horseface'' and all such captains of armchair snuggeries as they shuffled slowly inside the train, he realized that it had happened, and he felt the nausea rising again.

Hurrying down the ramp with his hand over his mouth he ran to the iron bench in the town square and threw up. Out came the hot, bitter, reeking liquid, in retching, convulsive waves, forming a stinking puddle between his feet. He felt faint, seizing the iron seat on both sides of him to steady himself. A rage of resentment seized him again, and he put his hand to his shoulder to tear away the silver eagle there, until he felt a huge warm hand fall gently on top of his. Looking up, he saw Sergeant Durkin standing over him.

''Nah, nah, sir,'' the big man said, almost crooning. ''Don't do it. The men are watching you, sir. They know how you feel and all, and Jaysus they love you fer it. They need you, sir. 'Twould be the divil's own doin' if yez let them down now.''

Duggan nodded silently and withdrew his hand from his shoulder. "It's George Meadows," he said with quiet bitterness. "It's him and the whole Pershing clique. They're a bunch of desk soldiers, Pat, and they hate field soldiers. We know combat, Pat, and they don't—so they hate us for being what they are not." He swung wearily around on the bench to watch the last of the men entraining. His eyes were tender as he spoke, but his voice was bitter. "Staff officers always complain that they never get any credit or glory, but I tell you that their only fit reward is the creature comforts that they cherish. They solve their problems with pencil and paper in heated offices, and we solve ours with fire and steel in mud and blood."

Duggan shook himself and got heavily to his feet. Characteristically, he had transferred his resentment from General Pershing, whom he did admire—and who also had the power to end his career—to George Meadows, whom he now despised and considered his chief enemy.

The train whistle blew, and Duggan began walking toward the locomotive, where he always rode. He and Durkin swung aboard, nodding politely to the little Frenchman at the controls. Sergeant Durkin stared at the man in momentary incredulity.

"Jaysus save me wit," he whispered to Duggan, "but fer a minute I thought it was Eduardo himself sittin' there. Remember him, sir?"

Duggan nodded. "War was a pink tea in those days, Pat," he said, gazing reflectively at the ruined town they were leaving.

"It was indeed," Durkin said. He pointed to the still-standing chimneys. "'Tis the safest place to be when they're shootin' at you, sir—right on top of the chimney."

Colonel Duggan tried to smile but could not. He was wondering if submitting his resignation wasn't the best thing to do, after all.

A week after the division arrived in Champagne, an official packet arrived from AEF headquarters in Chaumont. It contained orders for the Rainbow to prepare to join defense of the

Champagne-Marne region, and it also contained Mark Duggan's commission as a brigadier general.

Duggan was dumbfounded. He had believed that the incident at Charmes had put the cap on his career. Now, here, over Pershing's signature, was the offer of a star! Should he take it? For days he pondered his decision, divided between his wounded vanity telling him he should not accept without an apology, and his better judgment warning him that the star probably had not come from Pershing in Chaumont, but from Newton D. Baker in Washington. In the end, he accepted; and a week after he did, another communication arrived from GHQ ordering him to return to the States to take command of a brigade in a new division then forming in Camp Meade, Maryland.

Duggan was stunned. He had hoped that his promotion would bring with it command of one of the Rainbow's two brigades. He yearned to lead one of them in combat, in the new action preparing in the Champagne-Meuse. Although Duggan had already won three Silver Stars, a Distinguished Service Cross, and an oak leaf cluster symbolic of his second Croix de Guerre, his insatiable thirst for glory was far from being slaked. He hungered for the Medal of Honor, the highest award of all—the one his father had won—and he craved combat command because that was the surest means of obeying his father's injunction to carry the Duggan name higher.

But now, to return to America to join a green division that might never get to France, or might not get there until the war was over—this was the surest means of frustrating his thrust for glory. Was Pershing behind it? Perhaps George Meadows? Of course! The star had come from Chaumont! It was the bait, and he had bitten; and because there was no command in the AEF now open for one of his new rank, he was very properly being shipped home where one was available.

Oh, why hadn't he thought it out! he groaned inwardly. How could he possibly appeal now? Even if he had the temerity to approach Black Jack Pershing again—which he admitted he did not—he knew that the buck would be passed to the War Office. He could see Pershing irritably fingering his brush of a mustache, "Goddammit, Duggan, you should know better than to come to me with this. The chief of staff requested an experienced brigadier, and you're the only one available. You're it.''

Desperate, Duggan went to General Corrigan, the Rainbow's commander. Corrigan was furious.

"Goddam those busybodies in Chaumont!'' he swore. "When will they stop meddling with my division?'' But he held out no hope. "Sure I'm going to protest, Duggan. But it won't do any good. You're too much rank to stay on as my chief of staff. And both my brigadiers are fine commanders. I wouldn't relieve either of them, not even for you.''

Duggan nodded glumly. "I guess the only thing I can do is to start packing.''

"Maybe we can stall,'' General Corrigan muttered.

Duggan tried to smile. "I wouldn't recommend it, sir. Not after looking into General Pershing's eyes in Charmes.'' He arose. "Thanks anyway, sir,'' he said, and returned to his office.

Immediately, he sat down to write to Betsy notifying her that he was coming home and would probably arrive sometime in July. Then he dictated a letter to the division's two brigadiers, informing them that he could not accompany them on a tour of the Champagne-Meuse front next day, as he had planned, because he had to remain in camp to await his relief. The next few days were spent tidying up his office. On the morning he was to leave, he sent for Sergeant Durkin to begin packing his things.

Durkin came into the room with a long face. "Sad thing about General Sommers, sir,'' he murmured, seizing a duffel bag and opening it.

"General Sommers?'' Duggan asked, puzzled.

"Didn't you hear the news, Gen'ral? He's dead, sir—killed yesterday on the Champagne front.''

"My God!'' Duggan exclaimed. "I was going to go there with him. What happened?''

"'Twas a French short round, they say. Lucky for General Forbes he stopped to talk to some French officers, or he'd be gone too. They do say the Frogs are all cut up about it, sir.''

Duggan made no comment. He turned away from Durkin, anxious to conceal the thrill of hope that coursed through his body, which he knew would be reflected in his face. Sommers gone! It was a shame that he was dead, of course, but those were the fortunes of war. Now, command of the Eighty-fourth Brigade was open!

"Hold up on the packing, Pat," he said, going to the door. "I'm going to see General Corrigan."

The Rainbow commander looked at him sharply when he entered his office. "You've heard," Corrigan grunted.

Duggan nodded. "Yes, sir. I am truly sorry that Alan Sommers is dead. He was a fine officer and a true Christian gentleman, but—"

"But you'd like to have his brigade," Corrigan interrupted dryly. "Well, under the circumstances, I don't blame you, Duggan. And I'm going to do my damnedest to see that you get it." He glanced at his wristwatch. "I have an appointment with General Pershing for this afternoon. I'll be leaving in ten minutes. I will call you tonight at six o'clock."

Duggan nodded and left. That night, over a telephone crackling with static, Corrigan said, "The Eighty-fourth is yours."

At once, General Duggan thought of sending a telegram to Betsy informing her of his great reversal of fortune. But then he decided to write to her instead. A few weeks delay wouldn't make any difference. He could say much more in a letter; and besides, a telegram might frighten her.

Betsy Duggan received her husband's first letter as she and Virginia and the new governess, Mrs. Delaplace, were going down the walk of their home toward a taxicab awaiting them at the curb. The postman was coming up the walk with the mail, and Betsy took just Mark's letter and told the postman to hold all subsequent mail until she called for it in two weeks. She was going to Atlantic City for a brief vacation, she explained.

Betsy did not open the letter while they drove to Union Terminal, because she spent the time questioning Mrs. Delaplace, a very cheerful round little lady who was unfortunately frequently forgetful, to be sure she had brought all the bathing dresses and bathing slippers and sun hats and all the other "basics" needed for a stay at the seashore. They had to hurry at the terminal, collapsing into their seats a scant thirty seconds before the train pulled out for Philadelphia. Then Jinny got trainsick and she wouldn't let anyone but her mother take her to the rest room at the end of the car. In Philadelphia they had to rush again to change trains for Atlantic City. Once there, Betsy had to dash about in the crush of arriving vacationers to find a redcap to get their bags and find them a cab.

At last they reached their hotel on the boardwalk. It was the same hotel where she and Mark had stayed on their delayed "honeymoon" four years ago. Betsy wore the same white cotton dress and broad-brimmed white silk hat she had worn then. She was pleased to see the men in the lobby look up with interest when she came in to register. Betsy had kept her weight so well that it was almost impossible to tell that she was almost seven months pregnant. The old dress had needed to be let out only about two inches.

Upstairs, in the room adjoining Jinny's and Mrs. Delaplace's, she stood in front of a big brass-bound mirror, sucking in her stomach and smoothing it with her hand. Two more months! Betsy thought, grimacing. And the hot ones too. Well, it was better to take her vacation now, before she became really obvious. Everything had been arranged. Betsy had gone to a Catholic home for foundlings in Hoboken, New Jersey. She had told the sister who interviewed her that she was acting for a friend. Betsy could not be sure, but it did not seem that the nun had believed her. Otherwise, she had been very sweet and understanding and cooperative. Prospective foster parents of the same race and religion had already been found. Betsy needed to pay only for the cost of delivery and the few weeks she would be there. She had scrimped the money together by heroic economies. No new clothes, a spartan diet, and the cheapest sherry she could buy. Mark would have been pr—

Mark! The letter!

At once, she ran to the bureau to seize her pocketbook and take out the forgotten letter. She sat down on her bed and began to read.

Betsy's face froze in horror and the letter fell from her hands.

Mark was coming home.

He would be leaving five days after he mailed the letter. That meant that he would be arriving in another week or so.

Her husband was coming home after an absence of ten months, and she was not quite seven months pregnant.

Betsy picked up the fallen letter and read it through. But the rest of it was meaningless. She let it fall again, and got up and walked mechanically back to her pocketbook, removing a full pint of sherry. She went into the bathroom for a water glass, went back to the bed and began to drink.

She was caught. There was no way out, around, or through. Even if she wanted it, it was too late for an abortion. She could not pretend that the baby was overdue: No human baby in history had ever been twelve months in gestation. Betsy began to cry. She did not sob in despair, as on that morning when she realized that she was pregnant. Rather, she wept softly, like a keening kitten. She had been untrue to the most faithful man on earth. She had dishonored him, him who had said to her on their first day of married life: "I could not love thee, dear, so much, loved I not honor more." She cried helplessly, pitifully. She cried, and she drank. No! She would not dishonor him! She would kill herself first. Kill herself and the baby in her belly.

But how to kill herself and not let them find the unborn child of disgrace? She could not take poison or load one of Mark's pistols and put it to her head. They would find her body then—and the baby. How to get rid of her body? She filled her water glass again and drank. She felt a cool breeze on the back of her neck. Turning, she saw the white organdy window curtains standing taut toward her, like pennants, and behind them, the bright blue of the ocean. There! she thought. They couldn't drain an ocean, she thought with an odd, macabre satisfaction, and filled the glass again. She drank it quickly, put the empty bottle on the dresser, and bent, swaying slightly, to pull her bathing dress from a bureau drawer. She put it over her arm and arose, catching sight of herself in the big mirror. She seized the empty bottle and hurled it against the glass.

"Take that, you guardhouse whore!" she screamed, hurrying from her room to the hall elevator. Within seconds she was in the lobby, walking at a moderate pace so as not to attract attention.

Betsy went to the bathhouse under the boardwalk and changed. Then she knelt down to pray. Her prayer was a confused gibberish. Between the drink and her despair, she could not think clearly or for long. Sometimes she prayed to

God, sometimes to Mark. Always, she asked forgiveness, pleading that her "trespass" had been singular and impulsive. Still swaying, she went out the door and down the beach to the surf breaking gently on the hard wet sand. She paused, confused again, unsure whether she was playacting or serious. She felt giddy, and thought she heard voices shouting at her.

There were. Two men on the boardwalk to her right had jumped to their feet and were yelling at her and waving. There had been a shark scare that day and the lifeguards had ordered all bathers out of the water. The men were trying to warn her. But Betsy was too confused to listen to the distant shouts. She walked slowly through the murmuring surf of an outgoing tide.

The water was warm with the day's sun. She felt it caressing her as she swam with strong steady strokes toward the blue and violet sky of the eastern horizon. The men had run down to the edge of the surf to shout at her with cupped hands.

But now she did not hear them. She swam on . . . She swam on, waiting for her strength to wane; to sink . . . to sink slowly and forever and without care into that peaceful warm sanctuary of the sea. She felt herself going down and thought of Jinny. Jinny! She screamed her name aloud and gasped and choked on the salt water filling her mouth and making her retch. No! She could not leave Jinny. She churned her feet and arms and surfaced and saw with horror the huge black fin sliding by. It vanished. She put her face in the water and saw the torpedo shape climbing toward her, rolling . . . She stiffened in terror, but she did not panic. Suddenly, her brain cleared. She wanted to live. She clung to the life she had wanted to end. Now she saw the deadly white underbelly . . . the jaws opening and the teeth slashing toward her . . . Instinctively, she cringed, and the great shape flashed by her, seizing some other object in its dreadful reddening jaws, some fish, some other prey. . . .

Betsy began to swim toward shore. Slowly, careful not to excite the huge predator now gliding around her in narrowing circles, she swam breaststroke, raising her head only to suck in air, relying upon the warm feel of the setting sun on her forehead to guide her. Soon she felt the surf boiling around her. A breaker seized her from behind and rolled her onto the beach. She felt herself tumbling end over end, bumping her head on the bottom, her mouth filling with sand, and then nothing. . . .

The two men who had watched her ordeal with horrid fascination saw her burst from the surf, and grabbed her by the legs and pulled her free of the water.

"Oh, my God!" one of them cried. "Look! Look!"

"Jesus!" the other breathed. "She's having a miscarriage."

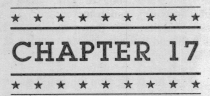

CHAPTER 17

Brigadier General Mark Duggan examined himself in the mirror of the music room in the magnificent medieval chateau at St. Benoit. The mirror was a large, opulent one of carved wood and gold leaf, curved in the Louis Quinze style characteristic of most of the chateau's heavily upholstered pink-and-blue furniture.

Duggan had chosen the castle as his brigade headquarters when the Rainbow had gone into reserve after almost two months of action in the Aisne-Marne and St. Mihiel offensives. Once again the division had distinguished itself, and Duggan, now celebrated in the Stateside newspapers as "the greatest front-line general of the war," had won his fourth, fifth, and sixth Silver Stars.

He wore his decorations as he stood before the mirror, examining himself from every angle. A photographer from the *New York Times* was to photograph him that afternoon, and in the evening there would be a lavish dinner for the brigade commanders and staff officers. Duggan wanted to look his best. His uniform and gray A scarf—which he still wore to protect his throat from the autumnal dampness of the chateau's stone walls—had been carefully cleaned and pressed by Sergeant Durkin, who had found an ancient black kettle in the kitchen and used it to steam the battlefield muck from the cloth. Durkin had spent hours polishing the general's boots and puttees and Sam Browne belt until they gleamed like glass.

Drawing himself to attention, Duggan saluted in the mirror. No, he thought, frowning: much too trite. Every shavetail in the AEF posed like that. His frown made him realize how prominent his forehead had become. He wondered if he really shouldn't do something about his receding hairline. Perhaps he should be covered for the photograph. He picked up his punctured campaign hat lying atop the grand piano and placed it on his head. Next, he put his gold cigarette holder in his mouth at a jaunty angle. No, much too flamboyant. My God, what would Black Jack Pershing say if he saw him photographed like that!

Duggan put the hat back on the piano and turned to study himself in the mirror again. His mind strayed and he thought of Napoleon and *his* hat . . . At Nice the upstart little artillerist from Paris had met the veteran generals of the Revolutionary Army of Italy, and had used his hat to subdue them. Removing his hat, they had removed theirs; and then, restoring his to his head, he had fixed them with the direct gaze of his astonishingly fierce eyes and had mastered them in an instant. They had not only remained bareheaded, they had quailed. Even the grizzled, impassive Massena had said later: "The little bastard scared me."

Mark Duggan sighed. Times were different now, he thought wistfully. No man of twenty-seven could rise to command his country's armies in today's world—no matter how capable he might be. And Duggan believed he was every inch the equal of Napoleon Bonaparte. He sighed again and put the cigarette holder alongside the gold cigarette box his staff officers had presented to him on leaving division headquarters to take charge of the Eighty-fourth. He read the inscription: "The bravest of the brave." His eyes filled with tears. That was what Napoleon had said of *his* best commander, Marshal Ney. Still uncertain of how he should pose, he caught sight of an ornate, thronelike chair beside a heavy music cabinet. He dragged it in front of the mirror and sat in it. Perfect! Elegant, his slim legs crossed, his body inclined slightly to his right on the arm of the chair. The medals were in full view, his handsome face sensitive and thoughtful. Because he was seated, his forehead seemed high, noble, framed by a natural hairline—it was exactly as he wished to appear.

There was a knock on the massive door of carved oak and Sergeant Durkin entered. "The photographer from New York is outside, Gen'ral," he said.

"Send him in, Pat," Duggan said, shifting his weight to the left side of the chair so that the wound stripe on his left cuff would also be in view.

At dinner that night, General Duggan was unusually charming and captivating as he moved from table to table to speak to his officers. He had been informed that the Rainbow was returning to combat the next day. The division was to take part in the massive Meuse-Argonne offensive by which General Pershing hoped to break through the center of the Hindenberg Line, take Sedan, and bring about the collapse of Germany. Exhilarated by the approach of action and the chance to win new glory, Duggan chatted gaily with his commanders, exchanging toasts with them.

Just as the soup plates were being cleared and the next course was being served by tiny Annamese stewards from French Indochina, there was a horrid, screeching whistle and a shattering crash. The chateau shook. Every man in the room dived for cover—everyone except Duggan. He sat alone at the head table, calmly twirling an empty wineglass.

"Come gentlemen," he called good-humoredly. "All of Germany cannot fabricate a shell that will scratch Duggan. Come, finish dinner with me."

Sheepish, laughing to cover their embarrassment, they returned to their seats. Service of the fish had been resumed when the door to the dining room flew open and the officer of the day hurried inside. He went immediately to Duggan.

"General, that shell just killed one of my orderlies," he cried.

"I am sorry to hear that," Duggan murmured.

"But sir," the young officer went on in agitation, "the men have just come back from the raid on Marimbois Farm. They took prisoners. The prisoners say the Boche are planning to destroy the chateau. They've moved up a big gun—a 280-millimeter, I think—and they're bragging that they're going to drop St. Benoit right on top of you, sir."

Duggan smiled grimly. "When?"

"Any minute, sir."

As though to punctuate the lieutenant's answer, a second screeching whistle was heard overhead. But this time the explosion came from a point a few hundred feet beyond the chateau. Duggan compressed his lips angrily. The Germans were firing for registry. The next shell would probably come between the other two—right on top of St. Benoit!

He filled his glass and raised it. "Gentlemen, the barbaric Hun is preparing to destroy another of his neighbor's works of beauty. Let us drink to the evening that might have been."

A murmur of approval came from his commanders. They drank in silence, and then, one after another, followed their general's lead in hurling their glasses against the stone wall.

"I think, now," Duggan said calmly, "we'd better leave."

They filed out. General Duggan was the last to depart. With Durkin beside him, he walked to the edge of a wood to await the bombardment. In a moment the third shell struck. It hit the roof with an orange crash. The earth beneath their feet quivered and showers of stone splinters fell around them. One by one, at intervals of two and three minutes, the huge projectiles came screaming, crashing into the old chateau. Fires began. In their flickering light Sergeant Durkin could see the tears in General Duggan's dark eyes. Within less than two hours the bombardment was over and the Chateau de Saint Benoit was no more.

Next morning, the general and Durkin returned to examine the smoldering heap of rubble. Tufts of pink-and-blue cloth from the upholstery and draperies nestled among broken stones. Duggan looked for the music room, searching for his gold cigarette box, which he had forgotten. He scraped his foot among the shards of the shattered mirror looking for it. Under the wreckage of the grand piano, beside the twisted, blackened chair he had sat in the previous day, he found a scrap of gold metal. He rubbed it and read the letters: AVE. That was all he found. Slipping it into his pocket, he murmured, "I owe them one for this, Pat," and walked slowly back to his staff car.

That night, the division moved by motor convoy to a reserve area in Mountfaucon Woods. General Duggan watched his men climbing into the small trucks and noticed that some of them beat their hands together for warmth. He heard teeth chattering. Duggan ground his teeth. It had turned cold early. After the St. Mihiel Offensive, he had personally begged Pershing for winter clothing. But it had not come. Duggan's soldiers were going back to battle in summer issue. Once again Duggan's memory strayed back to the dockside scene at St. Nazaire. He had tried to provide for the Rainbow, and George Meadows and Chaumont had thwarted him. Now his men were cold, and who would they blame?

"Son of a *bitch*!" he swore, getting into his staff car beside Durkin. The sergeant glanced at him in surprise. The general almost never used profanity. He must really be upset, he thought, letting out the clutch and driving slowly toward the head of the column.

Passing the trucks, Duggan could hear the Annamese drivers chattering away in cheerful singsong. *They* must be warm, he thought bitterly. He thought of Betsy. He had had a long-delayed letter from her that morning. She had been in the hospital, she wrote. A shark had chased her in the ocean off Atlantic City, and the shock had put her in the hospital. But now she was better, writing to say how Virginia had enjoyed her second birthday party and how she loved Mrs. Delaplace, her new governess. Betsy said she was delighted to hear that the transfer to the States, which had so depressed him, had been canceled. "Write soon, darling husband!" she had finished, and Duggan made up his mind to write as soon as they reached Mountfaucon.

When they did arrive in those bitter woods, however, Duggan's resolve was lost in dismay. Mountfaucon had once been a lush preserve of stately oaks and bright, luxuriant undergrowth. Now, only a few days after the beginning of the Meuse-Argonne offensive, it had been turned into a hideous labyrinth of beheaded trees and dangling limbs. Shellholes as deep as fifteen feet, and that wide across, were filling with water in the cold driving rain that had begun to fall. Over all floated the sticky-sweet reek of death.

General Duggan studied his soldiers climbing stiffly down from their trucks. They stamped their feet and swung their arms to restore circulation to their numbed bodies. He could hear them muttering angrily. They knew that they were about to be fed into a meat grinder not nearly so "short and sweet" as the St. Mihiel salient. Duggan walked wearily to his muddy and wet little dugout, wrapping himself in a blanket Durkin brought, falling asleep without another thought for Betsy.

In the morning, he drove to the front to watch the Seventy-ninth Division launch a frontal attack against the Hindenburg Line. The typical massive artillery bombardment had preced-ed the assault. Allied observation balloons drifting above the forest were directing the shelling. Watching through field glasses from an old churchyard on a hill, Duggan could see the terrain seem to come alive, leaping into the air in giant clods and splinters. His ears were full of the thunder of the guns to his rear. The barrage lifted. He could see waves of diminutive figures in khaki run forward. They advanced perhaps fifty yards and then vanished. He could not tell if they had fallen or taken cover. But they did not arise. Dismayed, he swept the now-silent woods below with his glasses. A hand fell on his shoulder and he turned around to see a tall, blue-eyed cavalry major standing behind him with a grin.

"We meet again, General Duggan," George Peyton said.

"Peyton!" Duggan exclaimed. His eyes fell on the pearl-handled pistol at the major's hip and he grinned. "Still as regulation as ever, Major?"

Peyton also grinned, studying Duggan's hat. "Same as you, sir, if I may beg the general's pardon."

Duggan smiled, adjusting his hat. "Don't tell me the cavalry is coming into this, Peyton."

"No more cavalry, sir," Peyton said gloomily. "I'm in tanks now. That *was* the last charge down at Ojos Azules, you know."

"I thought Haig used horses at the Somme."

"Haig." Peyton spat the name out contemptuously, and came to stand beside Duggan, focusing his own glasses on the attack below. He grimaced. "And they're all Americans," he muttered. He glanced at Duggan in momentary appraisal. "If what I'm about to say disturbs you, sir, please tell me to shut up."

"Go ahead, Peyton," Duggan said gently.

Major Peyton gestured helplessly at the smoke-filled forest beneath him. "The Germans have been there for four years, General Duggan. They've fortified it. The Argonne was a natural hedgehog to begin with. Now it's a crocodile's back. The French, at least, had the good sense never to touch it. And now we're trying it." He grimaced again. "On foot."

"Do you think your tanks could do it, Major?"

"No, sir. Never! The terrain's too cross-grained, sir. You need dry, level country for tanks to maneuver. They'd be sitting ducks in the hills and gullies and streams down there."

"Then why do you say it can't be done on foot?"

"It can't be done at all! I mean, not without an unnecessary expenditure of human beings. Oh, sure, it can be done, sir—and probably will be done, if only on sheer courage and the weight of human flesh."

Duggan's voice was soft. "Like Grant whittling Lee in the Wilderness?"

"Exactly, sir." Peyton grew agitated. "Before, when you mentioned Haig, I guess I made it plain I didn't think much of him. I *don't*, sir. I don't think much of *any* of them." He glanced in sideways apprehension at his listener, saw no sign of rebuke on his face, and continued: "They don't *understand*. In a war without flanks and with both sides dug in, it's just not *possible* to achieve a penetration with foot soldiers. Machine guns and rapid-fire cannon just chew you to pieces."

"I agree," Duggan said quietly, placing his glasses to his eyes again at the sound of renewed artillery behind him.

"But tanks can do it. A tank is an armored gun welded to an internal combustion engine. Tanks provide the shock you used to get from cavalry. Machine guns can't stop them and shrapnel can't hurt them. You have to have a direct hit to stop a tank—difficult against a moving object." Duggan nodded. "But Haig had tanks up there in Flanders last fall," Peyton went on, growing agitated and bitter again. "And what did he do? He sent them in *after* the infantry, and through mud two feet deep!" Peyton's face turned mournful. "So they got bogged down and the Germans knocked them out like fish in a barrel. And now Sir Douglas Haig tells the world tanks are not the answer."

"Well, they haven't done anything yet, Major."

"Oh, yes, they have, sir!" Peyton cried eagerly, dropping

a slender gloved hand on his white pistol butt. "At Cambrai, right after the Flanders bloodbath. Haig tried to stop it, but Byng risked his career and went ahead with it. The country at Cambrai was ideal—dry and with a downslope. Byng massed nearly four hundred tanks, General, and hit the Hindenburg Line without a single shell fired in advance." Major Peyton brandished his fist. "They cracked it! Cracked it open like an eggshell. Four miles in a day!" he cried jubilantly. "Not much less than Haig gained in four months at Ypres. How's that for proof, General Duggan?"

"But I thought Cambrai was another defeat," Duggan said, puzzled.

"It was, in the end," Peyton replied gloomily. "Byng didn't have any reserves. Haig had wasted them all at Ypres. He couldn't exploit the breakthrough, and the Germans counterattacked and retook what they'd lost." Peyton's blue eyes shone fiercely. "But, by God, sir, the tanks broke through!"

Duggan nodded pensively, field glasses to his eyes again. Peyton stepped forward to stand beside him, focusing his own glasses.

"Pinned down again?" Peyton asked.

Duggan nodded. He looked at the observation balloons drifting above the forest. "They'll probably call for more artillery." He shook his head in discouragement. "And the Germans will go below ground again. And the moment the barrage lifts, they'll come back up and jump on their Maxims and seventy-sevens again." He shuddered. "And in two more days I have to go in there my—"

Engines growled overhead. A squadron of Fokkers with black crosses on their fuselage dived out of the clouds. Machine guns chattered. Spent cartridges tinked musically on the hilltop shale, and within less than a minute every one of a dozen balloons had plummeted earthward in flames. Banking, the planes flew over the two officers. Duggan could see their yellow scarves flowing backward in the wind.

"Von Richthofen!" he exclaimed. "It's the Flying Circus." Then he realized that Peyton had drawn his revolver and was shooting at the Fokkers. Waving derisively, the Germans flew out of range.

"*Goddammit!*" Peyton fumed. "How the hell long did

GHQ think the heinies were going to let those balloons stay up there.''

He flicked the cylinder of his pistol open and blew through the smoking barrel. Putting the weapon back in its holster, he pointed grimly toward the vanishing Fokkers. ''There's the other answer to the front without flanks, sir,'' he said. ''That's the other gun welded to an internal combustion engine. Only this one doesn't go through the line—it goes *over* it.''

Two days later the men of the Rainbow went down into the Argonne themselves. They relieved two divisions in front of the Côte de Chatillon, a series of strongly fortified hill positions forming the pivot of the forbidding Kriemhilde Stellung, one of the Hindenburg Line's key sectors. The men were somber, walking through terrain even more hideous than Mountfaucon. The corpses were more numerous and more recently dead, and because it was cold, their decomposition was slower, so that the stench of decaying flesh was more persistent and pervasive. Here, too, the Germans had laid down heavy barrages of mustard and tear gas. With no wind stirring, it lay at treetop level in greenish-yellow mists. The men wore their gas masks. The hoses running from nose and mouth into the respiratory boxes at their breasts looked like huge snouts, giving them the appearance of grotesque, armored pigs.

General Duggan wore no mask. He could not abide being seen in one, for which foolish vanity he had almost paid with his life the night before. Driving to the headquarters of the 167th Alabama, he had been caught in a gas attack and become so violently convulsed that he nearly died. Nevertheless, weak as he was, he had arisen that morning to take command of the Eighty-fourth Brigade moving to the attack on the Rainbow's right.

''Did you see your old friend Ames last night?'' he inquired of Sergeant Durkin, walking through Romagne Woods beside him.

''I did, that, sir,'' Durkin replied in an unhappy tone.

Duggan glanced at him sharply. ''How is he?'' he asked, breathing heavily as they began to climb the hill from which he planned to watch the assault. "I haven't seen him since he brought me my hat and scarf."

"Strange, sir. My darlin' little snake's a changed man. He doesn't even drink, Gen'ral, would you believe that?"

"Ames?" Duggan cried in disbelief. "Ames not drink?" His mind went back to the wharf in San Francisco seventeen years ago, and he shook his head in disbelief.

"God's truth on it. Since the day he brought yer hat and scarf, I've been after him to come out to headquarters and have a sup with me." Durkin shook his head mournfully, turning, as he reached the crest of the hill, to give the general a helping hand. "But he won't. He says its sinful. Every time I mention it, he gives me a lecture on hellfire and the devil, Jaysus, yez'd think the poor man was a bloody priest, an' him goin' on that way about sin and retribution."

"Retribution, eh?" Duggan murmured, taking his field glasses from the leather case hanging at his breast. "Sounds like our old friend's Southern Baptist background is catching up with him."

"Ames, sir? Not him! He's not even a proper Christian, sir. Back on Samar in the old days, I used to rag him about bein' an unwashed heathen headin' straight fer hell. An' he'd laugh, sir, he would—an' he'd say bein' a heathen in hell was a lot better'n bein' a Catholic in heaven."

Duggan smiled faintly. Beneath him the assault platoons had reached the jump-off tapes and were quietly lying down, waiting for the artillery barrage to begin. In another minute it began. Half an hour later it lifted. Below the hill whistles blew, and into the swirling smoke of the forest went Duggan's soldiers, running at a lope, half bent, bayoneted rifles outthrust. Soon Duggan heard rifle shots and wild yells, then the dreadful chatter of the Maxims, and screams. Occasionally an orange flash and a crash sounding like the biting of a monster apple marked the explosion of an enemy seventy-seven shell. Gradually, an eerie quiet enveloped the battleground.

Below him, running hard out of the smoke, Duggan saw the lumpy figure of a soldier emerge. It was a young lieutenant. He came up, panting. "Colonel Buncie begs to report that both his assault battalions have been pinned down, sir. The enemy seems to be preparing a counterattack."

Duggan frowned. The 168th Iowa on the right had been stopped. "Can he hold?"

"He says he can with artillery support."

Duggan frowned again. Artillery. That's all anyone thought of in this war. "All right. Tell him to pull both his battalions back a hundred yards. That way he'll be clear of the Germans' preattack bombardment and we'll surprise them with a little more ground to cover. You understand me, Lieutenant?"

The young officer nodded, and Duggan continued: "The moment the enemy barrage lifts, we'll bring in our own. That ought to break up their counterattack." Saluting, the lieutenant turned and plunged once again into the smoke-filled forest.

Duggan's ruse succeeded. The Germans did lay down a preassault bombardment, and they did come on in field-gray waves the moment it lifted, only to be caught in the open by the surprise American shelling and driven back to their own lines. Nevertheless, when the Doughboys resumed their assault, they again encountered fierce resistance. By dusk the Eighty-fourth Brigade had reached only the forward slopes of the Côte de Chatillon. Both the Alabamans on the left and Iowans on the right had been halted and were once again withdrawing to stronger positions in their rear.

Casualties had been heavy. Throughout the afternoon, a procession of litter bearers had climbed the hill where Duggan stood, transferring their groaning and sometimes delirious burdens to mule-drawn ambulances waiting in the rear. Disconsolate, General Duggan walked back to his farm headquarters in silence. He sat at his field desk, thinking. He refused the food Durkin offered him, taking only a cup of warm soup. At midnight General Corrigan came into the farmhouse. He seemed tired and weary. He took a cup of steaming hot coffee from Durkin and sipped it slowly, his bloodshot blue eyes fixed on Duggan. At last, with an effort, he spoke.

"Duggan, give me Chatillon tomorrow night, or a list of five thousand casualties."

Duggan arose from his desk and came to stand before Corrigan. "General, if you do not have Chatillon tomorrow night, you shall have your list. And my name will be at the head of it."

Corrigan glanced up at him. His face worked and tears came into his eyes. Returning the empty coffee cup to Durkin, he went out the door as silently as he had come in.

Duggan's eyes were also moist when he turned to Durkin and said, "Please have Captain Fox notify my regimental commanders to come here at once." Durkin nodded and left.

Half an hour later the two colonels entered the headquarters and took the seats that Duggan pointed out to them. The general arose and began pacing in front of them, speaking to them in a husky, throbbing voice, jabbing his smoking cigarette in its holder in the air as he spoke.

"Gentlemen," he said, "the Germans are excellent soldiers. Thorough, efficient, brave. Perhaps their greatest virtue is their doggedness, their ability to stand firm in the face of adversity. However," he continued, puffing thoughtfully on the holder, "the defect of that virtue may be inflexibility, or, rather, a fixed habit of mind. They do not often improvise. They are doctrinaire. In the past few days, gentlemen," he said, placing one gleaming foot on his swivel chair, crossing his arms on his knee and leaning toward them, "I have been studying the enemy defensive tactics. I am convinced that the moment his center is threatened, he strengthens it with forces from his flanks. This leaves his flanks weakened, particularly, I would guess, his right. Now, gentlemen, think: all of our attacks—all of them, and on every level—have been frontal assaults. All at the enemy center and all repulsed with heavy loss." He paused to fit another cigarette into the holder. "It's high time," he said, "we hit him on his flanks. You, Buncie . . ." He pointed the holder at the shorter of the two colonels. "I want you to take two battalions of your Iowans tomorrow morning and hit the center of the Côte de Chatillon. Put your reserve battalion at your rear and a little to your right. You, Yancey," he said to the other colonel, "I want you to move two battalions of your Alabamans opposite the German right. Move under cover, before daybreak." General Duggan grinned. "You're an unreconstructed Rebel, Yancey— you must remember Jackson's flank march onto Hooker's right at Chancellorsville."

The tall colonel grinned with happy malice. "I do, General," he drawled. "And I still say Lee and Jackson could lick any Yankee general afloat."

Duggan laughed. "All except my father," he said, putting the holder between his teeth and lighting his cigarette. "All right, Yancey—you've got to be in position before Buncie moves. Hold your third battalion in reserve. Buncie, you're going to go in behind the customary artillery bombardment. I want the Germans to feel that they're being hit by the typical frontal assault." His voice turned grim again. "I'm afraid you're going to take casualties. But you've got to keep the pressure on the German center." Colonel Buncie nodded silently, and Duggan turned to Yancey. "You'll be going in with bayonets. No noise, no warning. Just like Mad Anthony Wayne at Stony Point. An hour after the barrage lifts, you attack." Yancey also nodded, and Duggan said, "All right, gentlemen, I'll see you in the morning."

Two hours before dawn, the Alabama assault battalions were in position on the American left. The Iowans were ready in the center, with their reserve battalion on the right, ready to strike the German left. A half hour before dawn the American artillery ranged in. General Duggan stood on the hill watching. At dawn it lifted and the Iowans attacked with wild yells. To Duggan's delighted surprise, their momentum carried them halfway up the Côte de Chatillon. But then the Germans counterattacked in force and pinned them down. A runner from Colonel Buncie reported that casualties were heavy. Litter bearers began plodding across the hill toward the mule ambulances.

General Duggan swept the Côte de Chatillon with his field glasses. He was plainly worried. It seemed much too early for the Germans to have brought in reserves from their flanks. Yet they had struck back in force . . . He stiffened. To his left—the German right flank—he thought he saw points of light glittering in the rising sun.

"Here, Pat," he shouted, handing Durkin the glasses. "See if you see movement over there on the German right." Nodding, the taller man took the binoculars and screwed them into his eyes. He, too, stiffened. "Glory be to God," he muttered, and then, looking around him for higher elevation, he saw a mule ambulance standing on the hilltop and scrambled up on top of it. " 'Tis them!" he cried excitedly. " 'Tis the dirty heinies indeed, Gen'ral—movin' toward the German center. I can see the sun dancin' on their bayonet points, sir."

Duggan struck his hands together in delight. He called for a runner. None answered. The last had been sent to Buncie and had not yet returned. Duggan was dismayed. Yancey *had* to attack the German right immediately. His eye fell on the mule ambulance being loaded with wounded.

"Undo those animals!" he shouted to Durkin. At once the big sergeant ran and began to free the mules from their traces.

The little Annamese driver shouted at him angrily. One of the American litter bearers pushed him away. General Duggan strode up, and the soldier cried: "My buddy's in there with his leg blown off, General. If you take those mules, he'll die!"

Duggan placed a gentle hand on the overwrought Doughboy's shoulder. "I'm sorry, soldier," he murmured. "But we need those mules so that a thousand of our other buddies may live." Shaking his head helplessly, the man began to sob—and Duggan swung himself up on one of the freed mules. With Durkin, he galloped off toward Yancey's post of command.

They found the Alabama headquarters under a clump of shell-torn trees to the left of the Côte de Chatillon. Yancey was seated on a large flat stone, drinking coffee from a canteen cup and studying a map spread out on his knees. His aides and runners were scattered around him, sitting on their helmets while they smoked and talked in low voices. Colonel Yancey glanced up in astonishment when his mud-spattered commander galloped up.

"Quick, Yancey!" General Duggan called. "The German right is moving. If you hit them now, while they're pulling out, there'll be the greatest slaughter!"

Yancey jumped to his feet, nodding eagerly. He put a hand on the neck of Duggan's mule. "Mind if I borrow your mount, suh?"

Duggan's answer was to vault to the ground, followed by Durkin. Instantly, Yancey and an aide galloped off toward the front. His headquarters followed, with General Duggan and Sergeant Durkin striding after them.

Suddenly, a Doughboy barred their path. It was Sergeant Beauregard Ames, and he was shaking his head doggedly.

"I cain't let y'all go up there, General," he muttered. "Y'all could get kilt."

"So can a lot of my men, Ames," General Duggan said, laughing. "How have you been?"

"Right good, I guess," Ames drawled. "But I cain't let y'all go up there, General."

Sergeant Durkin stepped between them, seizing Ames's shoulder and shaking him so that his helmet slid askew, revealing his thick blond hair. "Beau, lad—is it daft yez are? 'Tis the Gen'ral yer talkin' to."

"I cain't help it," Ames said, the set look returning to his face. "I got a call from the Lawd to watch out for him, Pat, and I cain't let him go up there."

Durkin turned to Duggan in amazement, and the general shook his head warningly. "All right, Ames," he said amiably, taking his arm. "I'm sure the Lord won't mind if we go up there together. You can watch out for me better that way."

Before the bewildered man could reply, Duggan propelled him gently forward. Soon the three of them were hurrying toward the sound of rifle fire and the high fox hunter's cry of the attacking Alabamans. Occasionally a Maxim chattered—but there was no crack of a seventy-seven or crump of a mortar shell, suggesting that the Germans had been taken by surprise.

Suddenly, on their right, among a pile of big gray rocks, a machine gun stuttered steadily. Bullets keened around them, kicking up spurts of mud.

"Down, sir," Durkin cried, pulling the general down beside him. " 'Tis a bypassed machine-gun nest."

The sergeant was right. Six or seven Doughboys were crawling on their bellies toward what appeared to be a cave mouth among the rocks. Staccato flashes issued from it. The Americans began hurling grenades. They exploded harmlessly among the rocks. The gun chattered on. Duggan jumped to his feet to watch, and moments later a German potato-masher grenade somersaulted through the air to fall sputtering at his feet.

"I'll take it!" Beauregard Ames shouted, and flung his body over the explosive. Almost instantly it exploded—and Ames was hurled into the air. He rolled over, screaming. His hands clutched his belly, clawing at his entrails, trying to contain them. But they slipped through his fingers, bloody and white.

Duggan and Durkin rushed to kneel beside him. Ames gritted his teeth.

"I'm goin', Pat, I'm goin'," he moaned.

"No, no, lad," Durkin cried, tearing his first-aid pouch from his cartridge belt, opening it, seizing a morphine syrette, and injecting it into the dying man's arm. Ames's contorted features began to relax. His blond head sank backward into the mud.

"I—I'm sorry, suh," he mumbled.

"Sorry!" Duggan exclaimed. "My God, man, you saved our lives."

"I . . . I owe you one . . . mebbe more . . . tell . . . tell Betsy I'm sorry . . ."

Startled, Duggan glanced at Durkin inquiringly, and the big sergeant shook his head.

"Your family, Ames," Duggan said hurriedly. "Your family— is there anything I can do?"

"My . . . my son . . . he . . . wants . . . to be . . . a . . . officer . . ."

"He'll be in West Point the day he turns seventeen. I promise you that, Ames—I swear it."

Beauregard Ames tried to smile. But his lips stiffened, and in the next instant he was dead.

Patrick Durkin began to weep softly. He took his canteen from his belt and opened it. Pouring water on the dead man's forehead, he made the sign of the cross over him.

"I baptize thee in the name of the Father, Son, and Holy Ghost," he whispered, bending his head to kiss Ames's closed eyelids. He arose. "He'd've never let me do that to him alive, sir," he murmured. "But they do say the soul takes two hours to leave the body." He shrugged. "Who knows? Maybe it's true."

Durkin tore his eyes away from the lifeless, crumpled body at his feet. He stared toward the front where a ragged volley of rifle shots had broken out. His face went white with rage. His blue eyes gleamed murderously in his livid flesh. Grasping his rifle, he ran toward the enemy with a wild, fierce cry of anguish.

But the battle was over before he got there. With their right collapsed by Yancey's yelling Alabamans and driven in on their confused center, and their terrified left rolled up by Buncie's reserve battalion of Iowans, the Germans had withdrawn in disorder. They left behind them their dead and wounded, their guns and many prisoners—and the Côte de Chatillon in American hands.

The impenetrable *Kriemhilde Stellung* had been penetrated. Next morning, a weary General Mark Duggan stood atop the Romagne Heights to watch another fresh division of Americans pour through the gap in pursuit of the retreating Germans. Soon the race was on for Sedan and the Belgian border. To Duggan's surprise and delight, an order arrived from Chaumont gazetting him to command of the Rainbow Division.

He was in command at Buzancy that night—the eleventh hour of the eleventh day of the eleventh month of the year 1918—when a sudden stillness came upon the front. It was an eerie quiet, to ears accustomed to violent sound; almost an alien intruder. Slowly, cautiously, like moles creeping from their holes, the Doughboys clambered up from their trenches. They stood erect, walking gingerly back and forth, casting anxious glances in the direction of no-man's-land. But no guns spoke. Matches flamed. Cigarette ends glowed in the dark. Soon the Western Front was winking and glowing as though infested by hordes of fireflies. Men began to talk, to laugh, to sing—to cheer.

General Mark Duggan walked among them, chatting, puffing on his own cigarette in its gold-and-ivory holder. The clouds overhead thinned and cleared, making a pale sickle moon visible. It reminded Duggan of the same moon the night of the raid, when the brave young German officer's eye had popped onto his scarf. He thought of Beauregard Ames, buried beneath a tree on the Côte de Chatillon; of the thousands of Rainbow soldiers lying forever still in alien soil. Tears came into his eyes as he reflected in anguish on the wantonness of war, on the hideous, horrible horror of it, of its victims, the young and beautiful, now maimed and mangled and gone. But then his eye fell on the pale moonbeam lighting the single star on his shoulder.

If he wanted more stars, he realized, he would need another war.

★ ★ ★ ★ ★ ★ ★ ★ ★ ★ ★ ★ ★ ★ ★ ★

WEST POINT

★ ★ ★ ★ ★ ★ ★ ★ ★ ★ ★ ★ ★ ★ ★ ★

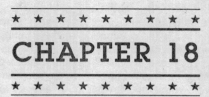

CHAPTER 18

In late April of 1919 the transport *Leviathan* sailed slowly into New York Harbor. Its rails were dark with Doughboys of the Rainbow Division eagerly searching the harbor for signs of the tumultuous welcome they expected. They had talked of nothing else all the way across the Atlantic from Brest, and now they were where they had yearned to be so poignantly since the moment they had heard their first shell explode.

Their ears hearkened for the sound of ship's whistles screeching them a welcome, but they heard none; their eyes sought the white plumes of seawater spouting skyward from fireboat hoses, but they saw none; and the cheeks that awaited the grateful kisses of pretty maidens saluting the heroes of their nation went uncaressed.

New York City did not seem aware, or even to care, that the Rainbow had come home. Ship traffic moved heedlessly up and down the Hudson and out into the bay, ferryboats plodded their bovine trails between the Manhattan and the Jersey shores, and the pier alongside where the *Leviathan* was eventually tied up was silent and deserted, except for a street urchin clutching a bundle of newspapers who gaped at them in curiosity. "What's yer outfit?" he called.

"We're the famous Forty-second," a Doughboy yelled back proudly.

The newsboy lifted a dirty, pinched face. "Ya ever see action?"

A sullen, angry silence ensued on the weather decks of the *Leviathan*. Then, so disgusted that they could not even curse, the men went below to get their gear.

On the bridge deck, Brigadier General Mark Duggan watched them go with sadness in his large dark eyes. Throughout the Rainbow's service in the occupation of the Rhineland, he had known that the men were bitter about not being repatriated immediately. They had resented the puritanical prohibitions against drinking or fraternizing with the German frauleins. They had even voted not to march in any victory parades upon their return. But in their secret hearts, Duggan knew, they yearned like artists for recognition. So had he. He had seen the welcome given to President Wilson in Paris when the American chief had arrived for the peace conference. He had never heard such cheers. Standing on the Champs Elysées, he had seen generals pass, Foch pass, Clemenceau pass, Lloyd George, troops of all nations, bands, banners—and heard cheers. But when Wilson's carriage came into view, he had heard an outcry that was almost inhuman, as though the war-tortured people of Europe were beseeching the Savior reincarnate. Of course, Mark Duggan, for all his immense vanity, had anticipated no such salute for himself and the Rainbow. But they had been entitled to something, he thought bitterly; certainly more than to come home to a blank stare. If, in Christian moral theology, he thought, one of the three sins crying out to Heaven for vengeance was to deprive a working man of his wages, what was to be said of robbing a soldier of his glory?

Turning to walk to his stateroom, he thought bitterly of Woodrow Wilson. Duggan now despised his commander-in-chief. Throughout that long, cruel winter of 1918–19, while American soldiers were dying by the thousands of influenza epidemics scourging crowded, unsanitary debarkation camps, the President of the United States had held a huge ocean liner pierside at Brest. Tens of thousands of men could have been ferried home on that great ship, but Wilson kept it for himself against the chance that he might wish to bolt the peace conference and sail home.

Duggan could not forgive him for that, even though he did

League of Nations. But it looks like a losing battle, he thought glumly, opening his cabin door: It looks like Senator Lodge is going to be too much for him.

"All ready to go, Gen'ral," Sergeant Durkin called.

Duggan reached for his punctured campaign hat lying on top of his luggage. He paused and looked at Pat. "Better give me my regular hat," he said quietly. "I don't think our country's in the mood for war heroes."

Not a quarter hour later, Duggan realized how perceptive his remark had been. Half the people they passed walking through Pennsylvania Station stared at them coldly or with open hatred and contempt. Sitting in the diner of their train speeding toward Washington, they encountered the same hostility. Even the black stewards reserved their smiles for civilians only. Duggan was dismayed at the contrast between this postwar enmity and the war years when he rarely rode between New York and Washington without basking in friendly smiles and admiring glances. Then, he and Durkin never dined alone. The opposite chairs were always filled by civilians of substance, eager to shake their hands or buy their meal or fill their glass. Now, he saw with a rising bitterness that he could not down, they would fill his glass with hemlock.

He also became aware that his country was not only in the grip of an antimilitary reaction, but also by a hysterical fear of Bolshevism. Bolshevik-inspired bombings or attempted bombings of public officials were frequent. The very newspaper that he read in the parlor car carried banner headlines reporting that the mayor of Seattle, a crusader against labor radicalism, had found a bomb in his mail. Next day, when Duggan reported to the War Office, a package addressed to the chairman of the Senate immigration committee exploded in the hands of the servant who opened it. The following day, thirty-six bombs were discovered in the New York post office. The packages containing them were addressed to high-ranking federal officials.

On May Day, while Mark and Betsy strode hand in hand among the cherry blossoms on the Potomac Tidal Basin, police and communist marchers fought each other in major cities. Throughout the spring and summer there were frequent strikes, all blamed on the Bolsheviks. Labor riots were common, and General Duggan, ever careful of his career, feared that he might be ordered to command the soldiers frequently sent to put them down. His old idol and mentor, General Leonard Field, had no such compunction. He joyfully came out of retirement to lead nine hundred soldiers into Omaha to quell a riot, and he commanded another fifteen hundred against rioting steel workers in Gary, Indiana.

General Field heartily approved of the famous—or infamous—"Palmer Raids" begun by Attorney General A. Mitchell Palmer after his home was shattered by a bomb. Palmer believed that all the social disturbance was the calculated work of Bolsheviks, and he sought to jail or deport them all. General Field, who was seeking the Republication nomination for President, agreed.

"Get rid of them!" Field roared. "Put them aboard ships of stone with sails of lead, and give them the wrath of God for a breeze and Hell for their first port."

Mark Duggan thought that General Field was just a bit too enthusiastic in his denunciations of the Bolsheviks and the labor radicals. "It won't do him any good at the convention," he said to Betsy one night after dinner. "For better or worse, the labor movement is here to stay. They've got a voice now, and even if it's mostly Democratic, there'll be some labor leaders at the Republican convention. They'll remember what Field did in Omaha and Gary."

"But who else can they possibly nominate?" Betsy asked, lifting her wineglass. They had eaten and were finishing the last bottle of Pommard that Mark had brought home with him from France.

"I don't know," Mark said, unhappily watching her empty the bottle.

Since his return, he had been startled by the amount of alcohol Betsy consumed. She saw his glance and flushed, but said nothing.

"But I certainly hope it's General Field," he continued. "Having him for my commander-in-chief wouldn't do us any harm."

Betsy nodded, sipping again. "What about General Pershing?"

Mark laughed. "Black Jack struck out, dearest. He and George Meadows took to the hustings a month ago, and they turned out to be the most inept soldier-politicians since

Winfield Scott. Now, I understand, Black Jack has let both parties know he'll sit it out and settle for chief of staff.''

"Will that hurt you?"

"Not if General Field is elected. I don't see how the Democrats can stop him. They don't have anybody. And even if Wilson wanted to challenge tradition and run for a third term, he couldn't do it.''

"Poor man," Betsy murmured.

"You don't hate Wilson anymore?"

"How can you hate a man when he's down like that? Mrs. Delaplace was telling me this morning she heard he's completely paralyzed. No one can see him but his doctor, his wife, and his secretary. She's friendly with one of the White House maids. She says when they told him about the Senate voting down the treaty, he just turned his face to the wall like he wanted to die.''

Mark nodded sympathetically. "It must be awful to end your days in despair and defeat. It's so much better to get your lumps when you're young.''

"I still think it was horrible the way the American people let Wilson down. They were all for the League of Nations in the beginning. And then they turned their back on him.''

"Our people just don't understand war and foreign policy," Duggan said moodily. "They treat war like a football game. It's over, we've won—and now we can all go home and celebrate.'' He sighed. "I think they were disillusioned by all that talk about preventing wars in the future. They'd just lost 126,000 young men in 'the war to end wars,' and here Wilson was talking about future wars. I think they thought they'd been hoaxed. They wanted no part of Europe anymore. Besides, the Red Scare was on. There was a Bolshevik under every bed. The Allied intervention in Russia had failed, and Tukhachevsky was getting ready to march on Warsaw. Really, who could blame them?''

Mark looked up sharply. His wife had risen to go to the breakfront and open a cupboard from which she took a bottle of sherry.

"Betsy, dearest," he said gently, "you're not going to have another drink?''

She flushed again, glaring at him momentarily. Looking quickly away, she opened the bottle. "J-Just one, Mark," she said, faltering. "Honestly, some nights I can't sleep, and then I begin thinking of that awful shark." Her eyes sought his pleadingly. "I . . . if I take a drink before bedtime, it helps me to sleep."

"Of course!" Mark cried in commiseration. He went to her side and put his arm around her. "I understand perfectly, dearest. I . . . I didn't mean to offend you." She squeezed his hand and raised her face to his. He bent to kiss her. "Go ahead, dearest—I have some reports to read in my study."

Betsy smiled, and Mark went into the other room. Occasionally, as he worked, he heard the clink of glass and the gurgle of liquid. Then he heard Betsy's footsteps on the stairs. After he had finished, he went into the dining room. The table was cleared. Apprehensive, hating himself, he went into the kitchen and lifted the lid of the garbage can. Inside were the empty bottle of Pommard and an empty sherry bottle. He put down the lid slowly with tears in his eyes. He remembered, as a boy on the plains, he had overheard his father talking with his mother about an officer's wife who drank. "An officer's wife who drinks," his father had said, "is worse than an officer's wife who sleeps with enlisted men. A man can get rid of a whore with honor. But a drinker, no. She clings to you and your career like a barnacle. And just like a barnacle, she'll drag you down."

The tears were still in Mark Duggan's eyes when he slipped silently into bed beside his sleeping wife.

General Leonard Field did not win the Republican nomination for President. It went instead to Senator Warren Gamaliel Harding of Ohio, and the Republican candidate, as Duggan had predicted, was elected. For his chief of staff, President Harding chose General John J. Pershing, and one month after his appointment, General Pershing sent for General Duggan.

"Mark," Black Jack snapped, fingering his mustache, "West Point is a mess."

Duggan nodded, pleased to hear the chief of staff call him by his first name again. "It certainly is, sir. During the war, they turned it into just another officers training school. Those one-year classes were ridiculous."

"Disgraceful—and I want you to clean it up."

Duggan was stunned. "*Me*, sir? I'm not an educator,

General—I'm a field soldier. Why, half the professors there taught me when I was a cadet.''

"That's the trouble. They're hidebound and hoary. You can hear their arteries hardening halfway down the Hudson. No, Duggan," he grunted, his thin lips compressing, "you've got to go up there and clean house. They can't fault you academically, because they gave you the highest grades in the Academy's history—and they know that you were an excellent combat leader. That's what the Academy's for, isn't it—to train successful combat leaders?''

"Yes, sir," Duggan murmured, still slightly stunned.

"I'm announcing your appointment as superintendent this afternoon," Pershing continued. "I'd like you to take charge in two weeks. That should be time enough to move your family. By the way, how is your family?''

"Fine, sir," Duggan said, and then, to his astonishment he saw an incredible tear glistening in Black Jack's stony gray eye. When he remembered that Pershing's wife and three little daughters had died in a Presidio fire in 1915, he understood—and looked away.

"That will be all, Mark," General Pershing said, coughing in embarrassment.

"Right, sir," Duggan replied. "Thank you, sir," and he left the office.

Walking home from the War Department that evening, Duggan decided that the West Point appointment was fortunate, after all. By law, the superintendent of the U.S. Military Academy could be no less than a brigadier general, and that meant his star was safe. Because of the antimilitary reaction, and the pacifist, penny-pinching mood of Congress, officers throughout the Army were losing as many as three grades in rank. George Meadows had already dropped back two grades from full colonel to major, and even Black Jack Pershing had reverted from general of the armies to full general. Duggan knew he was now the youngest officer of flag rank in the U.S. armed services, grades ahead of all his classmates, and even superior to West Pointers ten and twelve years his senior. With a minimum of luck, he reflected, without even another war, he should be able to carry out his father's last wish and carry the family name all the way up to the four stars of the chief of staff.

Betsy was delighted when she heard of his new assignment. "Oh, boy, West Point!" she cried, with all her old girlish enthusiasm. "Now we can see all the Army football games."

Mark smiled. "Yes, and if I have my way, we won't be losing to Notre Dame and the Navy so much, anymore."

Stepping quickly to the breakfront, Betsy said, "Let's celebrate with a drink before dinner."

Mark studied her uneasily. "Just one," he said warily. Betsy nodded, taking out two bottles and going into the kitchen. "What are you making?" Mark called, bending to open the liquor cupboard.

"A Manhattan."

"What's that?"

"It's a new cocktail, the best drink to come out of Prohibition. Sweet vermouth and whiskey."

"My God, Betsy, where did you get all this liquor?"

"The British embassy. They bring it in in their diplomatic pouch and there's no trouble."

"But, Betsy! Why do you need so much? There must be a case in here."

Betsy came back into the dining room and handed him his drink with a wry grimace. "You have to get it while you can, Mark." She preceded him into the living room and sat down. "You can't depend on your bootlegger anymore." She made another face. "Prohibition!" she snorted. "Pooh! It's enough to make you wish you weren't a Baptist. All those Christian Temperance women with their Eighteenth Amendment and their hatchets . . . Hatchet faces, too. They have some nerve telling people they can't drink." She sipped her drink. "They should all drown in their favorite beverage!"

Mark tried to smile, sitting beside her. "I suppose you mean water," he murmured. He sipped his drink. "Very good," he said. "Strong too."

"Just the fir—" Betsy began and caught herself. "Well, now that we're moving," she said quickly, "what shall we do with the house?"

"I hate to sell it," Mark said musingly. He got up and walked back to the kitchen, gazing at the same table at which his father had sat on that fateful hot morning eight years ago. He returned to the living room. "I can't bear to sell it, Betsy. It has too many memories. I'll always want to have it to come back to."

"Do you think we can rent it?"

"I don't see why not. There're so many new nations in Central Europe now—all carved out of the carcass of the old Austro-Hungarian empire—and they're all opening embassies here. It should be snapped up right away."

Betsy nodded. "What about Jinny? Don't forget, she's five now, and ready for school."

"There's a good school for Army brats at the Point." A yearning look came into his eyes, and Betsy glanced away. She knew that when he looked like that, he was thinking of his stillborn son and the son that was yet to come. At such times, she always brought Virginia in to see him, and this time she went to the stairs and called, "Virginia. Come on down, honey, Daddy's home."

Virginia ran downstairs and up to her father. Standing on tiptoe, she kissed him. He smiled and lifted her onto his knee, stroking her chestnut hair and looking into the large dark eyes exactly like his own.

"We're going to move, honey," he said.

"Oh, boy! Where?"

"West Point," Mark said, chuckling at a style of enthusiasm that might have been her mother's. "I'm going to be in charge."

Virginia's eyes widened. "Do they have guns there?"

"Yep. Guns and lots of kids. There's a lake you can swim in, and we can go boating on the Hudson River. And every Saturday morning, honey," he continued, his eyes twinkling, "I'll make the corps of cadets parade in your honor."

Her eyes grew wider, and then solemn. "Will you let me shoot one of the guns?" she asked.

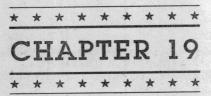

CHAPTER 19

There was no difficulty in renting the house. The Czechoslovakian ambassador snapped it up two hours after it was listed. Under the supervision of Sergeant Durkin, two new Army motor trucks moved the Duggans' furniture into storage and transported their personal belongings to the rambling old house built almost a century ago for the first superintendent, Sylvanus Thayer.

Betsy loved "old Vinny's house." She spent almost an entire week in New York City buying curtains and drapes for its scores of windows and picking out material for bedspreads and to reupholster the furniture. Mark was also delighted with the new assignment. He had moved into his office without a moment wasted in ceremony, not even a review of the Cadet Corps, much to the cadets' relief and gratitude. Duggan's staff more than pleased him. He was delighted to find that Major George Peyton was his commandant of cadets.

"Put your white pistols away, eh, George?" he said with a grin.

"Yes, sir! Right into the foot locker on top of your hat."

Duggan laughed. "Until the next war, George?"

Peyton's even white teeth flashed in his ruddy face. "Until the next war."

Duggan's aide was a first lieutenant named Michael Bauer.

Mark was attracted to him immediately. Lieutenant Bauer had the brightest cornflower-blue eyes Mark had ever seen, and although he was prematurely bald, his smooth round skull seemed to complement his wide, homely face. When he grinned, it was as though a candle had begun to glow behind his face.

"Call me Mike, sir," he said after the general had greeted him in his office. "They've always called me Mike wherever I've been: Texas, Kansas, West Point—everywhere."

"I thought I detected the twang of the plains in your voice," General Duggan said. "What class were you in here?"

"'Fifteen," Bauer said ruefully. "A little too late for France." He grinned infectiously. "But wars are like trolley cars, sir—there's always another one coming along any minute."

Duggan nodded, studying him thoughtfully. "You mean Versailles, Lieutenant? You think the fruits of victory are rotten with the seeds of war? Clemenceau imposed a Carthaginian peace?"

Mike Bauer shook his head, a puzzled look on his face. "I . . . I just meant that the world always seems to have one, sir."

Duggan nodded again, but said nothing. Evidently, his good-humored young aide was not as perceptive as he was personable. Nevertheless, Lieutenant Bauer was a devoted assistant. Together with Captain Peyton, he worked tirelessly to put into effect Duggan's plans for a new and modern West Point.

"We've got to produce an officer," Duggan told them at their first meeting in his office, "one who is capable of commanding in a democratic army." He lighted the cigarette in his holder and waved it at them like a baton. "When I was in France, I found all too many officers who thought it was enough to be a strict disciplinarian, a martinet. They acted as though they were commanding the professional soldiers of old, the desperadoes who were recruited by judges and press gangs and educated in the guardhouse. The kind of men Wellington called 'the scum of the earth.'" He smiled wanly and drew on his cigarette. "I never thought that was very gallant or grateful of Wellington. After all, the soldiers he called scum held the farmhouse at Waterloo and beat Napoleon. They beat him on the Peninsula too,'' he said musingly. ''It was the same kind of scum that conquered our frontier and tore over a million square miles out of the heart of Mexico. But they're gone now, gentlemen,'' he said, his dark eyes sweeping both Bauer and Peyton. ''We've got a new kind of soldier—the citizen-soldier. He doesn't like to be kicked or yelled at. He won't let you call him stupid. To train him,'' Duggan said, bending forward in his chair to stub out his cigarette, ''we have to develop a new kind of officer.''

Lieutenant Bauer's bright blue eyes were solemn as he asked, ''How will we do that, General?''

''Broaden the curriculum,'' Duggan said. ''Train him in the social sciences—politics, economics, social psychology— as well as in military studies.''

Peyton coughed politely. ''I couldn't agree with you more, General,'' he said respectfully, and then, his high voice rising, ''but I don't think they'll let you do it.''

''*They?*'' There was a chill in the general's voice. He had already noticed that of his two aides, Lieutenant Bauer rarely disagreed with him, always seeming to try to gauge his mind first before he spoke, but that Major Peyton was perhaps a bit too opinionated for a subordinate. ''They?'' he repeated icily.

''The academic board, sir,'' Peyton replied, flushing slightly, his tone respectful again. ''The board and the rest of the entrenched Neanderthals around here. General Duggan,'' he went on, pleadingly, ''remember I spoke to you frankly once before . . . on that hilltop above the Argonne? Do you mind if I—''

''Go ahead, Peyton.''

''Thank you, sir. You see, I've been here almost a year now—and it's dreadful the way they cling to the past. When I suggested to the military department that they put in courses on armored and aerial warfare, they told me there was no such thing. But there *is,* General, there is! In England, Colonel Fuller and Captain Liddell Hart have already published books on it, and in France there's a fellow named de Gaulle.''

General Duggan nodded. ''I've read them,'' he said. ''What did the military department say, when you told them that?''

''They quoted General Pershing as saying he'd seen both aircraft and tanks in France, and neither had had any effect on the outcome of the war.'' Duggan pursed his lips and glanced out the window momentarily, and Peyton rushed on. "That's just *it*! They didn't! They didn't because they weren't used right. Remember, sir," he said, lowering his voice again, "remember how we talked about that at Mountfaucon, and the Red Baron and his Flying Circus dropped out of nowhere and shot down all our balloons? Who could ask for better instruction in the warfare of the future? But here," he said moodily, "here in this primeval muck of an educational mire, they're actually talking about bringing Haig and Foch over to lecture on the tactics that won the war. Haig and Foch!" he cried in exasperation, his ruddy face deepening in color. "My God, sir—the Army might as well start issuing spears!"

General Duggan chuckled. "Your old bête noire, eh, George? Well, you needn't worry on that score. They won't be lecturing here while I'm around. And we *will* let some fresh air into the old place."

"I sure hope so, sir," Peyton said, getting to his feet with Bauer. "You know, I went through the library the other day and I couldn't find a single work by von Clausewitz."

"Von Clausewitz?" Bauer asked, a puzzled frown wrinkling his broad forehead. "Who's he?"

"See!" Peyton cried triumphantly. "Here's a graduate of the United States Military Academy who never heard of the most perceptive military writer of all time."

Bauer's homely face turned crimson, and Peyton put a soothing hand on his shoulder. "I didn't mean anything personal, Mike. It's not your fault. It's—"

"It isn't," General Duggan broke in musingly. "It's the fault of the curriculum. And that, gentlemen, I am going to change."

Betsy Duggan found life at West Point boring. She had expected a gay social whirl—cocktail parties and military balls, weekends in New York City—but she found that without Virginia and Mark to care for, her life would have been one of complete tedium. Mark seldom went out. His attempt to change the curriculum had plunged him into a bitter battle with the old-line, tenure-holding professors of the academic board, and he had little time for socializing. The only occasions on which she wore an evening dress were at official functions that required the presence of the superintendent. Otherwise, she had to be content with occasionally having the Peytons and Mike Bauer and his young wife Mimi over for dinner. Of course, she might have played afternoon bridge with the other officers' wives, but she did not like cards. Sometimes, Mimi Bauer came over in the afternoon, and they would have a few drinks and chat. One good thing about West Point, they agreed, was that it was so close to Canada and real, honest-to-goodness Canadian whiskey. None of that bootleg booze made in a Stateside bathtub.

Betsy's greatest pleasure was going to the Army football games. Next to that, she enjoyed watching the team practice. The sight of strong, handsome young athletes grappling with each other or racing up and down the bright green gridiron in pursuit of the football pleased and thrilled her. She was also fond of Coach Charley Bailey. Whenever he saw her sitting in the stands alone, he would turn the practice over to an assistant and come up to chat with her. On the Monday after Army lost to Notre Dame again, Coach Bailey noticed Betsy in the stands and came up to sit beside her.

"We never should have lost!" Betsy exclaimed hotly. "Honestly, I almost cried when it was over. The boys tried so hard. You ask me, that referee was the pope in disguise."

Bailey grinned. "It wasn't that bad, Mrs. Duggan. I will say, though, there were a couple of calls that could have gone the other way."

"And the crowd! Why don't we play them up here sometimes, so we could have somebody to cheer for our side? Does the game always have to be in Yankee Stadium?"

"We make about ten times more money playing down there, ma'am."

"Well, yes . . . I guess so . . . But that awful crowd. Is everyone in New York City Irish and Catholic?"

Coach Bailey grinned again. "I'm one, too, Mrs. Duggan."

Betsy laughed, coloring slightly. "Yes, but you're nice. Besides, you're on our side. Anyway, I think it's unfair that our boys have to play in front of that huge crowd with only a couple hundred Army officers to cheer for them."

"You're right there. But General Duggan's changing that, too, ma'am. Next year the entire Cadet Corps is going to the game, and they're going to parade between the halves too. That ought to give our kids a lift." He glanced at Betsy sideways. "Your husband has been awfully good for West Point athletics, Mrs. Duggan. We've never had a superintendent so interested in sports."

"Well, you know he just loves sports."

"I know. So did the other supers. But they never did anything about it. Maybe the academic board had them buffaloed. You know, West Point must remain simon-pure and all that baloney. Hell's bells, Mrs. Duggan, how do they expect me and my kids to go out and play on even terms with a coach like Knute Rockne and that football factory they've got out there at Notre Dame? And the Navy! They've got twice the student body we have, and they never hesitate to make things easy for a kid who can pass that football."

Bailey frowned. Something he saw on the field disturbed him. He put his whistle to his lips and blew a piercing shriek. Cupping his hands to his lips, he shouted: "No! No! *No!* Kogel. *Never* throw in the flat. That's what you did Saturday, and you know what happened." He turned back to Betsy. "Well, now, thanks to your husband, *I'm* getting a few horses of my own to run with. You know, our plebe team is undefeated. And we've got a plebe fullback who'll make them forget all about Elmer Oliphant." He got up to leave. "Really, Mrs. Duggan—you ought to go over to plebe practice some day. This kid's from Alabama. His name is Ames." Betsy Duggan's eyes widened and her hand flew to her throat, but the coach did not notice. "You can't miss him," he said. "He plays without a helmet and he's got thick blond hair."

Early the following afternoon, even before the plebe players were on the practice field, Betsy Duggan had taken a seat in the small tier of bleachers above it. She was immediately noticed by Lieutenant Yardley, the plebe coach.

"Well, this is a surprise—and an honor too," Yardley said. "Come, you've got to sit on the bench with me." Flushing with pleasure, Betsy followed and sat down beside him on the end of the players' bench, just as two elevens of uniformed plebes ran onto the field and lined up for a kickoff.

"We're having a scrimmage today," the coach explained.

"Wonderful," Betsy said. Then, pointing to the sturdy blond youth waiting to receive the ball, she asked anxiously, "Won't he get hurt without a helmet?"

"Not him! That kid's made of iron. He's our star player,

Mrs. Duggan. Beau Ames. Beauregard Stonewall Jackson Ames.'' He grinned. ''They're still fighting the Civil War down there in Alabama.'' Betsy smiled, and the coach chuckled. ''But let me tell you, Mrs. Duggan, that kid's going to be the best ball carrier Army ever had.''

A whistle blew. There was a thud of a foot striking leather and the football tumbled through the air into the arms of young Ames. Betsy Duggan was on her feet, screaming, as he started up the field. Again and again he shed or dodged tacklers, twisting and spinning until he was in the clear and returned the kickoff for a touchdown. Betsy was almost hoarse, she had yelled so hard. She turned scarlet when she realized that the other plebe players on the bench were staring at her. She began fumbling in her purse to cover her confusion. Lieutenant Yardley chuckled. ''Don't be embarrassed, ma'am. He does that to everybody. You can't help yourself. The moment he gets the ball, you're on your feet.''

Betsy nodded gratefully. It was true. Beau Ames was an electrifying athlete. He ran with reckless abandon, his blond head sometimes disappearing in a crowd of tacklers, becoming visible again, like an oriflamme, as he broke free. Before the scrimmage had ended, he had scored two more touchdowns and made some shattering tackles. The players began trotting from the field, and Betsy rose to leave.

''Would you like to meet Cadet Ames, Mrs. Duggan?'' the coach asked.

Betsy nodded, unable to speak, turning quickly away to conceal the tears at the corners of her eyes. She seldom thought of Beau without tears. She had startled Mark with her weeping the night he had described to her, dramatically and with great emotion, how the old soldier of Samar had laid down his life for him and Sergeant Durkin. Surprised as Mark had been, he had suspected nothing, surmising that his account merely had touched Betsy's warm and generous heart. Now, she felt the quick hot tears again, and she put her hand over her eyes as though shielding them from the autumn sun.

''Cadet Ames,'' the coach was saying, ''allow me to present Mrs. Duggan.''

The boy came rigidly to attention and bowed. Betsy was astonished. Though clad in a football uniform, his face streaked with grime, and with a bruise on the point of his chin, the young man did not seem in the least self-conscious. When he bowed, he might have been wearing full dress at a military ball. Betsy smiled, studying him, her heart pounding. He looked just like Beau! No, not actually. His eyes were blue, even hard blue, where Beau's had been grayish flecked with yellow, like a cat's; and he was bigger, probably less sensuous than his father, more intellectual. But he did have Beau's features and that beautiful thick tawny hair. Betsy longed to run her hands through it.

"You were simply marvelous out there, Beau—may I call you Beau?" He nodded, and she said shyly, "I knew your father, Beau."

Now it was the youth who was astonished. He ran a hand over his hair, stammering: "You . . . you knew my dad?"

"Yes, Beau," she said gently. "When I was a girl at Camp Robinson, Wyoming—and he was a young soldier."

"He . . . he never told me. You see, I . . . I'm his only child. My mother died in childbirth." He swallowed. "Dad never had a picture of her. He just told me about her. Excuse me, ma'am," he said, reddening, "but you look like what I always thought she looked like."

Betsy felt her eyes go moist again. "That's very sweet of you, Beau. Did you know that your father saved General Duggan's life?"

Beau's eyes widened. "No, ma'am. I never heard that."

"In France. He threw himself on a German grenade to save my husband and Sergeant Durkin."

The boys hands clenched and unclenched. "I always knew that he was one of the few men to win two Medals of Honor. He . . . he was a brave man, my father. The first one was in the Philippines, before he came home and got married. And then . . ." He swallowed again, and his face worked. "And then when he was . . ."

Betsy yearned to embrace and console the young man. But she knew it would embarrass him. Instead, she stepped forward and kissed him softly on the cheek. "I . . . I'm sorry, Beau," she murmured. "If I were to ask you to dinner at the superintendent's house, would you come?"

He grinned. "I guess that's an order, ma'am," he said, and Betsy smiled again.

She turned to go, and paused. "You haven't a trace of a southern accent. How's that?"

"My dad. He wanted me educated proper so's I could become an officer. He left everything he had for me to go to school up North. I was playing for Peddie when the Army scout saw me."

Betsy nodded. She did not think it was necessary to tell him that he would have been at West Point, football prowess or not. Mark had arranged for that a week after he arrived in Washington from France.

"I see," Betsy said. "Well, you'll be hearing me cheering for you when the plebes play Navy next week."

"Mark, I met the most wonderful plebe today."

"Yes?" Mark replied absently, sinking wearily into a chair. Betsy studied him in amazement. Rarely, if ever, had she seen her husband look so dejected. "He's the best football player I've ever seen," she went on, "and guess what his name is."

"Ames," Mark replied, chuckling, momentarily forgetting the day's frustrating meeting with the academic board. "Beauregard Stonewall Jackson Ames. I guess I forgot to tell you he was here. Honestly, dearest, those people on that board are so exasper—"

"Here, I'll make you a Manhattan. It'll make you feel better."

"But, dearest, we're having dinner with the Peytons tonight. You know George Peyton's heavy hand."

"Just one, Mark. You seem so tired. It'll cheer you up."

Mark took the cocktail and sipped it gingerly. "You know who the boy's father was?"

"I do, Mark," Betsy said, almost draining her glass in one gulp. "That's why I'm so surprised you never told me."

"Well, you know I had arranged for him to come here. But then one of our scouts saw him playing for Peddie and brought him here on a football scholarship. The scout didn't know about the duplication, of course. But he's a ten-strike, all right—the best I've seen since Elmer Oliphant."

"Is he a good student?"

"Yes and no. George Peyton tells me the boy is actually brilliant in history and literature and languages, but he's having trouble in math. He's got one of those fast, intuitive minds. He comes up with the answer before the instructor has finished presenting the problem.''

''What's wrong with that?''

Mark Duggan sighed. ''That, my dearest, is in essence exactly what is wrong with West Point. The faculty wants it done their way. By rote. Dreadful, dull, deadly rote. Believe me, I know—I was here for four years, and it was no different in my day than it was in Vinny Thayer's day. And it's the same today—rote, front-board recitation. I have told the board again and again that I want to make a cadet's education interesting and exciting, with classroom discussions, lectures, laboratory work, and oral drills, and they call me a dangerous innovator. Rote, they say, front-board recitation, the traditional way of teaching at West Point.'' He sipped his drink reflectively. ''Tradition!'' he snorted. ''What they really mean is atrophy. Black Jack Pershing was right. You can hear their arteries hardening halfway down the Hudson.''

''But Mark, you are the superintendent. Can't you make them do what you want?''

He shook his head in disgust. ''I thought I could. I thought it was going to be so easy. Just tell them what I want changed, and they'll do it. Tell them I want to drop useless courses such as geology and mineralogy and put in instruction in internal combustion engines, electricity, radio communications, aerodynamics, and so on. But no, my dearest, I have discovered that at West Point the superintendent proposes and the academic board disposes.''

''Is that what happened today?'' she asked, rising to pour herself another cocktail.

He watched her in dismay. ''You're not having another drink, are you dearest?''

She shrugged, flushing slightly. ''Just a halfie. George may have a heavy hand, but Marilyn always manages to hide the bottle.''

Mark frowned but said nothing. ''Yes, that's what happened today,'' he said. ''Same old frustration. George and me and one of the younger department heads voting one way, and the graybeards the other. Final score: them, six; us, three.'' He grimaced wryly. ''General Pershing never told me the super had only one vote, same as everyone else on the board. If I'd've known that, I doubt if I'd've come up here. Actually, the only real power I have is calling a meeting of the board. Like today. I told Lieutenant Bauer, Mike, to convene the board at four-thirty this afternoon. 'Four-thirty?' he said. 'The board usually meets at eleven to fix an agenda, and then breaks for lunch.' 'Not today,' I told him. 'I want them to come here hungry. And I'll starve them until I get what I want.' '' Mark pulled out his gold graduation watch and studied it. "I've got an hour to change," he mused. "Anyway, I didn't get what I wanted. They were obdurate. Old Colonel Goetzel interrupted me so many times while I was talking, I had to tell him to sit down and be quiet."

Betsy lifted her eyebrows in surprise. "Mark," she began slowly, carefully placing her empty glass on the end table beside her, "do you remember how President Wilson and the Senate were forever at each other's throats?"

"Of course," he said, puzzled.

"Then does it occur to you that the superintendent and the board might be just as hopelessly alienated? Each despises the other, and each is provoked by the other's tactics." Anger glinted briefly in Mark's dark eyes. But then an expression of patient control returned to his handsome features. "Please, Mark," Betsy continued. "Think: If you tried to win them over, maybe you'd be more successful. Perhaps you could take some of the less obstinate ones into your confidence."

Mark shook his head vehemently. "I am a general, Betsy, and a general has no confidants."

"But that's just the trouble, Mark. You used to be so gay and charming with people. But now . . ." She lifted her shoulders hopelessly. "Now, you're so . . . so aloof . . . You don't have any real friends."

"I am a general, Betsy," he repeated patiently, "and a general must be fair. And if thou wouldst be fair, my dearest, give up all hope of friendship."

"That's it!" Betsy cried, jumping to her feet and taking her empty glass to the sideboard to refill it. "That's just it! When I came here, I thought it was going to be wonderful. I always dreamed of being a general's lady, and at West Point my dream was coming true, the very place where we were married, the post I've always loved the most. But what happens? We go to a ball or a reception or whatever, and you dance the first dance with me and say a few words publicly, and then withdraw into yourself. Or else you excuse yourself because you have work to do, and leave me in care of Mike Bauer.'' She tilted back her head and drank. ''It's no dream, Mark, it's a nightmare. We have no friends . . . we don't socialize . . . we only go out when we have to . . . And all I do is sit here and . . . and . . .''

''And drink!'' Mark flung at her angrily, jumping erect and glaring scornfully at the glass in her hand. Grinding his teeth, he turned and strode toward the stairs. Behind him he heard a crash of glass. Turning, he saw Betsy standing in front of the fireplace, hands to her cheeks and sobbing. On the hearth in front of her lay the glittering shards of her smashed glass. Still sobbing, she eluded his outstretched arms and ran up the stairs to their bedroom.

Mark stood transfixed at the foot of the stairs. He could hear Betsy weeping. Then he heard Virginia's childish voice in the kitchen, and he became mortified, fearing that his daughter may have overheard the quarrel. He strode quickly into the kitchen. Sergeant Durkin was at the sink, alternating between drying dishes and fiddling with a crude crystal set on the windowsill. Virginia sat at the kitchen table, playing cards with Mrs. Delaplace.

''Six of diamonds,'' Mrs. Delaplace called, and Virginia pouted, took a card from her hand and flung it petulantly on the table. Mrs. Delaplace chuckled as she picked it up. ''Seven of diamonds,'' she said, and Virginia giggled. ''Go fish,'' she said. Mrs. Delaplace frowned. ''Now, Jinny,'' she scolded, ''I know you have that c—''

''Daddy!'' Virginia cried, seeing her father enter the kitchen. She jumped up, ran to him, and sprung into his arms. He kissed her and put her down, and she returned to her seat.

''Guess what we had in school today Daddy? The Civil War. The teacher let me tell the class all about Granpa. I told them how he was the youngest colonel in the war and all.''

''Attagirl! You're a Duggan through and through.'' Mark walked toward Sergeant Durkin, satisfied that Virginia had heard nothing. ''What's on the air, Pat?'' he asked, pointing to the squawking set on the windowsill. ''Jaysus, Gen'ral,'' Durkin muttered, ''I can't tell if it's a prizefight or a bull-fight. Them jabberers at the end, you'd think they'd learn the language before they put their fat flannel mouths up to the micryphone.''

"Pat," Mark said quietly, "I'd like you to call Major Peyton and tell him that something urgent has come up and Mrs. Duggan and I will be unable to dine with them tonight. Please convey my regrets." Durkin nodded and turned off the set. "Then bring the Pierce-Arrow around, Pat. I'd like to take a little drive."

A few minutes later General Duggan walked down the front steps to enter the sleek olive-green limousine waiting at the curb. He fitted a cigarette into his holder, lighted it, and blew smoke.

"Drive toward Storm King Mountain, Pat," he said. "I want to do a little thinking."

Durkin could see the glowing tip of the general's cigarette reflected in the rearview mirror. He slid shut the window separating the front from the rear seat and let out the clutch.

Mark felt slightly nauseous. He could stand hostility or conflict with anyone except someone he loved, and the quarrels with Betsy had been coming too frequently lately. Always, they were about her drinking. Every time he mentioned it, she flew into a white-faced rage. There was no reasoning with her, no way he could ever discuss what a drag a drinking wife could be on an officer's career. Nor could he explain that he had deliberately limited their social life for fear that she might make a fool of herself. So far, of course, Betsy had never staggered or fallen. But her speech was often thick and slurred, and she did use Sen-Sen to sweeten her breath. Mark always dreaded coming home from work, afraid that he might find her drunk on the kitchen floor. What to do? His wife was unquestionably what Colonel Wurzer called an "alcoholic."

"It is a sickness, like dementia praecox," the rotund little physician had explained to him. "They cannot help themselves. The only way they can control themselves is to stop. Completely. Forever."

But what to do? Douglas thought, winding down his window and thumb-flicking his cigarette out into the night. Divorce? Not in the United States Army. A divorced officer was an officer passed over. Besides, he was still fond of Betsy. And what of Virginia? But they couldn't go on like this. Obviously, it was going to get worse. There had to be some sol—

Tires screeched and Mark felt himself flung against the front seat. The car had braked to a stop, and Durkin was cursing savagely. Raising his head, Mark saw a pencil of light pierce the darkness ahead. It came toward them, around to the driver's window. A beam of light illuminated Durkin's angry face. Then it fell on a .45 service automatic pointed at the sergeant's head. Durkin wound down the window rapidly.

"What the hell is this?"

"Communist Collection Agency," a nasal voice called cheerily. "Hand me your wallet, please."

Mark was about to lower himself out of sight, hoping to open the farther back door quietly and slip up behind the highwayman—until he felt his own face framed in light.

The man with the pistol chuckled. "Naughty, naughty," he said, menacing Mark with the pistol. "Oh, my goodness, if it isn't an American army general. One of the mainstays of the established order."

"What's this all about?" Mark inquired evenly. "What's this 'Communist collection agency' business?"

"Simple, my dear general. I am the treasurer of the New York Chapter of the Socialist Workers Part—"

"You mean Bolsheviks," Mark cut in contemptuously.

"If you will. At the moment, we are out of funds. The easiest way to get money is to take it, the way Comrade Stalin kept the Russian party solvent by robbing banks. Therefore, my dear general, will you please be kind enough to give me your money?"

"No," Mark replied quietly.

"Give it to me," the man snarled, "or I'll fill you full of lead."

"Go ahead," Mark said evenly. "And when they catch you, they'll fry you in the Big House down below. Tell you what, though, bad man—I'll fight you for it. You'll never get it any other way, not as long as my name is Duggan."

"*Duggan!*" the man screamed "General Duggan? You filthy swine! You killed my best friend." Both men in the Pierce-Arrow stiffened, hearing the click of a hammer being drawn back. "I ought to shoot both of you dead," the man snarled.

"But my dear fellow, I don't understand," Mark said gently, softly sliding his hand toward the door handle.

"Yes, you do. That day at the Côte de Chatillon . . . When you and that other stinking coward in there took the ambulance mules and rode to the rear to save yourselves . . . My best friend died in the ambulance before we could get him to the hospital."

Mark was astonished. Instantly, he remembered that heartbreaking scene, and the skinny soldier sobbing and screaming curses at them as they rode away.

"I remember," he said. His voice was calm. The handle was firmly in his grasp now. But he wanted to keep the man talking. "Your friend's leg needed amputation. He was losing blood. But, soldier, you're mistaken. We didn't take the mules to save ourselves. We had to get to the front fast to give the order that won the victory and saved thousands of lives."

"Victory!" the man said scornfully. "What victory? You know damn well we fought the war to bail out the big bankers. You capitalist carrion!" He was shouting again. "We're going to kill every goddammed one of you. Generals! Bankers! Lawyers! All you bloated purple leeches sucking on the blood of the people."

"I see," Mark said, slowing turning the handle . . . "In the new order, you won't need generals or bankers or lawyers?"

There was a pause, as though the man were thinking of an answer. Then Mark flung the door open and jumped out onto the road. The pistol flamed and roared and Mark heard a smash of glass.

"After him, Pat!" he shouted as the pistol exploded again. Mark felt a painful thud on his forehead and thought that he had been shot. Then he realized that the man had thrown his flashlight at him.

"This way, sir!" Pat Durkin cried. "He's runnin' down through the woods."

Both men went thrashing through the underbrush, stumbling over the rocks and roots, clutching each other to keep from falling. Then they found a smooth path winding down through the trees and they realized that the gunman had escaped.

"Ah, give over, sir," Durkin wheezed. "He knows where

he is, and we don't. We'll never find the foul-mouthed son of Satan in these hills.''

"I guess you're right, Pat," Mark said, leading the way back to the limousine.

"Are yez going to notify the State Police, sir?" Durkin asked, closing the rear door behind the general and getting into the driver's seat.

"No, Pat. They'd never find him either. Anyway, I want to find him myself, my own way."

"In the sweet name of Jaysus, Gen'ral, how will yez be doin' that?"

"You remember Captain Baugh?"'

"Indeed I do. 'Twas his company made the raid at Luneville. And a darlin' fighter he was too."

"He was. And he is now a successful New York stock-broker, besides being a National Guard major and the president of the Rainbow Division Association. I want you to go down to see him, Pat. You remember that day at Chatillon. Buncie's Iowans were attacking on the right. This man sounds like an Iowan. You could almost smell corn growing in that twang of his. Buncie had two battalions in assault. Judging from where we found the mules, this man and his buddy must have come from the left battalion. Of the battalion's companies, only two were in assault, and of them, only four platoons, and maybe, in the end, only eight squads or less than a hundred men in the point were actually fighting. So it should be easy to locate the Iowa soldier whose leg was torn off that day and died from loss of blood, and then his buddy. Those Rainbow regiments were all National Guard, you know, all with close hometown ties. This company came from this county, and this squad from this town. That sort of thing. It shouldn't be hard at all to find our man."

"The way you put it, sir, it should be easy indeed. When would yez like me to go?"

"Tomorrow morning, Pat," Mark said, gingerly fingering the bruise on his forehead.

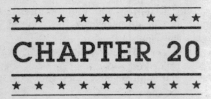
Within a few weeks of the incident at Storm King Mountain, General Duggan had the information he desired. Major Baugh called him by telephone from New York City.

"His name is Henry Hawkins, sir," Baugh said. "He comes from a little college town in Iowa called Grinnell. In fact, he was graduated from Grinnell just before the war. When you saw him at the Côte de Chatillon, General, you probably didn't realize he was an officer. A second looey. The man who died was in his platoon." Baugh paused. "Do you want me to go slow, sir, so you can write this down? Or do you want to have someone else write it?"

"Neither, Major," Duggan said, unconsciously fingering the thick scab on his forehead where the flashlight had struck. "I'll remember this a long time. Incidentally, Bill—how's the market doing?"

"Beautiful! Boom! Boom! Boom! Day after day. I'm making so much money, General, it's hard for me to believe I used to sweep up the sawdust in the Fulton Fish Market." Duggan laughed and Baugh continued: "Anyway, this Hawkins fellow, he seems to have been okay as a kid. No police record or anything like that. He was always joining movements, though. A big La Follette fan, street-corner protests, passing out political pamphlets—that sort of thing. Very active in campus politics too. How the hell he ever wound up in the AEF, I'll never know. His father, now, was a little different. A real scamp. A boozer and a pool-hall hustler. Apparently, he never worked a day in his life. Spent his time hustling the college kids. Gave his wife just enough money for herself and her son, and spent the rest on booze and loud clothes for himself." The captain paused again, and Duggan could hear the rustle of notepaper over the phone. "The mother, now, sir, she was a different kettle of fish. Very active in the local Methodist church. A temperance crusader. In fact, she was the Iowa delegate to the national convention of the Women's Christian Temperance Union."

Mark Duggan chuckled.

"Excuse me, sir?"

"Nothing, Baugh. Nothing at all. It just fits so perfectly, that's all. Go on, please."

"Some friends of mine on the force located him in the city, sir. He's living in a cold-water flat on the East Side. it's what the Commies call a cell. The local cops call it the Zoo, though. They're all in there together—free love, eat from the common pot, that kind of stuff, sir. This fellow Hawkins, a couple of niggers, a Russian sailor, a French waitress, and a rich kid from Radcliffe College in Boston. At least she was rich, sir. She was the angel for this cell, until her old man threw her out. The old man owns a textile mill in Massachusetts, and they just had a strike there. So he doesn't like Commies. Anyway, General, I guess that was when Henry Hawkins oiled up his forty-five and hit the highway."

"Probably. Thank you, Baugh. A very good job. Excellent. In fact, I'm so pleased, I'm going to have this bit of intelligence work accepted as your project in the Guard this year."

"Oh, thank you, sir."

"Not at all. Come spring, Baugh, those gold leaves of yours will be changing into silver."

"I can't tell you how grateful I am, General. Do you wish to move in on this Hawkins, sir? I mean, if you want to prefer charges or anything, I have a lot of friends on the force."

"No, thank you. I have what I want now. Thanks again, Baugh," he said, and hung up.

That night, before dinner, Mark told Betsy of Baugh's

report. They had forgotten, or at least they had pretended to forget, Betsy's tantrum of two weeks ago. And Betsy no longer drank before dinner. She did, however, make frequent trips to the kitchen to check the meal being prepared by the cook, going from there to the pantry, where she kept a pint bottle with a vanilla label on it filled with Canadian whiskey. She also kept a bottle in the water tank of the toilet off their bedroom. Because of his immense relief not to see Betsy with a glass in her hand, Mark neither suspected nor questioned her kitchen visits.

"A born hater," he said to Betsy after he had finished telling her about Hawkins. He touched the scab on his forehead. "The pages of history are full of neurotics like him. I tell you, Betsy, the broken or disturbed home is the nursery of the revolutionary. He grows up off balance and hating. Like that half-mad consumptive who killed Archduke Ferdinand. Full of pain and hatred, he fires the shot that kills twenty million people."

"Twenty *million*," Betsy repeated, aghast.

"Yes, twenty million—and that's not counting the German civilians starved to death by the British blockade. but I tell you, you find the unstable mind—usually the *brilliant*, unstable mind—overturning things everywhere in history. Occasionally for better, but usually for worse. Look at that fellow Ulyanov, or Lenin, as he calls himself. The czar executes his brother, so he hates the established order. He destroys it, with nothing to put in its place. So the commissar replaces the czar and he beats the people with scorpions instead of whips. Just like Jonathan sa—"

"—Roboam," Betsy interrupted, giggling.

"All right, Roboam. Same with this Stalin. A shoemaker's son forced to study for the priesthood. But he hates the society that scorned his father, and breaks out of the priesthood hating religion. Same with Talleyrand. They make him take the priestly oaths and he swears under his breath he'll make 'em regret it. And indeed he did, after he busted out as a bishop in the French Revolution. Hatred, Betsy—that's what turns the world upside down. If you ask me, hatred is more efficacious than love."

"I don't know, Mark—what about Jesus?"

"True. But he had a lot of hatred, or at least anger, in him too. He was always talking love and meekness, but he was sure handy with a whip himself. And the names he called the Pharisees!''

''Blasphemy!'' Betsy cried in mock horror. ''Be careful you don't get stoned, Mark. Anyway, forget Mr. Henry Hawkins and his hatred for a minute, and listen to the great news I have for you.''

''What's that?'' Mark said, sticking a cigarette in his holder and lighting it.

''Charley Bailey has found a way to beat the Navy.''

''You don't mean it!''

''I do. He's going to bring Beau Ames up from the plebes.''

''But he can't do that! Plebes aren't allowed to play varsity sports.''

''Yes they can,'' Betsy said stoutly. ''Charley says they can. He wants to talk to you about it.'' She got to her feet, preparing a visit to the kitchen—and to the pantry. ''He's coming over after dinner.''

''I got the idea this afternoon, General,'' the football coach explained. ''Babcock, our regular fullback, snapped his achilles tendon. You could hear it go up in the bleachers. The whole team groaned when they realized what had happened. It'll take months to heal, sir—and Navy's only two weeks away. Well, that was when one of the kids said, 'Let's put Babby's number on that Ames kid and let him play in his place.' That was when I got the idea, sir. Not that way, of course—that wouldn't be right.''

''But Charley,'' Duggan interjected, slowly rolling the Havana cigar the coach had given him between his fingers, ''plebes can't play varsity ball.''

''Freshman can't at all the other colleges,'' the coach said. ''But at Army, plebes can. It's been done before.''

''When?''

''During the war, and when Oliphant was here. He played four years at Purdue and four years at Army. In fact, I remember the Notre Dame kids used to tease Oliphant about the stripes on the sleeve of his jersey. They said each one stood for a year of college football.''

''You're sure, Charley—there is a precedent?''

"Dead sure." Bailey grinned slyly. "All we need is the superintendent's okay."

The general smiled again, taking the cigar from his mouth and studying it with approval. "They're both okay, Charley," he said, chuckling. "This—and that."

The news that the plebe football star would play against Navy in the varsity game of the year electrified the Cadet Corps. A week earlier than usual, jubilant cadets began turning bedsheets into banners. Soon the window ledges of the gray stone neo-Gothic dormitories blossomed with hanging squares of white linen beseeching the team to SINK THE NAVY! or SWAB THE GOBS! One standard said briefly, GO BEAU! General Duggan saw them next morning as he strode to his office clad in his smart, nonregulation short coat, swinging his swagger stick.

Major George Peyton was waiting for him inside. "The corps seems happy, George," Duggan said.

Peyton frowned. "They won't be, sir, when they hear what I have to tell you." He closed the office door and said: "Professor Goetzel has accused the plebe football team of cheating on their test."

Duggan went behind his desk and sat down, silent and aghast. He fitted a cigarette into his holder and lighted it, quietly smoking and thinking. A cheating scandal was the worst thing that could happen to a superintendent at West Point. He knew, if only because he had lived through one. A West Point cheating scandal had the unhappy faculty of binding together the country's queerest bedfellows: nudists, antimilitarists, isolationists, free-silver advocates, pacifists, homosexuals, Quakers, vegetarians, feminists, teetotalers, millenarians, nature lovers, anarchists, religious fundamentalists, food faddists, single-taxers, and so on—all joined in a common hatred of the United States Military Academy, and all crying for its elimination as the first step in their own programs.

Duggan passed a hand across his forehead. As he remembered, cheating scandals usually ended in the relief of the superintendent. To head off such a development, one of his first acts as superintendent had been to appoint a committee of cadets to draw up their own honor code. They had, and at the heart of the code was the stipulation that no cadet would lie or cheat or tolerate such dishonesty in another cadet. And here it was being challenged scarcely a year after its adoption! Duggan looked up at Major Peyton, standing expectantly in front of him.

"What does Colonel Goetzel say?" he asked in a low, controlled voice.

"He says he thinks that Cadet Beauregard Ames is the ringleader."

"Ames?" Duggan repeated in a voice choked with disbelief. But then, aware of Major Peyton's blue eyes studying him, he lifted a hand and said, "Go on, George."

"He says that Ames and others gave answers they couldn't possibly give, judging from their prior performance. He particularly suspects Ames because he says he has been especially inattentive in class the past week. He's been yawning, and twice he actually fell asleep."

"Has he any hard evidence?"

"None that I know of, sir. You see, the problem was a variable one. You could come up with a single answer—a perfect, or beautiful, solution—or a series of related answers. Either would be correct, but the beautiful solution, of course, would be . . . well, beautiful. That's what Ames and about a half dozen other football players got. Goetzel swears that they could only have gotten it by copying."

Duggan frowned. "All right, George. Please tell Colonel Goetzel not to mention this to anyone. I will be in touch with him. In the meantime, send Ames in to see me."

For perhaps ten poignantly agonizing minutes, Mark Duggan sat in his chair reflecting. His mind traveled back twenty years to the paddle wheeler in San Francisco Bay and the bruised and battered corporal swaying on the dock above him. He could see Captain Courland standing in front of the company at Balangiga calmly ordering the execution of Ames and Durkin . . . He could still hear the chattering roar of the spinning Gatling gun and the screams of the toppling Insurrectos . . . He could see Sergeant Ames come reeling out of the melee at Camp Mills and hear his choked, dying voice gasping: "My . . . son . . . he . . . wants . . . to be . . . a . . . officer." And now that son stood accused of a transgression, which, if proved, would destroy forever his father's dying hopes; and which also might irrevocably wreck the career of

General Mark Duggan. Duggan knew that if the slightest imputation of favoritism was attached to him, he was finished. Momentarily, he also realized how much the Cadet Corps' desire for a victory over Navy depended on the presence of Beau Ames in the Army backfield. In the next instant he dismissed the thought as trivial by comparison. Winning a game could never compare to ruining a future or wrecking a great career.

The office door opened, held by Lieutenant Bauer. Beau Ames marched past him to snap to attention in front of General Duggan. His gray cap held proudly under his arm, he saluted briskly. Duggan studied him. Although his blond hair was close-cropped, as required in a cadet, Duggan knew that when it grew out, it would be like the luxuriant tawny mass that had crowned his father's head. Duggan felt sad.

"Cadet Ames," he said sternly, "Professor Goetzel has made serious charges against you. He has accused you and other members of the plebe football team of cheating on your tests."

Beau Ames turned white. His blue eyes widened in horror. "Ch-Ch-Cheating?" he stammered. "Me, sir?" His chin lifted proudly. "I've never cheated in my life!"

"Colonel Goetzel says you and the others gave perfect answers you could not possibly have given on your own. He believes you copied from someone else."

"But, sir—there was a monitor in the classroom all the time!" Ames sucked in his breath. He seemed to be recollecting something. "I can explain, sir," he burst out eagerly. "Professor Goetzel summoned me to his quarters a few days ago. He was angry with me for falling asleep in his class. He wanted an explanation." Cadet Ames looked at General Duggan appealingly. "May I . . . may I explain to you why, sir? I never did get a chance to tell Professor Goetzel." Duggan nodded, and Beau rushed on. "You see, Coach Bailey had me practicing with the varsity all week. I had to learn new plays and how to play Babcock's position. Day after day, sir, he had me carrying the ball." Once again the youth's eyes were appealing. "Some nights, sir, I'd fall asleep at the mess table, I was that tired."

General Duggan spun in his chair and looked out the window. It *was* unfair, he knew it was unfair, to subject the football players to those grueling daily practices and then expect them to maintain the same academic standing as the other cadets. But he betrayed no sympathy. "Go on," he said gruffly.

"That's what I wanted to tell Professor Goetzel, sir. Only he wasn't in his quarters. There was a corporal there who told me the professor had turned his ankle and had gone to the infirmary. I was to wait for him." Beauregard Ames swallowed. "Well, sir, there was this problem on the blackboard. I studied it. I don't know how long it took me, sir, but I think I got the answer pretty quick." He blushed, stammering shyly. "I . . . I have a kind of thing that way, sir. Music and math . . . I just seem to understand them. Then another corporal came in and said they'd taped the professor's ankle and sent him home. The corporal told me I could leave. And I did." He swallowed again. "The . . . the problem I saw—that was the one on the test." Once again his chin lifted proudly. "But I'd've got the same answer, sir! Whether I'd seen it before or not, I just would've known the answer."

"I believe you," General Duggan said simply, impressed by the young man's sincerity. "But what about the others? How did they get the answer?"

Beau Ames reddened. "I . . . I don't know, sir."

"Now, I don't believe you," Duggan said sharply. "Either you told them in advance, or they copied from your paper. Which was it?"

Beau shook his head doggedly, unaware that his hands at his side were clenched into fists. "Neither, sir," he said. "I just don't know."

Duggan felt sorry for the youth standing so miserably before him. He knew that the cadet's loyalty to his corps went even deeper than the code of honor. He remembered his own ordeal as a cadet before the hazing board of inquiry more than two decades ago. He had refused to obey the order to name his tormentors, escaping expulsion only because he had become sick and fainted. Now the dreadful command was issuing from his own lips.

"Cadet Ames," he said sternly. "I am ordering you to tell me the truth."

"I . . . I am, sir."

"Cadet Ames, I am suspending you and the other plebes suspected in this matter from the Academy. Until I—"

Duggan stopped in astonishment. Thick tears were rolling down the youth's cheeks. His lips and nostril were quivering. "You mean I can't p-play against Navy? The whole c-corps is depending on me."

"If you obey my order you can."

Beau Ames said nothing, standing there stony-faced.

"Until the board is ready to conduct a hearing, you will remain in your quarters."

Beauregard Ames saluted, about-faced, and left. Duggan watched him go, his own large dark eyes full of misery. Why had he been forced to choose between himself and the son of the man who had saved his life?

"But why, Mark—why?" Betsy Duggan sobbed that night. She had begun to cry the moment her husband had started to tell her about suspending Cadet Ames.

"Betsy, I do not understand you, the way you're taking this."

"His father saved your life," she shot back reproachfully.

"For his son to wreck my career?"

"Career!" she snorted, dabbing at her reddened eyes with a balled-up handkerchief. "Can't you forget just once that you're a general, and try to be a human being?"

"Betsy!"

"Oh, I'm sorry. I . . . I didn't mean . . ." She began to cry again. "Do you *have* to suspend him? Can't you wait until after the Navy game? The whole corps will hate you."

"I can't help that. It's my duty. Don't forget the motto here: 'Duty, Honor, Coun—' "

"Oh, I know," she cut in dully, dabbing at her eyes again. "I found out about that on the first day of our honeymoon."

"I don't understand you, Betsy," he cried in exasperation. "You know very well what old Colonel Goetzel would do if I let them off."

"That horrid old hermit! He hasn't been off the reservation once since the day he got his tenure. He's just jealous of Beau's popularity."

"That may be, but he has influence. He's been teaching here for decades, and he keeps up an enormous correspondence with his old pupils. He could make trouble for me." He looked at her in bewilderment. "Why does this boy mean so much to you? You'd think he was..." His voice trailed off.

Betsy rose from her living room chair and walked to the window. "I knew his father," she said dully, over her shoulder.

Mark was dumbfounded. "*You knew* Beau Ames?"

"Yes. When I was a young girl out in Camp Robinson." She turned to face him. "Oh, there was nothing between us. You know that." She paused, blushing. "You know what happened on our wedding night." Now Mark blushed. "I was just a lonely young girl, and he was young, too, for a soldier. I guess I had a crush on him."

"Why didn't you tell me?"

"Have I ever told you of anyone before I met you?"

He said nothing, still amazed that Betsy had known Beau. She walked toward the kitchen, and he put out a gentle hand to restrain her. "No, Betsy," he said softly, "there's real vanilla in the vanilla bottle now." She swung on him in white-faced rage. "When you were over at Mimi Bauer's the other day, Jinny and I decided to bake a cake. When I opened the vanilla bottle, it smelled funny."

Betsy seized an ashtray from an end table and drew back her arm to fling it against the fireplace. Then she dropped it, covered her face with her hands, and began to whimper.

"I... I can't help it, Mark. I have to have a drink or I won't go to sleep... If, if I don't sleep, I see that awful shark again... I *see* him, Mark!" she wailed. "I actually *see* him."

He put a protective arm around her quivering shoulder. "I understand, my dearest," he murmured, stroking her hair. "But please, if you stop, or at least try to stop, I'll do what I can for young Ames." She put down her hands and looked at him eagerly through her tears.

"R-Really?"

"Yes. I'll lift his suspension and face it out with old Goetzel." He shrugged. "I don't know about the others. They'll have to prove how they got the answer. But I do believe that Ames came by it honestly. He's got that kind of mind. George Peyton says he has."

"Oh, Mark!" she cried, hugging him, beginning to weep

again, but this time tears of happiness. "I promise! I really promise!"

That night, he came to her bed for the first time since she smashed the cocktail glass against the fireplace. When he returned to his own bed and fell asleep, Betsy went to the bathroom to take a drink from the bottle in the water tank.

Beauregard Ames did play against the Navy, and the Army football team did gain its first victory in years. He played an inspired game. His bare blond head could be seen all over the field, plunging into the line, making tackles, catching passes—bringing the cadets repeatedly to their feet, leaving them hoarse and limp and delirious with joy.

The following night at dinner, after the corps had returned to West Point, word passed quietly among the still-joyous cadets that there would be a "shirttail parade" to celebrate the triumph. Such demonstrations, of course, were expressly forbidden; yet, promptly at midnight, the cadets gathered boisterously on the Plains. Their shirttails flying, shouting in delight, they snake-danced past the superintendent's and the commandant's house and then onto the site of old Fort Clinton. There, they built a huge bonfire and put out sentries against the chance that authority had not abdicated for the occasion. But it had. Unmolested, the cadets produced musical instruments and a bottle or two of Canadian and celebrated until dawn.

In the morning, Commandant Peyton came into General Duggan's office for his regular morning conference. Duggan grinned at him. "Was that your party I heard last night, George?"

"No, sir," Peyton said, grinning himself.

"You didn't skin 'em, did you, George?"

"Hell, no, I didn't! I damn well wanted to go over and join 'em!"

Duggan chuckled, then his voice turned serious. "It was great while it lasted, George—but now I've got bad news." He spun in his chair and looked sadly out the window, toward Trophy Point and the broad gray Hudson. "I'm leaving, George," he said in a voice husky with emotion.

"No!"

"Yes. General Pershing called this morning. He congratulated me on the victory over Navy, and then he told me that old Goetzel has been writing letters." Peyton flushed and opened his mouth to swear, but Duggan held up a hand. "He's threatening to press charges against me for what he calls covering up a cheating scandal. Goetzel isn't easy to ignore, George—he has influence. Anyway, as you know, General Pershing doesn't waste words. He told me straight out that a cheating scandal was the last thing he could stand right now, with the trouble he's having with Congress getting funds for the Academy. He didn't thank me, or anything like that—not Black Jack Pershing—but he did tell me that I was being reassigned without prejudice."

"Take you out of the impact area, is that it, sir?"

"Probably. And placate Goetzel at the same time." He sighed. "Just when we were making headway. Just when we were letting a little fresh air into this musty old military convent."

Major George Peyton nodded ruefully. "It's a goddam shame," he muttered angrily, but then he grinned, his white teeth flashing in his sunburned face. "But, goddammit, General, at least we beat the Navy!"

WASHINGTON

CHAPTER 21

"Are you nervous?" Betsy asked, settling back beside Mark in the rear of the White House limousine.

"No," Mark said, chuckling. "Why should I be? I always knew I'd get there."

"Maybe you're not nervous, Daddy, but I am," Virginia Duggan said.

Mark chuckled again, and Betsy spoke up sharply. "Did you get rid of that chewing gum, Virginia?"

"You bet. I wasn't going to take any chances on swallowing it when I met old Frozen Face."

"Virginia!" Betsy exclaimed sharply, glancing at the chauffeur. "That's no way to talk about the President."

"Oh, I don't care," Virginia said petulantly. "I still think he's made of ice."

Betsy said nothing, if only because she knew Mark would take Virginia's part. After all, she thought, it just wasn't proper for a fifteen-year-old girl to be sitting up front with the chauffeur like that. But Virginia had insisted, and Mark, as usual, had let her have her way. It still wasn't very ladylike, Betsy thought, especially when you realized that in half an hour President Hoover would be swearing in Mark as chief of staff of the United States Army.

"You know, I never lost confidence," Mark said musingly, gazing out the window of the limousine.

Again, Betsy kept silent. Maybe you didn't, Mark dear, she thought, but I did.

These had been the desperate years—between their departure from West Point and the wonderful letter from the White House. In 1924, when the War Department gave Mark leave to lead the U.S. Olympic team to Holland, she had thought he was being gently pushed aside and his career was over. But not Mark. He had regarded the assignment as an opportunity to shine from a different angle. His handsome face had been so often in the newspapers, and the United States team had done so well, that even sports-indifferent President Coolidge had sent him a public letter of congratulations. And so, his second star!

Betsy, meanwhile, left alone with Virginia, had begun to drink heavily again. And then the dreary years in the Philippines, with nothing but Jinny and Spanish brandy to console her. It was in Manila that Betsy regularized her drinking. She was careful not to get drunk, at least not falling-down drunk. She rose early, singing and whistling in the kitchen, starting each day with orange juice laced with two ounces of brandy. By noon she was slightly tipsy, and she would retire for a long nap. Rising in the late afternoon, she needed only a few nips to last until dinner with Mark, after which she retired again.

Betsy had clever hiding places for her brandy all over the house. Besides the toilet water tank, which Mark never discovered, she also had a bottle tied to a rope lying in the thick shrubbery under her window. The other end of the rope was coiled around a nail outside her window. Betsy knew that Mark had Sergeant Durkin search her room periodically, but Pat never did think to look outside the window. Why should he? She never hauled up the bottle until after dark. Usually, she was alone at night, while Mark spent his evenings with Manuel Quezon, the rising Nacionalista leader. He seldom took her anywhere, except to some official function at which her absence would be noticed. Their personal relationship was not yet cold, even though they slept in separate bedrooms. It was cordial, sometimes warm again, when they would talk together, either about Mark's career or Virginia.

Betsy's eyes strayed to Virginia in the front seat. It was in Manila that Jinny had become spoiled rotten, she thought. All those servants . . . and never a harsh word from her doting father. That was the defect of his virtue of confidence, Betsy decided: He would not believe, did not want to hear, bad news; nor would he suffer criticism of anyone or thing he loved or cherished. So Virginia had become a beautiful and spoiled creature—forgetting her own neglect and preoccupation with the bottle—spoiled and promiscuous. Betsy glanced again at Virginia gazing rapturously at the handsome young chauffeur in White House livery. That was Virginia! Anything good-looking in a uniform . . . Betsy remembered how Jinny, even at six, actually adored young Beauregard Ames. She remembered, too, the day she found her in the kitchen necking with the Filipino houseboy. She was only twelve then. Betsy had not dared to mention it to Mark. He would have been furious—at her, not Jinny. He simply would have refused to believe it. There were similar incidents, with Virginia growing more brazen each time.

When she had begun to menstruate, Betsy had deliberately taken her to her old friend and physician, Colonel McCarthy; ostensibly for an examination and instruction in vaginal hygiene, actually to find out whether or not Virginia was still a virgin. Damn Mike McCarthy and his parochial education, Betsy thought—he wouldn't tell her anything. But she could guess from his evasiveness that her daughter was an experienced wo—

She heard Mark gasp beside her, his hand gripping her wrist. "The New Willard!" he cried, pointing outside. "Where my father died . . . where he . . . where he told me to . . . where I took you to lunch . . . It's gone!" There was sadness in his voice. "It's all different," he murmured. "The Washington we knew is gone." A trolley car rattled past, and he waited for the noise to subside. "Remember the last time we drove down Pennsylvania Avenue to the White House?"

"I do indeed," Betsy said. "It was at the reception for General Bean."

"We rode in a horse-and-carriage then," he said wistfully, watching with unhappy eyes as the chauffeur patiently guided his vehicle through the late-afternoon press of motor traffic. "Remember all the footmen in livery and the royal crests, the horses and the plumed helmets? All the dynasties . . . all that pomp and privilege . . ."

"Yep. All blown away by Big Bertha, just like you said. My, you were in a philosophical mood that night, Mark. I've never forgotten it."

"I wish I'd been wrong," he said gloomily. "The old regime is gone, and in its place we've got less freedom and less bread. Just like I said." He sighed. The limousine had stopped for a red light. "Traffic lights," he muttered. "I think the horses were faster. Anyway, the men at Versailles had it all backward. Nationalism, they said—that would give the world more freedom. So what have we got? Nationalism that's dictatorial—what Mussolini calls Fascism. The enemy of freedom."

"There's that awful Hitler in Germany too," Betsy put in.

"Yes. I remember when I took the Olympic team to Holland. The Dutch were terrified of that fellow. You know, they regard the Germans as their cousins. They understand them. They kept telling me that a mad mystic like Hitler would be bad for Germany, for the world, if he ever came to power. And now he's reaching for it. He was in jail then. He'd tried to pull some crazy coup in Munich and failed. But he's out now—"

Mark stopped. The White House porte cochere was in view. He felt faintly nauseous, thinking of the swearing-in ceremony. "Japan's caught the disease too," he muttered. "That's the last thing Manuel Quezon said to me when we left Manila. 'Go with God, my friend,' he said, 'but I think you will be back.' When I asked him why, he said: 'Japan. You will have to fight Japan. She needs oil and raw materials, and you are raising your prices. Soon, rather than go bankrupt, she will take what she needs—and you will have to fight her.'"

"I always liked Manuel Quezon," Betsy murmured. "He's smart."

Betsy gasped. They were passing in front of the White House. A soup kitchen had been set up on the broad sidewalk alongside the iron fence, and a long silent file of gaunt-faced men and women in ragged clothes moved slowly through it. They held out bowls and metal army canteen cups to be filled with a thick, steaming gruel ladled out to them from huge tureens.

"My God, Mark, look!" Betsy cried in a quavering voice. "I can't believe it! In Washington, practically on the steps of the White House—a soup kitchen!"

"Yes," Mark said grimly. "And if you go out to the edge

of the city, you'll see the hobo jungles and the shantytowns. All along the railroad tracks. Every city has them. And half the men who live there wear business suits—like the laborers we saw building the retaining wall in San Francisco Bay. Manual labor was the only work they could get, and they were glad to get it."

Betsy shuddered, tearing her anguished eyes away from the defeated faces of her countrymen. "Less freedom in Europe," she muttered, "and now, everywhere in the world, less bread. Do you think the Depression will ever end, Mark?"

He shook his head, leaning gently sideways as the limousine turned into the White House grounds. "No," he said grimly, "not without a war, it won't."

President Hoover tried to smile cheerfully when he entered the Oval Room where General Duggan and his wife awaited him. But he could not—he was in a somber mood. There was a hint of sadness in the cold blue eyes sunk in his puffy, muffin cheeks. He, too, had seen the soup kitchen, set up only that morning on his orders. Herbert Hoover, however, would do nothing or next to nothing to alter American society. He might prescribe a palliative, like a soup kitchen, for the hunger that was one of the symptoms of unemployment; but he would not attack the disease itself by creating jobs. Government intervention in the country's economy was anathema to him, stinking of socialism. Hoover was a rugged individualist. He had, in fact, written a little book eulogizing that simple creed. And so, clinging stubbornly to an era as outmoded as the high, hard collars that he wore, he had sorrowfully called for the soup kitchen.

The President did smile wanly when General Duggan introduced his wife and daughter. "These are for your husband," the President said, handing Betsy four gold stars.

While photographer's bulbs popped and flashed, Betsy stood on tiptoe to pin two more stars next to the pair on the shoulder lapels of her husband's uniform. Then she kissed him fondly. Mark glanced at the four stars on his right shoulder and smiled. He shook hands with the President. Hoover was surprised to see tears in the eyes of his chief of staff.

"It was my father's wish," General Duggan explained.

"You see, sir, eighteen years ago he died in my arms right up the street in the New Willard Hotel. His last words urged me to carry the family name higher. He was a lieutenant general then, Mr. President—three stars." Duggan's proud dark eyes fell once more on his shoulder strap. "Now I've got four."

President Hoover nodded agreeably. But he was still surprised. Religious pacifist that he was, he found tenderness in a military man really inconceivable.

Mark Duggan took over as chief of staff with the greatest enthusiasm and the highest optimism. He saw his task as being essentially one of modernizing and reorganizing the Army. He soon found, however, that his real struggle was to save it from the onslaughts of the pacifists and the penny-pinching members of Congress. Again and again, his voice grim, he would tell Major Mike Bauer and Colonel George Peyton, both of whom he had brought to Washington: "Our job is to save the Army."

However, he quickly discovered, as he had at West Point, that saying was much easier than doing. The growth of the pacifist movement in America amazed him. It was not merely pacifist or antiwar, it was, with all the belligerence seemingly inherent in pacifism, violently antimilitary. Within a few weeks General Duggan and his aides put aside their uniforms for civilian clothes, rather than continue to endure the hostile glances and muttered insults of their countrymen. Again and again, Duggan was horrified to hear reports of uniformed soldiers and officers being attacked by crowds of angry, ordinarily law-abiding, civilians.

Within months Duggan realized that he had become the chief whipping boy of American pacifism. Probably, this was because of his habit of traveling across the country to make speeches warning against the consequences of non-violence. He hammered away at one undeviating theme: "You cannot stop war by disarming yourself, any more than you can stop fires or crime by scrapping the fire and police departments." He had especial scorn for the Kellogg-Briand Pact "outlawing war." Pacifists and isolationists had been delighted when this Franco-American treaty "renouncing war" had been signed by nearly every nation in the world, including the Soviet Union, Germany, Italy, and Japan. By the time

Duggan became chief of staff, however, Japan had already invaded China in the province of Manchuria; Italy, where Mussolini had solved the problem of unemployment by putting all people out of work into the army, was manifestly preparing to invade Africa; Germany was about to march again under the crooked black cross of Hitler's Nazi Party; and the Soviet Union was rapidly arming, with emphasis on tanks developed from a discarded American design.

Whenever General Duggan reminded his countrymen of these unpleasant realities, particularly at the big universities, he found himself booed and heckled and pelted with rotten eggs and fruit. Sometimes his limousine was attacked by crowds of protestors, and once he had to shout at Sergeant Durkin and strike him with his swagger stick to keep him from leaping out of the driver's seat to seize a bearded student who spat on the windshield and called Duggan a "blood-drinking warmonger." Eventually, the liberal journals, and particularly, to Duggan's pained surprise, the liberal Protestant press, joined the outcry against him. He was regularly caricatured in the daily newspapers as a pair of small polished boots and the tip of a dripping sword peeping out from under a huge, bullet-riddled campaign hat, his cherished "war bonnet," which had become famous in the World War. Also, to his intense and bitter anger, a story had circulated stating that he had once run away from battle riding an ambulance mule, as a result of which a dozen soldiers in the immobilized ambulance died. Duggan knew where that came from.

Henry Hawkins, whose career he checked periodically, had became a columnist for a New York newspaper, before moving into the State House in Albany as a special assistant to Governor Franklin Delano Roosevelt. There was not much Duggan could do about a man under the wing of a protector as powerful as Roosevelt, who even then, in late 1931, was generally considered to be the front-runner for the Democratic presidential nomination.

Unpleasant as the pacifist outcry was to swallow, it did not equal the material challenge to the Army rising from congressmen who, alarmed at a treasury depleted by the Depression, sought to make the deepest economies at the expense of the armed forces. To them, General Duggan repeatedly appealed to history, gravely calling the roll of nations and empires, of captains and kings, who had gone down to death and defeat as a result of their reluctance to spend money on their armed forces.

"If you had nothing left in the national treasury but enough money to ensure your national defense," he told the House subcommittee on military appropriations, "you should spend it on national defense—or lose the freedom that we cherish, the freedom that is the one liberating, exhilarating difference between ourselves and most of the rest of the world."

Duggan's impassioned eloquence, however, did not persuade many congressmen, and there were some who resented it as a little too high-flown for their cracker-barrel tastes.

Other, unexpected, and perhaps more serious opposition, came from Representative Moss Connors of Mississippi, chairman of the powerful subcommittee on military appropriations. Connors was an air-power enthusiast and also a crusader for mechanization of the Army. He repeatedly clashed with Duggan, frequently parading his own truly extensive knowledge of military affairs.

"Are you familiar with the writings of Captain B. H. Liddell Hart?" he asked Duggan at a hearing one day.

"I am, sir. And with those of his commanding officer, Colonel Fuller, and those of Colonel Charles de Gaulle in France."

Connors nodded, his bright, beady blue eyes staring out of his red, foxlike face. "And are they not agreed that the next war will be one of mechanized forces, of speed and movement?"

"They are sir, And I happen to agree with them."

"Then why, General, does the Army's budget allocate so much for troops and officers and bases and so little for tanks and airplanes?"

"Mr. Chairman," Duggan said, breathing deeply in open exasperation, "I have answered that question a dozen times before. We simply do not have enough money for both. We do not even have enough money for troops and bases." Duggan fixed the ruddy Connors with the direct gaze of his expressive eyes. "You will remember, sir, that in 1920 Congress fixed the Army's minimum size consistent with national safety at 18,000 officers and 285,000 enlisted men. We are now down to 12,000 officers and 125,000 men. We have barely enough money to support this tiny army. Among the armies in the world, America's ranks the sixteenth in size. Yet, Mr. Chairman, we are fourth in population and first in wealth. Even so, Mr. Chairman, with so little money, we have tried to siphon off funds for tanks and airplanes. But we have never been able to do more than build a pilot model or two before we run out of money. One airplane, sir, can cost as much as an entire regiment."

"But General," Connors persisted, "wouldn't it be better, in the war of movement of the future, to have the tanks and airplanes rather than so many troops?"

"So *many*!" Duggan exclaimed in disbelief. Then, recovering his composure: "Mr. Chairman, I do not wish to go down in history as the Marshal of Oz. I do not wish to command a mechanical army that is defeated because there are no human beings around to wind them up or pump gas into them. Tanks and airplanes with no one to drive or fly them are of very little use. But a trained, disciplined, professional cadre army that can be quickly expanded into the huge conscript army of the future, that is worth every little red cent that we can get. In an emergency, I am sure, American industry can turn out the tanks and airplanes. But in an emergency, sir, no power on earth can make an efficient fighting force out of an untrained mob."

"Thank you, General Duggan," Connors said tonelessly, reaching for his gavel as though to bring the day's hearings to a close. But then, glancing at the itemized budget on the table before him, he put his finger on one line. "General," he said, "there's an entry here for $150,000 for sanitary tissue. What is sanitary tissue?"

"Toilet paper," Duggan replied evenly, ignoring the snickers rising faintly in the hearing room.

"Toilet paper!" Connors exclaimed, his crooked little teeth grinning evilly in his red cheeks. "What does the Army need all that toilet paper f—"

General Duggan rose to his feet. He quietly filled his briefcase and picked up the gray homburg hat lying on the seat beside him.

"Gentlemen," he said, "I have risen as high in my profession as you have in yours. When you are prepared to apologize and to conduct this hearing with dignity, I will return."

The subcommittee did not apologize, and General Duggan did not return. Also, perhaps because of the general's testimony and Representative Connors's smutty little joke, the subcommittee refused to go along with its chairman's proposal to cut the officer corps from twelve to ten thousand—a victory for the chief of staff. It was, however, only a defensive triumph: he had only kept what he had, gaining nothing. Moreover, the budget had been trimmed from $331 million to $304 million, the third successive decline.

"Everywhere in the world, Mr. President, military budgets are going up," General Duggan complained to Hoover a few weeks later, "except in the United States."

Mr. Hoover, who had called Duggan and Secretary of State Stimson to his office to discuss Japanese aggression in Manchuria, said nothing—merely making his small mouth smaller. General Duggan was not surprised. He had quickly come to realize that his pacifist commander-in-chief regarded the War Department as a necessary evil, and would shed no tears at the gradual diminution of his armed forces.

Nor was he especially surprised when President Hoover refused to accept Stimson's proposal to apply economic sanctions against Japan and to put pressure on other nations to do the same.

"No, no," the President said in a shocked tone. "It would lead to war with Japan." He need not have added, as he did add: "War is never justified. *Never*!"

Describing the meeting to Betsy that night, Mark shook his head in disbelief. "It's incredible!" he cried. "Worse, than that, it's terrible—for our country, I mean—and the world too, for that matter. Herbert Hoover is the only leader in the world who actually *believes* in the Kellogg-Briand Pact. And do you know why? Because he *wants* to believe. He wants to believe that you can stop war by refusing to fight. And now the Japs will reach out for more. If we don't stop them in Manchuria, and the European democracies don't, if we just apply *moral* sanctions, as Hoover says—whatever they are— the Japs will just laugh in their sukiyaki and overrun the rest of China. And what about the dictators? Hitler's in power, now—and Mussolini says he's going to resurrect the Roman Empire. Do you think they care a fig for moral sanctions?"

Betsy nodded in agreement. "And to think we voted for him," she murmured.

"Well, I admit I voted against Al Smith because he was a Catholic. I really believed that a Catholic was more responsive to his Church than his country. But Hoover! Did anyone ask him about his Quaker pacifism? He's actually incapable of conducting foreign policy. He loathes war so much he doesn't realize that war is one of the two instruments of foreign policy. Diplomacy's the other. The stick and the carrot. But Herbert Hoover's just got carrots, no sticks—and you can't move a mule with just carrots."

Betsy nodded mechanically. She seemed preoccupied. Mark paused, puzzled. "Are you all right, dear?" he asked anxiously.

"I guess so. Why?"

"You seem distracted. The past few days you've been acting as though you've got something on your mind."

"Well," she said slowly, "I guess I do. It's Virginia."

"Virginia? What about Virginia?"

Betsy drew breath. "She's boy-crazy, that's what."

Mark stared at her in astonishment, reaching for the pack of cigarettes on the table beside him to load his holder. "I don't understand," he said, lighting up. "What do you mean, 'boy-crazy'?"

Betsy paused. She had deliberately chosen what she thought was the softest word. She could have used a stronger one: like slut, or . . . or . . . For three days now Betsy had been searching for the courage to tell Mark what had happened.

The handsome young orderly from the War Department had arrived with Mark's uniform from the dry cleaner's just as Sergeant Durkin drove up to take Betsy shopping. Betsy had smiled, pointed inside, and the soldier had nodded and gone into the house as Betsy drove away.

Two hours later, Betsy returned to find him still there—hurrying down the stairs and buttoning his fly as he ran past her. Betsy raced up the stairs to find Virginia's bed rumpled and Virginia locked in her bathroom. She refused to come out. Betsy went through the sham of slamming the door and storming downstairs, but she tiptoed back and slipped inside and stood beside the bathroom door, waiting . . . In a few minutes, the door opened cautiously and Virginia came out . . . naked. The minute Jinny saw her mother, she began to scream in rage. She ran up to her and beat her on the breast with tiny fists.

"You spy!" she sobbed, the tears of anger flowing down her cheeks.

"You slut!" Betsy shouted.

"Don't you dare call me that!" Virginia wailed. "You drunk! Jump back into your bottle and leave me alone!"

Horrified at what she had said, Virginia wailed again and ran back into the bathroom and locked the door. Hours later, of course, mother and daughter had embraced tearfully. But Betsy knew, now, and Virginia knew that she knew. All the time Betsy had been wondering what to tell Mark, she had asked herself: What if she gets pregnant? What if she has a baby? He'll blame me, I know he will!

"I was only trying to say, Mark," Betsy said, "that Virginia is too fond of men. She adores them. Especially good-looking ones in uniform."

"I don't believe it," Mark said quietly. He arose and came to her side, putting a gentle hand on her shoulder. "You must be mistaken, my dearest," he said softly, patting her shoulder. "You know that Jinny would never do anything unladylike."

"I didn't say unlady—" Betsy began.

But Mark went on, murmuring, "Probably, you're exaggerating something. I know how much you love her and worry about her."

Betsy looked up at Mark desperately. Seeing the unshakable faith in his eyes, she despaired. *How can I tell him?* she thought. *He'll never believe me, and he'll never forgive me either. My God, what am I to do now? Keep my daughter supplied in contraceptives, just so she won't—*

"You're distraught, dearest," Mark was saying. "Tell you what, I know I've been neglecting you lately. Supposing I call Durkin and have him drive us to the movies?" Betsy nodded dully, and Mark said, "And let's have a drink. We haven't had a drink together in ages." She nodded again, brightening. Mark went into the kitchen and made the drinks.

"Guess who called me from Governor Roosevelt's office today?" Mark said, returning to the living room. "Our old friend Henry Hawkins." He grinned as Betsy gasped in disbelief. "He's Roosevelt's top aide now—but still, I couldn't resist the chance to twist him a bit."

"What did you say?" Betsy asked, eagerly sipping her drink.

"I asked him if he was still working for the Communist Collection Agency." Mark chuckled. "That shook him, all right. It was at least five seconds before he answered. And when he did, he was stuttering. He said he didn't understand me. So I said, maybe I was mistaken. But he did admit that he came from Grinnell and went to school there and served in the Rainbow. I think he was a little surprised I knew so much about him. But I stopped there. I figured I'd gone far enough. But now he knows I know, and I like that."

Betsy shivered. "It's terrible that people like that can get so far in the world. A holdup man!"

"I don't know," Mark said, grinning. "Those were probably his salad days. He probably swapped his gun for a typewriter long ago. Roosevelt's got a lot of people like that around him. Not outright communists, of course—just fellow travelers. Socialists and self-appointed saviors of mankind. Like Lenin. All for the common man. But when the common man refused to lie down in the utopia Lenin designed for him, Lenin put him in a Procrustean bed. That would be our Mr. Hawkins. I'm sure he has his own blueprint for America."

"What did he call you for?"

"He said Governor Roosevelt was requesting a top-flight infantry officer to train the New York National Guard." Mark grinned maliciously. "I said, 'Mr. Hawkins, you can tell the governor that I'm sending him the finest infantry colonel in the United States Army.' "

"Who is that?" Betsy asked, forcing an interest, trying to drive the tableau of naked Virginia from her mind.

"George Quincy Meadows."

"Mark! That's spiteful. You said yourself he needed field command, at least a regiment, or he'd never wear a star. This will end your old friend's career. You're shanghaiing him!"

Mark shook his head doggedly. "I am not. Besides, he hasn't been much of a friend the past fifteen years or more. Anyway, it's done—he's coming to my office tomorrow." A horn honked on the street outside, and Mark said, "There's Pat. Get your things, Betsy."

● ● ●

Colonel George Quincy Meadows was actually smiling when he entered the chief of staff's office. Meadows had just come from the Assignment Bureau, where he had received his orders to command the Fifteenth Infantry. Shaking hands jovially with Duggan, he sank into the leather chair opposite him.

"Well, Mark," he began, "I've finally got the infantry field command I've been looking for all these years."

"Congrat—" Duggan began impulsively. Checking himself, he looked directly into Meadows's eyes. "I've got better news for you, George. I'm sending you to Albany to train Franklin Roosevelt's National Guard."

Meadows blanched. His face went ashen and his heavy features seemed to sag. "Mark," he said in quiet desperation, "that will just about end my career. I've *got* to have field command."

"Nonsense," Duggan said easily. "This is a great chance for you, George. Roosevelt looks like a shoo-in for the Democratic nomination. And Hoover couldn't even beat Al Smith this time. No, George, this is a great opportunity. You can make some pretty powerful friends up there in Albany." He smiled with sham good humor. "Who knows? You might wind up the next chief of staff."

"I know I have no sense of humor, Mark," Meadows said, biting his lip angrily. "But I don't think you're very witty either." Duggan flushed, and Meadows went on. "Me, a colonel, the next chief of staff? If anything, Mark, I think this assignment will make it certain that I won't even make brigadier."

"I disagree," Duggan said sharply. "Wait and see, George." He rose and came around the desk to shake hands. Colonel Meadows pretended not to see the proffered hand. Instead, he stepped back, clicked his heels, and saluted.

"Thank you, General Duggan," he snapped, before about-facing and striding stiffly from the room.

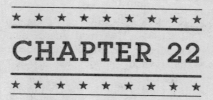

CHAPTER 22

The veterans of the Bonus Army had been streaming into Washington for weeks. They came in buses, in dilapidated old jalopies, on bicycles or on foot, and those who came an appreciable distance came in empty boxcars. A few even "rode the rods," crawling underneath standing boxcars to squirm up into the lying-down space formed by rows of bracing rods shaped like wide, shallow U's. They came without fear of being arrested and thrown into jail by railroad police, who were themselves victims of the Depression through reductions in pay and working hours. They'd long ago learned that all drifters in worn clothes were not bums or hobos, but frequently hungry, desperate men looking for work. Not satisfied with merely looking the other way, the railroad police actually directed the Bonus Marchers to the empty cars, or, having none available, slipped planks across the bracing rods so that the rod-rider might have a more comfortable journey.

There was not a fat man among them. They were in their early and late thirties, a time of life when middle-age spread usually plants a paunch on the ordinary man's middle. Yet, their worn and threadbare summer shirts or overalls fell from their emaciated shoulders in thin folds. Each day, the arriving veterans of the "Bonus Expeditionary Force," as they called themselves, massed outside Union Station, where they were issued placards saying CHEERED IN '17, JEERED IN '32 or WE WANT THE MONEY NOW! Then they formed ranks in military style and marched up Pennsylvania Avenue past the White House, singing their old World War favorite songs such as "Over There!" or "K-K-K-Katie" or "Pack Up Your Troubles in Your Old Kit Bag." Armed guards standing on the cleared sidewalks outside the chained and padlocked White House gates watched them parade past in silence, some of them with tears in their eyes.

Everywhere in America but in the White House and the Capitol, it seemed, there was sympathy for the desperate men of the Bonus Army. These were the war veterans who had come to Washington to demand immediate payment of the war-service bonuses that Congress had voted to be paid in 1945. They had set up a huge, sprawling, shantytown in Anacostia Flats across the Potomac, where some of them were joined by their families. When their number climbed past twenty thousand, many of them moved onto unoccupied land and empty government buildings on Pennsylvania Avenue.

Congress, however, rejected their petition; and yet, most of the hungry, jobless, aimless men of the Bonus Army stayed on in Washington, scrounging for food and employment. Gradually, as the southern sun tightened its stifling tentacles of heat around the city, many of the veterans left town. Others took advantage of a transportation fund voted by Congress for Bonus Marchers who agreed to go home. Some six thousand left by train. Nevertheless, by the time Congress adjourned in the middle of an unusually hot July, there were still ten thousand of them living in Anacostia Flats and on Pennsylvania Avenue. They were growing restive, resentful, irritable. Squatting in their squalid tent camps laced with networks of stinking, open latrines, angrily brushing away the hordes of black flies buzzing around them, they began to talk of marching on the Capitol.

Herbert Hoover was afraid of the Bonus Army. He firmly believed that the Bonus March was a communist conspiracy, that the ragged veterans whom he had refused to meet were dupes in a plot to take possession of the American capital. The past six months, he was certain, had given ample proof that the Reds wanted to foment revolution in the United

States. There had been a communist-led hunger march on Washington, a Pittsburgh priest with "dangerous ideas" had led twelve thousand unemployed men to the capital, and at a communist-inspired riot at Ford's River Rouge plant four workmen had been shot to death by panicking policemen. No, Herbert Clark Hoover did not believe the Bonus Marchers' protestations that they were not communists; from the depths of a White House that was now a kind of hermetically-sealed hermitage, he did not—and he wanted them out of town.

General Mark Duggan shared this conviction, but without sharing his commander-in-chief's morbid fear. He was deeply disturbed by the group of Red agitators led by John Pace, a bankrupt Detroit contractor who openly proclaimed his conversion to communism. Duggan had also been observing the spate of civil unrest that had erupted during the past half year, and he, too, was seeing Red. Unlike Hoover, however, who seldom appeared in public now, he had gone forth to warn his country of the menace. His last speech on that theme had been at the University of Pittsburgh's commencement exercises, where he was heckled seven times by student protestors, one of whom had screamed, "Why don't you mount your mule and go home!" They had all been arrested and fined, of course, but Duggan, stung by the taunt, was dismayed and disgusted to read upon his return to Washington that a county judge had lifted the fines.

It was on his return that Secretary of War Patrick Hurley informed him that the President wished him to prepare for possible disorders in the city. Duggan immediately ordered experimental models of a new tank to be sent from Aberdeen Proving Ground to Fort Myer outside the city. Ostensibly, they were intended for public exhibition of the latest mechanized equipment; actually, they were stocked with smoke shells, lubricated and fueled up, with their crews on an instant alert. Antiriot training was also begun at Fort Myer, with special emphasis on the use of cavalry to move against a mob.

"Maybe you'll live to see another charge, George," General Duggan said to Colonel Peyton, who commanded the antiriot force.

Peyton's white teeth flashed in his ruddy face. He looked

up from the "White Plan," the Army's outline for suppressing civil disorders in the capital, and chuckled. "Could be, General—but I'm really not too anxious to ride against our old comrades-in-arms."

"True. But we have to realize that if the President wants us to move these people out of town, we may have to use force." Peyton nodded grimly, while Duggan turned to a wall map of Washington. "Here are the critical points, George," he said, pointing to the center of the city. "The White House, the Capitol, the Treasury Department, and the Bureau of Engraving and Printing. They all have to be protected. If you come into town, you'll mass your troops in the Ellipse behind the White House."

"What if the veterans get violent?"

"We'll probably have to use tear gas. And we probably will have to get tougher with that nest of Reds under Pace."

"Tanks?"

"Not at first. We'll have them there to intimidate them, of course. But I would prefer horses."

Peyton grinned happily. "Now that's something I'd like—charging a crowd of Commies."

"No bloodshed, George. That's what the communists want. A bloodbath. Then they can wave the bloody shirt at the American people and start a revolution." He walked to his desk and sat down. "That's why they infiltrated the Bonus Army. They're out there in shantytown agitating every day. And the trouble is, except for Pace and his gang, we can't tell who's a Red and who's a loyal American." He studied the White Plan gloomily. "Let's hope the District police can handle them. Then we won't get our hands dir—" He looked up as his office door opened and Major Bauer came into the room.

"The leader of the Bonus Army is outside, sir," he said, handing the general a card. "He says he's an old friend of yours."

Duggan read the card in amazement. "Bill Baugh!" he exclaimed. "I never realized! I saw the name, but it never occurred—" He put the card down. "Send him in as soon as George leaves, Mike," he said, and then, turning to Peyton: "Remember, George: firm but friendly, tough but gentle. And pray that we never get called in."

• • •

General Duggan was as astonished by William Baugh's appearance as he had been to learn that Baugh "commanded" the Bonus Army. He must have been thirty pounds lighter. His once bull-like shoulders were bony knobs, and his bold eyes now were lackluster and beaten. Yet Duggan was pleased to see that he wore the Rainbow Division emblem pinned to his shirt collar.

"Good Lord, Bill, what happened?" he asked, offering his hand. "The last time I saw you was when I pinned those silver leaves on your shoulder. You sure were full of steam then."

"The Crash cleaned me out, General," Baugh said grimly, shaking hands and sitting down. "Everything. Down the drain. I had two million in stocks and bonds and a cool hundred grand in cash in the bank. Two Packards, a chauffeur, kids in private schools, and a big home in Montclair, New Jersey. Then—pow!—the iron ball hit and I was a pauper." Baugh sighed heavily, as though the recollection still pained him. "If it hadn't been for my parish priest, I guess I would have been another body splattering the Wall Street pavement. It killed my wife, though," he said sadly. "And the kids had to go back to parochial school."

"What about the hundred thousand in cash?"

"The bank folded," Baugh said simply. "Oh, I had it all, General. I even hit the bottle for a while and got myself kicked out of the Guard. The house brought me some money, though—but most of that went to pay my debts. So I wound up raking leaves and shoveling snow. Would you believe it? Some guy in Jersey came up with an idea for a handyman service he called Man Friday. I worked for him. Fifty cents an hour!" He snorted in contempt. "Christ, when I had it, General, I used to tip the waitress fifty cents for a nickel cup of coffee. But I was glad to get it. So when I heard of the Bonus March, I joined. I can use a thousand bucks, General."

"How did you come to take command?"

"They elected me," he said proudly. "I was the highest ranking veteran in the Bonus Expeditionary Force, and they wanted somebody to organize the encampment on military lines."

"Excellent," Duggan said. "So you see, Bill, you must still have some ability."

"It did make me feel better. And it's giving me back a lot of my self-respect. It's not so much the thousand bucks anymore. It's looking after those poor slobs out in Anacostia. That's what I came here for, General. Could you loan us some tents and rolling kitchens? Camp equipment and stuff like that?"

"From Army stocks?" Duggan asked in surprise. Gazing thoughtfully at Baugh, he loaded his cigarette holder and lighted up. "I'll see what I can do, Bill," he said, blowing smoke. "I just hope Congress doesn't squawk about lending out government property."

"What the hell's the matter with those bastards?" Baugh exploded angrily. "Christ, the way they've treated us, you'd think we were a bunch of wild-eyed communists."

"Well, I don't know, Bill," Duggan said slowly.

"Not *you*, General," Baugh said anxiously. "You don't believe the BEF's a Commie conspiracy too?"

"I would not say they organized it, Bill. But I do think they've infiltrated it and intend to exploit it."

"But goddammit, General—you know *me*! Am I a Commie? Me—a Brooklyn Irish Catholic. Christ, I still listen to Father Coughlin every Sunday night, and you know *he's* not a Red."

"I do indeed," Duggan said quietly. "He's a great American, and I wish we had more like him. But I still believe, Bill, that the communists intend to take over your movement."

"They can't! My men hate them. Christ, if it wasn't for the cops the other day, they would have cleaned out Pace and his crowd and put them all in the hospital. Every time there's a fight at Anacostia, General, it's between one of my men and some Red agitator." Seeing Duggan still unconvinced, he rushed on hurriedly. "Even when Congress turned us down cold, the Bonus boys didn't start tearing up the street and singing the Red hymn or anything like that. No, they were sore, all right, but they still formed ranks like I told them to, and then they sang the first stanza of 'America' and marched back to camp."

There were tears in Baugh's eyes when he concluded, and this time Duggan was impressed. "That was grand, Bill," he said gently. "I didn't know about that. But if none of them are communists, Bill, why don't they go home? It's all over. Congress has adjourned, and there's no hope until next year, when there'll be a new President."

"Half of them don't have a home," he muttered. "Oh, I don't know why, General," he began evasively. "They just want to stay in Washington. At least they're getting three hots and a flop out in Anacostia. Maybe they think their continued presence in Washington might bring Congress back."

Duggan gazed directly into Baugh's eyes. "Is there any truth to reports that you're planning to form your own army, Bill? The Khaki Shirts? Something like Hitler's Brown Shirts or Mussolini's Black Shirts?"

Baugh flushed and looked away, his manner again evasive. "Aw, that's a lot of baloney," he mumbled.

Duggan persisted. "Are you a fascist, Bill?"

"Hell, no!" Baugh cried angrily. "The only 'ism' I believe in is Americanism. But I do say that my men and myself and millions of other Americans are damned well fed-up with a system that lets the country keep floundering around in the mess it's in."

Duggan gazed at him thoughtfully. "What would you put in its place?"

"I . . . I don't know," Baugh said, his voice turning desperate. "But there's *got* to be a better way of making it work."

"All right, Bill," Duggan said evenly. "But please don't do anything rash like marching on the White House. I'd hate to use troops, but it's my duty to protect the White House. And that's what the communists want—a bloodbath."

"I don't," Baugh said doggedly. "And don't worry."

"Fine. And I'll see what can be done about the tents and kitchens."

The caller was Secretary of War Hurley. "The President wants you to evict the Bonus Army," he said succinctly.

Duggan looked at the telephone receiver in his hand in incredulous dismay. "But Mr. Secretary—he said only yesterday at the White House conference that he was going to let the Washington police do it."

"There's been bloodshed. Two veterans have been killed and three policemen are in the hospital. There's a wild mob of about three thousand Bonus Marchers gathered on Pennsylvania Avenue between Third and Fourth. I want you to clear the area immediately. Remember, General, use all humanity consistent with this order. Especially with the women and children."

"I will, sir," Duggan said, and put the receiver back on the hook. "Eviction," he muttered unhappily. "A job for the sheriff, not the chief of staff." He stared at Major Bauer, who had entered his office. Like Duggan, Bauer wore a white suit. "Better get your uniform on, Mike," Duggan said.

"It's come?"

"Yes. Two marchers killed, three policemen hurt. A wild mob getting ready to riot on Pennsylvania Avenue. Tell Peyton to move his force immediately to the assembly area." Duggan looked at his own impeccable linen suit. He turned to Sergeant Durkin, quietly pouring coffee from a silver service on a teakwood cart. "Better get my special occasion uniform, Pat." He smiled wanly. "My war bonnet too. Some of these poor, misguided veterans may remember it."

Major Bauer was dumbfounded. "Excuse me, sir—you're not accompanying the evicting force?"

"I am."

"But, sir—do you think it is appropriate for the chief of staff to be on the scene for such a minor operation? The public might misinterpret it."

"This could be a serious situation, Mike," Duggan said easily. "It might call for decisions beyond the responsibility of a subordinate commander. Besides, these are veterans. I think my presence there in uniform may ease their fears a bit."

A frown wrinkling his homely face and bald forehead, Major Bauer left the office to telephone Colonel Peyton.

The troops came clattering into the capital on trucks. They came from the four forts surrounding the District of Columbia: Myer, Meade, Washington, and Howard. In all, there were about eight hundred soldiers: two battalions of infantry, a squadron of cavalry, five tanks, and a National Guard coast artillery unit equipped with powerful searchlights.

General Duggan watched them assembling in the Ellipse, following them down Pennsylvania Avenue in a limousine driven by Sergeant Durkin. The car stopped at the head of the block between Fourth and Third. Duggan got out. He was elegant in his beribboned jacket and burnished Sam Browne belt above his famous "pinks"—breeches many shades lighter than the regulation tan—and gleaming, spurred leather boots reaching up to his knees. His campaign hat sat on his head at a rakish angle, and his cigarette holder stuck jauntily from his mouth. A murmur—half admiration, half hate—rose from the huge crowd of spectators lining the curbs on either side of the street. Major Bauer got out of the car next. The crowd watched him in silence. He stood beside the general, his jacket, bare of decorations, seeming to magnify the number of ribbons on Duggan's breast. Bauer glanced around him nervously. They stood there, side by side, contrasts in character—as though Audacity and Caution were together on the pavement.

Colonel Peyton rode up on a bay stallion. He saluted. "The veterans are back in the buildings, sir," he said, his hand resting on his pearl-handled revolver. "I'm going to clear the sidewalks before we move in." Duggan nodded, and Peyton cantered off, his horse tossing his head.

"Draw sabers!"

Sunlight danced on steel as the troopers' sabers flashed out of their scabbards with a hiss and came to rest upright against their shoulders.

"At a trot, forward!"

With a slow, steady clop-clop of horses' hooves, the cavalrymen rode toward the awed onlookers.

"Disperse!" the major commanding the squadron bellowed. "Disperse!"

From the crowd came a shrill boyish voice crying: "Hey, Major Pitcairn—this ain't the Battle of Lexington."

A derisive chuckle rose from the spectators, but then, as the horsemen quickened their pace, they retreated in a growling, muttering, sullen mass. Within ten minutes the sidewalks were cleared. The cavalry regrouped, and a battalion of infantry, advancing by companies, came down the street in close marching order, their rifles at right-shoulder arms. Bandoliers of tear-gas grenades were slung across the gas masks on their breasts.

"Bataaalll-yon, halt!"

Leather heels struck the pavement with a single, precise click—one-two.

"Orrrdeh, ahms!"

Flesh slapped against leather slings, and steel rifle butts struck the pavement.

"Fix bayonets!"

Again the flash and clash of steel as bayonets flew out of their sheaths, and the rasp of steel on steel as the soldiers fitted their blades onto the bayonet lugs at the rifle muzzles.

"Stack ahms!"

Moving quickly out of ranks in threes, each trio linked stacking swivels, falling in again and leaving neat triangles of stacked rifles in front of each unit. Now the company captains took over, striding easily along their company fronts, issuing instructions.

"All right, men, let's get those gas masks on. Check your tear-gas grenades. Be sure to have one in each hand when we go in." They waited until the men had put on their masks and seized their grenades. "All right, let's go in after them!"

With a rush, the soldiers in khaki raced into the buildings and the shanties the veterans had erected between buildings. Pulling the pins with their teeth, they hurled their grenades inside. Explosions racked the buildings. Black smoke belched from open windows, quickly followed by terrified veterans who were running before their feet touched the ground. They raced up Pennsylvania Avenue, many of them with bags of bricks they had not had time to throw. Soon, flames roared out the windows. The shacks crackled and collapsed.

General Mark Duggan frowned. "No one was authorized to use fire," he snapped.

Colonel Peyton galloped up to them, leaning down and cupping his hands to yell above the roar of the flames. "The goddam tear-gas grenades are defective. Half of 'em shoot flame instead of tear-gas smoke."

Duggan grimaced, brushing at the tears forced from his own eyes by drifting gas. "It may be accidental," he grumbled to Bauer, "but they'll fry us in the papers for it anyway."

Peyton made a face, wheeled his horse, and rode off.

Now the Bonus Marchers were a ragged, undisciplined horde, moving at a trot down Pennsylvania Avenue, heading for the Potomac and the Eleventh Street bridge. Reforming by companies, the soldiers pursued them, keeping them at a distance of about one hundred yards. Whenever the infantry drew close, the veterans turned to hurl bricks and captive grenades, booing and shouting profanity. Catching sight of General Duggan's limousine slowly following the soldiers, they began to chant:

> *Mule, Mule, General Mule,*
> *Ran from the battle on a medical mule.*

Duggan heard them but said nothing, staring straight at the back of Durkin's head, surprised to notice for the first time that the big sergeant's thick curly red hair was gray and thinning. Hearing shouting behind him, he turned to see a resurgent mass of spectators. There was a sprinkling of embittered veterans among them, as well as communist agitators who had earlier clashed with police. Provoked by the veterans and the Reds, about fifty of them detached themselves from the mass and attacked Duggan's limousine as it approached the Navy Yard.

"General Mule!" they screeched, hammering on the windshield with stones, hurling refuse cans against the side of the vehicle. "You goddam bloody butcher!"

Duggan ignored them with majestic nonchalance, staring calmly ahead and smoking. Major Bauer stared at him in open admiration, occasionally glancing out his own window. A stone crashed through the windshield, and Durkin stopped the car. He flung the door open and leaped outside, seizing the biggest of the attackers by the throat, knocking him down with a single blow and stooping to grasp the man by the ankles. Straightening, he swung the man around and around like a whirling discus thrower, sending the mob sprawling and clearing a circle around him. Then, completing his spin, he hurled the unconscious man high into the air and into the arms of the approaching crowd.

"There you are!" he bellowed. "Make *that* yer master, y' pack of yellow hyenas."

Returning to the driver's seat, he let out the clutch and drove away.

"Nice work, Pat," Duggan murmured. "It's always nice

to have a big harp like you around. I think I'm going to give you the Soldier's and Sailor's Medal.''

''Ah, don't do it, sir. 'Tis no pleasure beatin' sense into the skulls of mixed-up civilians. 'Tis out of their heads they are, sir, they're that sick of the Depression.''

Duggan said nothing. They drove on in silence, stopping just before they came to the Eleventh Street bridge.

Colonel Peyton was there, dismounted. ''Almost all of the vets are across the river in Anacostia, sir. Shall we go in after them?''

''No,'' Duggan said, stepping out of the car. ''Stop the men for dinner, and send in word that we're going to give them two hours to clear out so that no one will be hurt—especially the women and children.

A messenger from Army Intelligence rode up on a motorcycle and handed General Duggan a message.

The general read it, frowning. ''G-2 says some of the Bonus Marchers have weapons,'' he said to Bauer. ''They intend to fire on the first soldiers to cross the bridge.''

Another motorcycle messenger arrived, from the Secretary of War. Duggan waved him away.

''Do you want me to take it, sir?'' Bauer asked, surprised. ''It may be instructions not to cross.''

''It probably is,'' Duggan snapped. ''But I'm on the scene, and they're not. You heard about the guns.'' Bauer nodded, still visibly disturbed, and Duggan said, ''Come on, let's get some chow.''

Just before midnight the infantry moved cautiously over the bridge. They met no gunfire. Spreading out in skirmish lines, bayoneted rifles at port arms, they entered the encampment. They met no resistance. The camp was deserted, except for some women and a few harmless drunks, whom they pushed roughly aside. Infuriated, still stung from the profane taunts and bricks of the afternoon, the soldiers began firing the tents. Soon innumerable fires sprang up on the Anacostia bottomland, illuminating a mass of about two thousand marchers gathered at the southern end of the camp. The soldiers attacked them with tear-gas grenades and dispersed them.

Throughout the night, the embittered, weary, aching veterans trudged through the streets of the surrounding towns.

Sometimes sympathetic homeowners gave them shelter. Across the flats of Anacostia all was silent, save for the crackling of the flames, the low, controlled weeping of the women, and the sobbing of a seven-year-old boy who had been bayoneted in the leg when he ran back to his tent to retrieve his pet rabbit.

Mark Duggan walked slowly into the smoking rubble, followed by Mike Bauer.

"Well, they're gone." Duggan sighed, just as powerful searchlights switched on, crisscrossing the blackened earth with thick, ghostly beams.

A shadowy figure came toward Duggan and stopped in front of him. It was William Baugh. His eyes bored into Duggan's with a look of distilled hatred and contempt. His hand went to his shirt collar and he tore his Rainbow Division emblem from it and flung it in the muck in front of Duggan.

"After tonight, you son of a bitch, that emblem and your goddam flag don't mean a thing to me."

"Bill," Duggan said quietly, "I ought to have you arrested for what you just said."

"Screw you!" Baugh screamed, and turned and limped into the night, his hands over his eyes.

From the convulsive movement of his shoulders, Mark Duggan could tell that he was crying.

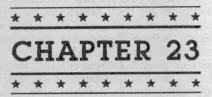

CHAPTER 23

The outcry succeeding the rout of the Bonus Army shook even Mark Duggan's invincible aplomb. From coast to coast, by editorial, by radio, by letter, and by voice, the Hoover Administration was denounced as a heartless tool of Big Business and an enemy of the American people.

Perhaps ninety percent of the American public was outraged by the "Battle" of Anacostia Flats.

The Washington *News* declared: "What a pitiful spectacle is that of the great American Government, mightiest in the world, chasing unarmed men, women, and children with army tanks."

Hatred of Herbert Hoover became so intense that it erased any chance he might have had for reelection. He was jeered wherever he went, jeered as no President in history. When he spoke, his face was ashen and his hands trembled. He was a beaten man.

The especially bitter invective, however, was reserved for General Duggan. He was caricatured directing artillery fire on children's nurseries or dropping bombs on veterans' hospitals. His caricature, once merely critical or mocking, was now full of contempt and hatred. The hat was ridiculously larger, the boots tinier, the spurs crueler, and the drops of blood bigger. One cartoonist went so far as to make him a minuscule figure perched on a huge mule. In Washington a syndicated columnist wrote a lengthy article entitled, "The Hero Who Turned into a Heel." Caustic and biting reference was made to Duggan's "gorgeous parade uniform" and to the presence of a personage so exalted as the chief of staff of the United States Army at an operation "fit for a corporal's guard."

Next to Herbert Hoover, Mark Duggan had become the most unpopular man in America. Unlike Hoover, however, he did not collapse. Not for a moment did he alter his conviction that the Bonus March was a communist conspiracy. Instead, with his unfailing capacity for transferring blame or disqualifying with an epithet, he concluded that half the writers and reporters in the United States were either communists or fellow-travelers. As the presidential election approached, he also began to wonder about his future. He had no doubt that Roosevelt would win, and that the people around him were no admirers of Mark Duggan. After Roosevelt's overwhelming victory, he was almost certain that when FDR took office in March 1933, the first casualty of the administration already being called "the New Deal" would be himself.

What, then, of the future? He was only fifty-three, the youngest chief of staff in history, and his capacity for work was still inexhaustible; in fact, he loved work almost as much as power. Should he enter civilian life? Remington Rand Corporation and a few international airlines had already offered him a directorship at a princely salary. For the first time, they could live handsomely without depending on Army vehicles, servants, and emoluments. Betsy would love it. Virginia would be overjoyed. They had had their fill of prestige long ago, and could do well without it.

And yet, Mark Duggan knew that he was a soldier, an Army brat trained from the cradle for battle. All over the world the war clouds were gathering. Hitler was rearming, Mussolini was rattling his saber in the direction of Abyssinia, and Japan was devouring China province by province—while the democracies slept! Front, flank, and rear, they were exposed to the teeth of the predators.

No doubt about it, he thought, within another decade there would be another world war. And when it came, where would he be? What then of his accumulation of wealth and his sated craving for comfort? What good the wheels of industry spinning beneath his hand when men were marching again? To be a tycoon when he could become a conqueror? He thought of the closing paragraph of Herodotus, how the Persians came to Cyrus and said that now that they ruled an empire, why did they not give up their own barren country and take the fairest land for themselves? *Then Cyrus, who did not greatly esteem the counsel, told them they might do so, if they liked—but he warned them not to expect in that case to continue rulers, but to prepare for being ruled by others—soft countries gave birth to soft men . . .*

No! Mark Duggan was a hunter, not a husbandman; not a worker, but a warrior. But what if the new President wrote finis to his career? General Duggan did not know, and he came to fear his first summons to the presidential office far more than the slings and arrows of his infuriated critics.

When it came, he had Sergeant Durkin drive him to the White House. Feeling faintly nauseous, he followed a black steward who led him past the secret servicemen into the office. Duggan was pleased, however, when Roosevelt greeted him with a radiant smile. They shook hands. Henry Hawkins was standing by one of the tall green-draped windows, gazing at the holly and boxwood border in the Rose Garden. Duggan was startled. The President's right hand man and alter ego was wearing a faded sweatshirt and a pair of blue jeans.

Roosevelt chuckled. "Henry feels that if I don't mind, there's no one else he needs to impress." Hawkins snickered and turned to face Duggan. Roosevelt introduced them.

"I believe we've met before, Mr. Hawkins," Duggan said evenly.

Hawkins flushed. "I don't think so, General."

"Well," Duggan said easily, his nausea disappearing, "I guess you impressed me more than I impressed you."

Hawkin's eyelid fluttered. "I've been wanting to thank you, General," he said, "for sending us Colonel Meadows. You were right. He is the finest infantry colonel in the U.S. Army."

"George and I were classmates together," Duggan said jovially, aware that Roosevelt's sharp eyes were on him. "We served in France and the Philippines together."

Hawkins nodded, hitching up his jeans as though preparing to leave, and Roosevelt said, "He'll be coming here, Mark."

"Excellent, Mr. President," Duggan replied, wondering, in momentary fear, if Roosevelt actually was going to replace him with Meadows.

"I asked you to come here, Mark," the President said as Duggan sat down beside the heavily carved presidential desk, "to ask you to stay on for at least another year."

Duggan was jubilant. "By all means, Mr. President!" he cried.

Roosevelt smiled. He loaded his cigarette holder, put it between his teeth, and lighted up. "I'm very much aware of your ability, Mark. Even without your record since the war, I remember it from our days together in the War and Navy departments." He blew smoke and grinned mischievously. "But not all of my advisers were for you."

"Because of the Bonus Army?"

"That and your well-known conservatism." Roosevelt grinned again. "Did you vote for me, Mark?" he teased.

Duggan turned scarlet. "I . . . I voted my convictions, Mr. President."

Roosevelt chuckled. "The American Legion was dead set against you. Mr. Hawkins and Mr. Tugwell think you're probably the most dangerous man in America."

"How so, sir?" Duggan asked, reddening again in consternation.

"They feel that the American people are so desperate for bread—for security—they might be willing to give up their freedom and turn to—"

"A man on a horse?"

"Exactly," Roosevelt said, frowning slightly at the interruption.

"I am a soldier, sir," Duggan said evenly, "a conqueror even. But I am not an enemy of the American system. It is the greatest in the world, and I, for one, would rather defend than destroy it. Above all, I respect civilian control of the military."

"Very good, Mark," Roosevelt said, blowing smoke again. "Fortunately for you, I think I have a broader understanding of foreign affairs than my predecessor." His lips tightened. "I'm counting on you to keep the Army strong. Once we lick this Depression," he said grimly, "we've got to think about strengthening our defenses."

"I agree wholeheartedly, sir. But France and England and the other West European democracies are preoccupied with the Depression too. That's how the dictators have been able to—"

"I know, I know," Roosevelet interrupted testily, holding up a restraining hand. "Thank you for staying on, Mark."

Duggan stood up and shook hands. At the door, he turned to look at Franklin Delano Roosevelt seated behind the beautiful old desk that Queen Victoria had given President Hayes. Roosevelt sat there, his big though crippled body filling the seat, his broad shoulders framed against the three tall windows, his cigarette holder rising jauntily from his lips, his commanding head thrown back confidently, and his good-humored chin lifted for blows.

"You're a fighter, Mr. President," Duggan said softly. "I have been in this office many times before, sir, and I want to tell you that the contrast between you and the former occupant is the difference between despair and hope."

Roosevelt looked up in pleased surprise. "Coming from you, Mark, that's the nicest thing I've heard since the election-night returns."

For a moment they studied each other. Two aristocrats, American patricians; both from old and famous families, trained in the "right" schools, born and bred to lead—Duggan, intelligent, aggressive, and inflexible; Roosevelt, shrewd, astute, and adaptable. Unconsciously, Duggan put his own cigarette holder in his mouth and began to smoke.

Roosevelt chuckled impishly, wagging his holder at Duggan. "This is *my* prop, Mark. From now on, if we are seen or photographed together, you will be smoking something else."

Duggan grinned and put away his holder. "As you say, sir," he said, and left.

Next day Duggan sent his holder to a jeweler to be engraved "Hail the Chief!" and sent it to the White House. He wrote a note to the President: "Churchill has his cigar, Stalin his pipe, and Roosevelt his cigarette holder. Next time you see Duggan, he'll be smoking a corncob." Then he sent Sergeant Durkin out to scour the tobacco shops for the biggest corncob pipe he could find.

• • •

Overjoyed at his new lease on the job he loved, General Duggan virtually hurled himself into his work with renewed vigor. His fear of becoming a civilian was dispelled. Roosevelt had said "for at least a year," and to the ever-optimistic Mark Duggan, that could easily be interpreted as two, perhaps even a full four-year term. By then, he was confident, the world would be so close to another great war that he could not possibly be shunted aside.

Duggan ate his dinner off his desk as often as he went home to dine with Betsy and Virginia. Almost always, he worked until the late hours, while the devoted Durkin sat in the outer office playing solitaire, drinking bootleg beer, and listening to the radio. The general shunned Washington social life. Because he despised Roosevelt's New Dealers and held them beneath contempt, he declined all invitations to dinner from the queens of capital society. His one abiding pleasure was the arrival in Washington of Captain Beauregard Ames in 1934. Beau had come to work in the War Plans Section under Brigadier General Meadows; eager to please Roosevelt and to placate Hawkins, Duggan had jumped George over a dozen colonels senior to him.

Duggan was fond of Beau. He enjoyed the company of the young officer, talking with him for hours about the Army they both loved. After Captain Ames's first night at dinner with the Duggans, Mark invited him to come and live with them. Ames accepted. Thereafter, Mark came home more frequently for dinner. Betsy was overjoyed and Virginia unashamedly enraptured. Prior to Beau's appearance, Virginia had customarily excused herself after dinner and had driven off in the little brown roadster her father had bought her to meet her friends. Unknown even to Betsy, Virginia had become one of the brightest lights among a group of well-born young Washingtonians whose lives shuttled gaily forth from the paddock to the speakeasy to the bedroom. Now, however, Virginia seldom left the dinner table, her large dark eyes fixed adoringly on Beau while he discussed the Army and foreign affairs with her father. Neither Duggan nor Ames noticed, sipping their brandy and smoking; but Betsy noticed, and was alarmed. The little hussy, she thought with unconscious jealousy. She's only nineteen and Beau is thirty. She'd better watch out!

Virginia had no intention of watching out. One night when

her father was working late, she came into the living room
where Beau sat listening to a comedy hour on the radio. She
laughed and said, "Let's have some music," switching to the
Artie Shaw band playing "Jalousie." She turned it up loud.
"Come on, Beausie—let's dance," she said, extending her
open arms.

Beau frowned. "Jinny, that's too loud. Your mother's
upstairs reading."

"Her? She's probably already asleep in a drunken bed."

"Jinny! You shouldn't talk that way about your mother."

"Oh, pooh." She turned the radio down. "Come on,
dance with me."

Beauregard Ames studied Virginia with growing interest.
Suddenly he realized that the little Army brat he had known at
West Point had turned into a beautiful woman.

He stood up. "Just once," he said warningly.

Virginia giggled and slipped into his arms. She pressed her
body against his and felt his penis growing hard. She pressed
harder against him and nibbled on his ear.

"Jinny!" he exclaimed, reddening, putting a hand on his
ear. "What's the matter with you?"

"Nothing. I love you."

Beau was astounded. He stopped dancing and stepped
back. "But, Jinny—I'm eleven years older than you."

"I don't care. I love you."

She slipped into his arms again, pressing against him once
more.

"Jinny," he cried in alarm. "This is wrong. What about
your father? I'm a guest in his house. It wouldn't be—"

"Oh, pooh." Virginia pouted, making a face. "He won't
know."

She gazed up at him rapturously, invitingly, and he bent his
head and kissed her. He kissed her again and again, his
masculinity now fully aroused, and she darted her little
pointed tongue into his mouth. At once, aflame with desire,
he swung her off her feet and carried her into the living room
and placed her on the sofa. She looked up at him.

"Beausie, have you—have you got a thing?"

"No," he panted. "I don't carry them. Do you want me to
go out and get some?"

She shook her head, and he entered her. Virginia wriggled

in ecstasy. He's so *big*! she thought, until her sight and hearing were engulfed to the greater profit of her other senses.

General Duggan had hoped that under the sophisticated and popular Roosevelt, both pacifism and Congressional penny-pinching would begin to abate. But they were growing stronger. In England, pacifism's greatest triumph was the Joad Resolution, where Oxford students, under the influence of a Professor Joad, declared that they would never fight for king or country. In America, the Ludlow Amendment had just missed passage in the House by a single vote. It proposed that the United States could only declare war by a popular referendum. The prospect of a menaced America springing to the ballot box instead of the parapet had been too much for Duggan to bear, and he had vowed to himself he would resign if the Ludlow Amendment passed.

And then Congress had meat-axed his budget again! It had granted him only $227,100,000—less even than the pacifist Hoover had proposed—and from this the Bureau of the Budget had just withdrawn $80 million. This, on top of the $143 million that Roosevelt had made the Army spend to organize his controversial Civilian Conservation Corps along military lines. Duggan felt betrayed. Even though Roosevelt eventually reduced the cut to $51 million, he still felt that the President had proved faithless.

"This will just about destroy the Army," he told Secretary of War Dern in his office.

"I know, I know," Dern said, nervously wiping his glasses. "I have just been on the telephone with the President. He has agreed to discuss it with me. Will you accompany me, General?"

"I'll be glad to," Duggan said with relief, but once he was inside the President's office again, he realized with dismay that the Secretary of War was not a warrior.

"Mr. President," Dern said, his voice faltering, "this cut in funds could be a fatal error for our country." Roosevelt lifted his jaw arrogantly, and the Secretary rushed on hastily. "I mean no offense, sir—I mean only that now is not the time to cut back on national defense, with the dictators rearming and Japan already embarked on a course of aggression."

"I see," Roosevelt said with biting sarcasm. "You want

me to spend a billion on bullets when the whole country is groaning for beans and butter.''

Dern was crushed. His shaking hand went to his quivering mouth.

Duggan could no longer contain himself. ''Mr. President, when you asked me to stay on, you asked me to keep the Army strong.''

''Yes, and I also told you that once we had licked the Depression, we would see to strengthening national defenses.''

''Mr. President, we cannot wait!'' Duggan's voice had risen sharply. Nausea was engulfing him again. It was the worst seizure since the scene with Black Jack Pershing at the railroad station.

''You will have to wait, Mark!'' Roosevelt snapped.

Duggan sprang to his feet. ''Mr. President,'' he cried, his voice husky and throbbing with emotion, ''when the next war comes and the last untrained American boy lies in the mud with his enemy's bayonet in his belly and his foot on his dying throat, I want his last curse to spit out the name of Roosevelt—not Duggan!''

Franklin Delano Roosevelt turned white. His face working in rage, he placed his powerful hands on the desktop as though struggling to come erect on his paralyzed legs. Sinking back in frustration, he pounded the desk with his fist and roared: ''You must not talk that way to the President!''

''You are right, sir,'' Duggan murmured, ''and I apologize.'' Sickening, his hand on his stomach, he turned to go. ''And you also have my resignation as chief of staff.'' He walked toward the door, beginning to retch.

Behind him, to his amazement, he heard Roosevelt say cheerfully, ''Don't be foolish, Mark—you and the Budget can work this thing out.''

Duggan hurried from the room, hastening down the long corridor toward fresh air. The moment he reached the White House steps, he began to vomit. His head bent, he stared dully at the beads and strings of puke clinging to his white trouser cuffs. A hand fell on his shoulder. It was Secretary Dern.

''Congratulations, General,'' Dern said, pretending not to notice his illness. ''Today, you saved the Army.''

• • •

If General Duggan had saved the Army, he was sure he had lost face with the President. He was certain that Roosevelt, a man who never forgave a foe or forgot a friend, would long remember the insult offered him in the presence of his Secretary of War. Once again he began to worry about the future. He knew that many of the President's closest advisers, especially Henry Hawkins, were urging Roosevelt to relieve him.

Secretary Dern, fast losing favor with the White House, told Duggan: "Hawkins keeps telling the President that you're a Hoover man. You're hated by the people, he says, and you think you own the Army."

Conversely, he also knew, other New Dealers were warning Roosevelt not to fire him until after the Republican convention. Bonus Army rout notwithstanding, they still regarded Duggan as a potential political enemy, a famous American admired by millionaires, whose magnetic personality and oratorical skill had the power to move the masses.

Nevertheless, Duggan was worried, and he began to pay closer attention to his correspondence with acquaintances in the business world—until his old friend Manuel Quezon arrived from the Philippines. Quezon was now president of the Philippine Senate, and he had come to Washington to discuss what he considered the proposed Philippine Commonwealth's primary problem: national defense.

"Mark," he said one night at dinner at the resident commissioner's, "do you think that the Philippines can defend themselves?"

"Manuel," Duggan said, blowing smoke from his favorite Philippine cigar, which Quezon had brought him, "I don't *think* that they can, I *know* it. Besides, when you gain your independence, we can't just walk away from you. We've spent more than thirty years trying to teach you all we know. The last thing we should do—which we should *have* to do—is to teach you how to defend yourself against a foreign foe."

"Excellent!" Quezon exclaimed. "And of course you know who that foe will be?"

Duggan smiled. "You told me nearly four years ago. Remember?"

"Yes," Quezon said sadly. "Japan will not stop with

China.'' He smiled. ''What would you think of being military adviser to the Philippines?''

''I can think of nothing better!'' Duggan cried. ''Manuel, you are like an angel from heaven! For the past six months I've done nothing but fret about my future. I'm far too young to retire, and I hate the thought of accepting subordinate command. My friends in the business world have been after me to come with them, but . . .'' He shrugged with elaborate disdain.

''I've talked to Secretary Dern and some congressional leaders. They think it can be done. As a matter of fact, would you mind drafting the bill for Dern to submit?''

''I'd be delighted!''

''And would you compose my letter requesting your services?''

''Indeed, I will.''

Quezon smiled, leaning across the table to shake hands. ''There is no general in the world I would rather have. And the salary, Mark,'' he said slyly, ''it is good. Eighteen thousand as military adviser, and fifteen thousand in allowances.''

''Thirty-three thousand dollars!'' Duggan exclaimed. ''And with my pay of eight thousand as a major general in the U.S. Army, that's forty-one thousand. Good Lord, Manuel, you're making me rich!''

''You will hold the rank of marshal.''

''Ah,'' Duggan grunted. ''Marshal Duggan. Sounds good.'' He grinned. ''Do I get a baton?''

Quezon laughed aloud, and the two friends parted, Quezon to enter the hospital for a minor operation, Duggan to hurry home with the great news. He found Betsy in the living room, sitting up waiting for him. He was surprised. Usually she was sound asleep by this time. She seemed distressed.

''What's wrong, dearest?'' he inquired anxiously.

She looked up at him wearily. ''Jinny and Beau want to get married,'' she said in a tired voice.

''Married!'' he repeated incredulously. ''But she's only twenty and he's thirty-one. You can't mean it. They . . . they must be teasing you.''

Betsy shook her head doggedly. ''No.''

He glanced around him as though struggling to hold on to his sanity, running a hand over his thinning hair. He sat down and stared at Betsy. ''When?''

"Right away."

Duggan sprang erect. "My God!" he stormed. "This isn't real! How can she do this to me? We need months to prepare. The bishop . . . the church . . . the invitation . . . the newspaper notices . . . Why are they in such an all-fired hurry?"

Betsy Duggan looked up at her husband dully. Should she tell him, or should she take the customary course and shield Jinny so that his anger would not fall upon her own head? No! she thought with sudden resolution born of years of growing resentment. No! she thought, gazing up at him, her eyes ablaze with defiance.

"Betsy," he said patiently, "please answer my question."

She spat out her reply: "Because she's two months pregnant."

* * * * * * * * * * * * * * * *

MANILA

* * * * * * * * * * * * * * * *

CHAPTER 24

As Betsy had expected, Mark refused to believe that his adored daughter would so dishonor him. He told himself that Virginia knew that he valued honor more than life itself, and would never do this to him. Nor would Beauregard Ames, the son of the man who had saved his life; the cadet to whom he had given a second chance when charged with cheating—the very apotheosis, in Mark's mind, of the West Point motto: Duty, Honor, Country.

Virginia came to him and explained that the reason she and Beau wanted to get married right away was because she was afraid her father's term as chief of staff would expire before he had the opportunity to detail Beau to the London embassy as a military attaché. General Duggan believed her, and acquiesced in her wishes.

He did not deduce, as his wife did, that Virginia—who had inherited much of her father's intelligence—was cleverly killing two birds with one stone. Virginia's story would save her daughter's reputation, and also take her overseas where she could tell her new friends that she had been married six months. When she met her old friends again, she could tell them that the baby was three or four months younger than it actually was. Betsy could just hear Jinny simpering: "Oh, yes, he is big for his age—just like his father."

Beau was assigned to London one month after the wedding, and in another month General Duggan and his wife left Washington and took ship in San Francisco for the Philippines. Manuel Quezon, who had just been elected as the first president of the new Philippine Commonwealth, was unable to be dockside to greet them, but he sent Vice President Osmena, plus an official limousine which he placed at the general's disposal. When Sergeant Durkin saw the Filipino chauffeur in a white uniform thick with gold braid, his blue eyes turned black.

"Jaysus, and what does that gold-plated little Goo-Goo think he's doin' behind the wheel," he muttered angrily to General Duggan.

Grinning, laying a quieting hand on the miffed sergeant's wrist, Duggan explained to Osmena in Spanish that he had his own chauffeur, who knew Manila well, and who was also his own bodyguard. Smiling now, Durkin replaced the dejected Filipino and drove Mark and Betsy to their new home.

Betsy was enchanted with their quarters, an air-conditioned penthouse on top of a new five-story wing of the Manila Hotel. She was delighted with the Spanish motif, the gold leaf, and the Moorish arches. With clicking heels, she walked down the long terra cotta hallway, opening the doors of the various bedrooms and bathrooms and exclaiming each time in rapture. Entering the formal dining room, she clapped her hands together. "Gorgeous! Look Mark, there are three views—the bay, the city, and the hills. And it's so *cool*!"

Mark nodded, pleased to see her happy again. They went out onto the terraces, flinching slightly at the reengulfing heat. Here the vistas were even more sweeping, more panoramic: one overlooking the old Spanish city, the other facing the harbor.

"I think I'm going to spend a lot of time out here," Mark murmured. "You can do a lot of thinking in a place like this."

Characteristically, Marshal Duggan began working at his new job that very afternoon. Sergeant Durkin drove him to his office in Malacanan Palace, and he spent the rest of the day chatting with his staff and organizing his daily schedule. Next morning, he was joined by Major Bauer. Mike had not wanted to accompany Duggan to the Philippines. He was eager for field command, which he had never held. Duggan, however, with customary charm and persuasiveness, convinced him that his career would benefit enormously by at least three more years of service under the former chief of staff. Together they plunged into the huge administrative task of building a Philippine National Army.

Their objective was a force of 400,000 citizen-soldiers trained over a period of ten years, so that, by the time the Philippine Commonwealth received its independence in 1946, the islands would be able to defend themselves. Supporting these ground forces would be a "mosquito fleet" of fifty torpedo boats and an air force of 250 airplanes.

Marshal Duggan's enthusiasm for his project was boundless. It did not, however, infect Major Bauer—at least not at the start. Bauer was convinced that the Philippines were indefensible. The islands had thousands and thousands of miles of coastline, open beaches over which any sea power such as Japan could easily conduct landings. Except for the sophistication and Spanish culture of Manila and a few other cities, the population of fourteen million was a polyglot of illiterate, ignorant tribesmen divided by differences in religion, language, and region. Most of the trainees who were inducted had owned little more than a loincloth and a bolo knife, and were absolutely unfamiliar with either discipline or a sense of order. Almost always, commands given in English had to be translated into at least a half-dozen dialects.

Major Bauer knew that when Duggan was chief of staff, his own War Plans division had categorically stated that the Philippines could not be defended and had recommended withdrawal of all U.S. forces stationed there. Duggan had known it, too, when he dined with Quezon on that memorable night. But his desire to remain in harness, his eagerness to accept a new challenge, had suppressed his better judgment. His optimism, feeding on hope and desire, had swelled out of proportion and become the mental monstrosity of wishful thinking.

Thus, when Bauer came to him with his fears, and his reminder of the War Plans' recommendation, Duggan derisively waved the big corncob pipe he now affected.

"Nonsense, Mike—the War Plans people didn't know what they were talking about. That's why I turned them down. Of course, I'm having trouble now. Every new project has bugs in it. But I'll iron them out." He fixed Bauer with glowing eyes. "Especially when I've got people like you working for me, Mike," he said softly.

"Thank you, sir," Bauer said, blushing slightly, hardly aware how swiftly his apprehensions had disappeared.

"Say, Mike," Duggan continued, "what happened to that naval lieutenant you introduced to me at the Manila Hotel last month? I liked that fellow. He understood right away when I told him that Japan was exhausting herself in China."

"Jim Duff?" Mike said. "Poor guy. He was playing golf with me one day and collapsed with a heart attack. He had to get out of the Navy."

"Too bad," Duggan murmured musingly. "I've been thinking of our mosquito fleet, and it occurred to me he might be just the man to organize it."

"He's coming back to Manila, sir. He wrote me he'd be taking ship from San Diego this month."

"Excellent. Send him to me when he arrives."

A month later Major Bauer stepped into Duggan's office, grinning widely. "Here's Jim Duff, sir."

Duggan came around his desk, jovially extending his hand. "Glad to see you again, Jim."

Duff sat down. He was a big, fleshy man, with a round ruddy face and thinning red hair. In an English police helmet, he would look like a London bobby.

Duggan studied him, picking up his corncob and sitting cross-legged on his desk. "How's your health?" he inquired, sticking the cold pipe into his mouth.

"Not too bad. I recovered pretty quickly. But the Navy wasn't taking any chances. Now," he said moodily, "I've got to start putting the pieces together again."

"Nonsense! I've got a project for you, Jim." Duggan got to his feet and began pacing the room, waving the pipe as he talked. "I need a navy of torpedo boats, Jim. I need them for offshore patrol. If I obtain the money, how many can you construct in ten years?"

"Oh, I guess about a million," Duff said, chuckling.

"I'm not joking," Duggan said sharply.

Duff swallowed and said in a strained voice, "Marshal, I've never even seen a torpedo boat."

"That's all right," Duggan snapped. "You will. You are a Navy man, aren't you?"

"I was."

"Then you know what to do. I'll fix up the appropriate rank for you, and you can start working on the Navy Department." Duff swallowed again, and Duggan put his pipe on his desk and strode up to him. "I'm counting on you, Jim," he said softly, his voice throbbing with faith and confidence. He put both hands on Duff's shoulders. "I *need* those boats. Without them, I have no navy."

"You'll have them, sir," Duff said, getting to his feet, mildly startled to hear the note of confidence in his own voice.

"I know I will, Jim," Duggan said simply, and Duff shook hands with him and left.

Outside, he encountered Bauer. Duff passed a hand over his hair. "Am I dreaming, Mike? I went in there a civilian, and now I'm coming out a commodore."

Bauer's wide mouth curved in a homely grin, and his bright blue eyes twinkled. "Makes you think you've been talking to Jesus Christ, doesn't he?"

"You're right! I swear to God, Mike, if he'd've ordered me to walk back to Diego, I think I'd've gone down to Cavite and taken off my shoes and socks."

Bauer grinned again. "You've only had a half hour of it, Jim. Think of me. I'm exposed to that voice and those eyes for hours every day." He shook his head ruefully. "You know, I came out here convinced the islands were indefensible and that building a Filipino army didn't have a prayer in hell. And damned if he hasn't turned me around a hundred and eighty degrees."

Duff studied Bauer soberly. "But that's like committing mental suicide," he said slowly. "You can't really change your mind like that, can you?"

Bauer shrugged. "When I'm with him, I can," he said.

Major Bauer returned to the States in 1939. Although Marshal Duggan had been able to persuade him to serve in Manila for four years rather than three, he could induce him to stay no longer.

"I've *got* to have field command," Bauer said doggedly,

and in the fall he and his wife Mimi sailed for the West Coast.

Duggan sincerely regretted his departure, but his disappointment was nothing in comparison to his joy when he learned that Bauer's replacement would be Captain Beauregard Ames. Both he and Betsy were as excited and nervous as children going on a trip as they awaited the arrival of Virginia and Beau and the little grandson whom they had never seen. The child had been named Kenneth, after his great- and great-great grandfathers. They had pictures of him, of course, from birth through every season until his third birthday. Elaborately framed photographs of Kenneth were all over the penthouse and in Duggan's office. He was a pretty child, with large dark eyes like his grandfather and mother, dark hair, and an oval face. There was a kind of fragile beauty about him, almost dainty, like a girl. At first Betsy had been mildly disappointed that Kenneth had not been blond like Beau and "her" Beau. (She now admitted to herself that Beau was her real lover, realizing, however, with the wisdom of age, that they never could have had a successful marriage.) But she soon forgot it in the joy of having a grandchild, and in seeing Mark's immense pride in having a grandson who would carry on the Duggan tradition.

The day the *President Coolidge* sailed through the mouth of Manila Bay, Marshal Duggan had Durkin drive him furiously down to Cavite, where he boarded one of the new British torpedo boats Commodore Duff had procured—Q boats, they were then called—and went roaring out toward it. Bouncing madly over the wind-whipped water, the powerful sleek boat shot across the *Coolidge*'s bow. Duggan actually stopped the ship. In full uniform, the gold marshal's baton that Manuel Quezon had presented him clutched in his hand, he went swaying up the Jacob's ladder. As he did, he recalled another ship he had stopped more guilefully in San Francisco Bay nearly forty years ago, and how he and little Kenneth's dead grandfather Ames had clambered up another ladder.

Captain Ames, Virginia, and Kenneth, clad in a sailor's suit, stood at the rail, watching the heavily braided top of his hat bob closer. Duggan vaulted lightly onto the deck and swung the child up in his arms. He gazed tenderly into Kenneth's eyes and kissed him full on the mouth.

"My grandson," he murmured softly, tears rolling down his cheeks. "Kenneth *Duggan* Ames, my grandson." Only after he had set the child down did he turn to embrace Virginia and shake hands with Captain Ames.

He turned, chuckling through the tears, when he heard Kenneth exclaim in a high, childish voice, "Mommy, why is Granddaddy crying?"

"Because he's so happy to see you, dearest," Virginia said.

Kenneth looked puzzled. "Do you always cry when you're happy, Granddaddy?"

Laughing again, Duggan swung the boy aloft once more and kissed him on each cheek. "You're a Duggan through and through, Kenneth," he cried. "Look at those beautiful Scots eyes."

"Well, sir," Captain Ames interjected, "there's a little bit of London and Alabama in him too."

"Right you are, Beau!" Duggan said, gripping the young man's arm fiercely. "He's got fighting blood, all right!" Setting Kenneth on the deck, he dug into his trousers pocket and pulled out a toy pistol, which he handed gravely to his grandson.

"Oh, boy!" Kenneth cried, seizing it, running down the deck and pointing it at the amused passengers. "Bang, bang!" he shouted. "Bang, bang!"

Noticing the gold baton Duggan held, Captain Ames said: "Did you hear who Roosevelt's new chief of staff is, General? I . . . I mean, Marshal?"

"No."

"Your old friend George Quincy Meadows. It was on the ship's radio just as we entered the harbor."

Duggan was about to remark, sarcastically, "Looks like Henry came through," but instead he turned to gaze at the city, remembering, once more, how he and George had stood on the dock in San Francisco Bay, watching the *General Philip Sheridan* sail away from them. Tears came into his eyes. They had been the closest friends then—eager young shavetails questing for adventure and glory—and out beyond the harbor mouth had lain the world that they would conquer. Duggan sighed heavily. Suddenly, all the rancor vanished from his breast.

"The President couldn't have made a better choice," he said quietly.

• • •

If Mark Duggan had adored his daughter, he worshiped his grandson. He insisted that Beau and Virginia live with them in the penthouse, and he personally supervised the decoration of Kenneth's bedroom, sending back to the States for early American wallpaper with battle scenes in red, white, and blue. Almost immediately he nicknamed his grandson "Duggie."

"Duggie," he would say to him each morning when he brought the little boy into the bathroom to watch him shave, "wherever you go, your name is Kenneth *Duggan* Ames. When you sign your name in school, or meet anyone, that's how it will be: 'Kenneth *Duggan* Ames.' Got it?"

The child would nod solemnly, laughing in delight when his grandfather began to sing old war songs and barrack ballads.

> *Mademoiselle from Armentieres*
> *Parlez-vous.*

> *Old soldiers never die—*
> *They just fade away.*

> *Over hill, over dale*
> *As we hit the dusty trail—*
> *And those caissons go rolling along.*

Marshall Duggan also taught Duggie all the movements of close order drill, how to wheel, about-face, salute, sidestep, and come to attention. Each morning when he had finished shaving, he would turn and shout: "Sergeant Duggie—tennnshun!" Stiffening proudly, the little boy would snap to. "About-face! Forrrard, march! Hut, right; hut, right . . ." Solemnly counting cadence, Duggan would march his grandson down the corridor until they came opposite Kenneth's room, at which point Duggan would cry: "Company, halt! Disss-misssed!" Then he would bend down, swing the laughing boy aloft, and kiss him good-bye for the day.

Duggan also lavished gifts upon Kenneth. For his fourth birthday, in 1939, he bought him a huge "war" set, a sandbox replete with hills, roads, streams, and forts, to be manned by toy soldiers in different uniforms, armed with toy field pieces, tanks, and trucks. He was also extremely protective of Duggie. Like many children his age, the boy was

afraid of the dark. Duggan let him sleep beside a lighted
bedlamp. This final piece of indulgence, however, aroused
the objections of his mother, his grandmother, and his Chinese
amah. One night when Duggan was working late, they put
Kenneth to bed and turned off the light. Within a few minutes
the boy began to whimper. They let him cry, retiring to the
living room. Stone-faced and silent, the three women sat
there playing mah jong.

Duggan came home. "Where's Duggie?" he asked.

"In bed," Virginia answered.

"But, good Lord—he's *crying*! Can't you hear him?"

Fixing them with a glance of cold fury, Duggan strode
swiftly down the corridor. He entered the boy's room, to
switch on the light and lift the sobbing child tenderly in his arms.

"Don't cry, Duggie," he murmured soothingly, kissing
him on the cheek. "Granddaddy's here, and everything will
be all right." Putting the child down, he left the light
burning, going straight to his bedroom without another word
for the three despairing, frustrated women.

Next day, Virginia came to him. "Daddy, you're spoiling
Kenneth rotten. You've got to stop."

"Spoiling him?" Duggan repeated. "Nonsense! You can't
spoil a Duggan."

"Daddy, his name is Ames."

"It's Kenneth *Duggan* Ames. And don't you forget it."

"Daddy, please . . . I can't do anything with him, he's so
spoiled. If I spank him or yell at him, he tells me he's going
to report me to the general."

Duggan chuckled, and Virginia's dark eyes blazed. "It's
not funny!"

"Jinny," Duggan said soothingly, "you sound just like your
mother when you were growing up. Now, did I spoil you?"

Virginia sighed helplessly. "Daddy, please—don't interfere
anymore. Please . . . ?"

Duggan kissed her lightly on the cheek. "Don't worry,
honey. I never did—and I never will."

Gradually, as the world drew closer to the great war that
Duggan had anticipated, he did see less and less of his
grandson. He saw him each morning, of course, but rarely at
night. By the time he came home, Kenneth was usually

asleep, without, eventually, a lamp to light his room. Consequently, Duggan was not aware that his protectiveness and the military milieu that he had created to make his grandson a "true Duggan" was having a reverse effect. Kenneth played less and less with his war set. At picnics or outings arranged by the base officers, he played more often with girls than boys, seeming to prefer hopscotch and "house" to football or baseball, and he never let his warrior grandfather find the dolls that his amah gave him and that he took to bed with him.

On September 1, 1939, Nazi Germany invaded Poland, after which Britain and France declared war on Germany; and Communist Russia, having attacked Poland from the east and divided that unhappy country between herself and Germany, invaded Finland. The terrible great conflagration Duggan had expected—not to say feared—was lighting the face of Europe in destruction and death. Certain, now, that he would one day don his war bonnet again, Duggan worked ever harder to forge a Philippine army. As he did, his confidence grew—probably because he seldom visited the training camps located throughout the archipelago at some distance from Manila. After the fall of France in 1940 and Japanese occupation of French IndoChina, he was still confident, reiterating his faith in the Filipino soldier in his messages to General Meadows and in his interviews with streams of visiting correspondents and dignitaries, who were drawn to Manila by the specter of war clouds drifting south from Japan. Some of the reports sent home were highly critical, including one highly uncomplimentary one from the Philippine adjutant general. Duggan dismissed all criticism with eloquence or countercharge. When *Time* magazine printed an article belittling the Philippine Army, he accused the press of a conspiracy to mock the Filipino as a fighting man and to destroy his self-respect.

In mid-1941 Duggan told a correspondent for the *New York Times*: "If Japan started a war in the Far East, the Americans, the British, and the Dutch could easily handle her with the forces they have deployed out here. The Chinese adventure has exhausted Japan. It had eroded the foundations of her economic and military structure. Half the Japanese army is now at third-class level. Out here in the Philippines we have twelve full Filipino divisions already trained. We are ready for any eventuality.''

A few days later President Roosevelt closed the Panama Canal to Japanese shipping and froze all Japanese assets in the United States. Japan now could neither sell nor buy in America. On the same day, General Meadows created a command called United States Army Forces in the Far East, combining both American and Filipino forces under Mark Duggan, recalled to active service with the rank of lieutenant general. Duggan was overjoyed, and he immediately began bombarding Washington with requests that the official war plan for defense of the Philippines be changed.

That plan accepted the loss of all the Philippines except the Manila Bay area, which was to be held until the arrival of the United States Navy and reinforcements. Duggan argued that the entire archipelago should be defended, and that it could be done by his growing Filipino Army together with American forces. With his customery eloquence, he convinced Meadows that he was right, and in November 1941 the plan was changed to suit Duggan. Delighted, the general divided the islands into separate commands and instructed his commanders to ''defend at the water's edge.''

Meanwhile, in Washington, the talks between Secretary of State Hull and Ambassador Nomura had collapsed. At the end of November, Duggan received a ''final alert'' notifying him that war with Japan was imminent. On December 6 he put his forces on a round-the-clock, full alert, and ordered his precious B-17 bombers—the famous ''Flying Fortress''—moved from Clark Field on Luzon farther south to Del Monte Field in Mindanao, where they would be out of range of Japanese aircraft on Formosa. Still confident that the Japanese would not attack until spring—when he would be ready for them—he went home early, had dinner, went out on the terrace to watch Kenneth riding the tricycle he had bought him—and went to bed.

At half-past three the following morning, the telephone beside his bed rang. It was Sergeant Durkin.

''Jaysus, Gen'ral—the Japs just bombed Pearl Harbor! 'Twas on the wireless.''

Duggan paused only momentarily. ''Bring the car around, Pat,'' he said quickly, and then added softly aloud to himself: ''The little yellow bastards.''

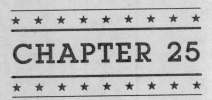
Half of General Duggan's precious B-17 bombers had not been sent south to the safety of Mindanao as he had ordered. By noon of December 7 they were still parked on Clark Field, inviting targets for the Japanese. Duggan's air chief had kept them there, hoping to send them in a raid over Formosa. Duggan's chief of staff had angrily rejected this suicidal proposal—not, however, because it was obvious that none of the Far East Air Force's fighter planes had the range to escort the Flying Fortresses to Formosa and back—but because he deeply disliked the air chief.

Three fighter squadrons from Iba Field assigned to protect the Clark bombers had been sent to intercept stations over the South China Sea, Bataan, and Corregidor. Another squadron was on the ground at Clark refueling. Three more fighter squadrons at Del Carmen Field between Clark and Manila were ordered to cover Clark, but could not take off because of dense dust clouds sweeping the runways.

At about half-past twelve Clark pilots walking from the mess hall toward their refueling planes halted in horror to hear the murmuring of many motors aloft. Air-raid sirens began to shriek. A V-shaped flight of enemy bombers, twenty-seven of them, flying at about 25,000 feet, came into view,

At once, the pilots ran for the protection of the slit trenches, while antiaircraft gunners sprinted toward their battle stations.

The bombs began to fall. They came down with the quavering high whisper peculiar to aerial bombs, and Clark Field heaved and bucked amid huge blossoming flowers of orange flame. The first bomb struck and destroyed the communications center. Some airplanes were hit and ruined. Then the Japanese flew off, the American antiaircraft shells exploding harmlessly beneath them. Soon after, a second flight of the same size arrived, bombing more accurately with the flames of burning buildings to guide them. Still, more than half the parked aircraft had escaped damage—until a flight of thirty-four Zero fighters swept in low with roaring engines and stuttering machine gunes.

That was the end of Clark Field's aircraft. Those that had survived the bombs collapsed in useless bullet-ridden heaps, and scores of burning aircraft sent plumes of black smoke spiraling aloft, like so many funeral pyres for General Duggan's Far East Air Force. The effective end of that unit came ten minutes later when fifty-four Japanese bombers and fifty Zeros wiped out the Iba Field facilities and destroyed a P-40 squadron that had returned from the South China Sea for refueling.

The Philippines now lay almost totally unprotected against enemy air attack.

Soon it lay defenseless to the sea. "Duggan's Navy," the much-vaulted and publicized mosquito feets, had been immediately useless. It did not attack because it had no ships to attack. The only Japanese vessels near the archipelago were aircraft carriers, standing hundreds of miles off the coast.

By Christmas, General Duggan was also without true naval support. On that day, the U.S. Asiatic Fleet sailed away from the Philippines to join Dutch and British forces guarding the Malay Barrier. On the following day a discouraged but still strangely confident Mark Duggan declared Manila an open city and moved with his wife and family to a house "Topside" on Corregidor, the tadpole-shaped island guarding the entrance to Manila Bay. Day after day in his headquarters in Malinta Tunnel, dug deep beneath "the Rock," he stared moodily at the picture of his father on his desk, while Major Beauregard Ames stuck colored pins into a wall map to trace the steady advance of the Japanese, who had landed in Lingayen Gulf on December 22.

Gradually, the trail of pins punctured Duggan's confidence in his ability to defend the Philippines "at the water's edge." Most of his poorly-trained Filipino divisions broke and ran at the first contact with the Japanese. Some stood their ground and fought bravely, but generally the Filipino Army was a failure.

Sick at heart, but nevertheless accepting reality, Duggan called to Major Ames, "Get a secretary in here, Beau—I'm pulling back from Luzon."

"Where to, sir?"

"Bataan," Duggan said, pointing to the peninsula just above Corregidor.

"Excellent, sir! That'll straighten the Japs up a bit." He, too, pointed to the map, where enemy pincers were coming ominously close to the rear of the North and South Luzon forces. "They're probably counting on a quick campaign. No more than a month."

"So Intelligence thinks," Duggan said grimly. "But if I can get into Bataan, they'll have to measure their advance in months, not weeks." He scowled. "With any help from the States, I'll stop them cold."

Picking up his pen, he began to write the order commanding Major General Jonathan "Bones" Cartwright to withdraw from Luzon.

For two weeks General Duggan paced his office like a caged lion. He walked perhaps ten miles a day between his desk and the wall map, actually wearing a path in the floor, watching with nervous apprehension the slow progress of the colored pins south to Bataan. He knew, as few men in the world knew, the grave risks of conducting a strategic withdrawal in the face of a vigorous, victorious enemy. Yet, he had chosen well in selecting Bones Cartwright to command the operation. In a series of well-conceived and superbly executed pullbacks made behind brave and determined holding actions, Cartwright extricated his troops and led them into the comparative safety of the Bataan peninsula.

"Bones, you did it!" Duggan cried, when the amazingly thin Cartwright entered Malinta Tunnel to report. He seized

Cartwright's bony hand in both of his and slapped him on the back. "I'm putting you in for the DSC, and recommending they make your temporary rank permanent."

"Thank you, sir," Cartwright croaked in his deep bass voice. His Adam's apple bobbed in his scrawny neck. He glanced at the icebox in Duggan's office. "Got any beer in there, General?"

Duggan chuckled. "Oh, I guess a few cans." He opened the door to draw out several cans, flipping one to Cartwright, who opened it, tilted his head back, and drank deep.

"Aaahh, that's good," Cartwright murmured, quickly finishing it and reaching for the second.

Duggan shook his head wonderingly. "I never will understand, Bones, how a man as skinny as you can drink all that beer."

"Simple, sir. I don't eat. Long ago, when I started in the cavalry, I was actually fat. I ate almost as much as I drank. So I had to choose between beer and beans—and I took the beer."

Duggan laughed. Getting up from his desk, he came around to gaze gravely down at the seated Cartwright. "Can you hold, Bones?" he asked.

"I'm going to try to, sir. But, I don't know . . ." He shook his head wearily. "Dysentery," he muttered. "Dysentery and malaria, beriberi and dengue. It's killing us. The Japs are nothing in comparison, sir. Basically, it's malnutrition. My men are just not getting enough to eat. And medicine is in short supply too."

Flushing slightly, Duggan looked away and said nothing. He was aware that some of his staff officers were criticizing him for having tried to defend the entire archipelago. Two priceless weeks were wasted, they were saying, which could have been spent in stockpiling Bataan. He knew, too, that when the Americans left Manila, huge stores of supplies were left unguarded on the docks, to be devoured by swarms of Filipino looters.

"I'll give you all I've got," Duggan said, his voice husky. Cartwright arose and Duggan placed both hands on his shoulders and fixed him with his eyes. "I'm counting on you, Bones. If Washington gives me one quarter of what they've promised, I'll pull it out yet."

Cartwright's Adam's apple bobbed again. He shifted the gaze of his own watery blue eyes to the map on the wall. He put down the empty beer can and said in a flat voice: "I'm sure you will, General. Thanks for the recommendations." He grinned weakly. "And the beer."

Duggan stared thoughtfully at the back of his departing field commander. He looks exhausted, he thought, wondering, momentarily, if he should relieve Bones. But with whom? No one else but Cartwright could have conducted such a masterly withdrawal. No, emaciated and worn as he looked—and he never did look healthy—there was no one else to be trusted. Putting the thought out of his mind, Duggan began composing another long message to Chief of Staff Meadows, appealing for reinforcements, supplies, and munitions—especially bombers. Day after day he sat in his stifling hot and suffocating Malinta lateral—barricade baffles at the tunnel mouth not only blocked bomb fragments, but also the flow of air—as calm and cool in his neatly pressed khaki as a clothing store mannikin. He fired off appeal after unrequited appeal, until, as the days of trapped frustration turned into weeks, the appeals became querulous requests and then haughty demands.

Just as regularly, soothing, unruffled replies came back from General Meadows: "A stream of four-engine bombers, previously delayed by foul weather, is en route, with the head of the column having crossed Africa . . . A stream of four-engine bombers started today from Hawaii, staging at new island fields . . . Two groups of powerful long-range medium bombers left yesterday . . . Pursuit planes are en route on every available ship . . ."

But none came. It was as though President Roosevelt and his chief of staff were physicians assuring a dying patient that he still had many years left, as though they feared that the truth would weaken the American will to fight on and upset the Japanese timetable of conquest. They knew the truth, of course, although perhaps not as bluntly as Brigadier General Michael Bauer, now General Meadows's deputy chief of the War Plans Division.

One week after Pearl Harbor, Bauer told Meadows: "It will be a long time before major reinforcements can go to the Philippines, longer than the garrison can hold out if the Japs commit major forces."

Yet, Bauer strove desperately to send relief to Duggan. He worked deep into the night trying to discover ways to get supplies into the islands. Blockade runners were hired in Australia and the East Indies. Ten million dollars was flown to Java for that purpose. Appeals to the Navy resulted in the overhauling of overage destroyers as blockade runners. Submarines were pressed into service. But only a driblet slipped through the iron net strung around and above the islands by Japanese sea and air power. Japan's grip on the Philippines tightened, until, at last, a despairing Bauer observed in his diary: "For many weeks—it seems years—I've been searching everywhere to find any feasible way of giving real help to the islands . . . I'll go on trying, but daily the situation grows more desperate."

Gradually, all of Mark Duggan's old rancor toward George Quincy Meadows returned. He blamed the chief of staff for all his failures and frustrations.

"It's the Chaumont clique all over again," he muttered to Ames, "the Pershing clique out for Duggan's scalp."

Sometimes, in the presence of Ames or Colonel Jim Duff, now Duggan's intelligence officer, he would deliver lengthy diatribes against Meadows, calling him "Genry Gawkins's errand boy." Duggan could compress a distillate of scathing contempt into the name "Genry Gawkins," which he now called Hawkins after FDR's closest aide flew to Moscow where the Russians, unable to pronounce the aspirate, put a guttural G in its place. Duggan's conviction of a communist conspiracy repossessed him—obsessively, this time—and not so much as a plot against America, as one to thwart Duggan in the Pacific. He stormed against Allied "Grand Strategy," which was to defeat the Axis first while containing the Japanese, after which it would be Japan's turn.

"Can't they understand that the Pacific has become the arena of world ambitions?" he exclaimed bitterly in the presence of Duff and Ames, his always-silent audience. "Don't they realize that Europe is tired of her greatness? Certainly the technocracy of Europe is a great prize, and her free-speech societies the greatest of values—but it is out here," he cried, his voice throbbing with emotion, "out *here,* in the Pacific and Indian Oceans, that the future of civilization lies. Out *here,*" he repeated grimly, striding to his globe, switching on the light and pointing to it with his gold baton. "Look, Beau, Jim—here are literally billions of human beings. Here are untold resources . . . most of the world's rubber . . . most of the oil . . . the rice . . . the ore . . . Name any treasure of the earth or sea—and you'll find it here." Jabbing his baton savagely at a point just below French IndoChina, he snapped, "Here's the Malay Barrier, the most vital narrow waters in the world. Here is the Straits of Malacca, the link between the Pacific and the Indian Oceans, between China and Japan, the Antipodes and the East Indies, and all the multitudinous, fertile islands of Oceania—between them and the East Coast of Africa, the Suez and all the oil riches of Arabia. And now Japan holds it! Since the fall of Singapore and the destruction of our own Asiatic Fleet, and the Dutch and British Asiatic fleets as well, the Pacific has become a Japanese lake. The Indian Ocean will be next. And they talk of Europe! Hitler! Mussolini! To hell with Europe!" he swore with unaccustomed savagery. "God damn Hitler and Mussolini! Out *here* is where Armageddon is! Out *here*!"

As bitter and frequent as General Duggan's disappointments were, he spoke of them to no one but Duff and Ames. To the rest of his staff, and especially to the troops on Bataan, he was the living embodiment of confidence and optimism. Playing the same game Roosevelt and Meadows were playing with him, his daily bulletins spoke cheerfully of "help" that was always "on the way." Clouds of airplanes . . . baysful of ships . . . acres of tanks . . . dozens of divisions . . . food . . . medicine . . . new rifles and helmets, shoes and socks . . . Daily, the emaciated scarecrows on the lines awoke to peer anxiously into the sky or out to sea for the "help" that never came. Eventually they became bitterly disillusioned and came to hate Duggan.

Back in Malinta Tunnel on the "Rock" of Corregidor, shielded from all criticism by the faithful Ames and Duff, Duggan was unaware of the reverse effect that his bulletins were having—until the day he visited General Cartwright on Bataan. Cartwright escorted him to the sector held by one of his two corps.

"Help is definitely on the way," Duggan told a group of officers there. "We must hold out until it arrives." There were a few scattered cheers, and then Cartwright asked,

"Would you like to take a look at our 155's, General?" Duggan shook his head. "I don't want to see them, Bones," he said, "I want to *hear* them!"

Driving back to Corregidor, Duggan's staff car was stopped by a traffic jam. Durkin got out to see what was wrong. Duggan lighted his corncob pipe, leaning back in his seat and puffing reflectively. He noticed a young soldier seated on an empty five-gallon can on the road beside him. He was reading a dog-eared sheet of paper and shaking with silent laughter.

"What's so funny, soldier?" Duggan inquired mildly. The youth glanced up and turned white when he saw who had spoken to him. He struggled to his feet, dropping the paper as he did. Duggan leaned down, picked it up, and began to read.

> *Bataan Cry of Freedom*
>
> *Dugout Duggy Duggan lies ashaking on the Rock*
> *Safe from all the bombers and from any sudden*
> * shock*
> *Dugout Dug is eating of the best food on Bataan*
> *And his troops go starving on.*
>
> *Dugout Dug's not timid, he's just cautious, not*
> * afraid*
> *He's carefully protecting the stars that Franklin made*
> *Four-star generals are as rare as good food on*
> * Bataan*
> *And his troops go starving on.*
>
> *Dugout Dug is ready in his Chris-Craft for the flee*
> *Over bounding billows and the wildly raging sea*
> *For the Japs are pounding on the gates of old*
> * Bataan*
> *And his troops go starving . . .*

Duggan glanced sadly at the horrified soldier standing beside him. "This is what the troops think of their general?" he asked gently. Visibly trembling, the youth gulped and said nothing. Duggan returned the paper with a shaking hand. "Son," he said gently, "I hope you live long enough to understand."

Motors began coughing into life, and the traffic ahead of Duggan's staff car lurched forward. Durkin came back and got into the driver's seat. In silent grief, Mark Duggan drove back toward Corregidor.

But he never returned to Bataan.

By late January 1942, General Cartwright's emaciated scarecrows still held the Japanese at bay on Bataan. Desperate, already behind schedule, the Japanese brought in reinforcements and resumed the attack.

On Corregidor some eleven thousand Americans and Filipinos cringed beneath daily bombing attacks and artillery shelling from Cavite. No one lived Topside anymore, except the crews manning huge coastal artillery pieces, after a series of Japanese air raids scorched the hilltops and left them a litter of collapsed and blackened buildings and twisted railroad tracks. Everyone now lived Bottomside, and General Duggan, with Betsy and Virginia and little Kenneth, moved into a crowded, airless lateral in Malinta Tunnel. Each time the enemy air raids arrived, however, Duggan left the safety of the tunnel and strode calmly out into the open, campaign hat perched jauntily on his head, binoculars glued to his eyes, watching the enemy approach and surveying the extent of damage.

Again and again staff officers and even antiaircraft gunners pleaded with the general to take cover. He always refused, pointing to his punctured hat. "They shot off the ones with my name on them forty years ago. Right here in the Philippines. Japan can't make a missile that'll harm Duggan."

One day, Duggan anxiously studied the parabola of the enemy's falling bombs, murmuring, "They're going to come close."

They did. One struck an antiaircraft emplacement twenty yards away. Duggan was lifted into the air and slammed against the ground. He arose, gasping, the wind knocked out of him. He heard screaming and ran for the emplacement. Its sandbags had been blown away. The gun mount was buckled and the gun barrel twisted as though bent by a giant hand. Four of the gunners were dead, each with his head torn off. Blood rose from the gaping holes between their shoulders like carmine fountains. The screaming came from the fifth gunner, a young soldier whose leg had been blown off. Blood spouted from the ragged stump of his thigh.

At once, Duggan pulled off his belt and ran to the youth. Winding it around his thigh, he pulled it tight to fashion a tourniquet.

"I'm going, General, I'm going," the soldier moaned.

"Nonsense, son," Duggan said gently, putting a hand on his forehead. "You'll live to stomp around on a leg of Tennessee ash."

A chaplain rushed up to them. He knelt beside the soldier and asked, "What's your religion, lad?"

"Catholic," the boy gasped. "I'm going to give you general absolution, son—just in case. Don't worry. It's not the last rites."

The boy nodded, and the chaplain took a dirty purple satin stole from his pocket, hanging it around his neck.

"Absolvo peccata te . . ." he began.

"I absolve you of your sins."

Duggan watched intently, amazed to see how the boy relaxed. Then he was thunderstruck when the chaplain finished and stood erect.

It was William Baugh.

"Baugh! Bill Baugh! What are you doing here?"

Baugh grinned at the unconscious banality of the general's question. "Tell you in a minute, General—as soon as I can get some stretcher bearers in here."

Duggan nodded. "Come to my office after you've finished," he said. He knelt to put a comforting hand on the wounded soldier's shoulder. "You'll be all right, son," he said, and returned to the tunnel.

Fifteen minutes later Baugh entered his office and sat down. "Surprised, aren't you, General?" he asked, grinning impishly again.

"I am, indeed," Duggan said, studying Baugh approvingly.

Although Baugh's close-cropped hair had turned iron gray, and a deep line—the mark of suffering—furrowed his face beside his nose, he had regained weight and self-confidence.

Duggan noticed the silver leaves on his shoulder. "Got your old rank back, I see."

Baugh nodded. "It's a long story." He studied Duggan. "When I left you that night on Anacostia Flats, General . . ."

he began, pausing significantly. "You know, sir, I have to tell you—I still think you were wrong about the Bonus Marchers." Duggan's eyelid flickered and his eyes glinted momentarily. But he said nothing. "Anyway, I walked all the way back to New York. I couldn't trust myself to ride a boxcar home. I knew the first bridge I'd come to, I'd jump off. So I walked, mowing lawns and raking leaves for my chow." He grinned again. "My Man Friday skills. When I got back, I went to my parish priest again. He'd just built a new high school, and he gave me a job teaching history. So I was able to put the kids through college. When they got out, I went into the seminary." Baugh frowned, and then smiled enchantingly. "It was a little tough at first. I'd forgotten how to study. And the padres weren't too keen on my language. They didn't mind a son of a bitch or two, but taking the Lord's name, they kept warning me about that. So whenever I'd forget myself and swear, like, 'Jesus!' I'd finish it off quick-like with, 'Savior of my soul.' Or if I'd swear, 'Keerist!' I'd say, 'is risen.'"

Duggan burst out laughing. "Bill, you're a corker!"

Baugh chuckled. "It worked, sir. So I was ordained, just about when Roosevelt pushed through the first peacetime draft. At about the same time, Cardinal Spellman was made Military Vicar of the U.S. Armed Forces. He was upset because there were so few Catholic chaplains in the service, and those that were in didn't have much rank. So when he saw my record and found out I'd been a light colonel in the Guard, he pulled a few strings . . ." He grinned. "Frankie's good at that, General. Anyway, he pulled the strings and got me reinstated, and here I am, your new chief of chaplains."

"Glad to have you, Bill. And the first thing I want you to do is to compose me a humdinger of a prayer for victory."

Baugh gaped in disbelief. "You aren't serious, sir?"

"Of course I am. You're a priest, aren't you? You can't compose a prayer?"

"Not really. The ministers are really better at it than we are. We generally stick to the Our Father and the Hail Mary. Besides, I remember in the last war how the German cardinal would bless the German banners and the French cardinal blessed the French banners. I always thought they were making it embarrassing for God."

Duggan smiled. "The French won, Bill."

"True—after we came in. Prayer is for spiritual welfare, sir, not material benefit. That's magic. That's what Simon Magi wanted from Peter—remember, General?" Duggan nodded, interested. "So all I can say, sir, is that if I turn out this prayer, it won't help very much without reinforcements."

"You surprise me, Bill."

"I shouldn't sir. Actually, you surprise me. I didn't think you would ask that. So many people come to us when they're in hot water, looking for a little bit of magic. They seem to think we have secret spiritual powers that'll get them out of trouble when they get their secretary pregnant or get caught with their hand in the till. But we don't. And then they get sore at us and swear they'll never go to church again. I'm a priest, sir," he said simply, "not a magician." He paused, as though weighing his next remark. "Are you religious, General?" he asked.

"Very much so."

"You believe in God?"

"To the very depth of my being."

"That's strange. I know you're an Episcopalian, and a very moral man—but I've never known you to go to church."

"It's true, I don't attend services very often. But I say my morning and evening prayers every day and try to read the Bible frequently." Duggan leaned forward gravely. "When I was a child, Bill, each night when I went to bed, my mother told me I would be a great man. She also told me that God was watching over me. I believed her. I still do. Out there today, when that bomb hit, only God Himself could have kept me alive."

"You really believe that, sir?"

"I do. I firmly believe that there is a special Providence watching over me. I didn't always believe in my destiny. But once that day in the Argonne, when Beauregard Ames laid down his life for mine, I have been convinced of it."

Chaplain Baugh sighed heavily. "People like you are rare, General. Almost unique. St. Francis had that same simple, unshakable faith. So do quite a few old women. But not many of the other saints, and certainly not many men. We believe, and we don't believe. Our faith is a checkerboard of doubt and belief. Funny, you'd think an athiest would have a checkerboard of denial too. But they don't. They never doubt their denial, never experience a faint glimmer of belief. You're like them, sir. You have no checkerboard—you just believe."

"I do. Do you doubt your religion, Bill?"

"Frequently. I mean no offense, sir—but a faith that has not conquered doubt is usually not very deep. And there's so much in Christianity that's difficult to swallow."

General Duggan tugged his graduation watch from his pocket and glanced at it. "This has been very interesting, Bill—but I have an appointment with Manuel Quezon shortly. Glad to see you again," he said with a grin, "and don't forget my prayer."

Defeat, black defeat, confronted Mark Duggan. Worse than defeat, disaster and disgrace: He might find himself compelled to surrender his command to the Japanese. Throughout January and into February the enemy had driven the Americans and Filipinos steadily before them. Far away in Malaya, they had captured Singapore, thus sealing off the Malay Barrier and freeing troops for combat in the Philippines.

At once, General Duggan—who had regained his fourth star—began making plans for conducting guerrilla warfare in the mountains. But then, Chief of Staff Meadows ordered him to leave the islands and flee to Australia. He ignored the order. It came again, and Duggan still paid no heed.

"I'm thinking of resigning my command," he told Colonel Duff. "Then I can stay here as a simple volunteer. Like Dr. Joseph Warren at Bunker Hill."

A frown wrinkled Duff's ruddy forehead. "I can understand your wanting to die a hero's death, sir," he began slowly. "But really, you're too valuable to be wasted that way. Who else but you can organize and lead the American counterattack?"

"I don't want to go," Duggan said stubbornly. "I'll send out my family, but I'm staying." He jabbed his corncob in Duff's direction. "Are you familiar with that scurrilous parody of the 'Battle Hymn of the Republic' that the troops are singing?"

Duff blushed. "I am, sir," he mumbled, surprised that his chief had seen it.

"Then you must remember the line, 'Dugout Dug is ready in his Chris-Craft for the flee.' Do you think I want to make a prophet of the scoundrel who wrote it?" he cried savagely.

"But, sir—" Duff began.

Duggan's chin lifted defiantly. "No, Jim—I'm staying."

But then General Duggan received a direct order from President Roosevelt commanding him to proceed as soon as possible to Australia to take charge of a new Southwest Pacific Theater then being formed. Duggan was shaken. He did not think he could disobey his commander-in-chief quite so easily as the chief of staff. Nevertheless, he hesitated for another two weeks, until Beau Ames came boldly to the general's desk one morning and said, "Sir, I must tell you that my father did not die for you to die in a Japanese prison." Saluting, he about-faced and left—and Duggan decided to leave.

That night, Duggan called General Cartwright to his office. "Bones, the President has ordered me to go to Australia."

Cartwright shook himself, like a boxer shaking off the effects of a blow. "I—I understand, sir," he said slowly. "You'll do our country a lot more good in Australia than you'll do here."

"Thank you," Duggan said. He opened his office icebox. "Here, there's a box of cigars in there you can have, Bones. No beer, though. Durkin drank the last can last night." Duggan grimaced. "No food either. I know the troops are saying I'm eating like a king. But look at me. I'm almost as skinny as you are. Twenty-five pounds! I've even put two extra holes in my belt." He peered inside the icebox. "There's a couple of jars of shaving cream in there, though. You want 'em?"

"I sure do. I had to borrow some this morning. Do you know, I met a colonel out on Bataan who told me he'd washed himself twelve times with the same helmet full of water."

Duggan grimaced again. "I can believe it," he said grimly. He came around his desk to stand in front of Cartwright. "We'll be leaving tomorrow night—by torpedo boat." His hands went to Cartwright's shoulders. "If I get through to Australia, Bones, I'll be back as soon as I can with all I can get." His voice became husky. "You've got to hold, Bones."

Cartwright's Adam's apple bobbed. "I'll hang on, General," he murmured, looking away. Taking the cigars and shaving cream, he left.

Shortly after dark the following night, General Duggan and his party assembled on the south dock of Bottomside on Corregidor. Fortunately, squalling rain clouds enshrouded the bay in darkness. Duggan was taking about twenty Army and Navy officers with him, the nucleus of the staff that would organize his new command. Colonel Jim Duff, his intelligence officer, was one of them. Sergeant Durkin was there too. As he came aboard, General Duggan was startled to notice that Durkin's graying red hair was now white.

"Good Lord, Pat, your hair's pure white," Duggan exclaimed.

" 'Tis the match of me soul, sir," Durkin said with a grin.

Durkin stared at the general's thin but still black hair and smiled mischievously. Durkin knew. Long ago in Manila, the general's wife had asked him to bring her some aspirin, and when he opened the medicine cabinet he had noticed the bottle of hair dye.

Colonel Ames was not going. Duggan had included him in the escape party, but he had refused to go. "I am proud to be your son-in-law, General," he said stubbornly, "and I want to stay that way."

Chaplain Baugh had also insisted on staying, although he did consent to come dockside and bless the torpedo boats.

Betsy and Virginia were going, of course, and little Kenneth and his Chinese amah. Four boats were required for the escape, and the flotilla was under the overall command of Colonel Duff, who had built the mosquito fleet and was now an experienced patrol-boat skipper.

Each passenger was allowed to carry one handbag, nothing more, although Virginia had brought a sleeping pad for Kenneth. Duggan and his wife stood silently on the deck of their gently rolling boat, watching the officers board their vessels.

Mark gestured toward the moored flotilla. "What do you think the liberal press will say about this?" he asked with heavy sarcasm. "They'll say I tied up four battleships filled with my own furniture, and Duggie's sleeping pad was stuffed with hundred-dollar bills." Turning, he went below.

Slowly, the four boats, moving with muffled engines, vanished into the darkness of the bay. Rain squalls swept the water. Lying face down on his bunk, Duggan heard raindrops hitting the water with the sound of machine-gun fire. Soon the boat began to sway violently, and Duggan guessed that they had slipped past the Japanese shore batteries and were safely in the South China Sea. He heard a roar of motors and felt the boat surge ahead, power pulsing through its hull. Now the flotilla was sailing in a diamond formation, making for the Cuyo Islands in the Sulu Sea.

The squalls turned into a storm. Great waves crashed the bow of Duggan's boat. Black water came flooding over the weather deck. Colonel Duff retreated to the safety of the bridge. Below, General Duggan had become seasick. So had everyone else. Little Kenneth lay whimpering on his pad. Duggan heard him, but could feel no pity, no compassion—he had become so ill himself. Not even the seizure at Luneville or the White House could compare to the double dose of nervous nausea and seasickness. Eventually, Duggan fell asleep, awaking, it seemed, instantly, although actually an hour later, all his senses keening, his cabin flooded with an eerie, bluish-white light. Leaping erect, his illness forgotten, he ran topside—halting in the blinding beam of a powerful searchlight.

Duggan turned away, shielding his eyes. He heard shells exploding around the torpedo boat; then a strange succession of thuds: *ker-plunk-plunk*.

"They're firing armor-piercing," Colonel Duff shouted. "They're going right through us without exploding."

"What is it?" Duggan yelled.

"Jap destroyer, I guess . . . Goddammit, get that friggin' fifty going," he swore at a seaman crouched up forward on the dual .50-caliber machine gun. "Shoot that goddam light out!"

His answer was a staccato stutter and a stream of red tracers curving through the dark before vanishing in the searchlight beam. Suddenly, darkness reengulfed the surface of the sea. There was a farway tinkling sound.

"Good shooting, swabbie," Duff called. "Goddam good shooting!"

Duggan could hear Duff coming toward him. He opened

his eyes, which he had squeezed shut to accustom them to the darkness. When he opened them, he understood what had happened. The storm had passed. Low clouds were scudding across the face of the moon. In ten more minutes there would be moonlight and the enemy would not need a searchlight.

"What's your plan, Jim?" Duggan asked as Duff came up to him, swaying in the darkness.

"I think we should scatter and run for it."

"Can you outrun the Jap?"

"No, sir."

"What can you do better?"

"Maneuver."

"Do you all have torpedoes, depth charges?"

"Yes, sir."

"Searchlights?"

"Yes—good ones."

"All right, Jim—we'll attack."

Duff was momentarily stunned. "Attack, sir? We're way outgunned. This is obviously a blockade ship. There may be more of them."

"Signal your other boats," Duggan said, ignoring the objection. "Tell them to set their depth charges at shallow depth and drop them. The explosions should catch the Japs' eye. Maybe he'll think we're blowing up our boats. Ten seconds later, switch on their searchlights toward the Japs' probable course. If they nail him—and, by God, I *know* they will—then you come in from the dark, and blindside him with your torpedoes."

There was another shocked silence.

"Got that, Jim?" Duggan asked calmly.

"Aye, aye, sir," Colonel Duff stammered, going back to the bridge to relay the orders.

Behind him, Duggan heard a tiny voice: "What's wrong, Granddaddy? Why have we stopped?"

Duggan turned and swept the child up into his arms. "For fireworks, Duggie," he said, laughing. "In a second we're going to have a big bang-bang regatta in my honor."

Duff's muted motors came slowly to full throttle as he swung the ship wide toward where the searchlight had been. A few seconds later there were muffled explosions on the port side. Some of the depth charges had been set so shallow that they shot up flames to light the pluming geyers of water shooting into the black sky. Darkness claimed the sea again, until three thick beams of light swept its obsidian surface. One of them picked up a long, low, dark silhouette, illuminating it. It was the enemy destroyer. Duff was coming in on his stern unobserved. A second beam lighted its port side.

"Port torpedo, stand by to fire," Duff called to his waiting torpedomen. "Starboard torpedo, stand by to fire." He paused, his heart beating. "Range, one thousand feet." He gasped. Machine-gun fire crackled from the destroyer. One by one the lights went out. But Duff had seen enough.

"Port torpedo, fire! Starboard torpedo, fire!"

Swishes, seconds apart, marked the entry of the torpedoes into the water.

Standing swaying beside Duff, his grandson in his arms, Duggan followed the iridescent bubbles marking their silent swift progress toward the unsuspecting Japanese.

The clanging of bells peeled across the water. The enemy had seen his danger and was swinging his ship wildly around—in time to take the full impact of both torpedoes on his port beam.

The sky came alight, glowing as though the shredding clouds were on fire. The emerging moon seemed to turn red. A giant explosion sent shock waves across the water. Little Kenneth Ames put his hands over his ears and dug his face deep into his grandfather's shoulder. Now, great sea swells rocked the torpedo boat, threatening to capsize it. Quickly, Duff turned the boat stern-to, and with a rising roar of power, sped south again for the Sulu Sea. Behind him came the other three boats, and the flotilla reassumed its diamond formation.

General Duggan remained topside the rest of the way, his grandson in his arms, his sickness vanished and his heart swelling with the exultation of the gambler who dares all and wins. Shortly after dawn they sighted the Cuyos. By seven in the morning they were dockside at Tagauayan. One by one the other boats straggled into port. Colonel Duff silenced his engines.

"Well, Jim, we made it," Duggan said, extending his hand.

"I know we did, sir," Duff said, removing his steel helmet

and mopping his sweating forehead with the back of his khaki sleeve. "But I still don't believe it."

At dusk the flotilla left Tagauayan, speeding over calm seas for the port of Cagayan on the north coast of Mindanao. Long after dark, a huge shape loomed across Colonel Duff's bow. Quickly, he cut his speed, and the shape surged on, unnoticing, frothing white water foaming away from its bow, its fantail churning white.

"Phew!" Duff exclaimed, resuming speed. "I thought that bastard would never leave."

Again two hours after dawn, the flotilla made Cagayan. Waiting staff cars sped the escape party to Del Monte Field, adjoining the huge Del Monte pineapple plantation.

There, two Flying Fortresses arrived to take them to Australia. Led by Duggan, still holding Kenneth, who had become ill, the officers went aboard. The airplanes took off, flying low over the water to escape detection by Japanese Zeros, heading for Darwin in northwestern Australia. An enemy air raid over that city, however, compelled the two B-17's to land instead at Batchelor Field, about forty miles south. From there a C-47 transport flew the exhausted party to Alice Springs, a frontier town of two thousand souls and perhaps two million ugly black flies, and from there a now-exhausted Mark Duggan, refusing to fly farther, took a slow, hot, rattling railroad train to the city of Adelaide in South Australia.

A crowd of reporters met Duggan at the station. They listened almost reverently as the famous American commander, already a hero in the Allied world, came to attention before them and said:

"I am here to organize an American counteroffensive against Japan. Chief among my objectives will be the defense of Australia and the relief of the Philippines. I came through, gentlemen," he said with quiet grimness, "and I shall return."

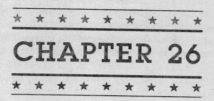

CHAPTER 26

I shall return.

The phrase electrified America and captivated the remainder of the Allied world. Messages of congratulations poured into General Duggan's headquarters in the Menzies Hotel in Melbourne: from FDR and General Meadows, from Churchill, Stalin, Chiang Kai-shek, Charles de Gaulle, and other heads of governments in exile.

I shall return.

The phrase infuriated the Japanese, who had desired Duggan's capture only second to the Philippines themselves. Thwarted, they howled with derision.

"General Duggan is now without question the most accomplished coward in military history," Tokyo Rose sneered in the nightly radio broadcast. "He has now run away from battle on a mule, a torpedo boat, and inside an airplane. We predict that the next time we defeat him, he will crawl away on his hands and knees."

I shall return.

It appeared everywhere in America: on colored "pinup" photographs of the general in his famous campaign cap and corncob; on stamps and lapel buttons; on dishes and enameled souvenir plaques; on the covers of *Time* magazine and *Newsweek* and Sunday rotogravure sections. "Quickie" biographies of the general were rapidly slapped together to become best-sellers. Publishers and movie producers vied with one another to obtain the rights to Duggan's ''life.'' Politicians also joined the adulatory scramble, introducing resolutions at every level—local, county, state, and national—praising the general. One congressman tried to have Corregidor's name changed to ''Duggan Island,'' while another more successfully had June thirteenth designated as ''Mark Duggan Day.'' Duggan was also chosen ''Father of the Year.'' Thousands of newborn babies were named after him; so were parks, streets, schools, and hospitals; flowers, drinks and dances. National polls found him the most popular of all possible candidates for the Republican presidential nomination, second only to President Roosevelt in overall popularity—a distinction which was not lightly overlooked in the White House.

Meanwhile, Sergeant Durkin's outer office in the general's hotel headquarters rapidly filled up with an accumulation of mementos and tributes that had become Durkin's daily despair.

''Mother of Divine Mercy!'' he breathed one morning after he had opened a crate and drawn forth a huge Indian chief's war bonnet of beautiful red-and-white feathers. ''This one's from the Blackfeet, Gen'ral. They've adopted yez, sir. Yer now a Sioux, a Cheyenne, and a Blackfoot. Ah, Jaysus, but they've given yez a fine name, sir,'' he continued, peering at the headdress. '' 'Mo-Kahki-Peta,' Chief Wise Eagle.'' Duggan chuckled, and Durkin returned the feathered headpiece to its crate, standing on tiptoe to place it atop a pile of boxes in a corner. He opened another package, examining an object in a heavy, gold-trimmed glass case. ''Just what you need, Gen'ral,'' he said wryly. '' 'Tis a first-class relic, sir—the bone of the little finger of Saint Thomas Aquinas.'' He began to laugh. ''The nun who sent it to you wants you to carry it when you return to the Philippines, sir.'' He shook his head in mock dismay. ''Sweet sufferin' Jaysus—fat Tommy's little pinky, no less, and him dead for sivin hundred years.'' He looked around him, puzzled, until he caught sight of a carton full of small boxes. ''Patrick, son of sivin Patricks, yer an organizin' genius,'' he said softly. ''I'll file it under 'Charms,' right in front of 'Citations and Medals.' '' He stooped to put the package in the carton. ''Right in here with all them African amulets and rabbits' feet.'' He straightened, shaking his white head. "Jaysus save me wit, Gen'ral, but there's enough rubbage in here to start a museum."

"Maybe we will after the war, Pat—and you can be the curator."

Durkin grinned. "Would yez let me carry yer baton, sir?"

Duggan smiled. "It's a deal, Pat," he said, and went into his office.

He sat down and began to study reports of American troops strength in Australia. He was shocked. There were barely 25,000 Americans available. Most of them were service troops. He hadn't a single fighting-strength division to spearhead his celebrated "return" to the Philippines! Dismayed, he studied Australian army strength. It was more reassuring, a total of seven divisions, but of these only two were veteran; a third was till in the Middle East. Duggan groaned inwardly. The Australian force was not even large enough to defend the continent!

At once, and almost every day from February until June, he sat down to compose an urgent request to Washington for reinforcements. He was assisted by Australian Prime Minister Curtin, who spoke so bluntly of his nation's needs and dependence on the United States rather than the United Kingdom that he angered Winston Churchill.

"Let me repeat," Churchill wrote to Curtin, "I have not become His Majesty's first minister to preside over the liquidation of the British Empire."

The British prime minister was provoked, of course, because at that moment the American president was veering away from the "Europe First" policy. Half of the men and material now leaving the United States were going to the Pacific.

Even so, Duggan still complained. Half of the Pacific half, he protested, was going to Admiral Nimitz in Hawaii. Convinced, as always, that *his* theater was the focal point of enemy ambition, he argued that the Japanese intended to attack Australia. Not even receipt of the Medal of Honor, for which he had yearned so many years, appeased his rage at being "neglected." In a "simple" ceremony, covered, of course, by three-dozen war correspondents and photographers representing all the media of the Allied world, Sergeant

Durkin pinned the star-spangled blue ribbon with its star-shaped metal pendant on the general's breast.

"Now I'm even with you, Pat," Duggan quipped, while photographer's bulbs popped and flashed. Pointing to the same blue ribbon on Durkin's tunic, Duggan said, "Pat won his Medal of Honor out in the Philippines forty years ago, gentlemen." He paused dramatically. "Forty years ago," he said, his voice sinking to a whisper. "Those very same islands. That was the beginning of our country's entry into world affairs, gentlemen. Before we annexed the Philippines, we lived in splendid isolation. All our wars were fought at home. But after the war with Spain, and the Philippine insurrection, America became a world power." He paused. The photographers had retreated to the rear of the office and the reporters had moved forward, their pencils moving rapidly across their notebooks. "Manifest Destiny, it was called then. And our destiny in the Pacific is still manifest. Here is the arena of world ambition, gentlemen. Here is where the future lies." Sticking his cold corncob into his mouth, he began to pace the room—his eyes, shrewd and watchful, on the correspondents. "Here is where the full weight of American might must fall." He paused again for effect. "And soon! We cannot wait! We *must* not wait!" he exclaimed, his voice beginning to rise. "Too late, gentlemen—all failure in war may be summarized in those two words: too late. Too late in realizing the enemy means business. Too late in preparing. Too late in striking." He signed heavily. "And I'm afraid, gentlemen, that it may be too late in the Pacific. By the time we turn to Japan, she will have constructed such a formidable ring of island forts around her stolen new empire that it may be too late for us to break through it."

There was a silence of perhaps a minute, while the excited correspondents completed their notes. They looked up, as though preparing to ask questions. Duggan shook his head. "That will be all, gentlemen," he said. Newsmen shot to their feet, their chairs scraping the floor. Turning, they actually ran for the door, sprinting down the corridor for the street and the telegraph office.

What the *New York Times* called "Duggan Manifesto" infuriated the leaders of the Allied world. Stalin, frustrated in his demands for a "Second Front" to relieve German pressure in Russia, sent off an openly bitter protest to Washington. Churchill sarcastically inquired if General Duggan had succumbed to "General Grant's disease," an allusion that was not lost on an outraged FDR.

"If he'd been drinking, he'd have an excuse," Roosevelt snapped to a smoothly sympathizing Henry Hawkins. It was on the tip of Hawkins's tongue to suggest that perhaps a new commander should be found for the Southwest Pacific, until he saw the shrewd, calculating glint in his chief's eyes and realized that Roosevelt was already weighing the risks of firing the second most popular man in the country. Ultimately, FDR decided against it, even though Duggan's powerful friends in the American press—William Randolph Hearst, Colonel McCormick, and Henry Luce of Time-Life, Roosevelt's most bitter enemies—had launched a loud "Pacific First!" campaign. Instead, he contented himself with a curt note to Duggan, ordering him to make no more public pronouncements on grand strategy or top-level policy without first clearing them with the Pentagon.

General Duggan was undismayed by the thinly-veiled rebuke. Instead, he rejoiced in the conviction that he had successfully dramatized the "neglect" of his theater. "We won't be orphans much longer," he told Colonel Duff, and reiterated his warnings to Washington that Japan intended to invade Australia.

In the Pentagon, however, the Joint Chiefs of Staff knew differently. American cryptologists had broken the Japanese code and knew for an indisputable fact that Admiral Yamamoto was even then leading the most powerful naval armada ever assembled toward Midway Island. It was to Admiral Nimitz that all available strength was frantically being rushed. On June 4, Nimitz's forces won a resounding victory at the Battle of Midway. American flyers sank five Japanese aircraft carriers, while the U.S. Navy lost only one. Parity in Pacific carrier power had been restored at six to six.

Two days later, however, General Jonathan Cartwright surrendered American and Filipino forces in the Philippines.

It was dark on the concrete seaplane ramp at Monkey Point on Corregidor. Starlight glinted faintly off the bay. The water

lapping gently at the edge of the ramp seemed to counterpoint
the heavy breathing of hundreds of American prisoners who
lay sleeping on the concrete. Colonel Ames was one of them.
Beside him lay Chaplain Baugh. The chaplain was dreaming
of better days in New York City, when he'd bought his wife
her first mink stole. A file of Japanese with bayonet-fixed
rifles slung on their shoulders moved silently among the
sleepers, kicking them brutally awake. One of them stopped
in front of Baugh and Ames.

"Oki naoru," he growled, jabbing Baugh in the rump with
his bayonet point. Sit up.

Stifling a cry of pain, the chaplain scrambled erect. The
man seized Baugh's throat, and the chaplain, fearing the man
planned to kill him, tensed to run. Then he felt the Japanese
rip the gold cross from his lapel, and he relaxed. The flat tan
face came close to his. "Pahkah pen?" he inquired softly.
Baugh shook his head. "Hamirton watch?" Baugh nodded
and held out his left hand. The soldier wrenched Baugh's
watch away, sliding it over his sleeve just below a dozen
others wound around his bicep like gold and silver bracelets.
Now Beau Ames had been prodded erect by another soldier,
who took Beau's watch and West Point class ring. Both
soldiers pushed the two Americans roughly forward.

"Ugokasu!" they cried. Move!

Baugh and Ames stumbled down the inclined ramp toward
the water. Ahead of them, the pale light of dawn glowed
faintly over the mouth of Manila Bay. In its light they could
see thousands of Americans and Filipinos sprawled over the
concrete. No Japanese were in sight. Even their own tormentors had disappeared.

"Just a goddammed looting expedition," Ames grumbled.
Baugh nodded, putting a hand on his behind. It was sore but
there was no cut. The bayonet had not penetrated.

"Yardbirds," Baugh muttered contemptuously. "When they
do kill us, Beau, I'm afraid they'll chop us up with dull
sabers."

Ames nodded. They glanced around, still searching for
signs of Japanese authority. On a hill crest to their right,
overlooking the ramp, they could see mushroom helmets.

"Maybe I can find out something up there," Ames said,
walking slowly up the ridge with his hands in the air.

Halfway up, a burst of machine-gun bullets pinned him to the ground. He came rolling wildly down, his face bruised and bleeding. "Trigger-happy monkey," he growled. "Thank God they can't shoot."

"You'd think they'd have some sort of setup to take care of all these people," Baugh said. "Hell's bells, there must be seven or eight thousand of us." He took his canteen from his belt and opened it, putting it to his lips and tilting his head back. "Empty," he said, grimacing, turning the canteen upside down. "Got any water, Beau?"

"Not a drop."

"Hell's bells, are they going to let us go without water until we blow our stacks? That's worse than starving, you know. One more day without water in this heat, and we'll be drinking in the bay. And you know what that means."

Beau shrugged. "I don't think they care. To them, a prisoner's life is of no value. If a Jap surrenders, he disgraces his family. His old man might even commit hara-kiri, to atone for the insult to the emperor. Unless they figure they can get some work out of us, they'll probably let us starve to death or go crazy with thirst—whichever is quickest."

A faint cheer arose from the waterfront to their left. Suddenly hundreds of men got to their feet and ran to form a line.

"Let's go, Beau," Baugh said. "I don't know what it is, but those yardbirds aren't queueing up for nothing."

At the end of the line a captain standing in front of them explained what had happened. "Some smart engineer opened a water point. Those friggin' Japs dropped eight thousand men down here without water, but the engineer tapped the main and got a faucet running."

It took three hours for Baugh and Ames to reach the head of the line, where they eagerly filled both their canteens and their canteen cups with warm brackish water. They walked back to the pup tent they had erected, sipping slowly.

"Let's take inventory, Beau," Baugh said, crawling under the canvas. Beau followed.

It was stifling inside, but nonetheless cooler than outside, where the bare concrete turned the humid, hundred-degree heat into a blazing, enervating inferno. Ames and Baugh quickly discovered that they possessed ten cans of C-rations—

about eight ounces each—mostly meat and beans, together
with three and a half cartons of Camels.

"Where'd you get all the smokes, Beau?" Baugh asked.

"Hoarded them, I guess. I don't smoke that much, and I
just kept drawing my ration. I had a hunch they'd come in
handy someday. What do you say we trade a couple cartons
for food?"

Baugh shook his head slowly, soberly. "No, Beau—I don't
like the idea of taking food from our buddies. Anyway, if the
Japs don't feed us, we'd never get enough to stay alive.
Maybe there'll come a time when you'll cherish a smoke
more than a bite." Baugh grimaced wryly. "Hell's bells, here
I am a prisoner hardly a full day, and I've already got a
problem in moral theology."

"How so?" Ames asked, rolling over on his back.

"Well, I'm a priest. A chaplain. The men need me. I can
intervene for them, comfort them. To those who believe, I
can bring hope. But now, what do I do? Do I give them of my
own small sustenance so that they can sustain life, thus
probably ending my own, or do I hoard my food—even deal
with them for theirs—so that I may live and fulfill my
function?"

Beau Ames rolled onto his belly and stared at Baugh in
disbelief. "Gawd'a'mighty, damn, Father," he swore, lapsing
into his father's drawl and echoing his favorite oath, "how
can you squat there in this heat and work up crazy, no-count
problems like that?"

Baugh chuckled wryly. "It's easy. For a while, there, I
thought of giving away my C-rations. But then I caught
myself."

"Doing what?"

"Courting a martyr's crown."

Ames snorted in disgust, and Baugh got to his hand and
knees. "Don't worry, Beau," he said, crawling outside,
"I've decided to stay awhile."

He got to his feet, dizzy in the suffocating heat of the
ramp. The line at the water point was now twice as long.
Probably takes five hours in line now, he thought—making a
mental note to get up early for water. There you go again,
chaplain, he thought—thinking of yourself. How can I help

it, Lord? he countered. I'm a soldier, and that's how soldiers think. Shrugging, he walked down the ramp toward the bay.

Some of the men he passed were gasping for breath. Others were already prostrate, sunk in a lolling torpor, their tongues protruding from their mouths. He looked around for a latrine and saw none. Some of the men were using craters and fissures in the concrete. They had no toilet paper either...Cone-shaped swarms of black flies were already hovering over the piles of excrement, raising an angry buzzing that some of the men found unendurable. Walking toward the waterfront, Baugh caught sight of a squatting Filipino.

"*No benjo, Padre*," the man called in embarrassment. No toilet, Father.

Baugh nodded gravely, noticing that many of the Filipinos were showing symptoms of dysentery. He continued on to the bay, where crowds of soldiers were standing chest deep in water to cool off. Baugh stripped down to his underclothes and joined them. The water was tepid, but nonetheless much cooler than the concrete ramp. Baugh moved farther out, hoping to find colder water, standing immersed almost up to his chin, but returning to shallower water in disgust after clots of fecal matter drifted past his lips.

God in heaven! he thought in despair—and this is only the first day. What will it be like in a week or two?

Within five more days, life on the ramp was even more hideous than Chaplain Baugh had feared. Men had begun to die at the rate of fifty a day. Mostly they died of malnutrition aggravated by dysentery. Malaria and beriberi also took their toll. Baugh was heartbroken to see how many youths perished. Most of the officers and the old soldiers knew how to take care of themselves, clinging desperately to their hope and self-respect. But the young simply gave up, turning their faces toward the hot concrete and dying.

Baugh's purple stole was now a faded, tattered rag, and he no longer needed to take his missal with him to the cratered burial ground on Malinta Hill, for he had come to know the Office of the Dead by heart. Because of the filth lying in the open, the flies had multiplied by the million, flying over the ramp in clouds, getting into the men's ears and eyes—even their mouths. Dysentery was epidemic, and the shallow waters of the bay, crested with floating excrement, no longer became a sanctuary from the sun.

On the seventh day of captivity a truck drove into the enclosure occupied by Baugh and Ames. A Japanese major got out and climbed on top of the hood.

"I am Major Hara," he said, gazing contemptuously down at the Americans and Filipinos gathered beneath him. "You are my prisoners."

He paused, and Ames gasped and grabbed Baugh's arm. "Do you know who that monkey is?" he hissed. "That's the Jap who owned the Manila camera shop. No wonder the Nips had our ack-ack guns pinpointed. I used to see that little bastard walking Topside every Sunday afternoon, up to his ass in cameras."

Baugh nodded, and Hara spoke again. "Your lives are of no value," he snapped. "If you work, we will feed you. If you do not, we will let you starve." He pointed to the loaded truck. "I have brought rice and cooking equipment," he said, grimacing in contempt at the feeble cheer rising from the prisoners. "You will now unload it."

Quickly, Colonel Ames organized work details to drag the heavy sacks off the truck and set up a kitchen. Others found firewood and drew water. By dusk the rice was cooked and each man was issued a mess kit full and one tablespoon of rock salt. Baugh was amazed at the effect the rice had on the men. Their shoulders lifted and their eyes shone. They even began to talk about the future, or about women. Some of them began to sing.

Colonel Ames, however, was not so impressed. "Americans need two thousand calories a day to live," he said grimly. "We're getting five hundred. That's not nearly enough to arrest our physical decline, let alone reverse it. And if the Japs keep working us, it'll just be a matter of time before we're all planted on Malinta Hill."

Baugh nodded, his somber eyes on the grave-digging detail forming in the dusk.

Next day, the rice truck arrived early. Major Hara got out and spoke to Ames. "You will cook rice now and stand by for sea voyage," he snapped, turning to study two rusty little freighters gliding into the bay.

Two hours later the prisoners, their legs bent under the load of bedrolls and packs, staggered down the seaplane ramp to waiting barges, which ferried them out to the ships. Prodded by Japanese bayonets, they clambered painfully up cargo nets hanging from the gunwales, tumbling on the grimy steel decks in an exhausted heap.

"Hell's bells, Beau," Baugh panted, "I counted at least five fellows who couldn't make it and fell into the bay. Do you think . . . ?"

Ames got slowly to his feet and hobbled to the rail. A glowering guard forced him back at bayonet point.

"They're gone," Ames muttered, sinking down beside Baugh. "Maybe they're the lucky ones."

"*Chimmoku no!*" the guard shouted. Be silent!

Other guards joined him and began herding the prisoners down a hatch. They packed them into three foul-smelling, murky holds, a thousand men to a hold that normally might accommodate two hundred bunks and two hundred men. When a canvas tarpaulin was dropped over the hatch, the holds became dark and airless. Engines sputtered and throbbed and the little ship shuddered. Anchor chains came clanking up the hawse pipes and the vessel began to move. The prisoners stood in the silent, fetid darkness, belly to back, urinating and defecating where they stood. Many men became seasick and vomited. Others suffered leg cramps of excruciating pain, forcing them to scream aloud. Some tried to die, deliberately relaxing and hoping to sink to the deck; but the pressure of the surrounding bodies held them erect. Gradually, all but a few of them sank into a coma. Their breath came slower . . . slower . . . long, shuddering gasps in the reeking dark.

When the Japanese guards opened the hatch five hours later, they recoiled in repugnance from the stench rising from below. It was a full quarter hour before they could bring themselves to descend the ladders, forcing their zombielike prisoners, with blows and kicks, to ascend to the deck, and then to stagger down ramps into waiting garbage barges. Fifty yards offshore the barges ran aground and the prisoners were compelled to wade ashore through waist-deep water. The water refreshed

them, and their spirits rose—until they were marched to a
railroad siding and crammed into tiny, rusty boxcars.

"I can't believe it!" Baugh muttered to Colonel Ames.
"They must be packing 150 men into a single car. Hell's
bells, the forty-and-eights in France were a pink tea compared
to th—"

The boxcar's sliding door crashed shut. The train jerked
ahead, lurching and gathering speed. Almost immediately the
temperature inside the boxcar began to rise. Within a half
hour it was well above 120 degrees. Now the ordeal of the
ship was repeated, except that the men now vomited from
motion sickness and sank more rapidly into a torpor. Three
hours later the train stopped, and the boxcar doors slid open.

It was raining heavily. Many of the prisoners had to be
pulled from the boxcars. They lay in the mud, gasping, their
parched mouths open to admit the blessed raindrops. Shouting
angrily, the guards jerked them to their feet and formed two
columns.

"*Koshin!*" the guards yelled. March! The columns un-
dulated slowly forward. Now the rain poured down in tor-
rents, turning the road into a slop of mud clinging to the
prisoner's feet with every step, sometimes sucking off their
shoes. Men began to fall. The guards beat them with rifle
butts. When they did not rise, they bayoneted them and left
them for dead. Trucks sloshing slowly along in the rear of the
marching columns picked up the bodies, alive and dead. At
nightfall, when the column halted in a village of nipa huts,
the trucks dumped their grisly loads into a huge carabao
wallow and the guards forced the prisoners to bury them
there, both the living and the dead.

There was no food that night, except for the Japanese
guards who ate their meal in shifts inside the nipa huts.
Lying beside the road in the rain, the prisoners could smell
the rice cooking. They began to mutter in anger. Soon they
were on their feet roaring. Major Hara ran out of his hut
screaming orders. The guards scattered and set up Nambu
light machine guns. They fired into the mob, killing twenty
or thirty men, wounding as many more. These bodies also
went into the wallow. So did the forty others who died
during the night.

In the morning, Major Hara mounted a truck. "You must

march to Cabanatuan Prisoner Camp,'' he shouted. ''You must not more riot. You must now form line for rice.''

In sullen silence the prisoners received their helping of steaming rice, spooning it quickly from mess kits held close to their chests for fear of spilling even a grain of their precious ration.

''Goddam me!'' Colonel Ames swore, putting a hand to his jaw. ''My teeth are so wobbly in my gums it hurts to chew even rice.''

''It's the scurvy,'' Chaplain Baugh grunted. ''You should chew grass.'' Ames stared at him in incredulity. ''That's right,'' Baugh went on. ''Grass is full of vitamin C. The lack of it is what causes scurvy.''

Without another word Ames put down his empty mess kit and walked to the roadside, where he pulled up a handful of greens and began chewing them. The guards stared at him in amazement, but Ames ignored them, filling his pockets with shoots and continuing to chew.

''It's tougher than rice, but I'll give it a go,'' he murmured. He bent to fill his canteen from a roadside puddle.''The rain's stopped,'' he said to Baugh, ''and that's a hot sun up there.''

Most of the men ran to follow his example, just as a motorcycle sputtered into life and Major Hara appeared in its sidecar, waving his hand to signal renewal of the march.

Now it was the sun that was the enemy. By comparison, the rain had been a benevolent tormentor. The sun hung high above the road in a round yellow ball. Soon the jungle to either side of the marching columns was steaming. Within an incredible two hours, the muddy slop of roadway had dried into a hard surface which eventually became dusty. Dust clouds settled on the marchers, clinging to their flesh and coating parched mouths and lips already cracked and bleeding from scurvy. The men drank off their water recklessly. Ames shouted at them to stop, but they paid no heed. By mid-afternoon many of them were crazed with thirst. They ran to lick at mud puddles or carabao wallows, gulping down any filthy wet. Baugh and Ames had to knock down two pitifully weeping soldiers who were trying to urinate in each other's mouth. Again, men were collapsing in exhaustion, this time by the hundreds. Again, the guards beat and bayoneted them. Now the macabre ''meat trucks'' raised huge clouds of dust at the end of the columns, and the flies that fed with noisy greed upon their dreadful cargo were eventually joined by croaking black vultures.

At sundown the columns were halted at another village. Once more there was no evening rice except for the Japanese. Clouds of insects attracted by piles of bodies waiting to be buried swarmed over the sleepless prisoners lying gasping in the village square, their ears full of the far off chattering of jungle monkeys. In the morning there was rice.

"I don't know if I can go on," Ames said to Baugh, quickly finishing his ration. He unbuttoned his fly. "Look at my crotch. It looks like a hunk of hamburger."

Baugh nodded. "I know. I feel like a leper myself." He leaned closer to Ames. "But one of us has got to get out of here." Ames's bleached white eyebrows rose questioningly. "The world has to know what they're doing to us," Baugh continued grimly.

"Who?" Ames whispered.

"You," Baugh replied.

"I can't! The men need me!"

"Shhh!" Baugh said, noticing a guard staring at them. He walked to the roadside to relieve himself. "Look, Beau, there's plenty of other colonels to take charge. A fat lot of authority Hara gave you, anyway. But *you're* the one. You're still in good shape. You've got the constitution of a horse, and it's you who's got to make the break to tell the outside world what these people are like."

The guard came toward them, and they both fell silent. "Christ, go ahead and talk!" Ames said with sudden ferocity. "That shithead can't understand us."

"Okay," Baugh said. "I know where we are. I came through this village on the retreat from Lingayen. There's an estuary over there to your right and a fishing barrio. Outriggers. I'm sure the Japs haven't had a chance to do anything about them. If you can make it to the village, maybe you can find a Filipino to take you down coast to Mindanao."

Ames frowned. "What's down there?"

"Guerrillas. There's a bunch of them around Linao Bay on the southwest coast. They've probably got radio contact with Australia. If General Duggan hears you're free, he'll turn the Pacific upside down to get you out."

Ames pursed his lips. "Sounds great—but how do I get away from this bunch of ghouls?"

"Simple, we'll create a diversion."

Ames chuckled. "You mean *you'll* create a diversion." The chaplain blushed. "What's the difference who does it?"

Ames patted Baugh's shoulder fondly. "You still bucking for a martyrs' crown?"

Baugh shook his head. "Not this time. This time it'll be the right deed for the right reason."

The guard who had been watching them began shouting in Japanese, pointing toward the pile of dead prisoners where Major Hara stood. Hara crooked a finger arrogantly, and Ames walked slowly toward him, followed by Baugh.

"You make prisoners bury dead," Hara snapped.

"Go fuck yourself," Ames replied with a grin.

"You tell that to me?" the astonished Hara roared. "I give you order! You do as I tell!"

Ames shook his head. "Not until you give my men enough rice and water to live on."

"They just eat rice."

"Not enough to live on, let alone march on and dig graves on."

Hara's right hand crossed to the hilt of the heavy samurai saber swinging at his left hip. "You do as I tell, or I cut off head," he warned, his black eyes flashing cruelly.

"Why don't you just kill us all and get it over with?" Ames replied. "Save you time and money, save us a lot of useless agony."

Hara's hand moved slightly, exposing a few inches of saber blade. Ames shrugged, turning when he felt Baugh's hand on his shoulder and heard him saying softly: "On your mark. This is it."

"What he say?" Hara roared, glaring fiercely at Baugh.

Smiling, the chaplain took Ames's place, and said, "I said, 'With your bark, you don't scare shit.'"

Out came Hara's saber with a flashing rasp. He brandished it wildly overhead. "How dare you tell me that way!" he bellowed.

"Because I'm in command here," Baugh said pleasantly.

"You just priest," Hara sneered. "You no command no thing."

"But my boss commands the universe," Baugh shot back. "And just for your information, you pompous little monkey, I'm a full captain in the United States Navy and the senior officer present."

"You kneel!" Hara screamed, swinging his saber high over his head.

"This body bends to no one on earth."

"We make you kneel," Hara panted.

"You couldn't make my sister kneel." Baugh snorted, his voice full of contempt. "One drunken Doughoy could handle five hundred of you paper asses between drinks."

Beside himself, Major Hara screamed out orders in Japanese. A dozen guards sprang forward to hurl themselves on the American chaplain. He fought them off, roaring like a wounded bull. But he had little strength. Exhausted within minutes, he was driven to his knees, where the guards wrenched off his jacket and held him fast for Hara's saber, now held in both hands high above his head.

"Oh my God," Baugh murmured softly, beginning the Act of Contrition, "I am heartily sorry . . . for having offended Thee . . . and I detest all my sins, because—"

The heavy blade whistled down, cutting halfway through William Baugh's neck. With a savage shriek, Hara yanked it free and swung again, completely cutting off the head this time. It rolled free. Frenzied, Hara swung his saber again and again, chopping the dead man's body into pieces. The guards joined him, lowering their bayonets to thrust and cut at the red-and-white litter of lifeless flesh. Suddenly they paused, astonished. The American prisoners had begun to sing.

"God bless America," they sang, their voices rising, as though singing a requiem for their brave chaplain, "land that I love. Stand beside her, and guide her . . . "

The astonished Japanese let them finish, merely shaking their dripping bayonets at them as though in warning, but making no move to silence them. Major Hara also stared wonderingly at them, thousands of human wrecks who should have been groveling at his feet, and yet, there they stood beside the piles of their own dead, offering their only possible defiance: a song.

Shaking himself, Hara cleaned his saber on the jacket torn

from Baugh's back, sheathed it, and went to look for Colonel Ames.

Moments after Chaplain Baugh had whispered "On your mark," Beauregard Ames had drifted slowly toward the pile of dead prisoners. Once he had the mounds of festering flesh safely between him and Major Hara and his guards, Ames began to run. His breath came sharply and his raw crotch burned like fire. His bouncing helmet caught him cruelly at the back of the neck. But he continued to run down the narrow path twisting through thick swamp grass rising six or seven feet high. He could hear Major Hara screaming faintly, and he realized that Baugh was deliberately goading him to gain time for his own escape. A half hour, he thought desperately, that's all I've got . . . The thought drove him forward in spite of his crotch, now seared with sweat, and the agony of his breathing. The tall grass gave way to low bushes and then palm trees, through which he could see blue water. He ran faster, almost sprinting through a deserted nipa village and collapsing in a panting heap among about five or six outrigger canoes drawn up on the beach. He drew himself to his knees and looked quickly around him. He saw nothing. But he felt a presence . . . He glanced wildly around for a weapon. Seeing a bolo knife lying in one of the canoes, he moved to seize it—freezing when a voice behind him said:

"You pushem hands along sky."

Ames raised his arms in despair.

"You allasame turnem toward me."

Ames spun in the sand on his heel to confront a bareheaded Japanese soldier covering him with a huge Mauser machine pistol. A bolo knife swung from his belt. Ames studied him, realizing that the man was a Filipino in a Japanese uniform.

"Quick, man!" Ames cried. "Let's get out of here. I'm Colonel Ames of the American army. The Japs are chasing me. Do you like the Japs?"

The man shook his head savagely. But he was still suspicious. "You talk true along me?" he said, warily lifting the machine pistol.

Ames pointed to his bleached white hair in exasperation. "How many Japs do you know with hair like this?"

The man grinned, lowering his gun. He stiffened. So did

Ames. They could hear the chattering of Japanese voices perhaps three hundred yards away. Ames thought he could identify Hara's voice shouting commands. Quickly, the man shifted the Mauser to his left hand and drew his bolo. He pointed with it to the one lying in the other outrigger and said, "You allasame catchem."

Ames grabbed the knife, wondering if the Filipino actually intended to make an impossible stand. But then, seeing him run among the canoes, overturning them to hack at their bottoms, he joined him. In a minute they had left all but one useless. The voices came neared . . . The Filipino ran to the one remaining outrigger, pushing it out into the water while motioning Ames to jump inside. With deft, sure skill, he hoisted its lateen sail aloft and began to paddle wildly. Ames seized a paddle up forward and joined him. They drew slowly away, increasing speed sharply when a land breeze caught the sail. His breath rising from his chest like a serrated knife, Ames dug his paddle furiously into the water. He felt an almost irrestible urge to turn around, but he kept on paddling.

Cries of dismay drifted out to the canoe. A ragged volley of shots whispered wildly overhead. In another minute they heard the sharp, staccato bursts of Nambu light machine guns. A few holes appeared at the top of the sail. Ames heard the faint plop of mortar shells leaving the tube, bracing himself for the bursts. But they exploded in harmless splashes behind them. Now the breeze had turned into a fair wind and the outrigger rose on its pontoon, almost flying from the water.

"No needem paddle now," the Filipino shouted joyfully. "Wind he allasame blow too much big."

Ames turned and dropped the paddle in relief, gazing in satisfaction at the shore line where little figures in mushroom helmets were dragging canoes into the water.

The Filipino grinned. "Jap he allasame sail along bottom." Then he spat in contempt. "Jap he shoot like drunk man."

Now is was Ames who grinned. "What's your name?"

"Francisco," the man said proudly, loosening his line to take in more wind. "Francisco Perez."

"Frankie, you're all right," Ames said, "My name's Beauregard Ames. Call me Beau." Francisco nodded. "What were you doing in the village?" Ames asked.

"Place belong me," Francisco grunted, his eyes warily searching the horizon for signs of Japanese ships.

"Oh, you were born there. Is that where you learned to speak Pidgin English?"

Francisco nodded. "Trader belong New Guinea, he stop long this place. Tradem." He grinned, his white teeth flashing. "Catchem marys belong us. Sleepem. Plenty fella pom-pom."

Ames laughed. His eyes also swept the horizon. Seeing nothing but low-flying gulls, he relaxed. "But what were you doing there, Frank? The village seemed deserted."

Francisco scowled. "Me prisoner. Me stop along Bilibid Prison. Jap he come, me allasame run away."

Ames was puzzled. "Are you a Filipino soldier?"

Francisco shook his head, scowling again. "No. Me convict." He stared hard at Ames. "Me killem Clara, mary belong me." Ames sucked in his breath slowly. "Clara, she work along Manila camera shop. She sleepem Mr. Hara. Me catchem." He pointed to the knife at his feet. "Me killem Clara," he said simply. He lifted his eyes skyward. "Clara, she stop long heaven now," he said sadly. His eyes blazed up fiercely. "Me kill Mr. Hara now!" he exclaimed.

Ames stared at Francisco in incredulity. "That's what you were doing in the village, looking for Hara?"

Francisco nodded. Ames looked away, toward the beach, now just a white line against the green of the hills. No, he thought, no way you can tell him that that's Hara back there. He's so full of hate he might turn around . . .

Aloud, he said, "How'd you get away from Bilibid?"

"Judge he say me die finish along rope," Francisco said, putting his hand to his throat. "Me stop long Bilibid. Jap he come, takem Manila. Bringem 'merican prisoners long Bilibid. Too much many. Number allasame grass belong donkey. Jap he maken me cleanem room belong shit. One day me lookem Jap he sittem along board belong shit. Me killem. Takem gun." He pointed to his Mauser and his clothes. "Uniform belong Jap now belong me. Bye-bye Bilibid. Me run. Me run like ass belong motorcar."

Ames grinned at the expression. "Frankie," he said slowly, "will you take me downcoast to Mindanao?"

A shrewd look came into Francisco's black eyes. "You pay Francisco?"

"I don't have any money," Ames said ruefully.

Francisco shook his head. "Me stop long Mindoro," he said.

Disappointed, Ames began to think. Suddenly he brightened and asked, "Have you ever heard of General Duggan?"

Francisco's eyes blazed scornfully. "You tink-tink me allasame bush Filipino? He great man. He come back by-em-by killem plenty fella Jap."

"Good," Ames said. "He's my father-in-law." Francisco stared at him blankly, and Ames explained in pidgin. "Daughter belong General Duggan now mary belong me." Francisco's eyes widened. "I'll give you something better than money, Frankie," Ames continued. "If you get me to Mindanao and I get to Australia, I'll have General Duggan get you a pardon from President Quezon."

Francisco's eyes gleamed and he bobbed his head in eager assent—just as the sudden roar of an airplane motor burst in their ears. A Japanese Zero that had glided with silent motor to a height of about five hundred feet behind them was now attacking with flaming wing guns. Francisco swung his outrigger sharply to starboard to elude the Zero and headed for a rain squall a few hundred yards away. Ames could hear the tinkling of the Zero's empty cartridges on the water as it roared past their port side. Now it was circling, coming again. Again the flaming wing guns and the tinkling cartridges . . . Ames watched its approach in fascinated dread. A bullet struck the bolo at his feet with a loud clang, ricocheting away in a shrieking visible red arc. Another shredded the gunwale at his wrist. The mast shuddered. A raindrop spattered on Ames's face . . . Another . . . Suddenly they were inside the safety of the squall.

"Frankie boy," an exultant Ames called jubilantly, "you're a goddam genius." And then a drenching rain made further communication impossible.

Francisco blamed Colonel Ames's thatch of bleached white hair for the Zero attack. He seemed to think that it had caught the pilot's eye. Ames did not attempt to explain to him that Major Hara probably had radio contact with Manila and had

called for an aerial search. At dusk they put into a sandy cove
and set up a camp.

"Me lookum barrio," Francisco said.

"I'll go with you."

Francisco shook his head, pointing again to the offending
hair. "Filipino talk-talk altogether too much. Jap he
hear."

Ames agreed. While Francisco was gone, he opened his
pack and took out a pair of scissors to cut off his hair. Then
he shaved the ragged ends smooth.

Francisco smiled when he saw what looked like a milk-
white cap over Ames's sun-browned face. "Good," he grunted,
handing Ames bananas and half of a small cooked chicken.
They wolfed the food down with silent satisfaction, taking
turns drinking from a skin of *tuba*.

In the morning they took to the sea once more—until Ames
felt the water blisters rising on his shaven scalp, and the
presence of Japanese sea and air patrols frightened them
ashore again. Thereafter, they sailed only at night, hiding in
the bush by day or on moonlit nights, living off food that
Francisco scrounged from the barrios, and proceeding slowly
south at the rate of about thirty or forty knots a night. Some
nights they lay becalmed and were forced to paddle. On
others they were compelled to stay ashore because of heavy
Japanese barge traffic moving along the archipelago's east
coast. Ames fretted at the delay, aware that in daylight, with
more sailing time and better winds, they could probably
double or even triple their speed. But the risk was too great.
Yet, Ames was delighted by his improving health. Francisco's
fresh fruits and meat gradually cured his scurvy and beriberi.
Ames's joints no longer ached and the body sores gradually
disappeared, along with the terrible inflammation of his crotch;
he could actually feel his teeth taking firmer root in his gums.

Nevertheless, it took six weeks to reach Samar, where
freshening winds finally sent them skimming over the night
seas. Passing the island's southern tip, Ames felt a twinge of
nostalgia, seized by an absurd urge to ask Francisco to make
for Balangiga, where his father, General Duggan, and Sergeant Durkin had fought more than forty years ago. He
suppressed it, however, in his eagerness to reach Leyte.

There, they found the mouth of the gulf much too wide to

cross in a single night. Rather than risk detection, they crept around the Leyte coast to enter the islet-studded waters above Mindanao. Soon they made the big island itself. A few miles south of its northern tip, a sudden storm piled the waves high. Their tiny craft was tossed on the crests like a leaf. Francisco swung the canoe hard to starboard, making desperately for the lee of the coast. He pulled violently against his wildly flapping sail, and the mast broke with a sharp snap. Unknown to both men, the Zero's bullets had pierced the mast and it had been steadily weakening since. The water beneath them began to rise in a giant breaker. It swept them shoreward, breaking on the beach with the sound of thunder and hurling them into a coconut grove, where the outrigger was smashed against a tree and broken into pieces. Ames and Francisco were thrown to the ground. They lay there stunned while the cold black water flowed back over them into the boiling surf. Scrambling erect, the two men ran deeper into the grove. They spent the night there, drenched and chattering. In the morning, when the storm broke, they saw no sign of their wrecked canoe.

"Looks like we'd better start walking," Ames said to Francisco.

Although they had lost their boat, they had held on to their bolo knives; Francisco still had his Mauser machine pistol, and Ames his pack filled with rice and matches. They needed them all. Almost immediately, as they began a trek of about four hundred miles in a climate and terrain that neither the Filipinos nor the Spaniards nor the Americans had been able to conquer, they blundered into a swamp filled with barriers of tall grass seven feet high and three inches wide. Spelling each other by turns, they hacked a passage with their bolos. As they moved, the water rose. By noon it was waist high, and by mid-afternoon it was at Ames's breast and just beneath Francisco's chin. They pushed despairingly on, guided only by the sun, striking southwest for Linao. Gradually, the water receded. By late afternoon it was again at Ames's waist. They halted in front of a huge fallen hardwood tree, perhaps eight or nine feet in diameter. Gasping, they dragged themselves up on top of it. Ames took bananas from his pack. They ate them in silence and fell asleep.

In the morning, they saw that the water beneath them had fallen. They jumped down. Francisco looked for dry wood while Ames took rice from his pack, filling his helmet with swamp water.

When Francisco returned with an armful of brush, he pointed to the helmet and shook his head. "Too much bad," he grunted. "Allasame poison. You die finish."

Ames was dismayed. "But how will we boil the rice?"

Francisco grinned. He emptied out the helmet and dragged his foot through the water, dredging up a vine one inch thick. Holding it high in the air, he cut off the bottom and let pure water run into the helmet.

Ames chuckled. "Frankie, you're not only a genius—you're an archangel."

They ate and plodded on. Days turned into weeks. They forded rivers or swam them when they were too deep. They crossed new swamps and climbed mountains. They followed dry creek beds and arroyos, always guiding themselves on the sun and the shadows it cast. Once, in an arroyo, a dreadful storm broke overhead. They hobbled on. Fifteen minutes later there was a wild roaring to their rear and a howling wall of water burst upon them. Francisco would have been swept away if Ames had not caught hold of a tree and seized the frail Filipino by his ankle. After that, they stayed out of arroyos.

When they came to a mountain, they climbed it eagerly. High in the immense quiet of the hills, where enormous trees formed a canopy hundreds of feet above their heads, they breathed easier in cool, insect-free air. But they hated to descend again into the lowlands, where serrated swamp grass slashed their flesh and horrible, sucking leeches attached themselves to their bodies. Each night in the swamps and lowlands, they pulled the disgusting blue worms, bloated with blood, off their flesh. When their rice ran out, Ames began to shoot monkeys. He put the Mauser on single shot to conserve ammunition. Then he would slip softly into the jungle, waiting to hear the chatter of a monkey above the raucous screaming of the macaws and parakeets flitting in and out of the trees in jade and scarlet flashes. A monkey would last them one or two days, depending upon its size. One night, in a rainstorm, when they could not light a fire, they tried to eat raw monkey meat. Even Francisco quickly spat the indigestible flesh out of his mouth.

The passage of time was marked each morning by Ames, using a pencil mark on the back of a letter from Virginia which he kept in his pack. Ames thought often of Virginia and his son Kenneth, and what he would tell General Duggan when he reached Australia. Francisco also daydreamed: of the little black-eyed girl he had loved and murdered, of the exquisite tortures he would inflict on Mr. Hara when he caught him.

About a month after they were shipwrecked, they began to climb an unusually steep mountain. High in the trees they could see abandoned huts.

"This Ata ground," Francisco said, stamping the earth with his feet. "Atas," he said, pointing to the empty huts. "They stop long tree." He stuck out a level hand about four feet above the ground. "Atas too much small."

Ames nodded wearily. He had been growing steadily weaker for the past few hours. Now his eyes burned. His vision was blurred. A dull ache had begun in his bones. His throat was sore and his mouth dry. Hot flashes convulsed his body. Yet, he toiled on; until, an hour later, halfway up the mountain, he sank gasping to the earth, unable to continue. He knew then what was wrong with him, and he despaired. Francisco knew, too, the moment he knelt besides Ames and felt his burning forehead.

"Malaria," Francisco muttered. Slinging the bigger man over his thin shoulders, Francisco carried him upward to a level of grass under a banyan tree. He cut Y stakes from surrounding small trees and pushed them into the ground, cutting saplings to lay in the Y's and form a bed six inches above the earth, lashing the poles together with creeper vines. Placing Ames on the bed, he found cold water and began to bathe his forehead. Francisco knew, however, how little that would do. He realized that Ames's fever had only begun and would get much worse, and that he would die unless he could get him medical help.

In the morning, Francisco took his own and Ames's bolo and went searching for Atas. He found them only a few hours away, building new tree huts around a little blue lake. They would live there until the lake was fished out, and then move on again. Francisco noticed with misgivings that there were no women present when he entered the clearing by the lake. That meant that they did not trust him and that his approach had been observed. There were about twenty of them, none more than four feet high or ninety pounds in weight. They stood around a youth of about sixteen, the tallest, who was obviously the chief. All of them were armed with primitive spears and quivers of darts that were probably poisoned.

Francisco quickly laid his bolos and Mauser on the ground and went up to confront the young chieftain. The others formed a circle around them. A few of them muttered threateningly, but the youth raised a hand to silence them. In pantomime and sign language, Francisco explained that he needed litter bearers to carry Ames to Misamis on Linao Bay, where American guerrillas had a headquarters. He signed to the chief to follow him to the bolos and the Mauser, indicating that he would give them to him if he agreed. The youth lifted a bolo with interest, gently feeling the edge and testing its weight. The Mauser he pushed away with contempt. It was merely another piece of white man's magic, like his machines that rolled over the ground or flew through the air or sailed over and under the sea. White man's magic did not impress him. But the bolos! He bobbed his head in assent. Ten minutes later the chief and three others, clad only in loincloths, betel-nut bags swinging at their wrists, followed Francisco to the tree under which Colonel Ames lay.

For the first three days of the journey, Beauregard Ames lay unconscious on the litter being carried by the four Atas. On the fourth day he awoke, and Francisco gave him water. Immediately, Ames expelled it in a stream of yellow bile. His spleen had become distended and he could not hold water. Gradually he became conscious of being borne on a pallet. He could see the tops of the heads of the two forward bearers, and felt the litter sway gently to the rhythm of their movement. Occasionally he would try to see more, but he was too weak to rise, and sometimes his head would loll helplessly over the side of the litter and Francisco would have to lift it gently back on top. Then the fever reclaimed him. He felt as though his body were baking in an oven. His bones ached horribly, as though they were being cracked in a vise. Then he lost consciousness again.

The Atas toiled on. They were incredibly strong for their size and possessed apparently inexhaustible stamina. They spoke to each other rarely, pointing to the sun to indicate the time of day, chewing stoically on their betel nut as they swung along the track. They also astonished Francisco by their sureness of direction. Proud as he was of his own bush craft, he could not understand how they could halt in a seemingly impenetrable forest of trees and rocks, sweep the terrain with their eyes, and almost immediately discover a trail within twenty yards or so. At night after eating, they sat around the fire drumming with their fingers on narrow tom-toms. The beat was soft at first, rising slowly until it reached a wildly pulsating staccato. Sometimes when Colonel Ames heard the wailing drums through the burning mists of his fever, he thought that he was in Hell.

Two weeks after the journey began, the Atas crossed a high grassy plateau and began a sharp descent to Misamis. A day later they entered weed-grown roads leading to stone-walled estates. Beyond the walls they could see the white arches and patios of stately Spanish homes peeping through the trees. Apparently, they were all deserted. At one high-walled estate, however, they encountered an armed Filipino guard who halted them. He covered them with a submachine gun while ringing for an officer. A Filipino major came through an iron gate set in the wall. He spoke sharply to Francisco in dialect, and Francisco pointed to the pallet held aloft by the four silent Atas and told him who the sick man was. At once the major signed to the Atas to follow him through the gate to a small outbuilding with a red cross painted on the door.

Inside, an American doctor had Ames transferred to a cot. Filipino girls took off Ames's filthy clothes, washed his body, and put a cotton nightgown on him, while an American nurse taped a tube to his forearm and began to give him an intravenous feeding.

The doctor turned to Francisco, standing quietly a few feet away from the cot. "Are you all right?"

"Me fine," Francisco said. He pointed to the unconscious Ames. "He livem?"

The doctor nodded. "I think so. He's a strong man. You did well to bring him here."

Francisco bowed slightly, turning to look for the Atas. They were gone. Francisco went back out the iron gate and looked down the road toward the beach and a cluster of empty houses on stilts. He could see the Atas standing there, solemnly studying the bay. Then they turned, betel-nut bags swinging at their wrists, the bolos dangling from the loincloths of the chief and another youth of his age, and trudged back the way they had come.

Two weeks later Beauregard Ames was well enough to request a meeting with Brigadier General Diego Cox, commander of American-Filipino forces in Linao Province. Ames remembered Cox as the son of a Spanish mother and an American father who had been educated in the States as a mining engineer. General Duggan had commissioned him to build a railroad in Mindanao. Ames could not be sure whether or not the general's rank was self-conferred or authentic, but he did realize, when he sat down in the chair nailed to the floor opposite General Cox's huge carved mahogany desk, that this tall, cold, sad-faced man had no doubts about his being head man.

"I have heard of your remarkable escape, Ames," he said stiffly. "Allow me to congratulate you." He paused, his thin lips pursing. "I can use you here."

"Oh, no, sir," Ames burst out. "I have to get back to Australia. I've heard you have radio contact with GHQ."

"I do. But I need you in my command. Moreover, I do not often contact GHQ except on urgent matters. To do otherwise is to risk discovery."

"This *is* urgent. I've got to tell the outside world what the Japs are doing to our people."

"Surely, Ames," Cox continued in a condescending tone, "you do not expect me to radio General Duggan to tell him that there's a colonel here demanding a submarine to Australia."

Beauregard Ames smiled. It was a smile of tender gloating, which Ames could not forego. "I certainly do so, sir," he said evenly. "You see, General Duggan is my father-in-law."

Diego Cox's face darkened and he leaned forward in his chair. "This is not the time or place for bad jokes, Ames."

"No joke, sir. If you wish, you can inquire if Colonel Beauregard Stonewall Jackson Ames is not in fact the husband of Virginia Duggan. I've lived with General Duggan in Manila since 1939.''

General Cox's hooded eyelid flickered and he lifted a long thin hand. "I will be back to you in a day or two," he said curtly.

A few days afterward, a courier arrived in Ames's quarters with a carbon copy of a message from GHQ, reading:

COL. AMES AUTHORIZED BOARD SUBMARINE WEEK OF JAN. 10–17. WELCOME HOME, BEAU!

DUGGAN

A later message pinpointed the time and place at January 16, directly off Misamis. Early that morning, Colonel Ames and Francisco shoved an outrigger filled with fruit into the water and paddled out onto the bay. They sat there for hours, facing each other, staring at the horizon, eating bananas and drinking water from a canteen. At noon Francisco's eyes widened and his jaws worked soundlessly. He pointed in dread over Ames's shoulder, and when Beau turned around he saw a huge black snout—like a whale's—slowly emerging from the water.

It began climbing the sky at a forty-five degree angle, and Ames saw that it was a submarine. At a height of about fifty feet it shuddered and fell forward into the water with a monstrous slapping sound, lifting its stern to the surface. Decks awash with water and deck guns dripping, it lay there bobbing gently. Ames and Francisco came quickly alongside, just as the conning tower rattled open.

Ames took Francisco's hand fondly. "Frankie," he said, "you're not only a genius and an archangel—you're even better: You're a good ol' boy."

Francisco's teeth gleamed white in his face. "You allesame numbah one fella, Beau. You no forgettem pardon belong me?"

Ames shook his head and brushed at his moistening eyes. "Never," he said, and climbed carefully aboard the swaying submarine, turning to wave good-bye to Francisco before entering the conning tower and climbing down the hatch.

As he descended, a voice came over the bullhorn: " Take Colonel Ames to the wardroom while we take the fruit aboard.''

A sailor led Ames through the mess hall where bearded submariners were eating ice cream for lunch dessert. Ames was surprised at the overpowering smell of oil below decks, stopping momentarily to study the control center with its bewildering array of gauges, wheels, and valves. He entered the tiny wardroom just as bells rang and whistles shrilled, signaling descent. But he felt no sensation as the submarine went down.

A naval officer entered the wardroom. "I'm Commander Russell," he said, cheerfully extending his hand. "Glad to have you aboard."

"Thank you for going out of your way to pick me up," Ames said.

The commander smiled. "Not at all. We love a chance to get some fresh fruit aboard."

"How soon will we get to Melbourne?" Ames asked eagerly.

"Sorry, Colonel," the commander said. "We're headed for Guadalcanal. You can board a plane there for Aus—" He stopped, amused by the puzzled look on Ames's face. "You never heard of Guadalcanal?" Ames shook his head, and Commander Russell grinned. "Boy! You really were back in the boonies, weren't you? America is counterattacking, Colonel. Guadalcanal was our first victory. General Duggan stopped them cold in New Guinea and he's already kicked them out of Buna-Gona. We've got control of the air in the Pacific, and we've got them beat on top of the water and underneath it too."

"Wonderful!" Ames exclaimed. "How about the Philippines?"

"A year away yet," Commander Russell said soberly. "Maybe two. We've still got to take a lot of islands away from them before we can retake the Philippines, Colonel."

Ames sighed. He felt tired.

The commander studied him anxiously. "Anything I can do for you, Colonel?"

Ames nodded, pointing to the sailors outside finishing their dessert. "Yes," he said wistfully. "If I could just have a little dish of that ice cream . . ."

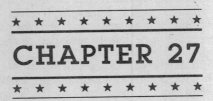

CHAPTER 27

General Duggan's large dark eyes blazed with anger when Colonel Ames finished describing Japanese treatment of their prisoners in the Philippines.

"They'll pay!" Duggan said with soft ferocity. "They'll pay."

When Ames told him of how William Baugh had deliberately sacrificed his life to enable him to escape, Duggan shook his head sadly.

"Life is strange, Beau," he said. "Your father died so that I might live, and Bill Baugh died for you. 'Greater love than this no man hath . . .'" he murmured. "Bill Baugh was a brave man. I'm going to put him in for the Medal of Honor."

Beau smiled wistfully. "I think he'd prefer a martyr's crown," he said.

Duggan did not seem to hear the remark. "Beau, I've got an important job for you. I want you to be my press officer under Jim Duff here at GHQ."

"GHQ!" Ames repeated in dismay. "But General, I'm a *combat* officer. I don't want a desk job. I want a *regiment*!"

Duggan smiled fondly. "Well spoken, Beau," he said, walking toward a roll of wall maps. "But for the time being," he went on, with faint bitterness, "there won't be much combat out here. Everything's going to Europe, Beau—

beans, bullets, and black oil; men and materials, and especially landing boats. We've been told to mark time in the Pacific, Beau—Nimitz and me—while Roosevelt and Meadows pull Churchill's chestnuts out of the fire." Reaching up, he rolled down a huge map of the Mediterranean. "North Africa!" he snorted. "What are we doing there? I'll tell you what: They decided they didn't have enough muscle for a second front in France this year. The British got a bloody nose at Dieppe. They put it out that it was just a raid, but I *know* it was a reconnaissance in force. Once they realized the German strength, they changed their minds. But the Allies had to do something, so Churchill talked FDR into North Africa. All those ships and planes and men could have come out here," he said bitterly. "Out here, where we've got the Japs on the run, where they could serve *America*." Using his corncob to trace a line across the Mediterranean, he said: "You see, Beau—that's the British lifeline. Through the Med, down the Suez, and into the Indian Ocean—the lifeline of empire. And we're securing it." He grimaced. "When we could be . . ." His voice trailed off and he glanced questioningly at Colonel Ames. "Have you heard who is in command in North Africa?"

Beau shook his head, and Duggan smiled maliciously and said: "Mike."

"*Mike?* I can't believe it! Why he was only—"

"Only a brigadier, yes—but he ran George Meadows's errands well. And Churchill has found him charming." He smiled again. "Not to say amenable. Genry Gawkins was helpful too. Three stars in nine months," he murmured. "Not bad for a super clerk." He stuck his corncob into his mouth and turned to the map again. "Well, they just met at Casablanca," he said, pointing to the Moroccan coast. "Churchill and Roosevelt. They've decided to go into Sicily next. And then, I suppose, Italy." He struck his hands together savagely. "Headline hunting, that's what it is," he snorted. "Italy! A crocodile's back. Cross-hatch fighting all the way. Just wait till they spend a winter in the Apennines. I'll say this, though, Beau—I'm glad I'm not in command. I saw enough of that kind of war in the Meuse-Argonne."

Beau came to stand beside him and study the map. "Do

you think," he began thoughtfully, "they may be trying to help Russia a little too?"

"Of course they are! That's just it! Ever since Genry Gawkins came back from Moscow, we've heard nothing but Europe first, Europe first. That's to take the pressure off Stalin. Don't you realize the tragedy of it, Beau? Nazi Germany invaded Communist Russia when both were the sworn enemy of the democracies. And what does Churchill do? He immediately rushes to Russia's side instead of letting the two 'isms'—both our enemies—destroy each other."

Beau nodded. "My daddy used to call that a pissin' contest between skunks."

Duggan grinned. "You rebels always did have an unprintable way with words." Rolling up the Mediterranean map, he pulled down one of Asia. "I don't mean to suggest that Churchill is Stalin's man. It's just that he hates Germans so much he can't think straight. He's already said he'd do a deal with the devil if it would help him kill Germans. Well, who dines with the devil must sup with a long spoon—and Stalin and communism are the devil incarnate. The moment Stalin realized that Churchill was actually going to help him—instead of doing what Stalin would have done, let his two enemies eat each other up—he began stepping up his demands for a second front in Europe." He pointed to Manchuria in Northern China. "What about a second front in *Asia*?" he snorted. "What about Russia attacking the Japanese in Manchuria and relieving the pressure on us in the Pacific?" Leaving the map, he began pacing to floor "I can't understand it, Beau," he muttered, jabbing the air savagely with his corncob. "The cornerstone of Anglo-American policy seems to be Russia first, not Europe first. Why? We've got the *power*! We've got the ships and the planes and the money and the materials and the capacity to outproduce the entire world combined. We've got everything that Russia needs, and yet we crawl to Stalin with our hat in our hand. Of course, he's got the manpower. But what good are mobs of men if he can't arm them with more than hammers and sickles? So *we're* arming them, and do you know, Beau, that when our ships sail to the Persian Gulf flying the Russian flag, the Japs let them pass. How's *that* for a mixed-up war?"

Beau glanced up at his father-in-law in disbelief, just as the office door opened and a captain came in to lay a newspaper still smelling of ink on the general's desk. Duggan picked it up, groaning aloud when he read the banner headline: ALLIES DEMAND UNCONDITIONAL SURRENDER. His face a study in horror and dismay, he sat down to read the story describing the joint proclamation by Roosevelt and Churchill at Casablanca. When he had finished, he sat still for a full two minutes, his hand over his eyes.

"I can't believe it," he said, removing his hand and staring dully at Beau.

"What is it, sir?" Beau asked, alarmed at the expression of gravity bordering on despair in the general's eyes.

"Churchill and Roosevelt—mostly Roosevelt, if you read between the lines—they've just announced a policy of unconditional surrender. In other words, the enemy can't sue for peace. He has to throw down his arms and beg for mercy, or else we'll destroy him. This will put steel in Hitler's spine, Beau—mark my words. It will kill any antiwar or antiHitler movement that may be starting in Germany. If they can't hope to negotiate with us, they certainly won't be able to arouse any interest in getting rid of Hitler. The same for the Japs. If they can't bargain, can't keep their emperor—they'll fight to the death. So, I'm afraid, Beau, that this foolish policy will prolong the war and cost many thousands of lives. Once Goebbels gets through telling the German people that we mean to annihilate them, once the Japanese warlords do the same, they'll produce a last-ditch desperation in them that will cost us dearly." He sighed. "You know, in the last war, Beau, Clemenceau of France said, 'War is much too important to be left to the generals.' To which I might add: and making peace is much too difficult to be left to politicians. If this policy is pursued, I promise you that Germany and Eastern Europe will be left in a leaderless vacuum just made for Communist Russia."

"And Japan, sir?" Beau asked.

"Not a chance, Beau," General Duggan said with calm majesty. "Not as long as I'm alive."

After the Casablanca Conference, the war in the Pacific slowed almost to a halt. Mark Duggan chafed at the enforced inactivity. He grumbled about being "downgraded" to command of "a sideshow." He repeatedly challenged the wisdom of concentrating on North Africa and European Russia and the skies over Germany. He made an enemy of Admiral King, Chief of Naval Operations, by making demands or proposing operations encroaching on Admiral Nimitz's authority or territory, and continued to exacerbate his relations with General Meadows by insisting that his theater receive top priority.

After the Quadrant Conference in Quebec authorized Nimitz to launch a Central Pacific campaign, and appointed Lord Louis Mountbatten to head the newly formed Southeast Asia Command, Duggan protested bitterly that he was being made to play second fiddle to a "glamor boy" and a "swab jockey." Infuriated, he began to entertain powerful senators at his headquarters in Brisbane, as well as influential publishers and owners of chains of radio stations, and soon a campaign was begun in Congress and the press to have Duggan named as the single, overall commander of the entire Asiatic war theater.

Gaining momentum, the drive was halted by Duggan himself after he was informed—through Henry Hawkins, who was always delighted to pour a few gentle drops of acid on the general's open wounds— that if there were to be a single Asiatic chief, it would be Nimitz. Embittered now, Mark Duggan considered resigning to return to the States to campaign for the Republican presidential nomination. He changed his mind, however, after President Roosevelt, shrewdly diving his intentions, publicly announced that there would be no single commander, while lavishly praising Duggan's conduct of the war.

Moreover, a new war hero had begun to captivate the American people: Michael Bauer. Bauer's unpretentious manner, together with his bright blue eyes and friendly grin—a style in sharp contrast to the Duggan hauteur—was proving irresistible to Americans who liked their demigods to be "just folks." Now it was Bauer's happy and homely face that grinned from magazine covers. Bauer was also adept at giving some of the credit to the enlisted men, a tactic that both endeared him to the soldier he was embracing for the benefit of the photographers, and to his family; if not also, by extension, to all the families of all those millions of enlisted men.

Mike Bauer's fondness for hugging private soldiers, however, infuriated Duggan. "Look at him," he exclaimed bitterly, shaking the newspaper at Beau Ames one day when they were scrutinizing the general's communiqué. "He's already running for President." He put a finger on a photograph of General Meadows and General Bauer taken after Casablanca. "The caption says they're inspecting 'the front.'" Duggan snorted, chuckling mirthlessly. "Neither of them has ever heard a shot fired in anger, and they're both wearing pistols. At 'the front.' That's a water fountain George is bending over. Ever see a water fountain at the front, Beau? My, my, George is a lot wider in the beam that he was when he played for Army. And there's Mike, hugging another soldier. Only the soldier's wearing glasses, his pants are pressed, and he's got a pocketful of pens and pencils. How many soldiers like that have you ever seen at the front, Beau?"

Duggan's jealousy of Bauer abated slightly, however, when the Allied attack in Italy became bogged down in the mud and mountains north of Rome. "Von Kesselring's giving Mike a few lessons in mountain warfare," he grunted in satisfaction, actually gratified to see his prediction of an Allied "bloody nose" in Italy come true. When Mike Bauer was relieved, however, returning to Britain to begin organizing the great cross-Channel invasion scheduled for the spring of 1944, Duggan had great difficulty concealing his envy. "How can he command armies when he never commanded as much as a pistol in combat?" he said scornfully.

Finally, in the fall of 1943, the Joint Chiefs authorized Duggan and Nimitz to renew their several drives toward Japan: Duggan up the Solomons ladder and along the northern New Guinea coast towards the Philippines, Nimitz north through the Marshalls and Carolines toward the Marianas. Obviously, the war in Italy was faring poorly. Even though the country had surrendered and Mussolini had been overthrown and assassinated, the Germans under Kesselring had reduced the Allied attack to a costly step-by-step, shot-for-shot advance. Churchill was already insinuating that the campaign had been someone else's idea, and Franklin Delano Roosevelt, ready to announce his intention of seeking a fourth term in 1944, was openly dismayed at the criticism in the press.

"I guess Franklin needs a victory or two," Duggan said archly to Beau Ames, after they had finished going over the general's daily communiqué. "And I guess that means that you'll be back in harness soon, Beau."

Colonel Ames smiled happily. During the past few months he had become deeply disillusioned with his assignment as press officer for the Southwest Pacific Theater. At first he had been pleased with the assignment. After the ordeal of his escape, it had come as a respite, almost as rehabilitation, and the work had been so undemanding and routine that he had been able to sneak an occasional flight to Melbourne for a few days with Virginia and Kenneth.

All that was required was to care for the press corps billeted at General Duggan's headquarters in Brisbane, to see that the general's strict censorship was rigidly enforced and to pass out the daily communiqués. Gradually, however, Colonel Ames became uneasy and distressed. To his astonishment, he quickly realized that the communiqués were actually written by General Duggan. His grandiloquent style was unmistakable. So were the Duggan name and the first person singular, almost as frequent on the pages as punctuation marks. Of the first hundred communiqués issued by Colonel Ames, eighty-one mentioned only one person: General Mark Duggan. Even the dateline was embarrassing: GENERAL DUGGAN'S HEADQUARTERS. Everything was General Duggan's: "Duggan's forces" . . . "Duggan's right flank in New Guinea" . . . "Duggan's brave young airmen" . . . "Duggan's navy" . . . No units were ever mentioned by name, simply because they all belonged to General Duggan.

"The Aussies are hoppin' mad," Jim Duff said to Beau Ames one night while they drank beer on the screened-in veranda of the theater headquarters. "The general has got them doing the dirty work, mopping up all those bypassed pockets in the Solomons and New Guinea. And he never gives them credit."

"I know, Jim," Ames said ruefully. "And today's communiqué dismissed enemy resistance there as 'negligible.' "

Duff wagged his huge red head with a dolefulness that was almost comical. "Ain't nothin' negligible what shoots at you, Beau."

"You can say that again. And boy! if you think the Aussies are pissed off—you should hear the *Marines*! A Marine colonel came into my office today screaming like he wanted to bayonet me. He said getting no credit was bad enough, but having Duggan steal their glory was too much. He said if we called his outfit 'Duggan's men' one more time, they'd start turning their weapons the other way.''

"Who can blame them?" Duff said musingly, reaching into a bucket of water chilled by a can of DDT insect poison and seizing another bottle of beer. "You know, I'm still from Annapolis, Beau," he said, opening the bottle, "and I damn near became a Marine myself. One night in Malinta Tunnel, I asked the general if he was going to cite the Fourth Marines for especial gallantry that day. You know what he said?" Duff asked, tilting his head back to drink. "He said the Marines got more than their share of the glory in the last war, and he was going to make sure they get no more in this one." Duff wiped his lips with the back of his hand and belched gently. "That just isn't fair," he said mournfully.

"You see what I've had to contend with, Jim?" Ames said, pulling the last bottle from the bucket. "Christ! Sometimes I think the correspondents are even worse. They're just a little too clever, you know. I have to pretend not to hear them when they take their communiqués and say something like, 'Well, well—another tablet from Mount Sinai. What doth the Lord sayeth today?' When I reported that the general had returned from a trip to Hawaii, some wise guy snickered and said: 'Have a nice walk?'" Ames groaned and clamped his forehead. "And those pamphlets, those goddam 'I Shall Return' pamphlets with the general's picture on them that we dropped in the Philippines. They keep coming up to me with them, asking if I'd have the Old Man autograph them."

Duff chuckled. "You know what the GI's say now when they go to the latrine?"

"I can guess."

"Right—'I shall return.'"

Ames grimaced. "Today was the worst," he said. "Maybe that's why I'm talking so much. Today we passed out photographs of the general inspecting the New Guinea front. And right in the middle of one of them is this goddammed Packard! A *Packard*! Out in the New Guinea jungle. They all began laughing and asking if the Packard belonged to one of the local tribal chiefs. I blew my stack, Jim—honest I did. I sent the sergeant down to take the pictures back, and when one of those scribblers refused to return his, I went up to him

myself and told him if he didn't cough it up, I'd personally
throw him on the first plane back to the States. So I got
them all back, and destroyed the negative too. But Jesus,
Jim—a Packard in the *jungle*?''

''Where was it really?''

''Out here,'' Ames said in disgust. ''One of the camps
near Brisbane. I guess the Old Man got so jealous of Mike
hugging GI's at the so-called front that he decided to get in
the act himself. So he drove out to this camp. Not that he
wouldn't have gone right to the cannon's mouth, if necessary.
You know him, Jim. Christ, he almost got himself killed at
Manus, he got so close to things. The sniper had him right in
his sights. But then when he realized who it was, he got so
excited, he fell out of the tree. Anyway, the general went to
this camp to shake hands with the GI's, and Sergeant Durkin
forgot to park the car out of sight.'' He finished his beer and
stared moodily at Duff. ''You know, it feels good getting all
this off my chest. You don't mind my sounding off like this,
do you, Jim?''

''Hell, no! I'm enjoying it. It's all going to go into the
book I'm going to write: 'Me and Duggan.' ''

Ames laughed. ''You better use a pen name, Jim, if you
don't want to be back sailing a ferryboat in San Francisco
Bay. The Old Man simply cannot stand anyone else in the
limelight. Oh, I know he's my father-in-law, and I'm fond of
him and admire the hell out of him. But here he is, a military
genius, the greatest commander in our history, and he has this
one silly hole in him.''

''What's that?''

''His vanity. He will not let anyone else near the cameras.
Like today. I went up to General Eichler and told him the
Time magazine correspondent wanted to do a cover story on
him. Christ! He looked at me like he'd been stabbed. 'Colonel,'
he said, 'I'd sooner have you slip a rattlesnake in my pocket.'
I couldn't believe it, until he told me he had just come from
General Duggan's office. The Old Man had copies of *Life*
and the *Saturday Evening Post* on his desk. Both of them had
articles praising Eichler's campaigns in New Guinea. And the
general shook them at Eichler and said: 'Do you realize I
could bust you down to colonel and send you home tomorrow?' That was enough for Eichler—enough for anybody, I

guess. So he thanked me and said: 'Colonel Ames, you above everyone else should know that there is only one general in the Southwest Pacific.' "

Duff grinned with mock ruefulness. "Guess I won't write that book after all, Beau." He reached into his shirt pocket and pulled out a folded slip of paper. "Now that you've made a clean breast of it, I'm not so leery about showing you this." He handed it over. "You know, there's all kinds of lampoons and travesties floating around on the general's communiqués. This is the sharpest. I think an Aussie wrote it." Colonel Ames nodded, beginning to read:

> *Here, too, is told the saga bold*
> *   of virile, deathless youth*
> *In stories seldom tarnished with*
> *   the plain unvarnished truth.*
> *It's quite a rag, it waves the flag,*
> *   its motif is the fray,*
> *And modesty is plain to see in*
> *   Dug's communiqué . . .*
>
> *"My battleships bombard the Nips from*
> *   Maine to Singapore;*
> *My subs have sunk a million tons*
> *   They'll sink a billion more.*
> *My aircraft bombed Berlin last night."*
> *   In Italy they say*
> *"Out turn's tonight," because it's right in*
> *   Dug's communiqué . . .*
>
> *And while possibly a rumor now,*
> *   someday it will be fact*
> *The Lord will hear a deep voice say*
> *   "Move over, God—I'm back!"*
> *So bet your shoes that all the news on*
> *   that last great Judgment Day*
> *Will go to press in nothing less than*
> *   DUG'S COMMUNIQUÉ!*

"Sad, but true," Ames said, handing the paper back to Duff with a wan smile. "And do you know, Jim, if you had shown me something like that six months ago, I'd've punched you in the nose."

CHAPTER 28

Throughout the late winter, spring, and summer of 1944, while his forces leapfrogged up the New Guinea coast, and those of Admiral Chester Nimitz island-hopped north to the Marianas, General Mark Duggan waged a renewed and intensive campaign to have himself appointed supreme commander in the Pacific.

Duggan was not aware of how much his jealousy of Michael Bauer, which rose almost to a level of insanity with the landings in Normandy, had become his motivating force. He would not, of course, admit to anyone, least of all himself, how bitterly he resented seeing his old aide—a commander whose perception of war was only slightly more than his experience of battle, which was zero—become his equal in rank while superseding him in popularity at home. Moreover, Mike Bauer held the title of "Supreme Commander," while Duggan was merely a theater commander. Duggan burned for that designation, "Supreme Commander, Pacific." He was like Henry the Eighth, chafing and sulking because the papacy had conferred titles on the thrones of France, Spain, and Austria while withholding similar honor from England.

Obsessed, then, with his fixation, Duggan began to leak articles to the press in which belittling comparison was made between himself and Admiral Nimitz. General Duff, who had assumed Colonel Ames's duties after Beau returned to action as a regimental commander, quietly arranged secret interviews with some "trustworthy" member of the "loyal press," as Duggan distinguished those publications sympathetic to his ambitions from those of the "opposition press," which were not. The first condition of these meeting was that General Duggan was not to be quoted directly or to be alluded to as a source of information. Usually, these highly explosive "inside" think pieces were reserved for release upon some special occasion, as when the last Japanese bases at Mar and Sansapor in Dutch New Guinea were seized in July of 1944. The following article then appeared:

SANSAPOR, DUTCH NEW GUINEA—When General Mark Duggan today cried, "Hoist the colors!" and the Stars and Stripes caught the breeze above this former Japanese bastion, the event commemorated not only the final eviction of the enemy from this, the second largest island in the world, but also celebrated a feat of arms unrivaled in military history.

In two months, Mark Duggan advanced no less than 1100 miles in the face of fierce enemy opposition. And he did this with minimal casualties and perhaps the most meager amount of supplies ever allotted an officer of his rank and command. In a word, since Mark Duggan began climbing the Solomons ladder and leapfrogging up the enormous New Guinea coast, he had accomplished nothing less than a military miracle.

At the outset of the war, Japan confidently expected the Americans to hammer away at their fortified bases in New Guinea and on the islands, base by base and island by island. In this way, they hoped to wear the Americans down and make the cost of reconquest so bloody that they would settle for a negotiated peace favorable to Japan.

Mark Duggan, however, did not gratify the Japanese in exactly this way. Instead he went what he calls "leapfrogging" or "island-hopping." Instead of going from Base One to Base Two, as they enemy anticipated, he went from Base One to Base Four or even Base Six. This left the forces on the intervening bases and islands neutralized and useless. It left them "to wither on the vine." Although the concept of bypassing is certainly not a new military tactic, it has never before been carried out on such an awesomely enormous scale.

Masterful as this advance of 1100 miles in less than a year has been, nothing reflects the flexibility of Duggan's genius so much as the fact that this original and daring concept was born of necessity. With the skimpy forces available to General Duggan, especially in aircraft carriers, most of which are under the command of Admiral Nimitz, it would have appeared that a victorious march over such vast distances would take years rather than months. Losses in men and material would be staggering. Yet, by his audacious decision to go leapfrogging, General Duggan made the impossible seem easy. He picked and chose his targets. A man fond of the game of baseball and its jargon, he simply "hit 'em where they ain't." And if he had possessed carriers in any number, he might have done it quicker! The range of his leaps might have been doubled or even tripled. Without them, however, each leap was limited to the range of the land-based fighter planes covering his amphibious forces: two hundred or four hundred miles, rather than a thousand or fifteen hundred.

Finally, all this was accomplished with truly minimal losses. When Mark Duggan successfully neutralized the formidable Japanese base on Rabaul by his operations in the Bismarck Archipelago, his combined casualties were less than Admiral Nimitz's single, opening operation at Tarawa.

With the appearance of this article, the Army-Navy rivalry in the Pacific, always seething behind an assumed facade of cooperation, erupted into open, acrimonious warfare.

At once, Admiral Nimitz protested to Admiral King in language ordinarily not becoming an admiral. The commandant of the Marine Corps, stung by the reference to Tarawa's casualties, called a press conference at which he angrily explained that Duggan's Solomons and New Guinea advance had been through hastily improvised "mud-and-log fortifications" and in areas where there was room for maneuver, while the Marines under Nimitz were compelled to make frontal assaults on mandated islands that the Japanese had been fortifying for twenty years. "Duggan's been moving through mud, while we've been hitting cured concrete and coral. As you know, gentlemen, concrete and coral are a little harder. Also, we took Guadalcanal at about the same time Duggan took the Papuan peninsula in New Guinea. We lost one killed in thirty-three men, he lost one out of eleven. Furthermore, the showpiece in his Bismarck operations, where there was room to maneuver, was accomplished by my old command: the First Marine Division."

Such fuel, poured recklessly on the fire by spokesmen for both sides, sent the flames of controversy flickering higher, until the entire nation seemed to be choosing sides. The bounds of reason were shattered when a squad of irate Marines stormed the city room of Hearst's San Francisco *Examiner*, demanding retraction of a pro-Duggan editorial entitled, "No More Tarawas." Tempers were also lost on much higher levels. When a meeting of the Joint Chiefs of Staff was begun by Admiral King's attempt to enter Admiral Nimitz's protest on the record, General Meadows brought his fist down on the table in slow fury, grating through his gritted teeth: "I will not tolerate this hatred," whereupon King snapped: "You wouldn't have it if you'd muzzle Duggan." At this, Meadows adjourned the meeting and requested an appointment with President Roosevelt "to discuss recent developments in the Pacific."

FDR ignored the appeal. He had already declared his candidacy for a fourth term, and he was not inclined to make a martyr of anyone so famous as Duggan, or Nimitz either, for that matter. Moreover, having successfully overcome the Washingtonian tradition of two terms per President, he had secured legislation ending the prohibition against voting by members of the armed forces. The vast majority of men in uniform were youngsters, youths who had known no other President, many of whom actually worshiped Roosevelt. FDR would never gratuitously alienate one half of thirteen million voting servicemen by taking sides. Instead, he scheduled a meeting with Duggan and Nimitz in Hawaii.

President Roosevelt actually sought to kill three birds with one stone at the Hawaii conference. He wanted to persuade Duggan and Nimitz to bury their hatchets, he wanted to hear final arguments on their opposing plans for approaching Japan—Duggan for the Philippines, Nimitz for Formosa—and more, much more than either of these, he wanted a few pictures of himself shaking hands with both of his victorious commanders.

Just before FDR had left the States, the Democratic National Convention had nominated him for a fourth candidacy, while the Republicans had named Governor Thomas E. Dewey of New York. The day before FDR boarded the cruiser *Baltimore* in San Diego, Republican Senator Everett Dirksen of Illinois sneered at "this picture-taking junket."

"Mark Duggan may not be a fourth-term threat this fall," Dirksen said. "But he is still exceedingly popular in America. Admiral Nimitz is only less so. In an election year it's a good idea to be seen as much as possible with as many popular people as possible."

General Duggan shared the senator's contempt. "Purely political," he snorted to Jim Duff the day he received a "summons" from General Meadows to be at Pearl Harbor to confer with the President. As a result, he took with him only Duff and Sergeant Durkin. He had no suspicion that the President intended to settle the Philippines vs. Formosa debate. Angrily pacing the aisle of his B-17 during the long twenty-six hour flight from Brisbane, he complained bitterly about being used as a publicity foil. "And he calls me away from the war for this: a political picture-taking picnic." He smiled grimly to himself: Maybe I'll upstage Franklin a bit, he thought, just as the airplane's landing alarm began to whine and Duggan felt the plane lose altitude. He went to the window and saw Hickam Field beneath him. Pulling his graduation watch from his pocket, he studied it. "Ten to two, Jim," he said to Duff. "The President's ship docks at Pearl at three. You've got a whole hour to find me the biggest open touring car in the islands."

Startled, but not really surprised, Duff ran for a waiting

staff car the moment the Flying Fortress touched down. An hour later he returned driving a huge bright red open limousine. A fire chief's hat was painted on the sides of both front doors.

"It's all I could get, sir," Duff explained apologetically, mopping his sweating forehead. "The only other open car in the islands belongs to a famous madam."

Duggan grinned. "Good choice, Jim. Now all I need is a motorcycle escort."

"That's been arranged, sir," Jim Duff said, pointing to a line of about a dozen military police motorcycles roaring over the airfield toward them.

"Excellent," Duggan said. "Have the staff car take you to Fort Shafter, Jim. Pat, let's get going." Entering the backseat with a grin, he looked at his watch again. "Ten after three, Pat," he said. "Maybe you'd better drive like we're really going to a fire."

President Roosevelt was not pleased. Minutes after the *Baltimore* had been made fast to the dock, Admiral Nimitz came aboard accompanied by Admiral Howley and other ranking Navy and Army officers in his command. FDR greeted them in the ship's wardroom, where he sat in a wheelchair propelled by a Secret Service agent. Admiral Leahy, his personal chief of staff, sat beside him. Drinks were passed out by black stewards in white jackets. FDR chatted amiably with his guests, exuding his irresistible charm, putting the lower ranking officers at their ease. From time to time he glanced at the wardroom; at first in expectation, and then in irritation. Leahy and Nimitz began to swap sea stories, hoping to entertain their chief, who was an avid sailor and had been an Under Secretary of the Navy in World War I.

"Where is Duggan?" the President snapped, ignoring the forced bonhomie.

"I can't rightly say," Nimitz replied in his faint Texas drawl, scratching his close-cropped pepper-and-saltish hair. "I know he landed at Hickam over an hour ago."

A rising wail of sirens halted all conversation in the wardroom. It was followed by a piercing screech of braking rubber. The braided commanders in the wardroom swung in unison toward the door, all suddenly pausing in embarrassment and turning to defer awkwardly to their immobilized commander-in-chief. Snapping his fingers angrily, the President was wheeled out the door ahead of them.

On the quarter-deck outside, they could hear thousands of onlookers jammed into a roped-off area cheering lustily. Below, behind a line of gently idling motorcycles, seated in the backseat of his open red touring car in majestic nonchalance, wearing a flier's leather jacket, his corncob pipe in his mouth while gaily lifting his campaign hat to the cheering crowd, was the tardy Mark Duggan. The admirals gaped while the President glared. Duggan stood up, waved his hat again to the throng, and strode calmly up the gangplank. Halfway up, he turned and waved his hat again. The applause was thunderous.

Even Franklin Roosevelt could not withhold his admiration. "Beautiful, Mark," he said, extending his hand. "I couldn't have done it better myself."

"Thank you, Mr. President," Duggan replied, momentarily stunned at Roosevelt's appearance. Obviously, the President was not in good health. His eyes were sunken, his cheeks sagged, and the gay sport shirt that he wore hung in folds on shoulders that were no longer brawny. My God, he's a sick man! Duggan thought. Aloud, he said: "You haven't changed a bit since the last time I saw you eight years ago, Mr. President."

FDR nodded, signaling to his attendant to wheel him back to the wardroom. Duggan came up beside him, after cordially shaking hands with Leahy, Nimitz, and the other officers.

FDR lifted his chin. "I suppose you think I brought you here just to take pictures," he said tartly to Duggan. "That's what your Republican friends are saying."

"Oh, no, sir. And by the way, sir, congratulations on your nomination."

"Thank you. What do you think of my chances, Mark?"

"I don't know about the folks at home, sir, but you're still the champion with the troops."

Roosevelt grinned. "I'm glad to hear that," he said. He grinned again impishly. "We *will* take a few pictures, Mark," he said. "That car of yours will be just right for you and Nimitz and me to be seen in." He grimaced. "Couldn't you have picked a quieter color?"

"I had no choice, sir. The only other open car in Hawaii is fuchsia, and it's owned by a famous brothel keeper."

"Oh, my God!" FDR groaned in mock dismay. "What the Republicans would have done with that. Anyway, Mark, I think I'll take that car."

"Go ahead, Mr. President," Duggan said, eyeing Roosevelt's cigarette holder. "You've got my cigarette holder, so you might as well have my car too."

The President chuckled. "Over there, Steve," he said to his attendant, pointing to a huge wall map of the Pacific. He began to cough, covering his mouth with his hand. A paroxysm seized his body and he coughed for a minute. When he spoke it was in a choking voice. "You see, Mark, I also came out here to make a final decision on our next step against Japan. The Joint Chiefs and most of the planners in the Pentagon favor bypassing the Philippines and attacking Formosa. The Navy is solidly for it. But I still want to hear from you and Admiral Nimitz personally before I make up my mind."

Duggan glanced around him in dismay, suddenly aware that many of the naval officers were not admirals, but captains and commanders with bulging briefcases under their arms; staff officers prepared to argue the Navy's case. Duggan fumed inwardly. A trap! He had brought nothing, no one . . . Meadows and King had sandbagged him. He would have to go it alone! He sat down, outwardly nonchalant, while Nimitz picked up a pointer and advanced to the map.

"We favor Formosa, Mr. President," he drawled, "because we believe it's the quickest and shortest approach to Japan proper." His pointer touched the Philippines to the south of Formosa. "We recommend that the Philippines be bypassed and all available forces, not only in the Central Pacific, but in the Southwest Pacific also, be brought to bear against Formosa."

"In effect, that would mean phasing out the Southwest Pacific Theater?" the President asked.

"I suppose so, sir," Nimitz replied, his light blue eyes shifting uneasily toward Duggan, grim-faced and silent, alone among the admirals. "Except for mopping-up operations against the bypassed bases, the theater would be quiet." He cleared his throat. "We would probably need all but one or two of the area's American divisions and all but a few air squadrons. Both fleets, of course, and all the aircraft carriers, would be required.'' Nimitz eagerly lifted his pointer to the Mariana Islands. ''Now that we have taken the Marianas, especially Saipan and Tinian, sir, we have advanced our land-based air to within less than two thousand miles of Japan. Soon, as you know, the big new B-29 bombers will be bombing Japan's home islands. Land-based air in the Marianas will give the Formosa operation invaluable support.''

Roosevelt nodded, impressed. ''What are the strategic benefits of Formosa over the Philippines, Admiral?''

''From Formosa we can cut the Japanese line of communications. We can clamp an aerial and sea blockade on the home islands, cut off Japan's industry from her sources of supply south of Formosa. We might even bring her to her knees without an outright invasion.''

Roosevelt nodded again, even more impressed. ''When, Admiral?''

''Next summer, sir.''

The President stroked his chin thoughtfully. ''Thank you, Admiral,'' he said cordially. Then, with a warm smile, he turned to Duggan. ''Your turn, Mark.''

General Duggan arose and strode to the center of the room, facing the President, his back to the map. He held his corncob in his right hand. ''Mr. President,'' he began, carefully choosing his words, ''my preference for the Philippines is based not only on military considerations, but on moral and political grounds as well. I will discuss the military first.'' Using the corncob to tick off points against his finger, speaking in a clear, crisp, controlled voice, he continued. ''First, the Philippines will cut the Japanese supply line every bit as effectively as Formosa. Much of what she needs comes from the archipelago itself, and most of the rest from the Dutch East Indies and the South China Sea to the south and west.'' He strode toward the map. Roosevelt leaned forward attentively, always eager for instruction in his favorite subject: geography. ''Second,'' Duggan resumed, striking his finger, ''Formosa is much too far from land-based air support. Even with the Marianas bases, the leap is in thousands of miles. Too far for land-based fighter support. And carrier aircraft would be insufficient. Third, who will contain the 300,000 enemy troops in the bypassed Philippines? Fourth, Formosa has a hostile population, unlike the Philippines, and staging operations against Japan from there probably would prove difficult. Fifth, to wait until next summer for the final approach to Japan is much too long. It will give the enemy time to strengthen his defenses. Moreover, we should be attacking the home islands themselves by next summer. Now," he said, beginning to relax, "the arguments for the Philippines. First, they are much closer: With completion of the Morotai and Palau operations this September, we will be within seven hundred miles of Leyte, five hundred of Mindanao. Second, the population is friendly and we have appreciable guerrilla forces there which are even now working on the enemy's communications. Third, there is at present sufficient shipping and troops in the area to take Leyte. Fourth, it can be done much sooner—no later than this fall."

Pursing his lips thoughtfully, FDR asked: "Exactly when?"

"October, sir." Duggan was about to add, "before the elections," until the calculating glint in FDR's eyes told him that he had made his point. "From Leyte, we would go to Luzon, sir," Duggan continued, his voice turning husky. "Luzon and Manila. And now I come to the political and moral considerations." Fixing Roosevelt with his dark eyes, he said: "I believe that abandonment of the campaign to relieve the Philippines would provoke an enormous adverse reaction among the American people. Our people want to free the Filipinos, they feel they have a moral obligation which they wish to honor, and no military considerations other than the life or death of our action itself would change their mind." Roosevelt's eyes glinted again, and Duggan's voice rose in confidence, beginning to throb. "Morally, Mr. President, we *must* relieve the Philippines. Seventeen million Filipinos who have remained loyal to the United States, enduring the greatest privation and suffering to do so, *expect* us there. Will we deliberately bypass the Philippines—nay, abandon them—leaving these loyal millions and our own sick and suffering prisoners to the mercy of a cruel enemy whose predilection for murder and torture, robbery and rape, places him in the forefront of the most malevolent tormentors of mankind? No! Mr. President, we *cannot*—we cannot make true prophets of those lying Japanese who each day tell the Filipinos that we have abandoned them and will not shed a single drop of American

blood to redeem them. We cannot, sir,'' he whispered, his
voice sinking, ''for if we do, Mr. President, our name will
be a stink in the nostrils of Asia for a hundred years to
come.''

There was silence in the wardroom. Every eye was fixed on
Duggan, standing there trembling, his eyes flashing. Once
again there was open admiration in the eyes of Franklin
Delano Roosevelt.

"All right, Mark," he said. "You win."

The night was dark and moonless. On the ghostly great
shapes gliding slowly into the Leyte Gulf, sailors walked the
weather decks cautiously, peering anxiously into the black,
carefully holding on to the gunwales or the cable railings of
their ships. Lookouts strained their eyes, calling to the helms-
man with loud warning when another ship appeared with
quiet suddenness beside or before them, vanishing just as
quickly, with only the soft swishing of their unseen wakes to
mark their course.

Aboard the cruiser *Nashville,* General Mark Duggan stood
at the rail, meditating. He had just come from his quarters,
where he had been reading the bible, searching for passages
to comfort him and give him strength. *"Not only sentinels
wait for the dawn..."* Generals, too, Duggan mused, relieved to see the first faint bluish blush of day staining the
horizon astern. We made it without mishap! he exulted.
Thank God for the clouds! *"And the young men put on them
glory and the robes of war."* How many young men, he
thought sadly, how many of them will not see another dawn?
Dear God, he prayed, be merciful. Spare them... Duggan
walked slowly forward, watching the light creeping across the
gulf toward the city of Tacloban. *"What king, about to go to
make war against another king, doth not first sit down, and
think whether he be able, with ten thousand, to meet him
that, with twenty thousand, cometh against him?"* How well
put, he thought, how well had Jesus expressed the wisdom of
avoiding battle with a superior foe. Duggan, with 200,000,
was now going against Yamashita, with 300,000. But Duggan's
force was concentrated, and Yamashita's was distributed throughout the islands. Duggan was hitting him where he was not.

Leyte, with its valuable plains and airfields, was not so heavily defended as Luzon.

Mark Duggan was proud that the armada carrying his troops to battle was the most powerful naval force yet assembled, even stronger than Bauer's at Normandy. Now it was full daylight, and the Japanese air still had not risen to strike the Americans. Duggan deliberately strode around the cruiser, exulting again in what he saw—ships everywhere, everywhere ships; from the horizon to the shore, where the rooftops and church spires of Tacloban were now visible beyond the beach, with the dark green hills of the jungle rising behind them.

Duggan studied the Leyte shore, a tender poignance aching in his breast. The Philippines again! How deeply his family had been associated with these islands. It was here that his father had been a victorious general, had become the archipelago's first governor-general. He thought wistfully of his own tour as the infant Commonwealth's first field marshal, and of his old friend, Manuel Quezon, its first president, who had died of cancer two months ago. Duggan's hand strayed to his campaign hat. He took it off, fingering the bullet holes, smiling to himself as though hearing Durkin chuckling again and remarking, "They already used up all the bullets with your name on them." He turned to his right to stare northward toward Samar, toward Balangiga, where he had first looked the Medusa of battle in the eye and found that she had no terrors for him. He thought of the *General Philip Sheridan*, the stinking cavalry transport that had brought them there; of all the ships he had sailed on, of the misty gray morning they had entered the Loire at St. Nazaire, of the evening off Vera Cruz when Durkin fancied that the setting sun was touching the snowcapped peak of Mount Orizaba. Duggan shivered slightly, and sighed—just as "General Quarters" came blaring over the ship's bullhorn.

At once, the *Nashville*'s decks became crowded with sailors and Marines sprinting for their battle stations. Helmeted and wearing life jackets, they climbed rapidly into gun mounts, sweeping the sky with their glasses. Below, Duggan could hear the sound of bulkhead doors being slammed shut and dogged down, sealing off the compartments. The ship quivered and rolled. A series of great explosions almost forced Duggan to cover his ears. The *Nashville*'s six-inch guns were firing at the Leyte shore, joining the great bombardment that had begun all around her. Duggan could hear the sixteen- and fourteen-inch shells of the battleships behind him wailing overhead, sounding like flying boxcars. Inshore, destroyers swept in close, their sterns digging into the water like rearing thoroughbreds. Rocket ships released flights of missiles with a dreadful hissing sound, darkening the sky. Duggan put his binoculars to his eyes, watching the puffs of smoke and flame grow larger and more numerous. Now he could hear the whine of dogfighting planes overhead. A fighter with a huge red ball on its fuselage came twisting downward, trailing flames, plummeting into the sea like a stone—and the *Nashville*'s crew cheered above the caldron of sound in which their ship seemed to be immersed. Now the drifting smoke had fused. An enormous white pall darkened by dust hung over the beaches, sometimes winking pink or becoming suffused with yellow by the explosions beneath it. Dauntless dive-bombers dived down through the smoke, releasing their bombs and climbing upward with a screech. Gull-winged Corsairs flew low firing rockets, followed by land-based Havoc attack bombers.

Once more Mark Duggan felt his spirits soar in exultation. He turned to see Durkin grinning at him, lifting his joined thumb and forefinger high in the gesture of perfection. Instantly, it was quiet. The cannonade had lifted and the aerial bombardment had ended. The pall of smoke was lifting to reveal fires on the beaches. Duggan raised his glasses again, watching tensely as the first wave of troop-filled amtracs churned shoreward. He braced for the sight of enemy shells exploding among the amtracs. He saw none, and turned to Durkin with a smile.

"Perfect, Pat," he said. "They never laid a glove on us."

At noon General Duggan prepared to go ashore. He put on a fresh set of pressed suntans, his campaign hat, and a pair of sunglasses, clambering down a ladder into the *Nashville*'s motor whaler. Behind him came Jim Duff, Durkin, and the ranking commanders of the Southwest Pacific. Making for a nearby transport, Duggan picked up Sergio Osmena, the new president of the Philippines, and his official party. Then Duggan and Duff climbed atop the whaler's engine house while the boat bounced over choppy water toward beaches already piled five and six feet high with thousands of tons of equipment and supplies. Loaded trucks roared inland, raising clouds of dust, yet the hills of boxes and cartons of fuel drums rose higher. Landing craft of all sizes lined the beaches, their ramps down, while offshore hundreds of others bobbed in the swells with idling motors, awaiting their turn to unload, watching for the signal from harassed beachmasters who strode up and down the beaches gesturing angrily and bellowing through their bullhorns.

Duggan's boat sought to land on the left flank of the invasion force, where Beauregard Ames, now a brigadier general, was an assistant division commander. A scraping noise beneath the keel, however, forced the dismayed coxswain to back off.

"Too shallow, sir," he yelled to an aide-de-camp, and the young officer telephoned the beachmaster to send a small craft to which the general and his party could transfer.

"Not a chance!" the beachmaster yelled into the astonished aide's ear. "Let 'em walk!"

Feeling the general's expectant eyes on him, the aide turned scarlet and mumbled: "I—I'm sorry, sir—there are no other boats available."

Duggan scowled, looking down at his spotless suntans. Then he grinned. "Well, Jim," he said to Duff, jumping down from the engine house, "they've been wisecracking for years about me walking on water. Maybe I'll give it a try."

He strode forward and stepped off the bow into knee-deep water. Duff and the others followed.

"No luck," Duggan said jokingly, his good humor returning the moment he saw the photographers on the beach. "Now I know how St. Peter felt."

Duggan knew instinctively that pictures of himself and his party striding through the surf would receive wide publicity, and he was in high good spirits when he reached the beach. Leaving Osmena and the others, he walked inland, accompanied by Duff and Durkin. Occasionally a sniper's bullet from the wooded hillside peeped overhead.

"General," Duff said anxiously, a worried frown on his red forehead, "don't you think you've gone far enough? I mean, if the Japs ever suspected you were here... After what we did to Yamamoto, they'd sacrifice a whole division to get you."

Duggan chuckled, pointing to Durkin. "Pat'll tell you— there's no power on earth can harm me in the Philippines. Anyway, I want to see how Beau is doing. I promise you, Jim, I won't go farther than his command post."

They continued on, pausing to examine two dead Japanese soldiers, apparently killed by shrapnel. They lay twisted in that limp, almost boneless sprawl peculiar to the violently dead.

"That's the way I like to see them," Duggan muttered, striding on.

The farther they walked, the more dead bodies they saw, perhaps a third of them Americans. Graves Registration personnel were already at work, ticketing the corpses. Duggan shook his head sadly.

General Ames's command post was in a huge crater dug by an exploding 16-inch naval shell. Beau was crouched at the bottom speaking to a regimental commander by walkie-talkie. Beside him a captured Japanese colonel lay on the ground under the ungentle knee of an American soldier. The soldier held a knife at the colonel's throat. Ames was astounded when he looked up and saw Duggan standing above him.

"My God, General, what are you doing up here?"

"Same as you, Beau. You know I've got to get the feel of the fighting. How's your outfit doing?"

"All right now, sir. We should be on our first day's objective well before nightfall. We had a stiff fight on Red Beach, though. Heavy casualties..."

"I saw them," Duggan said, his face grave. He came down into the crater, glancing down at the captive colonel.

Beau Ames grinned. "I've got a prize for you, sir. This piece of carrion is none other than Colonel Hara, the snake who murdered Bill Baugh. He turned to the soldier. "Let him up."

Reluctantly, the soldier arose and put away his knife, pulling Hara roughly to his feet.

"Easy there, soldier," General Duggan said. "Let's not be like them."

The soldier gaped in incredulity. So did Hara.

Ames studied Hara in disgust. "Too low to step on, too wet to kick," he muttered. His voice rose. "Colonel Hara, I think I'm going to turn you over to a Filipino named Francisco Perez." Hara's eyes widened in horror and he swallowed. "I ought to," Ames grumbled, "but I can't. We were raised differently. We don't torture and murder prisoners like you do. We try to live by law. And that's where you're going, Hara—to trial as a war criminal."

Duggan nodded approvingly. "He'll have company, Beau. Homma, Yamashita, all of them . . . they'll pay." He glanced up at Duff and Durkin, still standing warily on the rim of the crater above him. "We'd better be going back." He pulled out his graduation watch. "I've a broadcast scheduled for two o'clock." He clambered up the slope, scorning his son-in-law's attempt to help him. "Keep up the good work, Beau," he said, and began trudging back to the beach.

By the time they got there, it had begun to rain. Duggan climbed up on a weapons carrier on which a portable radio transmitter had been mounted. It was linked to the *Nashville*'s master transmitter, which could broadcast on several wavelengths to guerrilla forces in the archipelago and those Filipinos who still had radios. Duggan seized the microphone with shaking hands.

"People of the Philippines," he cried in a trembling voice, "I have returned. By the grace of Almighty God, our forces stand again on Philippine soil." His voice broke, but he continued on, speaking louder above the roar of motors around him, the sound of the rain and the rattle of battle inland. "Rally to me! Let the indomitable spirit of Bataan and Corregidor lead on. Rise and strike! For your homes and hearths, strike! In the name of your sacred dead, strike! Let no heart be faint. Let every arm be steeled. The guidance of Divine God points the way. Follow in His name to the Holy Grail of righteous victory!"

Mark Duggan came down from the weapons carrier, trembling with emotion. His drenched, mud-spattered suntans were plastered to his body, and even his campaign hat dripped water. But his eyes shone with a holy fire.

"Well, Pat," he said to Sergeant Durkin, "we're back."

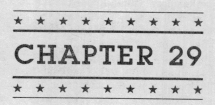

CHAPTER 29

"President Roosevelt is dead, sir," Jim Duff said, coming into General Duggan's Manila office. "It was on the radio. Cerebral hemorrhage."

Duggan stared at him in disbelief. He had known that the President was ill, and he had seen from the photographs taken at the Yalta Conference in February 1945, that he was much worse than when they had met in Honolulu seven months previously. Nevertheless, for Franklin Delano Roosevelt to be gone . . . for someone else to occupy the White House . . .

"Oh, my God," Duggan groaned. *"Truman!"*

"Jesus!" Duff swore. "I never thought of *that*! You don't think much of Truman, sir?"

"I never met him. Roosevelt never said anything about him to me either. All I know is what I've seen in the paper: a little man in a bow tie playing the piano for pretty movie stars. Well, at least it won't be that Commie Henry Wallace. We can thank God for that. He's even worse than Genry Gawkins."

"I always wondered why Roosevelt dropped Wallace," Duff said musingly.

"It wasn't Roosevelt so much as the Democratic National Committee. Wallace was too much of a leftist even for them. They must have known that FDR would never live out his term, and they couldn't stand the thought of Wallace in the

White House. Besides, FDR was thinking about all the post-war treaties the Senate would have to ratify. He didn't want the Senate to do to him what they did to Wilson. So he picked Truman because Truman had the Senate's respect and was popular there.''

''Well, I admit he doesn't look too commanding, sir—but maybe he'll rise to the occasion.''

''It's possible.'' Duggan stared at Duff thoughtfully. ''That's one of the great things about our country, Jim. We don't have many great leaders, but we do have great institutions. Even a mediocrity like Truman can make them work.''

''Do you think Roosevelt was a great man?''

''I can't say. He was a fine man, maybe even a great one. I'll never forget the thrill of hope that lifted American hearts when he took office in 1933. But in foreign policy . . . that crazy Unconditional Surrender . . . all those concessions he made to Stalin at Yalta . . . the way he let Churchill hypnotize him . . . his naive belief that he could charm a clever brute like Stalin . . . I just don't know, Jim.''

Duff nodded and left—returning almost instantly with a message in his hand. ''Admiral Nimitz wants to know if you'll release the Seventh Fleet to Admiral Spruance at Okinawa.''

''Not on your life!'' Duggan snapped. His voice softened. ''Tell him I'm sorry, but I need the fleet here for our own operations and protection.''

A troubled expression crossed Duff's round, red face. ''I don't know, sir—the Kamikaze are sure kicking the hell out of Spruance's ships.''

''No, Jim,'' Duggan said. ''Remember all those hungry years when we pleaded for ships and carriers and got turned down? I don't know what's keeping them at Okinawa anyway. Until they secure that island, I can't do very much about planning for Olympic.''

''Olympic'' was the code name for the massive invasion of Japan scheduled for November 1945. Far and away the greatest amphibious force in history would seize Kyushu, the southernmost island of Japan. In the following spring an even greater operation, code-named ''Coronet,'' would assault the Tokyo plain on the huge capital island of Honshu.

Both operations were to be under the overall command of Mark Duggan.

Duggan was immensely proud of his forthcoming command, and of the title that would soon be his: "Supreme Commander, Allied Powers." Once the war in Europe was over—and in that mid-April of 1945 it seemed only a matter of weeks—there would be a vast shift of Allied power to the Pacific. Duggan would command it all, in cooperation with Nimitz on naval problems. Not even his receipt of the new five-star rank of General of the Army pleased Duggan as much as the rapid rise of his fortunes since the Leyte landings the preceding October.

In January his forces had landed on Luzon, and in February they entered Manila. Gradually, the remaining islands were reconquered and the restored Commonwealth government under Osmena had called for the reconvening of a new Congress in June. In April, then, Duggan was jubilant—as well as secretly pleased that the end of the war in Europe would undoubtedly mark the peak and ensuing decline of Michael Bauer's popularity and the resurgence of his own. He was confident that Bauer's image was already smudged.

"The Battle of the Bulge didn't make Mike look too good," he had remarked to General Duff after the German penetration of the Allied line in January. "I never could see why he insisted on advancing toward Germany on a broad front. He's violating the cardinal rule of assault: concentration. Sure, he's forcing an inferior foe to defend at every point—but he's got so much more than they have! And he's got the Russians pounding them from the other side. Good Lord, Jim, he could have been in Berlin last Christmas if he had any imagination, any audacity. Hold them with his right and swing hard with the left. Mass on the left, the north, and step on the gas."

"They did try something like that in Holland last September, sir—but it didn't work."

"With *Montgomery*?" How could it work with Montgomery? He's a set-piece fighter. He likes six-to-one superiority, or even more. He won't move until the last shoelace is tied. For what I'm talking about Mike needed someone like George Peyton. Look what George did in Brittany and Bavaria. If Mike had massed his left and put Cowboy George in charge, he'd've eaten his Christmas breakfast in Berlin.'' Duggan sighed. ''Poor George. I guess he'll go into history as the general who slapped a private soldier in the face. But he's still tops with me, and I certainly hope he comes out here when the war ends over there.''

The war in Europe did end three weeks after the death of Roosevelt, and Okinawa was secured the end of June. Now, a huge tide of men and arms began flowing toward the Pacific. Duggan was overjoyed. For Olympic alone he would command more than forty American divisions, to say nothing of the Australian, New Zealand, British, French, and Canadian forces that would follow. American naval power had grown so great that in July surface forces had begun to bombard the Japanese islands, joining the dreadful scourging from the skies that had already begun to batter beaten Japan to her knees and, in a single night, had reduced much of Tokyo to ashes. Soon Duggan began to receive intelligence reports indicating that Japan was prostrate and was frantically trying to persuade the Soviet Union to negotiate a peace.

''They can't surrender unconditionally,'' Duggan explained to Duff. ''They want to keep their emperor. So the carnage continues.''

That same month, President Truman, Prime Minister Attlee, and Chiang Kai-shek issued the Potsdam Declaration calling upon Japan to surrender unconditionally or else face ''prompt and utter destruction.'' The phrase puzzled Duggan, until he learned of the detonation of the world's first atomic bomb on July 16, 1945. Still, the Japanese did not surrender. And then, on August 6, the mushroom cloud rose over Hiroshima; and again, three days later, over Nagasaki. On August 11, Japan agreed to a conditional surrender—and on August 19 a delegation of Japanese officials flew into Manila.

Jim Duff stared at Beau Ames in disbelief. ''Atsugi,'' he repeated. ''He's not going to Atsugi!''

''He is indeed.''

''But Beau—he'll be killed! Christ, I talked to those delegates from Japan. They're scared silly that a civil war will break out. All the young officers—especially the Kamikaze—are against the surrender. They want to fight to the bitter end. There's been fighting already. They had to fight to capture the remaining airplanes and remove the propellers. The Kamis swore they'd crash-dive the *Missouri* the moment she enters Tokyo Bay. Every day these crazy suiciders are mailing severed fingers to the Imperial Palace with notes that hands and heads will follow if Hirohito doesn't call off the surrender. Christ! All they have to do is kill Duggan and start the whole thing boiling again.''

''I know, Jim, He knows too. Even the Japs don't want him to go to Atsugi. It used to be a Kamikaze training base, and there's still a lot of them living there. The Old Man knows that. But he also knows the Oriental mind, or at least he says he does. He's confident they'll treat him with respect. Like a conqueror, he said.''

Duff grinned ruefully. ''He would say that. Well, *I'm* not going to try to change his mind. I like it here.''

The following morning, Duff and Sergeant Durkin were with General Duggan when his Flying Fortress took off for Atsugi. They arrived in the afternoon of a bright, sunny day. Duggan could see heat waves rising shimmering from the runway. He shook hands with General Eichler, who came up the ramp to welcome him.

''The end of the road, Bob,'' Duggan grunted, taking his corncob from his mouth. He pointed at a line of ancient and decrepit vehicles headed by a faded red fire engine parked a few hundred feet away. ''What in the name of God is that?''

Eichler grinned weakly. ''Our motorcade, sir. That's the best they could give us.''

Duggan shook his head pityingly. ''They must really be hurting,'' he said.

Duggan's automobile was a ten-year-old American Lincoln. He got into it with Duff and Durkin. A sharp explosion made Duff and Durkin jump. They looked at each other sheepishly when they realized it was the fire engine starting. Lurching slowly forward, the ramshackle vehicles of the supreme commander's motorcade drove toward Yokohama fifteen miles away.

To either side of the road stood armed soldiers standing at attention with their backs turned. Duff studied them apprehensively. They could easily wheel and massacre the motorcade.

''Why do they have their backs to us, sir?'' he asked Duggan.

"A mark of respect," the general said. "They do that when they're guarding the emperor. Only him." He paused, smiling gently. "Or a conqueror."

Yokohama was a ruined, silent desert. It had been eighty percent destroyed by B-29 raids. The surviving shops were either boarded up or had window blinds drawn. The sidewalks were empty, the streets full of rubble. The Americans drove in silence to the New Grant Hotel, which Duggan had chosen for his temporary headquarters before boarding the *Missouri* to preside over the surrender ceremonies.

His party went at once to the dining room, where they were served a steak dinner by silent, bowing, softly hissing waiters. General Duggan reached for a glass of sake beside his plate.

Duff shot out a hand. "Let me test it first, sir," he pleaded.

Duggan chuckled. "Jim, you're the kind of guest that gives poison banquets a bad name," he said, sipping the wine appreciatively.

Before retiring that night, Duggan received the welcome news that General Jonathan Cartwright had been found in a prison camp in Manchuria and was flying to Atsugi. The following night, as Duggan sat at dinner, Cartwright entered the dining room, limping on a cane. He was so thin he looked like a scrawny, elongated bird. His shiny new suntan hung on his body in folds, and his Adam's apple seemed as large as his beaked nose. Duggan rushed up to him and threw both arms around him. He tried to speak but his voice choked with emotion and the tears rolled down his cheeks.

"Bones . . ." he whispered hoarsely over and over, gently kneading Cartwright's frail arm. "Bones . . ."

Next morning, General Cartwright was with General Duggan and Admiral Nimitz when they went aboard a destroyer and made for the *Missouri*, anchored six miles off Yokohama. More than 250 Allied warships of all sizes, shapes, and functions lay anchored around the giant battleship. Mists rising from the water underneath low gray clouds drifted across decks white with sailors.

Aboard the *Missouri*, except for a cleared space occupied by an old mess table covered with green felt cloth, on which the documents of surrender lay, every inch of standing or sitting space was filled. Sailors sat precariously on gun turrets and on the huge sixteen-inch rifles themselves; on gun mounts, in crow's nests, atop hatches. Throngs of Allied generals and admirals crowded the quarter-deck below them. Cheers broke from every throat when the five-starred flags of Nimitz and Duggan were flung to the breeze, and a mighty roar arose after the American flag that had flown over the Capitol on Pearl Harbor day was unfurled triumphantly above them. Shortly after eight o'clock Nimitz and Duggan came aboard. A hush came over the *Missouri*. The two commanders went immediately to a cabin, and the buzz of conversation rose again. Shortly before nine, the Japanese delegation arrived: seven top-ranking Japanese generals and admirals, four civilians of the Foreign Office dressed in swallow coats and top hats. Foreign Minister Mamoru Shigemitsu led the party. He limped painfully on the wooden leg that had replaced the one he lost to an assassin's bomb years ago, making straight for the surrender table.

Nimitz and Duggan came out of their cabin, followed by Admiral Howley. They went to the table. General Mark Duggan, Supreme Commander, Allied Powers, stepped up to the microphone. General Jonathan Cartwright stood behind him.

"We are gathered here," Duggan said, "representatives of the major warring powers, to conclude a solemn agreement whereby peace may be restored. The issues, involving divergent ideals and idealogies, have been determined on the battlefields of the world and hence are not for our discussion or debate. Nor is it for us here to meet, representing as we do a majority of the people of the earth, in a spirit of distrust, malice, or hatred. But rather it is for us, both victors and vanquished, to rise to that higher dignity which alone befits the sacred purposes we are about to serve, committing all our people unreservedly to faithful compliance with the understanding they are here formally to assume.

"It is my earnest hope, and indeed the hope of all mankind, that from this solemn occasion a better world shall emerge out of the blood and carnage of the past—a world dedicated to the dignity of man and the fulfillment of his most cherished wish for freedom, tolerance, and justice."

Duggan's voice was trembling when he finished, and

his hands shook when he signed the surrender documents as the first of the Allied signatories. Stepping back, he watched the other representatives sign. China . . . the United Kingdom . . . the Soviet Union . . . Australia . . . Canada . . . France . . . New Zealand . . . the Netherlands. Above him the sun was breaking through the clouds. It shone brightly upon that vast armada of Allied ships, upon the single destroyer that was the lone survivor of the once-mighty Japanese navy. An approaching murmuring of many motors became a loud buzzing drone rising to a deafening roar as four hundred monster B-29's and fifteen hundred carrier aircraft swept over the bay. Momentarily, Mark Duggan thought of that moment of hesitation in his life when his tour as chief of staff was ending and his military career seemed over; when he had thought seriously of entering the business world. It was then that he had resolved that he would not be a tycoon but a conqueror. And he had. He remembered again his dying father's words: ''The name . . . the family name . . . carry it higher.''

And he had.

KOREA

CHAPTER 30

On June 24, 1950, Mark Duggan celebrated his seventy-first birthday. A quiet family party was held at the Duggan quarters in the American embassy. There was a birthday cake with seven red candles, each representing a decade, and one white one. Little Kathleen Ames, who had marked her own first birthday only two months ago, helped her grandfather blow out the candles. When she puffed up her cheeks, puckering her mouth into a rosebud, both Betsy and Mark laughed in delight, remembering how Kathy's mother had done the same on her first birthday thirty-four years ago.

"Thirty-four years!" Betsy exclaimed, staring at Virginia. "I can't believe it."

"Don't remind me," Virginia said, beginning to slice the cake.

"It was just before Wilson asked Congress for a declaration of war," Duggan said. "I can still see him—pale and shaking life a leaf."

Virginia began passing out the cake. "None for me, honey," Beau Ames said. "I'm getting too heavy."

Virginia glanced pointedly at the half-empty glass of beer beside his plate. "Not from cake, you're not."

Ames chuckled good-naturedly. "Give my piece to Kenny,"

he said, and his son cried out boyishly: "Pass her over, Mom—can I have Kathy's too? She always makes a mess."

"No, you can't—greedy-guts. I'll feed Kathy hers."

Young Ames made a face. General Duggan studied him thoughtfully, pleased, as always, to see how the handsome boy had fulfilled the promise of his childhood beauty. Duggan did not notice, of course, that the youth's good looks were almost feminine, how his large dark eyes were just a trifle too large, his lips a shade too full, and his smooth clear skin a bit too delicate.

"Well, Jinny," Duggan said to his daughter, "have you made up your mind about sending Kenneth to school in the States?"

"Oh, I don't know, Daddy," Virginia said in mild protest. "The service school here is actually very good."

"I think military school would be good for him," Duggan persisted.

"I don't want to go!" young Ames burst out petulantly. "I hate mili—" Feeling his father staring at him sternly, the boy fell silent, his upper lip quivering.

"We'd better be going," Virginia said hastily. "Kathy's asleep already, and Kenny has to study for a test tomorrow."

The Ames family arose. General Duggan accompanied them to the door, puffing a cigar from the box of Havanas his son-in-law had given him for his birthday. After they left, Mark and Betsy returned to the table. Duggan dipped the end of his cigar into the brandy inhaler at his plate. He rolled it luxuriously between his lips, puffing on it thoughtfully.

"Forty-nine years," he murmured. "It's been that long since George Meadows and I left West Point for San Francisco and the Philippines. If I do say so myself, Betsy, it's been quite a career."

"It has indeed," Betsy said, pouring herself a second cup of tea, "and if I do say so myself, it's time to end it."

Mark said nothing, staring at his wife meditatively. Betsy's face had softened since she stopped drinking six years ago. She had never told him why, although Virginia knew. It was Virginia who had found her mother drunk and drowning in the bathtub of their Melbourne hotel suite. She had pulled her out and given her artificial respiration. Betsy never drank again.

"But, Mark," she said, trying to break in on her husband's reverie, "you're not listening. I said it's been fourteen years since we left the States."

"True. It would be nice going home. One more year, Betsy," he said consolingly. "The peace treaty will be signed then, and Japan will be on her own. I can step down then."

"Promise?" Betsy cried eagerly.

"I promise. They probably wouldn't let me stay on active duty anyway."

"We could sell the house in Washington, and locate somewhere along the Hudson near the Academy. You'd love that. So would I. We could go to all the games and the affairs at the Point and go into New York on weekends."

Mark smiled. "I'd rather be President."

"You're not serious."

"I am."

"But Mark—you're too old! By 1952 you'll be seventy-three. Americans have never elected anyone that old."

"I don't *feel* old," Mark said doggedly.

"I know you don't—and you don't act it. But both Senator Taft and Mike Bauer are ten years younger than you are. Honestly, Mark—I don't think you'd have a ch—"

"Damn, Mike!" Mark swore viciously, stubbing out his cigar. "I don't know how he does it. All he does is grin, and they go gaga over him. If I'd've been in command in Europe, I'd've been in Berlin before Christmas. But they still like Mike. You know what Alanbrook said in his diary, that I was head and shoulders over Mike, and Meadows too. But look at him! He never read anything deeper than a dime Western in his life, and now he's head of a great university. He never heard a shot fired in anger, and they put him in command of armies. He never voted in his life, either—and now they'll probably make him President. How in the name of heaven does a mediocrity like that—a super clerk—get away with all that?"

"It's the common touch," Betsy said soothingly. "You said yourself that the American people distrust majesty."

"They do," Mark said bitterly. "They want all their eagles to be sparrows like themselves."

Still in a bitter mood, Mark went to bed. But he could not sleep. He lay awake reflecting on his nearly five years as

Supreme Commander, Allied Powers. In the weeks following
the surrender ceremony, he had enjoyed a brief renaissance of
popularity, eclipsing even Bauer. But then, as he took up his
duties in Tokyo, his image had begun to fade. It was as
though he were a man stood up against a cellophane wall to
be fired at by both sides. First the Russians, seconded by the
British, complained that he was "too soft" on the Japanese.
They demanded a four-power commission and zones of occupation similar to the Allied division of Germany. Duggan
refused. Although the Soviets did not declare war on Japan
until four days before she surrendered, they nevertheless laid
claim to the big northern island of Hokkaido, almost a third
of her territory. Duggan again turned them down. At one
point General Kuzma Derevyanko, chief of the Russian
military mission to Duggan's headquarters, entered the supreme commander's office and in abusive language informed
him that Russia would secure his dismissal. Derevyanko also
threatened to bring in Russian troops on his own.

"If you do," Duggan said quietly, "I will throw you and
your entire mission into jail."

Astounded, the Russian mumbled, "I believe you would."

Duggan was proud of his achievement in holding the
Soviet bear at bay on the doorstep of Japan. The Central and
Eastern European countries exposed to the same communist
takeover tactics had vanished one by one behind the Iron
Curtain. He was dismayed and deeply wounded to find
himself the target of a torrent of caustic criticism at home.

Lying sleepless in his bed, Duggan reflected bitterly on
how viciously he had been attacked for his "uncompromising
attitude toward our Russian ally," by those same writers and
professors who had watched in silence, if not actually silent
approval, while the Red tide engulfed Poland, the Baltic, and
the Balkans. He thought of how the same people who had
tried to destroy Germany by turning her into an agricultural
nation had sought to create civil war in Japan by bringing the
emperor to trial as a war criminal. They had derided the
supreme commander as "the first American pro-consul,"
calling him "Deep Purple" for his grandiloquent prose. That
very morning, a New York newspaper columnist had written:
"General Duggan is fond of telling us how well he knows the
Oriental mind. Judging from the number of persons he has

kicked out of office, he seems more familiar with the Oriental behind.''

Duggan had also found himself criticized for his support of Chiang Kai-shek in the civil war with the communists led by Mao Tse-tung. He had repeatedly warned the State Department that a Nationalist victory was vital to the future of democracy in Asia. He was ignored. Instead, the State Department and the American press were happy to receive the assurance given by George Quincy Meadows, the U.S. ambassador to China, that Mao and his followers were not communists but ''agrarian reformers.'' Duggan reflected bitterly on how the State Department arranged an armistice in China just as Chiang was closing on Mao. George Meadows was sent to negotiate a peace.

En route, he stayed with Duggan in the embassy in Tokyo. Duggan remembered how tired and worn George had appeared, and how little hope he had held for a real peace in China. He had been right. After seven months of fruitless negotiation, the war was resumed—but with the difference that Chiang's supplies from America had dwindled to a trickle, and Mao's—supplied by Russia from American stocks received in World War II—had increased massively. Duggan still had not entirely recovered from the shock of communist victory in China in 1949—only a year ago, the same year in which Soviet Russia, using secrets passed to her by American traitors, produced an atomic bomb.

''It is an unmitigated disaster for Asia and for the world,'' Duggan had said then of the Red victory in China.

He still believed that. Turning restlessly on his side, he recalled what Manuel Quezon had said to him one day in Malinta Tunnel when Japanese bombs were exploding overhead. ''I do not fear Japan, Mark,'' Manuel had said. ''Your country is much too strong for her, and you will beat her. No, I am afraid of China. She is a slumbering monster. She has been asleep for centuries. But when she awakes, if she becomes energized by some horrible movement such as Communism or Fascism, she will scourge all Asia.''

And now great China was communist—and awake. Which way would she move? Duggan thought anxiously of Korea to the west of Japan. Korea was also divided, as Germany was divided, as Japan would have been if he himself had not been so firm. Stalin's trained puppets had planted a Red satellite state north of the 38th Parallel, and the United States, working through the United Nations, had sponsored a free, elected one to the south. Both South Korea and North Korea had been arming, and both had vowed to unify the peninsula by force of arms. Would Korea be the world's next battleground between the open and the closed societies?

It occurred to Duggan that Stalin's blockade of Berlin last year, which had called forth the dramatic Berlin Airlift, might really be a feint, a distraction calculated at drawing freeworld strength and attention away from South Korea, the true object of his intentions. Yawning, he turned over again. He thought of what Betsy had said about being too old to run for President. But he really *didn't* feel that old. Maybe she was right . . . Maybe in another year it would be time to hang up the sword . . . Maybe it would be fun living on the Hudson near the Academy . . . Maybe . . . Mark Duggan fell asleep.

Shortly after dawn his bedside telephone rang. An excited aide in Duggan's headquarters in the Dai Ichi Palace informed the supreme commander that Communist North Korea had invaded South Korea.

At about the same time, the telephone rang in the library of President Harry Truman's home in Independence, Missouri. The caller was Secretary of State Dean Acheson.

"Mr. President," he said, "I have very serious news. The North Koreans have invaded South Korea."

"Oh, my God!" Truman exclaimed. "I'd better fly back to the capital right away."

"No need to rush, sir," Acheson said. "We don't have many details yet. But I do think we should call for an emergency meeting of the Security Council."

"Good idea," Truman snapped. "Are the Russians still boycotting it?"

"Yes, sir. They say they're not coming back until August, when the presidency rotates to them. That's when they're going to try to have the presence of Nationalist China ruled illegal."

"Wonderful! It could be that Uncle Joe Stalin goofed on this one, Dean. If we don't have to worry about a Russian veto, maybe we can get the UN to intervene."

"I think so, sir. The least we should get is a call for a cease-fire."

"Very good, Dean. Report to me in the morning."

Immediately, the Secretary of State contacted United Nations Secretary-General Trygve Lie in New York. "The North Koreans have invaded South Korea, Mr. Secretary. Could you summon a meeting of the Security Council?"

"I will, indeed!" Lie cried in a guttural Norwegian accent. "This is war against the United Nations!"

Next day, the Security Council, with Russia still absent in protest of the membership of Chiang Kai-shek's Nationalist China, passed a resolution calling for a cease-fire in South Korea and directing the North Koreans to withdraw to their own country. That same day Acheson called Truman's home again.

"The situation is very grave, Mr. President. General Duggan says the South Koreans appear to be on the verge of collapse.

"I'm leaving right away," Truman snapped, and ordered the presidential airplane—the "Sacred Cow"—prepared for a return flight to Washington. En route, the President reflected on the disgrace of the democracies in the years prior to World War II: how they had stood shamefully idle while Japan raped Manchuria, Hitler gobbled up Austria and Czechoslovakia, and Mussolini invaded Ethiopia. Not until it was almost too late had a hand been raised to deter the dictators. Now, Truman thought, if no one resists Red aggression, no small nation will be safe from a stronger Communist neighbor. Truman resolved to help South Korea. He cabled ahead to Acheson to assemble the military chiefs for a meeting in Blair House (the White House was being renovated). At that conference, Truman authorized General Duggan to protect Americans in South Korea and to prevent Seoul, the capital of South Korea, from falling "into unfriendly hands."

Truman also sent the Seventh Fleet into the Straits of Formosa lying between mainland Communist China and Formosa, to which Nationalist China had withdrawn after its defeat on the mainland the preceding year.

"We've got to keep Mao and Chiang off each other's throats," Truman said. "We've got to keep the war from spreading."

"What about Western Europe, sir?" Acheson asked in his

soft, controlled voice. "It's possible Korea could be a diversion for the true attack there."

"I know," Truman murmured, his gray eyes thoughtful behind their rimless glasses. "Better get out an alert to be on the watch for any buildups or changes in attitude."

Acheson nodded, fingering his mustache and reaching up to take a message from an orderly. "It's from Duggan," he said, putting on his spectacles. His voice turned grave as he read: "'South Korean units unable to resist determined Northern offensive. Contributory factor exclusive enemy possession of tanks and fighter planes. South Korean casualties as an index to fighting have not shown adequate resistance capabilities or the will to fight, and our estimate is that a complete collapse is imminent.'"

"No doubt about it now!" Truman exclaimed, hitting the tabletop with the palm of his hand. "We've got to help South Korea. If the communists win there, they'll be pointing a dagger at our Japan-Formosa-Philippines defense triangle." He adjusted his bow tie, staring at Secretary of Defense Louis Johnson, who sat next to Acheson, and the four uniformed military chiefs sitting next to him. "I don't want to commit ground forces," he mused aloud. "At least not until we find out what Russia intends to do." He glanced at General Hoyt Vanderveer, Air Force chief of staff, and Admiral Forrest Sherry, chief of naval operations. "Do you think we can do it with just air and navy?"

Both officers nodded in agreement.

"Then I'm ordering Duggan to use all available American air and sea power to attack North Koreans south of the 38th Parallel." He turned to General J. Lawton Connors, Army chief of staff. "Do you think we can contain them that way, Joe?"

Connors shook his head. "I'm afraid not. I don't think Duggan thinks so either. I understand your reluctance, sir. Sending in soldiers could bring in Russia and start a third world war. But I honestly think you're going to need ground forces in the end."

Truman sighed. "Well, let's try it for now." He shifted back to Acheson. "Is the Security Council convening?"

"Tomorrow, sir. We're hoping they'll put the UN into the war."

Next day—the day Seoul fell to the Reds—the United

Nations did pass a resolution momentous in world history, by which it recommended "that the Members of the United Nations furnish such assistance to the Republic of Korea as may be necessary to repel the armed attack and to restore international peace and security in the area."

A week later the Council authorized a unified command for Korea—a total of sixteen nations, eventually—and asked the United States to appoint a commander. By then, President Truman, deciding that Russia did not plan to enter the war, ordered American ground forces into action. By then, too, he appointed a Supreme Commander of the United Nations Command.

General Mark Duggan.

The day before Mark Duggan became the first soldier to command a United Nations army, he flew to Korea to reconnoiter the battlefield. He drove north toward Seoul, accompanied by Jim Duff and Beau Ames, with Sergeant Durkin at the wheel, cautiously crawling through the backwash of defeat that flowed south around them.

Soldiers without rifles or helmets stumbled by. Their round, flat, tan faces were scratched and dirty, and their sunken dark eyes beneath heads of thick, straight black hair were stunned and vacant. They stared uncomprehendingly at the American general in the punctured campaign hat who rode grim-faced through their midst. Women with tiny babies in their arms straggled along . . . Korean *yang-bans*, or gentlemen, patriarchal in their white robes and tall black stovepipe hats, swayed past, bent beneath the weight of loaded A-frames . . . younger men bearing great bundles of possessions on their backs, even, sometimes, with their aging and infirm mothers and fathers strapped there . . . others pushing little two-wheeled carts laden with household goods and small children, or prodding overloaded oxen . . . Sometimes an ox would pitch forward to the ground, its four legs sprawling, and the river of misery would part and flow around it. No one spoke or wept or cried out. Not even the babies or the children wailed. All that the Americans could hear was the panting of breath counterpointing the steady murmur of soldier's boots and the whispering of sandals.

Durkin stopped the staff car beneath a hill south of the Han

River. They climbed the rise and Duggan studied the Han and the city of Seoul on the farther bank. They could hear the hammering of pneumatic drills and the ring of steel on steel. Duggan swung his glasses toward the Han River bridges. They had been blown—all four of them—by the retreating South Koreans; blown while crowded with thousands of fleeing soldiers and civilians, almost all of whom had been toppled to their deaths.

"They're repairing the bridges," Duggan said. "Looks like they're getting ready to cross the Han. They probably want to end the war as fast as they can. If they can destroy the South Korean army and make all Korea communist, it may be too late to intervene."

"How is that, sir?" Beau Ames asked, craning his head to watch enemy aircraft circling over Kimpo Airfield.

"For one thing, they'll hold all the ports. From a military standpoint, landing over hostile open beaches or assaulting defended ports would be immensely more difficult. Politically, it would be even riskier. Attacking a communist-unified Korea could be damaging to our prestige. And I doubt if the UN could get many members to try to put South Korea on her feet again." He stared grimly toward the bridges. "I can't let it happen. I've got to hold the southern tip of the peninsula. I've *got* to keep the port of Pusan open."

The roar of rising aircraft led Duggan to turn to his left to study the area around Kimpo Airfield. Then he examined the roads running west from Seoul to the port city of Inchon.

"Inchon . . . Seoul . . . Kimpo . . ." Duggan murmured aloud. "What a counterstroke! Nothing like it in history . . . ever . . ." Putting his binoculars back in the leather case dangling from his neck, General Duggan strode confidently down the hill. He rode back to the airport in silence, speaking only when he entered his plane and sat down next to General Duff.

"Well, Jim," he said, smiling, "I think I've got them licked."

General Duff was puzzled by his chief's remark. He was aware, of course, of Mark Duggan's buoyant optimism. Few of the great captains in history could match his self-confidence. But Duff, as Duggan's chief of staff, was also aware of the facts. Since the end of World War II, American military strength had dwindled to about seven percent of its peak. General Duggan had only four understrength divisions in Japan, about fifty thousand men. They were mostly untrained garrison troops, the younger brothers and nephews of the Americans who had defeated Japan. They were eating the fruits of someone else's victory, drinking the heady wine of the conqueror, growing fat and soft. They had cars and mistresses and they called their officers by their first names.

General Duff knew this, as he also knew that the North Korea Army numbered 135,000 men, hardy peasant youths who had been well-trained by the Russians, who had put excellent weapons in their hands, teaching them to drive the big, terrifying Tiger tanks or fly MIG fighter planes. The South Koreans, called "ROK's" for the Republic of Korea, were 143,000 strong. But of these, only about 65,000 were combat troops, none of them as well-armed or trained as their brothers from the north. Why, then, Duff thought, is the Old Man so confident?

General Duggan actually did believe he could halt the North Korean juggernaut with his comparative handful of men. When he sent in the first American ground troops—a pickup force of only 406 officers and men—he described it to the press as "my arrogant display of strength."

The North Koreans brushed it aside and continued to rush south toward Pusan. "Young soldiers!" their commanders exhorted them, "the war must by won by August fifteenth, the fifth anniversary of our liberation."

Again Duggan sent in more troops, ordering them to delay the enemy so that he could build up a counteroffensive force in Pusan. These, too, were overcome. The Americans were unable to halt the dreaded Tiger tanks. Duggan's commanders in Korea pleaded desperately for tanks of their own . . . for antitank shells . . . for reinforcements . . . Ominous reports of enemy military prowess and of an imminent enemy breakthrough to Pusan crossed the supreme commander's desk. Shaken, Duggan radioed Washington.

> The situation in Korea is critical . . . The enemy's armored equipment is of the best, and the service thereof, as reported by qualified veteran observers, as good as any seen at any time in the last war. They

further state that the enemy's infantry is of thoroughly first-class quality.

This force more and more assumes the aspect of a combination of Soviet leadership and technical guidance with Chinese Communist ground elements. While it serves under the flag of North Korea, it can no longer be considered as an indigenous N.K. military effort.

I strongly urge that in addition to those forces already requisitioned, an army of at least four divisions, with all its component services, be dispatched to this area without delay and by every means of transportation available.

The situation has developed into a major operation.

President Truman and his military chiefs were shocked. Duggan had assured them he could halt the North Koreans with a two-division counteroffensive. They had believed him. American military self-esteem had grown so great since World War II that some of the more asinine blimps in the Pentagon were saying: "Once the Reds realize who they're up against—they'll change their minds."

"My God!" Truman exclaimed to Defense Secretary Johnson. "He told us he could do it with two, now he's proposing to use his entire four—and wants four more divisions from us!"

"Mr. President," Johnson answered in a grave voice. "If we give them to him, we won't have enough force left to defend the continental United States—let alone Western Europe."

The President stared at Johnson in disbelief. "Democracy," he murmured softly. "I believe in it . . . it's what it's all about . . . but I'm beginning to become convinced that you can't fight a police action or a limited war in a democracy. The people don't understand. They don't *want* to understand. They believe in that goddam minuteman," he swore, his voice turning harsh. "They myth of the citizen-soldier springing to arms. They hate standing armies. So when the last war was over, they beat their swords into cocktail shakers. They dismantled the greatest fighting force ever put together. And Russia didn't . . . And neither did China . . . Oh, I know," he muttered, his voice full of self-contempt, "I didn't try to stop them. How *could* I? It would have been political suicide, and it wouldn't have changed a thing." A gleam of hope came into Truman's eyes. "What about the United Nations forces?" he asked Johnson.

"They'll come, sir. But not in time to save Pusan. They'll never be much more than token anyway."

"They're going to hold our coats," Truman snapped. "Just like what Stalin's going to do for China and North Korea. Well, Mr. Secretary," he said, lifting his square jaw, "give Duggan what he wants."

Duggan was jubilant when he was informed that a Marine brigade had already taken ship for Pusan, and that an Army division would shortly follow. He was delighted when Chiang Kai-shek on Formosa offered 33,000 troops for use in Korea, but dismayed when President Truman declined the proposal.

"We would have to arm and equip them the same as we are now doing with the South Koreans," the President told Duggan. "To transfer them to Korea would weaken Formosa's defenses, and to use them would needlessly offend Red China."

Publicly, General Duggan agreed with his chief. Privately, he did not. "More State Department chop-suey," he snorted to General Duff. "How that striped-pants crew loves a Chinaman! Don't offend Red China," he repeated sarcastically. "Sounds like the old days under FDR and Genry Gawkins: don't upset the Russians. Now it's Red China we have to handle with kid gloves." He paused, sunk in thought, remembering the day in Honolulu when he had upstaged President Roosevelt. Why not the little man in the bow tie?

"Jim," he said, "didn't you tell me the Veterans of Foreign Wars were asking for a message for their national convention?" Duff nodded, and Duggan strode back into his own office. He came out a half hour later with a page of handwritten copy. "Send them this," he said.

Duff nodded, beginning to read: " 'Nothing could be more fallacious than the threadbare argument by those who advocate appeasement and defeatism in the Pacific than that if we defend Formosa we alienate continental Asia. Those who speak thus do not understand the Orient. They do not grasp that it is in the pattern of Oriental psychology to respect and follow aggressive, resolute, and dynamic leadership—to quickly turn from leadership characterized by timidity or vacillation. . . ' ''

President Truman was infuriated when he was informed of the message by the White House press room. It was not to be read to the veterans for two more days, but one magazine containing the full text was already in the mails. Harry Truman needed more than one prepandial bourbon to help him digest those bad marks in "Oriental psychology." At first he thought of firing Duggan, or at least of removing him as military commander in Korea and replacing him with General Gomer Brawley, Chairman of the Joint Chiefs. But, no, Truman thought, why make a martyr of a man whose renascent popularity was rivaled only by his ambition to be President? Besides, the Defense Department was undergoing a shakeup. Louis Johnson was on his way out as Secretary, and until Truman could persuade George Quincy Meadows to come out of retirement to take the job, he couldn't spare Brawley. Instead, the President sent Duggan a sharp note ordering him to withdraw the statement. Duggan obeyed. Obeyed with a smile . . . He had publicly challenged the policy of his chief and gotten away with it.

"Let's get back to the war," he said to Beau Ames. "I want you to go over to Korea as my personal representative. Report to Johnny Wallace in Taegu and tell him I'm sending him the rest of the Eighth Army, plus whatever comes out here from now on. And I want the Pusan Perimeter held!"

The Pusan Perimeter on the lower tip of the Korean peninsula was a rectangle roughly eighty miles long and sixty miles wide. Its front and left flank were guarded by rivers, its right and rear by the sea. Within it were two vital cities: the port of Pusan itself, to which a steady stream of men and arms had begun to flow, and Taegu, sixty miles to the north, where President Syngman Rhee had located his fugitive government, and where General Wallace had his headquarters.

When Beau Ames arrived in Taegu, he saw immediately that the enemy's strategy was either to seize the city itself, thus effectively destroying Rhee's government and the nerve center of its defense, or to cut the Taegu-Pusan road, thus cutting off Rhee and Wallace from the port.

To do this, a dozen North Korean divisions had been hammering at Wallace's defenses. Throughout August they took all the roads south, putting special pressure on the Taegu-Pusan road. To stop them General Wallace fought a "bucket-brigade" war. He was like a fire chief, rushing his forces to the points where the flames of battle leaped highest, allowing the smaller ones to flicker or die out. Beau Ames approved of what he saw, praising Wallace's conduct in his daily reports to General Duggan. Beau was also delighted to see the gradual buildup of United Nations strength inside the perimeter. A veteran Marine brigade had arrived, and scores of the big Pershing tanks that were more than a match for the Russian Tigers. Naval strength had also increased. Carrier aircraft gave invaluable support to the ground troops, implementing Wallace's land-based air, and gunfire ships bombarded the seaward flanks to disrupt enemy troop movements there.

Gradually the United Nations' strength overtook and passed the enemy's. By the end of August there were 180,000 men under Wallace's command, including 1500 men of a newly-arrived British brigade, and 91,500 ROK's. The rest were Americans. Against this force, the North Koreans hurled 98,000 troops in a final effort to push the UN into the sea. Wild fighting erupted on both banks of the Naktong River as it flowed west around Taegu, and then turned south to the Straits of Korea. It was a chaotic, shifting struggle. For days on end Beau Ames went everywhere with General Wallace, sleeping when and where he could, catnapping or dozing erect, living, as he said, "on coffee, fingernails, and cigarettes." Here the enemy would cross a river, there they would be hurled back. Here a UN force sat in peaceful quiet, like an island serene in an ocean of conflict; and there a unit would be struck repeatedly, assaulted by wave after wave of North Korean soldiers.

Gradually the enemy wore himself out. Nevertheless, the North Koreans hung on, commanded to gain the victory if it meant fighting to the last man. As they hung on, behind them General Mark Duggan struck one of the master counterstrokes of history.

CHAPTER 31

When Mark Duggan stood on the hilltop overlooking Seoul while the human debris of defeat flowed around him, he conceived the single stroke that would destroy the Red Army. It was this that had inspired the remark—"I think I've got them licked!"—that General Duff had found so mystifying.

At that moment, Duggan decided on the delaying action that would slow the enemy's rush down the peninsula, and then hold him in place for the blow deep in his rear that would crush him. At first, however, the very speed of the North Korean attack upset Duggan's plan. Not until it was slowed, and Duggan became confident that the Pusan Perimeter would hold, did he divulge his intention to Duff.

"*Inchon!*" Duff exclaimed, incredulous. "My God, sir, Inchon must be two hundred miles north of Pusan."

Duggan smiled, delighted at the effect his proposal had made. "It is indeed, Jim. And that's why I've chosen it. Inchon is the port city for Seoul, and Kimpo Airfield—the best airfield in Korea—is its airport. Everything the Red Army shoots, all its replenishment and reinforcement, comes through that triangle: Inchon-Seoul-Kimpo. History will show you, Jim, that when an army was destroyed, nine times out of ten it was because its supply line was cut. When I land at Inchon and take Seoul and Kimpo, the enemy will turn and try to get out of the trap. When he does, Johnny Wallace will break out of Pusan and pursue him. And our forces holding Inchon-Seoul-Kimpo will be the anvil upon which he will break them in pieces.'' Duggan smiled again and filled his corncob. ''It will reverse the war like a change in the wind. It will be the greatest single stroke in history, Jim—and I shall crush them!''

General Duff returned to his office buoyant, infected, as always, by his chief's irrepressible optimism. He immediately called a meeting of his staff to plan the Inchon operation. Duggan, meanwhile, cabled Washington requesting immediate dispatch of a Marine division. He was refused. General Brawley was a well-known opponent of amphibious warfare in general and the Marines in particular. He had already informed Congress that he doubted if large-scale landings from the sea would ever again be needed, and he had been among the leaders in the unsuccessful campaign to dismantle the Marine Corps.

Infuriated, but undismayed, Duggan cabled again:

> I strongly request reconsideration of my need for a Marine division. Its availability is absolutely essential to achieve a decisive stroke. If not made available, a much longer and more expensive effort, both in blood and money, will result. I must have the Marine division by September 10. I cannot too strongly emphasize the complete urgency of my request.

His appeal was successful. President Truman authorized the call-up of the Marine Reserve. An Army division was also selected for the operation, to come in behind the Marines and wheel south to assume the blocking position that would be the ''anvil'' on which General Wallace would wield his ''hammer.'' Nevertheless, General Brawley was still dubious, as were many of Duggan's own commanders, the world's foremost exponents of the art of amphibious warfare, the leaders who had served Duggan so well in the Pacific war. They were present at a meeting in Duggan's office, which the supreme commander called after he was informed that the Joint Chiefs themselves were flying to Tokyo in hopes of dissuading him from his plan.

''Gentlemen,'' Duggan said with a smile, seated behind his desk with General Connors and Admiral Sherry to either side, facing a semicircle of lesser generals and admirals, ''I am aware that everyone in this room but me has doubts or reservations about Inchon. Now, let's hear them." He pointed courteously to his amphibious commander, Admiral James Boyle, to be the first speaker.

"Sir," Boyle said, getting to his feet, "we have made up a list of every conceivable obstacle—natural and geographical— and Inchon has them all." He paused for effect, watching Duggan. The supreme commander began filling his corncob, saying nothing. "Inchon has every 'don't' in the amphibious textbook, sir. Chief of these are the tides. They're enormous— the second highest in the world—with an average twenty-nine foot rise and fall of the sea. Some days it's as high as thirty-six feet. The tide moves so fast, a ship can be stranded on the mud flats in ten minutes." Duggan nodded, puffing meditatively. "Next is the mud itself. The mudbanks run out from shore as far as six thousand yards. To clear them, the landing ships can only approach the shore on days when the tide rises at least twenty-nine feet. There's only two or three days a month when this can happen in daylight, sir. So the moon will dictate your D-Day. You may choose from September fifteenth, October fifteenth, or November fifteenth."

"September fifteenth," Duggan grunted.

Boyle said, "I figured that."

A chuckle ran around the room and Duggan removed his pipe and grinned.

"Also, sir, we don't know how much dredging has been done in the harbor. The facilities are limited. The pier and dock space is small. Inchon would never make a real logistics base. And there's only a four-mile stretch available for landing points—all of these are over piers or seawalls. Finally, the channel and maneuver space are too narrow for bombardment ships. They'll have to stay in the channel, even anchor there to hold against a five-knot current. It's like sailing a ship on a dead-end street, sir. There just isn't enough turnaround room. Our bombardment ships will be sitting ducks."

Perspiring slightly, the admiral sat down.

Duggan thanked him courteously and pointed to the commander of the Marine division, General Lionel Jones. Jones stood erect. He was a slender, silvery-haired man. "General Duggan," he said in a soft voice, "I don't like it because my men will have to land almost in the heart of a city and over a seawall that can be easily defended. Because of the tides, we can't go in until dusk. We'll have only a little more than an hour of daylight to fight our way into a strange Oriental city of a quarter-million people. In that short space of time we'll have to go up against warehouses and other buildings that can be easily fortified. Then we'll have to reorganize to fight off the enemy counterattack. It's not much time, sir—and we know next to nothing of what to expect when we land. We know more about the surface of the moon, sir, then we do about the defenses of Inchon.''

Duggan nodded, turning to General Connors on his right. "The Army chief of staff also objects, gentlemen. Will you tell me why, Joe?''

Connors compressed his lips grimly, speaking from his chair. "It's too far, General. The turning movement is much too deep to have the effect you envision. From what I've just heard, it's much riskier than I thought. I would recommend that you land instead at Kunsan, a hundred miles south of Inchon. Kunsan is a better port with far fewer natural obstacles.''

"Thank you, Joe. Admiral Sherry?''

The chief of naval operations also spoke seated. "I can only second General Connors," he said in a grave voice. "Also, what about the Communist Chinese? They've been moving troops north. They've got four armies around Tsingtao due west of Inchon across the Yellow Sea. They must know that if we succeed at Inchon, it means ruin for their fellow Reds down at Pusan. Will they sit by and let this happen? Or will they try to hit us when we're jammed up inside a narrow harbor?''

"I don't think they'll come in, Admiral," Duggan said quietly. "These North Koreans are Stalin's puppets, not Mao's." He fell silent. A hush came upon the room. Duggan deliberately allowed the tension to build. He removed his corncob. "Gentlemen," he said softly, "you have convinced me." All eyes registered surprise, and Duggan smiled gently. "You have convinced me more than ever that Inchon is the place. You have laid before me every conceivable obstacle—military, natural, and geographical—and you have not discouraged, but encouraged me." Jabbing with his pipe, his voice rising dramatically, he continued. "The enemy must also feel that Inchon is impossible. He must also feel safe.

And, gentlemen, if military history teaches anything, it is that he who relies upon a sense of security is already undone.

"Century after century, gentlemen," he said, his voice throbbing, "bears testimony to the crossing of impassable waters, the scaling of inaccessible cliffs, the march through impenetrable swamps or the breaching of unbreachable walls by guile or deception. Remember: Troy was deceived and undone by the wooden horse, Jericho was betrayed to Joshua by the harlot Rahab, Hannibal crossed the Alps, the walls of Jerusalem crumbled under the catapults of Titus, Quebec was surprised by Wolfe, Vicksburg succumbed to blockade and starvation—and in our own time the impregnable Maginot Line was turned when Hitler penetrated the impenetrable Ardennes, the fortress city of Singapore was taken from the rear, and Japan's island empire fell to my own strategy of island-hopping."

He paused, filling his corncob and lighting it. "Let us return to Wolfe and Montcalm at Quebec. Montcalm also felt safe. His defenses were secure. His cliffs were unscalable. But Wolfe found the chink in his armor—the narrow path leading up to the Plains of Abraham—and he seized it and won a half a continent for England. No, gentlemen, I am not discouraged. What you have just said convinces me that the enemy commander will reason that no one would be so brash as to make such an attempt." He put the corncob aside again, turning to Connors. "Kunsan is truly safer, General, but it is not deep enough. It will just make the North Koreans back up a few miles, and it will not cut off their supply line. Inchon will—and it will save a hundred thousand lives. I realize that it is a great gamble—perhaps five thousand to one—but I am used to those odds."

His voice sank to a harsh whisper. "I shall land at Inchon, and I shall crush them!"

A typhoon howled over the Sea of Japan. Heavy rains and 125-mile-an-hour winds lashed the surface of the sea, piling up great waves, threatening to destroy Joint Task Force Seven then setting out from Sasebo, Japan, for the Korea Strait. At midnight an anxious General Mark Duggan boarded his flagship, the *Mount McKinley*. He was swathed in a rubber poncho, bending against the wind and ducking his head to avoid the stinging raindrops, clutching his campaign hat firmly on his head with one hand and clinging to the gangplank rail with the other. Once aboard, he went immediately to his cabin and called for the weather reports.

They were encouraging. Typhoon Kezia had veered north. Nevertheless, a violent backlash struck at the task force ships, putting to sea one by one. The sea was wild and turbulent.

Duggan felt faintly nauseous. He lay down. His head swam. He began to worry about Wolmi-do. This was a little island in Inchon Harbor, directly west of the city to which it was connected by a causeway. Duggan's intelligence had discovered that is was heavily defended. Seizure of Wolmi-do—or "Moontip Island"—was essential to the success of the entire operation. Rising 352 feet above the water, it was the highest point of land in the port area. Its guns could scourge the Marines going over the seawalls to either side of it. It had to be taken—and well before the main assault landings.

With reluctance, Duggan had ordered three days of preinvasion aerial bombardment of Wolmi-do, thereby risking the loss of element of surprise he valued so much. Nevertheless, to deceive and distract the enemy, he also called for Kunsan to the south to be placed under fierce aerial attack, to be followed by an ROK landing raid one day before the Inchon assault. To the north a British task force was hammering at Chinnampo, while to the east a big American bombardment fleet, including the mighty *Missouri,* was prowling the Sea of Japan, preparing to strike at Samchok, directly west of Inchon, and make a diversionary landing there.

Everything that could be done has been done, General Duggan thought, feeling his nausea rise as the ship's rise and fall increased in violence. Supposing the enemy held firm down at Pusan . . . Would Wallace be able to break out? Would Inchon prove a fiasco then? Stop worrying, he told himself, remembering his father's frequently repeated admonition: "Mark, never take counsel from your fears. If you do, you will go down to defeat."

Duggan could hear the wind whistling outside his cabin. He staggered to his feet to go into his private head and throw up. Stumbling back to his bunk, he threw himself on it, actually thankful that he was seasick. He was too miserable to worry anymore, and in a few minutes he fell asleep.

There was consternation in the North Korean Military Command at Inchon. Consternation and disbelief. *Inchon*, not Kunsan or Chinnampo or Samchok was being attacked; Inchon the inaccessible.

"Ten enemy vessels are approaching Inchon," the military commander radioed the communist capital at Pyongyang. "Many aircraft are bombing Wolmi-do. There is every indication the enemy will perform a landing . . ."

The ten ships creeping cautiously up Flying Fish Channel were the gunfire group of Task Force Seven: the American cruisers *Toledo* and *Rochester*, the British cruisers *Kenya* and *Jamaica*, plus the American destroyers *Gurke*, *Henderson*, *Collett*, *Swenson*, *DeHaven*, and *Mansfield*. The destroyers were deliberately being used as "sitting duck" decoys. They were anchoring in the channel in broad daylight, hoping to draw the fire of Wolmi-do's uncharted guns. Because of this, the oldest destroyers in the Far East—but also the best gunners—had been chosen. The cruisers, meanwhile, would cover the destroyers from five to seven miles below them. They were too big to be risked in the narrow channel. If one of them were sunk there, the invasion force might not be able to get into the harbor.

Low tide had been chosen, to detect mine fields and to obtain maximum depression of the guns. In came the ships, steaming warily in tandem. At once, the leading *Mansfield*'s lookouts spotted a string of mines half submerged in low, muddy water. *Gurke*'s forty-millimeters chattered and the mines exploded in geysers of smoke and water. *Henderson* dropped off to destroy three more mine fields. Now the shores of the harbor islands had become thronged with white-robed Koreans, come to watch the battle. Now the tide was rushing in, covering the mines . . . The destroyers floated higher . . . *DeHaven*'s gunnery officer saw enemy soldiers running into a gunpit. The bombardment was to begin at two o'clock—in five more minutes—but the officer could actually see them through the bore of his guns. He had them bore-sighted . . . He pressed the firing key and *DeHaven*'s five-inchers belched orange flame and smoke. The Wolmi-do battery erupted in flame, smoke, debris and flying bodies—and the battle had begun.

For ten minutes the North Korean guns remained silent. But then they returned the American fire. Each time they did, they marked themselves for their own destruction. An hour later it was all over. Wolmi-do lay obscured beneath a quivering pink cloud of smoke and dusk. Many enemy guns had been silenced at a cost of three ships damaged, one man killed and eight wounded. Next day the gunfire group was back, battering Wolmi-do for an hour and a quarter. After they upped anchor and made for the harbor mouth, American aircraft struck at the island. At dusk the American invasion armada came creeping up Flying Fish Channel.

Half an hour after midnight the ships bearing the Marine battalion that was to assault Wolmi-do reached Inchon Harbor. Two hours later they sailed inside its mouth, following the long, ghostly column of gunfire ships. The Marines were amazed to see a lighthouse illuminated on little Palmi-do. They were unaware that a gallant naval officer had lighted the beacon and now sat atop the lighthouse, wrapped in a blanket and shivering.

Just before six in the morning the gunfire ships resumed their cannonade. Wolmi-do was again aflame. Rocket ships ran inshore to release hissing flights of rockets—a total of six thousand. Carrier-based Corsairs howled down from the sky to strafe Wolmi's beaches. Korean civilians again crowded the shores of the harbor islands, or scampered out onto the mud flats to watch the attack. Now the Marine landing boats stopped circling and fanned out into battle line. They went in with a concerted roar of motors, and at 0631—just a minute behind schedule—their ramps banged down on the beach at Wolmi-do.

Mark Duggan awoke at dawn, feeling calm and confident. His sickness was gone. He dressed quickly, hoping to eat breakfast before the bombardment began. In the wardroom, he waved a genial hand to the Navy and Marine officers who arose with a scraping of chairs. He went directly to the captain's seat at the head table. Admiral Boyle, seated next to him, hid a smile behind his hand. The captain of the *Mount*

McKinley, who had come into the room only a step behind Duggan, glanced down at him in dismay and consternation.

"Ex-cuse me, General," he stammered, "but in sailing tradition, the c-captain's chair is for him alone."

Duggan smiled up at him indulgently. "I understand perfectly, Captain," he murmured. "But someday you will be able to tell your grandchildren that on the day of his greatest victory, General Duggan stole your seat."

There was a chuckle in the room. Still confused, the captain took a seat next to Boyle.

"Good Lord!" Duggan exclaimed, staring at his plate. "What's this?"

"Steak and eggs, sir," General Jones on his right explained. "It's a Marine tradition we picked up in New Zealand and Australia. Whenever U.S. Marines make a landing now, they have steak and eggs for breakfast."

"I thought it was beans," Duggan said, beginning to eat.

"It was sir. And the surgeons wish it still was. They don't like sewing up guts full of steak."

Duggan chuckled, just as the bombardment opened. He arose, hurrying topside, where he sat in a deckchair with his binoculars focused on Wolmi-do. Beau Ames came to sit beside him. Both men were tense, watching the assault boats bounce shoreward. They could hear the sound of small-arms fire. Ten minutes later they saw a barge put nine tanks ashore: three of them armed with flamethrowers, three with bulldozer blades, and the others with cannon. They rolled inland into the obscuring smoke.

Beau clutched the general by the arm. "Look! Look, General—on top of that hill! It's the flag! The American flag!"

Duggan swung his glasses in delight. He could make out the Stars and Stripes fluttering from a stick nailed to a shattered tree.

"I've done it!" he cried in exultation. "I've won the war!"

Still jubilant, with Beau following, he went below to write the message: "The Navy and the Marines have never shone more brightly than this morning." Then he turned to his son-in-law. "Come on, Beau—let's go finish breakfast."

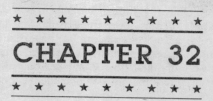

* * * * * * * * * * *

CHAPTER 32

* * * * * * * * * * *

Although the war against North Korea was not literally "won" the moment the flag was unfurled above Wolmi-do, the successful landing an Inchon that followed marked, at the very least, the beginning of the end for the Red Army to the south.

Within a week after the Marines seized Kimpo Airfield and began driving on Seoul, enemy assaults on the Pusan Perimeter ceased. A few days later the North Koreans began retreating—and Wallace sent his Eighth Army after them in pursuit. Quickly, the retreat became a rout. By the end of September the communist army south of the 38th Parallel was completely shattered. All order had disappeared. Some of its thirteen divisions had simply vanished. Fleeing North Korean soldiers, in small groups or in twos or threes, trudged furtively north—making for their homeland and moving mostly at night. There was no other way: All the escape routes were in United Nations hands, the sea was hostile, and from the sky American aircraft spat death at them.

Two weeks after the invasion, Mark Duggan flew into Kimpo Airfield and drove into wrecked and fire-blackened Seoul to restore the South Korean capital to President Syngman Rhee. Broken glass fell tinkling from the shattered skylight above Duggan as he stood in the legislative chamber with

Rhee beside him and spoke to a throng of United Nations commanders and ROK officials.

"By the grace of a merciful Providence, our forces fighting under the standard of that greatest hope and inspiration of mankind, the United Nations, have liberated this ancient capital of Korea. It has been freed from the despotism of communist rule, its citizens once more have the opportunity for that immutable concept of life which holds invincibly to the primacy of individual liberty and personal dignity." His voice quivering with emotion, he concluded: "I now ask you to recite with me the Lord's Prayer."

Slowly, faltering at first, but gathering strength and unison, the assembly intoned the prayer. Duggan then turned to Rhee, who seized his hand.

"We admire you," Rhee said, tears falling from his eyes and trickling down his ancient, wrinkled face. "We love you as the savior of our race."

After the ceremony, Duggan returned to Tokyo—and the adulation of the free world. It surpassed even the praise and plaudits that succeeded his escape from the Philippines. President Truman cabled: "Few operations in military history can match either the delaying action where you traded space for time in which to build up your forces, or the brilliant maneuver which has now resulted in the liberation of Seoul." Secretary of Defense George Quincy Meadows also sent his congratulations, and the Joint Chiefs of Staff reassured him of their unshaken confidence in him, also authorizing him to pursue the enemy into his own country to carry out "destruction of the North Korean Armed Forces."

With immense satisfaction Duggan began the pursuit into North Korea. He was jubilant. "Now it's our turn to unify Korea by force of arms," he said to Jim Duff. "It's been my greatest pleasure to provide free elections in Japan, and now, by God, Jim, I'm going to do the same thing in all Korea."

At dinner that night he was gay and relaxed. "Maybe we'll be getting that house on the Hudson sooner than you think," he said to Betsy, laughing. "We'll have a second honeymoon."

Betsy made a wry face. "Remember what happened to the first Hudson honeymoon."

The following morning, Beau Ames brought the newspaper

into his office. "China says she won't let us get away with it," he said, his voice grave.

Duggan took the paper, putting on his spectacles to read the warning issued by Chinese foreign minister Chou En-lai. "Nonsense, Beau," he scoffed, looking up. "If they'd have intervened at Inchon, they might have been able to cause trouble. But now it's too late." He smiled brightly. "I promise you, Beau—you and Jinny and the kids will eat your Christmas dinner in the States."

Throughout October the speed of the United Nations advance into North Korea seemed to justify Duggan's optimism. The ROK's were the first over the boarder, jubilant and exultant driving for the Yalu River, the boundary between North Korea and Red China.

"We will wash our swords in the waters of the Yalu," the ROK officers cried, and President Rhee declared: "I am going all the way to the Yalu, and even the United Nations can't stop me."

Within a week the UN General Assembly authorized Duggan to cross. He did, and soon the Americans and their allies were racing for the Yalu.

Red China, meanwhile, continued to issue warnings. "Chou En-lai was at it again, this morning," Ames told his father-in-law the day after American troops crossed the border. "He said you built a fascist state in Japan and are trying to do the same in Korea."

Duggan nodded, preceding him into the office. "Tune in the Hong Kong radio, Beau," he said. "I hear they've got a transcript of a huge Hate-America rally in Peiping last week."

Beau twirled the dials of a high-powered receiver.

"*. . . is the paradise of gangsters, swindlers, rascals, special agents, fascist germs, speculators, debauchers, and all the dregs of mankind,*" a voice was screaming, pausing for thunderous applause.

Duggan smiled wanly. "That'll be it," he said dryly.

"*The United States,*" the speaker continued, "*is the world's manufactory and source of such crimes as reaction, darkness, cruelty, decadence, corruption, debauchery, oppression of man by man, and cannibalism.*" A storm of yells and pounding feet burst from the receiver.

Beau Ames grinned. "He left out pederasty."

Duggan smiled sadly. "Why is the world so full of hatred?"

The speaker resumed: *"The United States is the exhibition ground of all the crimes which can possibly be committed by mankind—"*

Duggan switched off the radio, staring thoughtfully at his son-in-law. "What do you make of it, Beau?"

"Sounds to me like they're preparing their people for war," Beau said gloomily.

"Nonsense! It sounds to me like they're bluffing. The key resolution on Korea comes up in the General Assembly in a few days. I think Chou is trying to blackmail the UN." He paused reflectively. "I think I'll call their bluff," he said. "I'm going to broadcast an ultimatum to North Korea demanding their unconditional surrender."

Secretary of State Acheson stared ruefully across the desk at President Harry Truman. "I wish Duggan had never issued that ultimatum," he murmured. "Red China's up in arms, sir. The Indian ambassador just informed me that Chou got Pannikar out of bed for a midnight conf—"

"Pannikar?" Truman interrupted, his puzzled glance shifting to Secretary of Defense Meadows, seated beside Acheson.

"Yes, sir—the Indian ambassador to China. You must remember him."

"Oh, yes—he's hardly less a Commie than Mao, isn't he? What did Chou want?"

"He told Pannikar to tell us that if we didn't call off the invasion of North Korea, the Communist Chinese will enter the war."

Truman adjusted his rimless glasses, frowning. "What do you think, Dean?" he asked Acheson.

"Well, sir, Panikkar has played the communist game pretty regularly in the past. We can't really regard him as an impartial observer."

"That's what I think. They could be trying to blackmail the UN. The key vote on the Korean resolution is due tomorrow. It looks pretty much like a bluff to me."

"Very true, sir. But I don't think we can discount the possibility of Chinese intervention."

"Not at all," Truman grunted, swinging on Meadows. "George, I want you to tell Duggan to continue the action. If he meets Chinese units in Korea, continue the action—just as long as he thinks he can succeed. But in no case—repeat, no case—should he move into China without authorization from me." Meadows nodded with a heavy frown, making a note on the pad before him. Truman continued: "Tell him I want to confer with him personally." He studied his schedule and looked at a map of the Pacific. "On October fifteenth. Either at Honolulu or Wake. Tell him I want to get the benefit of his first-hand information and judgment."

Meadows nodded again. Both he and Acheson could guess the true motive of the President's visit. They both were aware that the Truman Administration had slipped in popularity, and that congressional elections were only a month off.

General Duggan was not quite as indulgent. "Well, well," he crowed to General Duff after receiving Meadows's message. "Must be election time, eh, Jim? The little piano player in the bow tie needs to bask in a little reflected glory. Just like FDR in 'forty-four." He paused with a reflective grin, remembering the borrowed red touring car. "Tell Secretary Meadows I'll meet him at Wake, Jim." He grinned again, and Duff glanced at him inquiringly. "Honolulu's about equidistant from Washington and Tokyo, Jim," Duggan explained. "But Wake's thirty hours from the White House and only eight from us." He winked. "Who's coming to whom?"

Harry Truman did not seem to resent having to travel four times as far as one of his generals. He was smiling, even in a holiday mood, when he alighted from the *Independence* at Wake, walking briskly toward General Duggan waiting on the ramp.

"I see you're still wearing your old campaign hat, General," he said with a friendly grin, extending his hand.

Duggan took it and smiled. "That's not a bad bonnet you've got on yourself, Mr. President," he said, pointing to the creamy-white five-gallon hat on Truman's head.

Immediately, photographer's bulbs began to flash and pop. Perhaps a half-dozen still photographers had accompanied the President, plus another half-dozen motion-picture cameramen from the newsreels and the television networks.

"Have yourself a party, fellows," Truman said, still grinning happily. Duggan said nothing, smiling a superior, indulgent smile.

After they had finished, the President and the general entered a rusty Chevrolet and drove to the office of the island's airline manager. They went inside alone.

"Well, General," Truman said, "things seem to be going very well in Korea. I heard on the airplane radio that the South Koreans are almost on the Yalu."

Duggan nodded. "Yes, sir. I believe that formal resistance will end throughout North Korea by Thanksgiving. I hope to be able to withdraw the Eighth Army to Japan by Christmas."

"Excellent!" Harry Truman said, rubbing his hands, thinking of the elections two weeks away. "Excellent!" His face sobered. "What about the Red Chinese, General? They're making an awful lot of noise. Do you think they'll intervene?"

"Absolutely not! Had they interfered in the first or second months, it would have been decisive. I no longer fear their intervention. I no longer stand hat in hand. The Chinese have 300,000 men in Manchuria. Of these, probably no more than a hundred to a hundred and twenty-five thousand are distributed along the Yalu. They have no air force. Now that we have bases for our air in Korea, Mr. President, if the Chinese tried to get down to Pyongyang, there would be the greatest slaughter."

Harry Truman rubbed his hands again. "I believe you're right, General." He put his hand in the pocket of his double-breasted blue suit. "I've got something for you, General," he said, grinning again and walking toward the door.

Duggan followed him, surprised to see the cameramen gathered outside again around a battery of microphones. Truman stepped toward them, motioning the general toward him.

"For the landing at Inchon," he intoned, "the greatest single counterstroke in military history, I hereby award General of the Army Mark Duggan his second Medal of Honor." Turning with a smile, he pinned the decoration on Duggan's breast. "I'd rather have this than be President," Truman said, while bulbs flashed and movie cameras whirred.

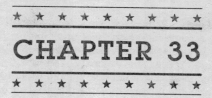

CHAPTER 33

General Chu Teh was brief. The commander-in-chief of the Communist Chinese forces had just come from a conference with Chairman Mao and Foreign Minister Chou, and he had immediately summoned his deputy, General Peng Teh-huai, to his office.

"It has been decided to enter the war in Korea," Chu said to Peng. "You will go immediately to Mukden and take charge of the operation."

General Peng flew at once to the capital city of Manchuria and drove from the airport to the headquarters of General Lin Paio, commander of the Fourth Field Army.

"Welcome, Comrade Peng," General Lin said, coming around his desk with a smile and offering his visitor his chair. "It is wonderful to see you again after all these years."

Peng sat down. His hard, brutal, peasant's face relaxed in an astonishingly friendly smile. "How long, Comrade Lin?" he asked, accepting a proffered cigarette and lighting it.

"Not since the Long March."

"Twenty years! It can't be!"

"It is, comrade. Remember when you saved me from drowning in the Great Grasslands. You gave me some wild vegetables to eat too. They kept me alive."

Peng's face hardened. "Those were the bad days," he

muttered. "No food, no shoes, no shelter. Rain, rain, rain—and swamps ... Water all around us and none fit to drink Remember, comrade, when we drank our own urine?"

"You did, comrade," Lin said with a shudder, "but I couldn't."

"That's right," Peng said, smiling again. "I forgot that you weren't a peasant like the rest of the army."

"But I was just as tough," Lin said proudly.

"Not at first. You were a visionary. You joined the party for intellectual reasons. You didn't hate the old order like we did."

Lin laughed, rising to pour tea from a silver service on a sideboard. "You're not going to tell me that story about kicking over your grandmother's opium pot again, are you?" he asked, handing a delicately enameled china cup to Peng.

Peng smiled ruefully, stirring his tea. "It's true—my family voted to kill me for it. My uncle's eloquence saved my life. Saved me for a coal mine at the age of nine." Peng sighed. "The young people today don't realize how it was in the old days. They grumble about not having enough freedom. They don't know that in the old days there wasn't *any* freedom and hardly any rice. At least we gave them rice." He glanced sharply at General Lin. "Did you know that Chu Teh's parents drowned the five children born before him because they couldn't feed them? They took pity on Chu and gave him away."

Lin nodded, leaning forward to set his empty cup on his desk. "How is our commander-in-chief?"

"He is well and sends you greetings. That is why I am here. It has been decided to enter the war in Korea. You will begin moving your forward elements over the Yalu at once." He paused, his cunning eyes glinting. "We will tell the world that they are not soldiers of our army. They are 'volunteers.' Eventually, you will move your entire field army across the Yalu. To deceive the enemy, you will classify your armies as 'units' and your divisions as 'battalions.' In this way, they will believe your strength to be a fraction of what it actually is. Also, all troop movement must be made at night. By day, the men will hide in railroad tunnels, village huts, caves, or mine shafts."

Peng arose and walked to a wall map of Manchuria and Korea. "You will stop the Yankee imperialists in two places. Here," he said, pointing to the east coast of North Korea, "in the area below Chosin Reservoir. And here," he continued, pointing to the west coast, "in the area of Chosan on the Yalu." His lips twisted. "You will probe for the South Koreans and strike them first."

Lin smiled. "They will run," he murmured.

"They are carrion," Peng muttered. "They are lower than the rice thrown to the dogs at a poor man's funeral." He sat down again. "When you have driven them back, you will withdraw yourself." Lin looked up in surprise. "Yes, withdraw," Peng continued. "This is only the First Phase Offensive. It is intended to warn the Americans and their United Nations lackeys." He smiled cruelly. "It is also intended to lure them deep to their own destruction if they do not heed the warning."

"Excellent, General Peng," Lin said. "And the supplies?"

"They are coming."

"I do not have enough to keep an army in the field for more than five days."

"You will get your supplies. The Soviet Union is providing them. We are providing the troops and the leadership, and Russia is sending the material. Including the new MIG fighters. It is a partnership."

"What about the North Koreans?"

"They are partners too." Peng's lips curved cruelly again. "Junior partners."

Lin grinned. "Horse and rabbit stew?"

"Exactly. One horse and one rabbit. They are the rabbit, and we, Comrade Lin," he said, getting to his feet, "are the horse."

General Duggan's optimistic forecast of an end to the war by Thanksgiving was shared by his entire command. Soldiers of the First Cavalry Division, advancing toward the Yalu on the left or western flank, boasted that they would parade down the plaza in Tokyo on that day, wearing their yellow trooper's scarves. Marines on the right or eastern flank vowed that they would "pitch a bitch" when they received holiday leave in Australia. The ROK's on both flanks, meanwhile, had actually reached the Yalu to make ritualistic washing of their swords in its waters.

North Korea seemed finished. Premier Kim Il-sung had fled into the forests, gathering remnants of his army around him for what his enemies confidently believed would be his last stand.

Bombardiers of the Far East Air Force's Bomber Command complained: "We have run out of targets." Only three bridges had been left standing in North Korea, and these were adjudged more useful to the UN than the enemy. Bomber Command's sorties fell from hundreds to dozens and then to none. Two bombardment groups began returning to the United States.

General Mark Duggan was himself so confident that he encouraged Betsy to write to a large realty house advertising Hudson River properties in the *New York Times*. He had the firm's catalog on his desk one morning in late October when General Beauregard Ames came in unannounced.

"Lightning hit the shithouse, sir—the Chinese are in."

Duggan glanced up irritably, as though annoyed at his son-in-law's coarse humor. Seeing the expression of gravity on his face, he let out his breath slowly.

"When?"

"Last night, sir. They hit the ROK's on both flanks and chewed them up. The reports suggest that they're still running."

"You're sure they're Chinese?"

"Positive. They're calling themselves 'the People's Volunteers,' but they're still Chinese soldiers. Whistles, bugles, padded cotton jackets, Russian rifles—and all."

"How is the situation?"

"Bad, but not critical. The right flank on the Sea of Japan isn't too bad. Everyone's backpedaling, but Tenth Corps has it under control. On the left, Wallace is fighting to save his right. The ROK's broke in a human flood and overflowed into some of the American units. Looks like they're trying to press him back into the Yellow Sea."

"What does Johnny say?"

"He thinks he can straighten out his line. But he'll have to pull back to Chongchon." Ames shook his head ruefully. "Now I understand all those forest fires in the north during a wet fall. They were moving their troops under cover of the smoke."

Duggan nodded mechanically. "Keep me informed," he said, pushing the real estate catalog aside.

That night, he ate his dinner off his desk, as he did for the next two nights, until he became satisfied that the Eighth

Army and Tenth Corps had successfully withdrawn from the Chinese trap.

Nevertheless, Duggan's offensive, begun with such ballooning optimism and confidence, had been hurled back. Red China was definitely in the war against the United Nations, and even though Duggan denounced her entry as "international lawlessness" in his special report to the United Nations, Foreign Minister Chou En-lai calmly admitted that "volunteer units formed by the Chinese people" had joined the North Koreans, coolly comparing China's decision to the aid given by France to the American Revolution.

Meanwhile, a strange lull came over the battlefield. The Chinese seemed to have melted away. Duggan was puzzled, until Duff provided him with reports that Red Chinese soldiers and supplies were pouring over the Yalu River bridges each night. At once, Duggan ordered the bridges destroyed by bombing. To his dismay, the Joint Chiefs informed President Truman of his intention, and Truman ordered the bridge bombing postponed until Duggan explained the need for it.

In anguish, Duggan replied: "I believe your instructions may well result in a calamity of major proportions for which I cannot accept responsibility."

Now it was the Joint Chiefs and the President who were shocked and amazed.

"A *calamity*?" Harry Truman repeated when General Brawley reported to him. "A calamity after he tells us three days ago that he's still optimistic?" Truman sighed and adjusted his glasses. "All right—tell him he can bomb the Korean side of the bridges only. And hands off on the hydroelectric plants," he added grimly. "I'm still going to limit this war."

General Duggan was pleased when he received permission to strike the southern end of the bridges—until he conferred with his air commander.

"It can't be done, sir," General Havemeyer said. "Washington must have *known* it cannot be done."

"Why?"

"They've built their antiaircraft defenses on their side—the safe side—of the river. They must have known that, too, sir—that they wouldn't be molested there. Our bombers can attack the Korean side of the Yalu bridges only along courses that the Chinese have got zeroed-in. So they'll have to bomb from eighteen thousand feet in winds up to one-hundred-twenty knots. Accuracy will be next to impossible. Even way up there, they'll have to watch out for MIG fighter planes. They take off from Antung across the border.'' Havemeyer smiled bitterly. ''In what you have so aptly called their 'privileged sanctuary,' sir—and they climb to about thirty thousand feet, before slashing down on our bombers. After they make their pass, they head for home and the privileged sanctuary again. And our own fighters aren't allowed to go after them.'' Havemeyer glanced appealingly at Duggan. ''It's—it's criminal, sir. Can't something be done about it?''

''I wish there were,'' Duggan said grimly. ''I've asked for the right of 'hot pursuit,' like policemen chasing bandits from one town to another. But it's been denied. 'Don't extend the war,' he said with bitter mimicry, 'don't bring the Russians in.' By God, Havemeyer, you have no idea of the restraints they've put on me. It's like fighting Joe Louis with one hand tied behind your back. They have the manpower, but we have the firepower—only we can't use our firepower. The piano player in the White House has decreed that we can't send our air into Manchuria to destroy their bases or cut their line of supply over these bridges. We can only strike them *after* they've arrived safely in the battle zone. From *China*, Havemeyer—from a land of almost a billion people! What do they care how many men they lose, as long as they can be assured that their line of supply—their matériel, which they value more than their soldiers—is safe. By God,'' he continued, grinding his teeth and making fists of his hands, ''sometimes I wish I could take the piano player by the bow tie and—'' Duggan cut himself short, realizing that he had said perhaps too much. ''All right, General,'' he said, ''see what you can do.''

There was, however, nothing that General Havemeyer could do, and the Yalu bridges remained standing. Meanwhile, the battlefield lull continued.

''I can't understand it, sir,'' Beauregard Ames said, frowning and running a hand worriedly through his thick graying hair. ''It has to be a trap.''

''Nonsense, Beau!'' Duggan cried cheerfully. ''I thought so, too, at first. But they've been inactive too long for just regrouping. I'm convinced they've made only a limited intervention. They've drawn a *cordon sanitaire* to protect Manchuria and the Yalu River power plants. That's what I've told Washington, and for once they agree with me. So do the French and British. They say the communists are fond of creating buffers.''

"I don't know, sir," Ames persisted, obviously unconvinced. "These intelligence reports bother me. Enemy units are identified only as 'units' and 'battalions.' No divisions, no corps, no armies. Some of the interpreters have reported that sometimes the prisoners get confused and do say 'division' or 'army.' ''

"What do you make of that?"

"That they're trying to deceive us as to their strength, sir. I think they're listing divisions as only battalions and so on. Jim Duff has enemy strength broken down to a hundred thousand: forty thousand North Koreans and sixty thousand so-called 'Chinese volunteers.' I think the Chinese strength is four or even five times that.''

"But there's been little aerial observation of enemy troop movement. Even the Yalu bridges are quiet.''

"That's because they've probably gotten all they need across the river by now. And North Korea is full of tunnels and empty mines, sir. Excellent daytime hideouts. I think they're moving by night. One of the prisoners said they never move by day unless they have to. If they do, and one of our planes appears overhead, they have to stand dead in their tracks until it leaves. Anyone who moves is shot.''

"Beau, I can understand your reservations," Duggan said gently. "If you really feel that strongly about it, then you had better put it in writing.''

Beau Ames flushed in miserable embarrassment. "You know I won't do that sir," he muttered, as though protesting his loyalty.

"I do indeed—and I'm sorry I said it. But don't worry, Beau—we're going to go after them again, and this time we're going to get them." He brought his fist down on his desk in slow savagery. "I won the first war against North Korea, and now, by God, I'm going to win the second one against Red China!''

Beau Ames nodded, trying to grin cheerfully, a though he were convinced. But he could not. For the first time, the Old Man's optimism had not infected him, had not assuaged his qualms and left him buoyant and full of radiant hope. Ames watched dubiously as the Eighth Army in the west and the Tenth Corps in the east again drove north, gaining as much as ten miles a day. Three days later, however, he was back in General Duggan's office, a sheaf of reports in his hand, his face ashen.

He could not bring himself to say, "It *was* a trap, sir." He could hardly bear the calm, expectant stare of the general's confident dark eyes.

"The Red Chinese attacked in strength last night, sir," he said in a hoarse whisper. "The Marines are caught in a trap, and Eighth Army is in full retreat."

General of the Army Mark Duggan sat at his desk in his headquarters in Dai Ichi Palace and read the letter from Representative Joe Martin, leader of the Republican minority in the House. Since the Red Chinese counterattack had driven the United Nations south of the 38th Parallel again, forcing the second evacuation of Seoul, Martin had become, with Senator Taft, the most bitter critic of the Truman administration on Capitol Hill. It was he who accused Truman of a "no-win policy," of being "soft on communism." Even after the United Nations Command had deflated Red China's military pride, hurling her armies out of Seoul and rolling them back north of the parallel with enormous losses, Martin had continued his attacks on the President.

"Why does he keep the Seventh Fleet in the Straits of Formosa?" he sneered. "Not to protect Chiang Kai-shek or limit the war as he says, but to protect Red China from an invasion by Chiang." Again: "The American people will not accept this shameful stalemate in Korea. They want victory! They want to win. Why talk of a cease-fire and a return to a divided Korea when we have the power to unify a free Korea? If we are not in Korea to win, then this administration should be indicted for the murder of thousands of American boys." And finally: "We must open a Second Front in Asia. We must support Generalissimo Chiang Kai-shek in an invasion of the Chinese mainland, and so relieve the pressure on our forces in Korea.''

It was this last theme, reiterated again and again, which so alarmed America's European allies in the United Nations, especially after Martin publicly declared: "I have good reason to believe that General Duggan favors such an operation." And now Martin had written to Duggan, asking him for comment on his speech, beseeching him to present the case for "Asia-first" as against "Europe-first."

Duggan reread the letter: "I would deem it a great help if I could have your views on this point, either on a confidential basis or otherwise."

Duggan put the letter down, reflecting. Should he reply, knowing full well that, "confidential or otherwise," if his "views" were controversial or critical of the President, they would inevitably reach the public ear? Should he recite his frustrations since the stalemate ensued in Korea? Should he place on the record the restraints placed upon him; how he had appealed again and again for the right of "hot pursuit," and been denied; how his protests against the enemy's "privileged sanctuary" had passed unheeded; how he had requested permission to bomb another enemy supply port, Racin, and been told it was too close to the Soviet Union; how his renewed requests to use Chiang's armies in Korea were also denied. He thought bitterly of how the Joint Chiefs, still thinking of European priorities, had panicked after the second retreat from Seoul, sending him instructions to prepare to evacuate his forces to Japan. And then, after he had angrily demanded "clarification" of Washington's military stance in Korea—whether it intended to remain there indefinitely, for a short time, or to withdraw—the response had been a long letter from the President reiterating his fears of extending the war, hinting again at possible evacuation.

"Passing the buck!" Duggan had snapped to Beau Ames. "He boasts that he's no buck-passer, but if you ask me, he's Number One. He's put me in a military straitjacket, and expects me to bail him out—with one arm. He's practically guaranteed the Red Chinese supply line, and he expects me to win the war. And if we get kicked out of Korea, who will he blame?''

Mark Duggan was not aware of how this morbid dread of

defeat had taken possession of him. It was worse even than the dark days in Malinta Tunnel. He despaired of ending his long, victorious career in ignominy. Privately, he considered himself the greatest commander in the history of modern arms, if only because America had fought more wars in the past half century than any other major power, and he, Mark Duggan, had commanded at every level, from the shavetail of Samar to the supreme commander of Inchon. He no longer thought of himself as a soldier responsible to his civilian commander-in-chief, as a professional whose skill in the art of war was only the instrument—not the end—of national policy. So he thirsted for victory, abhorring the idea of stalemate, or "no-win," as Martin called it, in the conviction that his countrymen, ignorant of war as an instrument of national policy, would construe it as defeat.

Duggan had even grown irritable and snappish at home. Although he now spent long hours at his office, when he did return to the apartment, he was no longer an attentive, gentle husband or an adoring grandfather. He was, rather, a frustrated and exasperated old man. He even spoke sharply to his grandson, and so frequently that Virginia packed Kenneth off to military school in the States.

"Get him out of the impact area," Beau told Virginia. "The Old Man used to idolize him, but now he's turning on even him." Beau also had aged in the past few months. His worried frown had cut furrows into his forehead. He sighed deeply. "I don't know how it's going to end, Jinny—but it can't go on this way."

Mark Duggan was thinking much the same thing after he picked up Martin's letter and read it again. It had to end! The chains of restraint that weighed upon his warrior's soul were unbearable. Something would have to give . . . Perhaps, he thought, picking up his pen, Martin's letter was the yearned-for opportunity . . . He did not, of course, allow himself to think that it might also provide the way out. He began to write:

> My views and recommendations with respect to the situation created by Red China's entry into war against us in Korea have been submitted to Washington in most complete detail. These views are well-

known and generally understood, as they follow the conventional pattern of meeting force with maximum counterforce, as we have never failed to do in the past. Your view with respect to the utilization of the Nationalist Chinese forces on Formosa is in conflict with neither logic nor this tradition.

It seems strangely difficult for some to realize that here in Asia is where the Communist conspirators have elected to make their play for global conquest, and that we have joined the issue thus raised on the battlefield; that here we fight Europe's war with arms, while the diplomats there still fight it with words; that if we lost the war to communism in Asia, the fall of Europe is inevitable; win it, and Europe most probably would avoid war and yet preserve freedom. As you pointed out, we must win. There is no substitute for victory.

Immensely pleased with the last line of his letter, General Duggan drew another sheet of paper toward him and began to compose an ultimatum to Red China threatening total destruction.

A clamor of protest among America's UN allies succeeded Duggan's ultimatum. The British ambassador telephoned Secretary Acheson, requesting a copy of "Duggan's latest pronunciamento."

"I . . . I haven't seen it yet," the usually impeccable and unruffled Acheson stammered.

"Lucky you," the ambassador murmured in a tired voice. "It is really quite extraordinary. He warns Red China that she has not the industrial capacity to conduct modern war, and he says, in effect, that if she does not give up her attempt to conquer Korea, the UN will very likely invade and destroy her."

"Oh, my God!" Acheson moaned.

"Quite. Is the general aware of our agreement that no action or public statement with regard to Red China will be taken by you without first consulting us?"

"Certainly. He has been reminded of it time and time again."

"Curious, I should say. Perhaps Duggan has it backward.

Perhaps he thinks that he is Washington and you are Tokyo. Well, Dean, we will say nothing publicly. But I shall be most grateful if you will convey to the President our most earnest concern.''

"I will indeed,'' Acheson said in a troubled voice, hanging up and immediately calling the White House.

"I've seen it!'' Harry Truman snapped. "It's a damned disgrace, that's what it is. It will scuttle the cease-fire we've worked so hard to get. I tell you, Dean, this is the end. Duggan is guilty of complete insubordination, and I will not tolerate it any longer.''

Acheson said nothing, privately doubting that the President would dismiss the general and bring on the political battle of his life. He was correct. Truman merely instructed the Joint Chiefs to notify Duggan to clear all future statements on policy with Washington. A few days later, however, Representative Martin read Duggan's "confidential'' letter to him on the floor of the House, and Harry Truman immediately called a meeting of the National Security Council.

"This passes insubordination,'' Truman said to the generals and secretaries gathered around the big table. "It is an outright challenge to our policy of containment. I have made up my mind to relieve him, but I want to hear your views first.''

"I agree with you, sir,'' Secretary Acheson said, fingering his mustache. "But I warn you, if you dismiss him, you will have the political battle of your life. This is what Taft and Martin and their people have been waiting for.''

Truman nodded, glancing at Secretary Meadows. "I would advise caution, Mr. President,'' Meadows began slowly. "Perhaps we should reflect more. If Duggan is relieved, it might make if difficult to get military appropriations through Congress.''

"George, I'm going to leave it up to you. I want you to go through all the messages between Duggan and Washington in the past two years, and then give me your advice. Gentlemen, we will meet again Monday morning.''

At that conference it was unanimously agreed to relieve General of the Army Mark Duggan of all his commands.

"After reading the messages, sir,'' Secretary of Defense

George Quincy Meadows said, "I concluded that you should
have dismissed him two years ago."

Truman compressed his lips grimly. "Thank you, George.
And I would like you to write the last message."

Meadows nodded. Truman stared at him in mild surprise.
His dour Secretary of Defense was smiling broadly!

The Duggans were celebrating Kathy Ames's second birthday
at a party in their quarters at the American embassy. Betsy
had baked a cake, and Kathy had blown out the candles with
delightful gusto. Then Sergeant Durkin went into the kitchen
to get a knife to cut it. Durkin came running back to the
dining room, his seamed face working in emotion, tears
streaming down his cheeks.

"He's sacked yez, sir," he cried. " 'Twas on the wireless.
President Truman's given yez the sack and replaced yez with
Gen'ral Ridgeley."

A hush came over the table. Betsy Duggan began to cry. So
did Virginia Ames. Beau Ames put a consoling hand over hers
and stared inquiringly at the general.

"Why are you crying, Mommy?" little Kathy cried. "Why
is Gramma crying? Granpa, why is everybody crying?"

"Because they're happy for you, honey," Duggan whispered
hoarsely, squeezing the little girl's hand and gazing up at
Durkin standing beside him. "It's been a long time, Pat," he
said softly, glancing at his punctured, faded campaign hat
lying atop the breakfront. Pat seized the hat and brought it to
him. Duggan gazed at it with nostalgia in his eyes, poking his
finger through the bullet holes. "Take it, Pat," he said. "It's
yours. You're the Irish druid who made fifty years of magic
for me."

Durkin shook his head doggedly, tears again in his eyes.
"Ah, Jaysus, sir, the spell wasn't strong enough for that
bow-tied, four-eyed runt of a pianny-player."

Duggan smiled wanly. His large dark eyes roved affectionately
over everyone at the table, caressing each of them lovingly.

"Well, folks," he said gently, "we're going home at last."

ABOUT THE AUTHOR

The author of *The General* was born in Philadelphia, the youngest in an Irish-Catholic family of eight children. Growing up in Rutherford, New Jersey, Robert Leckie got his first writing job covering football for the Bergen Evening *Record* in Hackensack. Upon hearing of the Japanese bombing of Pearl Harbor, Leckie joined the Marines and served nearly three years in the Pacific theater, winning eight battle stars, four presidential unit citations, the Purple Heart, and the Naval Commendation Medal with Combat V. His wartime experiences formed the basis of his acclaimed first book, *Helmet For My Pillow*.

Following World War II, Leckie continued his journalistic career, writing for the Associated Press and the *New York Daily News* and serving as an editor for MGM newsreels. With the publication of his first book, Leckie dedicated himself full-time to writing, and is the author of thirty-five fiction and non-fiction books, including *Strong Men Armed*, *Delivered from Evil*, and *None Died in Vain*. He and his wife Vera divide their time between South Carolina and New Jersey.

The history of man in flight....

THE BANTAM AIR AND SPACE SERIES

The Bantam Air and Space Series is dedicated to the men and women who brought about this, the era of flight -- the century in which mankind not only learned to soar the skies, but has journeyed out into the blank void of space.

- ☐ 1: THE LAST OF THE BUSH PILOTS
  by Harmon Helmericks   28556-4 $4.95
- ☐ 2: FORK TAILED DEVIL: THE P-38
  by Martin Caidin   28557-2 $4.95
- ☐ 3: THE FASTEST MAN ALIVE
  by Frank Everest and John Guenther 28771-0 $4.95
- ☐ 4: DIARY OF A COSMONAUT: 211 DAYS IN
  SPACE by Valentin Lebedev   28778-8 $4.95
- ☐ 5: FLYING FORTS by Martin Caidin 28780-X $4.95
- ☐ 6: ISLAND IN THE SKY
  by Ernest K. Gann   28857-1 $4.95
- ☐ 7: PILOT
  by Tony Le Vier with John Guenther 28785-0 $4.95
- ☐ 8: BARNSTORMING
  by Martin Caidin   28818-0 $4.95
- ☐ 9: THE ELECTRA STORY: AVIATION'S
  GREATEST MYSTERY by Robert J. Serling
                                     28845-8 $4.95

Available now wherever Bantam Falcon Books are sold, or use this page for ordering: